STRETCH, 29

Damian Lanigan was born in Coventry and brought up in Manchester. He currently lives in New York, where he is working on his second novel.

D0543575

# STRETCH, 29

## Damian Lanigan

HarperCollins*Publishers*

This novel is entirely a work of fiction.
The names, characters and incidents portrayed in it are
the work of the author's imagination. Any resemblance to
actual persons, living or dead, events or localities is
entirely coincidental.

HarperCollins*Publishers*
77–85 Fulham Palace Road,
Hammersmith, London W6 8JB

www.**fire**and**water**.com

A Paperback Original 2000
1  3  5  7  9  8  6  4  2

A catalogue record for this book
is available from the British Library

ISBN 0 00 651428 6

Typeset in Minion by Palimpsest Book Production Limited,
Polmont, Stirlingshire

Printed and bound in Great Britain by
Omnia Books Limited, Glasgow

For Matthew Batstone

# DOWNSHIFT

# Two hundred quid

I was walking towards Knightsbridge with two grand in my pocket, wondering how far it would get me.

*Scenario 1: I get the tube to Heathrow, buy myself a one-way ticket to LAX, hole up in a motel on Sunset, spend three sleepless days and nights hunched over the complimentary stationery, chewing down triple espressos. I emerge blinking and amazed with a movie idea so high concept that Fox kidnap me, stick me in a suite at the Beverly and forbid me to speak to anyone while they put the elements together. Tarantino wants to direct, Kidman wants to star, DiCaprio's falling over himself to play a cameo. I demand and get back-end points and a three-thousand-square-foot office on the lot. I'm a producer now.*

I liked it but I had some nagging concerns about the visa situation, so as I negotiated the painted ladies skittering between Gucci and

Armani on the slick December pavements, I swung my attentions eastwards:

*Scenario 2: I get the tube to Heathrow and buy a one-way ticket to anywhere in the European Union, let's say . . . Brussels. No, no, let's say Bologna. Never been there, but it's probably quite nice. I teach English for most of the year and spend the autumn picking grapes for food and lodging. I screw forty per cent of my female students, and fifty per cent of my grape buddies. My life is simple, but fulfilling. I am known as Crazy Inglese. I marry the daughter of the guy who owns the winery. I end up running for mayor. I win and get the public transport system sorted out in record time.*

Scenario 2 was getting a bit depressing. I was now right on top of the tube station, being offered a sprig of heather by some hairy gypsy child. I told her to piss off and in desperation flung my imaginings yet further east:

*Scenario 3: I get the tube to Heathrow and buy a one-way ticket to Goa. I sleep on the beach, do a stack of acid and become very wise. By the summer I'm wearing a long white dress and Tolstoyesque beard and live off freebies from gullible backpackers for the rest of my life. I sleep with many freckled Australian girls, one of whom is actually called Noeleen.*

Jesus, I couldn't even get a decent fantasy going.

This may have been because the two grand wasn't mine. It belonged to Bart, who owned the restaurant in which I slaved. In a fashion that was becoming habitual, he had summoned me from the restaurant in Battersea to the roulette table at the Sheraton Park Tower. A crackle on his mobile, in the background a whirring followed by the paradiddle as the ball bounced on to the wheel:

'Get me two grand. I'm blown down here.'

The calls were now coming about twice a week. I'd asked Tony Ling, the restaurant's Anglo-Chinese accountant, if it was OK, and he'd just laughed at me, showing his tiny unbrushed teeth: 'It's his train set.'

Tony wasn't on my side either.

And so, despite the dull feeling that there was something going on I didn't quite understand, and from which I could never benefit, here I was, in rich, clogged Knightsbridge, wondering what the hell I was doing here, having a curse put on me in Romany.

*Scenario 4: Take the two grand to my boss, and be quick about it.*

As I started to cross the road to the casino, a rich young mum in a towering 4 x 4 almost took me out. The gypsy curse nearly fulfilled instantly, but by a Range Rover rather than a horse-drawn wagon. I watched her as she swung through the red light, mouthing in the rear-view at the wriggling baby seat. The money, the bull bars and twelve airbags made her further away than Goa. Up there, in all that air-conditioned, insulated headroom, she was safe and sound with the object of her unconditional love: a smooth, fat midget who couldn't keep things down. I wanted to be her husband, and look after her.

*Scenario 5: Comfortable bourgeois tedium in old London town with a wife and a child and at least two cars.*

That's the one, and two grand gets you nowhere near it.

When I arrived at the casino, the door staff nodded me through with a combination of courtesy and disgust. I didn't hold it against them: the winter drizzle had coaxed an old-dog aroma from my Crombie and glued most of my hair to most of my face. I went through to the tables. The place was pretty empty: a couple of absorbed Chinese at the baccarat table, a group of cigar-ing pinstripes around one of the roulette wheels obviously in a post-lunch tailspin.

Bart was sitting at the marble bar on a black leatherette stool manically swirling a vodka tonic.

'Jesus, Stretch, you bin in a fuckin' road accident?'

'Yes.'

'Well, get on with it – where's the money?'

I retrieved the money from my inside coat pocket. He took it, put it between his teeth and hitched his jeans up round his roasting-dish belly.

'Go on then, what are you waiting for – get in a cab and fuck off back to work.'

'It's my evening off actually. I'm going home.'

'In which case don't get a cab. Well, you're welcome to get one, but I'm not paying for it.'

'Thanks, Bart, you've really made my day.'

'Don't mention it, Frank.'

Bart: he doesn't make it easier.

I went into the marble-and-mood-music toilet and let the codger spritz my wrists with Czech and Speake, to take away the Airedale twang rising from my coat.

It was nearly four and already getting dark by the time I was back out on Knightsbridge. There was now no point in me going home, because I'd been invited to a pre-Christmas drinks potty in Holland Park, and was expected there at six-thirty, an hour earlier than everyone else, to 'catch up we haven't seen you in ages'. I wonder why that was. I decided to spend some time with a paper, in a pub, smoking. I'm the world champion at killing hours. All I have to do is look at them and they die. By the way, 'party in Holland Park' sounds pretty good, doesn't it?

It lost a bit in the enactment, I can tell you. I *will* tell you.

I bought a *Standard* and inserted myself in The Duchess of Kent with a pint of Pride and inspected the catering jobs. I read every single one. The best I could do was a two-hundred-quid-a-year pay rise if I went to be a trainee manager at Kentucky Fried Chicken in Streatham. Nice opportunity. I turned it down on the basis of the cardboard hat.

I left the pub at five, big empty bags of time banging at my knees, going nowhere in particular. As I crossed Knightsbridge Green a figure leapt up off one of the benches: 'Frank! Frank Stretch!'

I looked into the man's face. Gaunt and swarthy, eyes slightly narrowed, he looked at me eagerly. It took me a few moments to lock on properly.

'Bill. Christ, how's it going?'

Bill Turnage, an old schoolfriend. I suddenly had a strong desire to escape. I couldn't bear the thought of having to talk him through the last ten years.

'It's fine. I'm just down for a couple of days, from Suffolk. On ... business.'

'Christ.'

We were both now pretty awkward. I looked at my watch and tried to look pushed for time.

'Listen, I'm in a real hurry, actually. Got to go to some drinks party, sorry to sound like such a yuppie.'

'No, no, that's fine. Let me take your number.'

Shit.

'Actually, I'm between apartments currently, but why not jot down an address. They can forward everything to me.'

'Sure, sure.'

He took out a notebook and scribbled down my address. Then he looked at me with a curious intensity.

'Take my card, get in touch, I mean it. I'd love to see you.'

I slipped his card into my coat and started rubbernecking for a taxi.

'God, yeah, of course. But really I'm in a tearing hurry, Bill. Ten minutes late already; look there's a cab.'

'Call me, Frank.'

''Course.'

I lobbed myself into the cab and asked for Notting Hill, thus blowing my evening's budget.

I decided that I'd walk from the Gate down Holland Park Avenue; I was still way too early. As we pulled away I looked back for Bill and saw him still looking after me. It started to give me the willies. When I was out of sight I took his card out of my pocket:

BILL TURNAGE

FURNITURE DESIGN & BUILD

Maybe having a business card would make things simpler. Everyone I know has a business card. It's the first thing people seem to do now, trade business cards: 'this is who I am', 'and this is who *I* am', as if what the card says about them clears everything up.

I turned over in my mind what my card would say on it: *Waiter?* That would be the most honest, and thus the most undesirable. *Maître d'?* Says either queer or sad. Besides, *maître d'* in a bar and grill in Battersea? Come off it. *Manager?* Oh, God, anything but that. Mimicking white collar language when you're just a fetcher, carrier and ferrier is so shaming. Forget the positive spin: if I had a business card there's only one thing it could say on it:

FRANK STRETCH

LESS SUCCESSFUL THAN HIS FRIENDS

## £14,273

Yes, it was pretty straightforward really. Frank Stretch, under-achiever, flop, relegation contender – outclassed by his friends. Now, you may think that you're less successful than your friends, and you may well be right. The difference between us, however, is that I have a system that proves it.

If you feel as if you're under-achieving, perhaps you'd be tempted to read a self-help book. Don't, because I've tried them, and the thing about self-help books is that they are all wrong. They make it easy on the reader and tell him from the outset that he's really a wonderful, successful human being. They refuse to acknowledge the hard and heavy truth, which is this: people who read self-help books are less successful than their friends, that's why they read self-help books. My approach to the whole issue is a lot more rigorous and a lot more honest. It goes like this: 'Admit it, you loser, you're less successful than your friends, and not only that, you can prove it.'

9

According to this inclusive and elegant system of classification of success in life, my best friend Tom scores 73, and my (ex) flatmate Henry 59. Lottie, his knitwear fanatic girlfriend, scores a moderate 46. Bart, my dear boss, weighs in with 68. I score a lot less than any of these people. In fact thanks to the system I am now able to make a broader statement about my standing in the world: 'Stretch, you're less successful than everyone you know.'

I'm aware that I am open to the accusation of being self-pitying, but I'd like to point out that it is closely scrutinised, finely calibrated, judiciously-arrived-at self-pity. If you were me, and thank Allah you're not, you'd be self-pitying too.

I call the system The Maths, as in, 'Ooh he looks as if he might put in some really good maths', when applied to a new acquaintance, or 'Pretty abysmal maths there', when applied to myself.

The principle is quite simple, really; scores for the ten important areas of life, out of ten. Let me talk you through it.

ONE: MONEY £ A more complex dimension than you might think. When you're doing someone's money score, make sure you ask all the difficult questions. The first golden rule is that people under the age of fifty always claim to be poorer than they are. (Whereas, men over fifty like to pretend they're richer than they are, particularly to their friends, but I don't meet them very often.)

The second golden rule is, don't forget family. A friend of yours, let's call him Henry, might complain that he's underpaid and over-mortgaged, and can't afford to go on holiday this year. You may feel entitled to a momentary moment of superiority. But hold on a second. You then find out that his dad's a sales director of a small slipper-making company in Preston. Still feeling chipper? Well, Henry Senior has share options worth £150,000 and pension rights running to two-thirds of his annual £48,000 salary. On his demise, that dough is only going in one direction, and that's to Henry Jun. This is by no means the worst example I could cite. I once shared a flat with a bloke who ate Safeway cornflakes with tap water for Sunday lunch and smoked Berkeleys. He was trying to get into the movies, like every other fucker. He chose as his mode of entry to this rarefied world working the late shift at the Brixton Blockbuster video store. It transpired that he had an obscure great-uncle who spent his days strapped into a leather wing-backed armchair in the Carlton Club, pissing himself with rhino force inside his tweed britches. When he finally had his coronary over the fashion pages of the *Telegraph*, my flatmate inherited half a million, as well as a sizeable tranche of Herefordshire and moved into a loft apartment in Clerkenwell. What looked like a dead-cert dowdy 1 turned out to be a big, airy, sky-lit 9.

Guess what? He's now in the movies.

In 1994, the year before all this started, I earned £14,273.00 and had no expectation of ever inheriting anything. My mother died fifteen years ago, and my dad had gone AWOL in the Mid-West or the West Midlands, where his last known employment was self-unemployment. Another half-arsed Thatcherite dream gone tits-up. I could go on, about postmen uncles and dinner-lady aunties, but any way you look at it, I'm skint and likely to remain so pretty much forever.

I'll just give you a ready reckoner:

| | |
|---|---|
| Rupert Murdoch down to the Queen Mother | 10 |
| Michael Heseltine down to Jeffrey Archer | 9 |
| Alan Shearer down to Cherie Booth | 8 |
| Some of my friends down to Preston slipper company director | 7 |
| Ken Livingstone down to your local GP | 6 |
| Most of my friends down to most of the rest of my friends | 5 |
| Car salesmen down to articled clerks | 4 |
| PAs to the MD down to binmen | 3 |
| Me | 2 |
| Over two-thirds of the UK population | 1 |

TWO: LOVE ♥ Compared to money, this one's a cinch. From where I'm standing a half-hearted Christmas card from an ex-girlfriend scores you at least a 3. Look around and you'll see that most people beat this score, just don't look at me. I scored another 2.

THREE: SEX ▮ Pretty easy to mark yourself, but often very tricky to mark others. Some couples spend their entire lives pawing one another in public, trying to create the impression that when they're alone it's an unstoppable gymnasm from dusk till the early afternoon. Very often such behaviour is a straightforward deception. Spend a night at their place and press your ear to the bedroom wall while maintaining a total unbreathing silence. What will you hear? The sounds of a hardback closing, a peck on an already dozing partner's cheek and the light clicking off. A milky, cuddly, dreary 2.

No, those to watch for high scores here are the ones who barely seem to look at each other at table apart from to exchange black, jaded insults. After dinner they nurse their hostilities at opposite ends of the room, while everybody else inwardly speculates on their imminent break-up. In the sack they're like a herd of satyrs home on leave to make a porn movie. Look for the flu symptoms: bleary-eyed and all sore and achy in the morning. And then watch them closely. They are already considering their next options: which orifice, which lubricant, which forearm, which piece of machinery. A 9, no question.

You may have noticed that the sex symbol is phallic rather than yonic, if you will. Now, the act of sex for me is a yoni thing rather than a phallus thing, simple as that. That is, in an ideal world it's a yoni thing. At that time, however, it was very much a phallus thing, and no prizes for guessing whose phallus. I regularly scored a fine upstanding 1, especially in the mornings.

FOUR: WORK ⚲ Quite easy to score, as long as you remember

the key question: Are you happy in your work? The ruddy-faced pinstripes larging it up in the City with their partnerships and directorships tend to score low marks in this system, despite the serial-number incomes. All the ones I know consistently wang on about early retirement or writing their novel or opening a surf shop in Maui. They hate their work, but also define themselves in terms of their work, and it's all writ large on their business cards. Oh dear. 2s and 3s all round.

Another example. You may think that Bill Clinton has a pretty good job, and most people would agree with you. I don't. I mean it's just one thing after another if you're the Leader of the Free World, isn't it? West Bank settlers one minute, a Republican majority in Congress the next, some woman broadcasting to the nation about distinguishing marks on your penis the next. Bill's welcome to it if you ask me. My (ex) flatmate Henry's girlfriend is called Lottie and she knits sweaters for a living, except that she doesn't get paid for it. I don't really want to do that either, but at least I'd sleep at night.

When I left university I had a question to answer. What becomes of a dissolute, immature ex-Maoist (the girls are prettier in the Communist Society), now patrician-Tory, broadly-not-deeply-read pseudo-intellectual when he has to get a job?

I initially took the conventional Oxbridge approach. I applied for jobs in American, Swiss and Japanese investment banks. I considered law, but in banks the girls are prettier. In fact, they're the Maoist girls, but now in £80 undies and mock-Chanel body armour. Needless to say I failed. I then applied to go on a journalism course in Harlow and succeeded.

A year later, the girls in the pricey underwear were just graduating into their first 3 Series when I took up an eight-and-a-half-grand glamour job on the *Streatham Post*. While they dealt in issues of world importance, like the exchange-rate fluctuations between the schilling and the escudo, I was scrabbling around with the trivia: births, marriages, deaths – that sort of thing.

I operated in a different world order from my peers. My world ended at Balham, Wandsworth, Chelsea Bridge. Nothing in which I was interested ramified outside this area: Chamber of Commerce Outrage at Red Route Plan, Lady Mayoress Opens New Texas Homecare, Woman Found By Son 'Had Been Dead Three Weeks'.

On the other hand, the people I knew were obsessing about the fate of the dollar from their striplit hangars at Salomon or Stanley. They were part of that process whereby some bureaucrat in DC says the word 'nervous' at a dinner party and six hours later little children are crying in the streets of Nairobi.

Anyway, I didn't last long. Journalism's all about getting your face around, cold calling, beer drinking, loud laughing, cock sucking. I just didn't have the necessary. Most of all it's about wanting it badly, and I've never wanted anything badly, nothing that wasn't human and female at any rate. So I sacked it. In fact, if truth be known, they sacked me. I'd captioned a picture of the local MP at a garden fête as follows: 'ANGELA HOWEY, MP, HOLDS ALOFT A LARGE PARSNIP BEFORE INSERTING IT INTO HER ANUS'.

Everyone at the paper missed it, and they got scores of furious letters, not least from Ms Howey herself, but I was long gone. It was, I can see, a puerile gesture, but momentarily enjoyable, and mentally I was way out of there anyway. I wasn't happy in my work, you see. At least I got out alive, if somewhat disillusioned with journalism for the time being. And now I wait tables.

So I would ask myself the question: Frank, are you happy in your work in a bad restaurant in Battersea? The answer? No, not really. Score? 3.

FIVE: HOUSE ⊞ One of the easiest of the lot, particularly if you're an owner-occupier. The property market has a strange and mysterious beauty to it, in as much as you always get exactly what you pay for. It's practically impossible for people to artificially inflate or deflate their scores here. Let the market decide, it has great wisdom in these matters. Again, a ready reckoner may help to elucidate:

| | Belgravia | Notting Hill | Fulham | Clapham | Tooting | Peckham | Leafy Surburbs* | Provinces (Rural) | Provinces (Urban) |
|---|---|---|---|---|---|---|---|---|---|
| Estate | n/a | n/a | n/a | n/a | n/a | n/a | n/a | 10 | n/a |
| Mansion | 10 | n/a | 8 | 7 | 6 | 5 | 9 | 7 | 6 |
| Detached | n/a | 0 | 8 | 7 | 6 | 6 | 7 | 5 | 6 |
| Townhouse | 10 | 0 | 8 | 7 | 6 | 5 | n/a | n/a | 5 |
| Terrace | 9 | 0 | 7 | 6 | 5 | 4 | 5 | 3 | 3 |
| Mews | 9 | 0 | 7 | 6 | n/a | n/a | n/a | n/a | n/a |
| 2 Bed Flat | 8 | 0 | 6 | 5 | 4 | 2 | 4 | 3 | 3 |
| 1 Bed Flat | 7 | 0 | 5 | 4 | 3 | 2 | 3 | 2 | 1 |
| Studio | 6 | 0 | 4 | 3 | 2 | 1 | 2 | 1** | 2 |
| Hovel | 4 | 0 | 2 | 1 | 1 | 1 | 1 | 1 | 1 |

* of London, obviously.
** Likely to be a barn (unconverted).

In all cases subtract 1 point if you're renting.

For owners of second homes, combine scores up to a maximum of 10.

For Islington, read Fulham, for Neasden read Tooting and so on. Zone 1 tends to beat Zone 2 which tends to beat Zone 3.

You may think that I have marked Notting Hill a tad unfairly, especially if you've just bought a plasterboard cubbyhole there for two hundred grand. I just say that if you live in Notting Hill you deserve all the unfairness you get.

If anybody else feels hard done by, and thinks this table undervalues their own property, I am afraid to say I don't yet operate an ombudsman system to mediate disputes.

I rented a room in Henry's cosy three-bed flat in Clapham, which was above a CTN and overlooked the public khazi. A roof-terraced, stripped-floored, *ficus-benjamina*-by-the-tellyed 4.

SIX: WHEELS 🚙 Cars, basically. With motorcycles, HGVs, tractors etc each case is treated strictly on merit, but basically I'm talking cars. Cars are complex in a way that houses aren't. Whilst in the case of new cars the market principle is broadly operable – a £13,000 Vectra always scoring more points than a £9,000 Punto – the second-hand market wreaks havoc. For instance, Marie, my ex-girlfriend, scores a solid 4 with her nearly-new Nissan Micra, whereas Henry, with his ancient Triumph Stag, scores a 5, despite the fact he paid about two grand less for it. More high marks might be scored by: a gubernatorial stretch Zil; a gold Roller droptop on white-walls; a cigarillo of crimson fibreglass with head-high tyre tread and 400 horses slavering at the nape of your neck; any Aston; anything American.

The acid test is whether or not your car evokes the comment 'Nice motor' (or ''smoter') from a black eighteen-year-old male. If so then you're 5 or above, if not, you're 4 or below. I drive a 1977 Vauxhall Cavalier. Oh! My Chevalier! ''Smoter'? No. Laughing stock? Yes. Score? 2. Better than a Daewoo, purely for the kitsch value.

SEVEN: PHYSICAL 🧍 You could never accuse me of being superficial here, as I always take care to look beneath the skin, as well as upon it. There are two dimensions on which to score; 5 for aesthetic beauty and 5 for physical health. Kind of, 'Yeah, not bad, but how long's it going to last?' Some examples: a Premier League footballer with a horse's face (getting rarer – most of them look like Zulu chiefs or boy band members nowadays): a 6. A supermodel with an aerobics video out is brushing 10. A supermodel with a syringe of smack lolling out of her eyelid as she goes hypoglycaemic in a nightclub toilet (i.e. most of them), more like a 6 again.

Despite the peascod gilet of Trex that I sport, I get two beauty points for tapering, sensitive fingers and a winning, lop-sided grin, and one fitness point for being able to go to the shops without the aid of a motorised wheelchair. I smoke Luckies, because hardly anyone else does, and binge drink whenever I get the chance, which I'm sure doesn't do me any favours, but I never go to the doctor's (on the same basis that I never open mail from the bank) so maybe I'm just fine. Thus, being in paranoid ignorance of my real state of health, I gave myself a rather unprepossessing ♀ score of 3.

EIGHT: POPULAR ♪ Do people spend their time at parties scanning the space over your left shoulder looking for someone they'd rather be talking to? How many invitations do you have on the mantelpiece? How many times this week did you spend your break time circling the programmes you're going to watch on telly tonight? How often do you sit there in the early evenings desperately flipping through your mental address book, wondering why no-one ever calls? My answers to these questions go like this: yes, 0, 5, very often. It's a painful area, and you may well be reluctant to be truthful to yourself. I could even forgive you for overstating your score a little bit. I did. My score? 3. Work friends score half.

NINE: INTERESTING ❗ Another difficult category, and one with several booby traps lying in wait for the inexperienced. Let's take an example. I have an acquaintance called Christophe who would give himself an 8 or 9 here. He would adduce as evidence the following: he plays the guitar to a high standard, goes to the theatre a lot, has one Californian parent, one Swiss, both of whom have had complicated and drawn-out nervous

17

breakdowns. He rides a Harley and lives for half the year in a villa in Fiesole giving English lessons to the children of rich Tuscans. Crucial to his impression of himself as a ravishingly interesting fellow is the fact that he has travelled widely 'amongst the peoples' of the Himalayas, China and the Arctic Circle, often, as he never ceases to remind one, in difficult and dangerous circumstances. He has eaten yak's bollocks. He is something of an authority on Taoism. There is no 'r' on the end of his name. A 9, Christophe? You must be joking. A 2? That's it.

On the other hand, my flatmate Henry is a computer scientist from Leeds. His dad is that slipper magnate I was telling you about. His mum's a housewife. For some reason he's a Crystal Palace fan, and rarely misses a home game. His interests include supermarket shopping and TV. He holidays in the Peak District. He likes Pink Floyd and Michael Bolton. Score? 8. A man should be judged by the content of his character, not by the colour of the stamps in his passport.

I scored myself a 7 here. Oh, all right then, a 6.

TEN: CACHET ♛ Not the same as popularity at all. A hundred years ago this section would have been called 'class' and everyone would have slotted into their given echelon with a kind of Buddhist acceptance: Lord Salisbury: a haughty 10; fresh-off-the-boat-at-Liverpool-docks-Irish-immigrant: a potatoey 1.

The prevailing convoluted, ironic system of social classification makes everything a lot more complicated. Whilst it remains very easy to score in the lower reaches (rapists and child abusers regularly put in low scores, as does Henry), there is always a lot of debate about the high marks. Low life is just as likely as high life to push scores northwards. Even winos (or 'dossers' or whatever we're supposed to call them nowadays) can score well, as long as they get a bit of media attention. Some other central figures in the new social order are surprising. Footballers can put in some *immense* scores. In the fifties they had the status of miners; it was good to know they were there, keeping things ticking along, BUT I´M NOT HAVING THEM FUCKING MY DAUGHTER. Now, they are like the young viscounts of the eighteenth century, taking their pleasure as it pleases them with the flower of European girlhood. The Grand Tour is somewhat dumbed down, however; Marbella and Mauritius replacing Florence and Venice, but they're generally the boys to beat for ♛.

Provenance is a key factor, e.g. Blenheim Palace is excellent, but so is a Glasgow tenement. A semi in Purley has retained its ability to put in a fair-to-middling if slightly shame-faced 3. Semis in South Manchester, Wigan, Poulton-le-Fylde, Stoke, St Helens and Salford are much the same as a semi in Purley, with the necessary London weighting discounted. Consequently, I also get a 3.

So let's tot me up.

| £ | ♥ | ▮ | ♟ | ⊞ | 🥽 | 🧍 | ✆ | ! | ♛ |
|---|---|---|---|---|---|---|---|---|---|
| 2 | 2 | 1 | 3 | 4 | 2 | 3 | 3 | 6 | 3 |

Grand Total 29.

Various ways of interpreting this, but the one I was going for at the time was as follows: 'I am 29% as successful in life as I could be, which is much less successful than my friends.' Putting a more positive gloss on it, I was a huge 71% as unsuccessful as I could have been. Much better than my friends. Fuck it.

Coincidentally, when this all started, I was 29 years old. So there it was. 29. The beginning and the end of Frank Stretch.

# Three hundred grand

Half an hour after fleeing Bill Turnage I was still crammed into the corner of the cab (non-smoker, inevitably) somewhere between High St Ken and Holland Park. The meter was clicking up remorselessly, like a digital stopwatch. I was speculating on Bill's maths. FURNITURE DESIGN & BUILD had a convincing ring to it, but there was something almost desperate-looking about Bill that made me baulk at anything above the high 40s. I tried to put him out of my mind. There was no chance of me ever getting in contact with him, no way he'd bother to write to me. We're at the end of the twentieth century, for God's sake, nobody has to do anything they don't *want* to do. And anyway, I had more pressing concerns, namely the guests at Tom Mannion's party and how they would bring home to me with force my irredeemable 29-ness. All of them would be my age, have, on paper at least, my background and education and all of them would have more money, nicer flats, more sex, better bodies, better jobs, faster cars, fuller diaries and fewer neuroses than me. What was worse was that they'd all know it and they'd know that I knew it. What was worse than *that* was that Tom and Lucy had invited some girl along they thought I might be interested in. I wasn't at my best.

Tom, though, is a good guy, he means well, he wouldn't hurt a fly. The only thing is, he's *different* from other people. He's sort of *better* than other people. He is my age. He is a public law barrister in what people describe to me as 'a sexy set'. (What can this possibly mean?) His father is very high up in the newspaper and magazine business, and a baronet. Tom is happily married to Lucy, a beautiful woman (Varsity sweetheart) who trades bonds. He drives an Alfa Spider. He got a rowing Half-Blue at Oxford. He wrote a novel about art theft when he was 26. As I was being reminded now, as the cab came to a growling halt outside his house, he lives in a mews house in Holland Park. He's funny, clever, charming and handsome. He speaks three languages. He's my 'best friend'. He scores 73. The maths in detail:

Nowadays, I have to mark him down on . The athleticism is atrophied, the belly is swelled by foie gras, Veuve Clicquot and summer pudding. He gets away with it, though, he's so damned handsome, and the podginess makes him *look* rich. Mine is strictly chip fat and sour beer.

He is my best friend as I say, but it is a friendship increasingly sustained by distant historical links, rather than current behaviour. I have somewhere a chart which illustrates our drifting apart. The salient points are as follows: in the first couple of years after university we saw each other on average 2.1 times a week. He moved in with Lucy, at this point, and the average over the next year went down suddenly to 1.3, but didn't further decline over the next year, in fact it held firm at 1.4. Then things started to go wrong; a sudden dive to 0.6, and a constant decline, until here we were at the end of 1995 and I'd seen him four times all year, and not since the summer.

The reason was simple: he was changing, I was staying the same. The best example of this was in our attitude to children.

My view was concise and uncontroversial: the process of acquiring children, as it takes place in the British middle classes, is an exercise in eugenics. Both parties in the enterprise spend their early sexual career sifting and sorting prospective mates on the basis of their appearance, bloodstock, prosperity, psychology, intelligence, hair colour, etc. It is not until it is felt by both parties that a satisfactory balance is struck on these criteria that any firm agreement on procreation is made, and this agreement is usually consecrated in a formal, social context. This gathering, setting the couple off in their best light, effectively invites the others in attendance to speculate on how *beautiful, intelligent and socially useful* the putative offspring will be. The male attempts to inseminate the female shortly after. If at any stage of the incubation period it is determined that the child is likely to be sub-standard in any of the crucial respects, it is 'terminated', and you start all over again. Preferences are for obedient, outgoing, straight-backed, easy-tanning, blue-eyed blonds who are capable of propagating the genetic inheritance into the distant future. A thousand years, perhaps. You can see where this is heading.

Tom, although perhaps not quite as visionary, was, in his early twenties, sceptical. He could see that children often represent dilution rather than increase, and place intolerable restrictions on freedom, and unforeseeable destructive pressures on existing relationships. Indeed, this view seemed to be increasingly widely held. Here was a generation on the cusp of their thirties, the women with their best gestating days behind them, and the slither, thud and squeal of childbirth was as yet utterly unheard. The difference was, amongst our disparate circle, that the book was now closed on who would be first to drop. Tom and Lucy had, it was rumoured, 'been trying' for six months, which was interesting as I had found them trying for somewhat longer. Tom was already an authority on school fees and IQ-enhancing dietary supplements. Interleaved with *The Economist* and *EuroMoney* in their magazine rack were copies of *Spawn, Your Foetus* and *Perineal Suture Today*, or whatever those baby-zines are called. Anyway, I stood there outside their Downing Street-style door, and as soon as Lucy opened the door, the beam on her face told me everything. The master race was goosestepping into town.

I managed a hurried, 'Oh, you clever girl!' and an awkward hug and air kiss before unconvincingly bolting up the stairs for their toilet to avoid unnecessary kerfuffle. When I reappeared I hailed Tom, who was unloading wine from a case.

'Well done, you grubby little fucker. I knew you'd muster a chubby eventually.'

Tom and Lucy were moving between the sitting room and the doll's house kitchen, laying out bottles and decanting snack foods, mainly those gnarled and weighty crisps that are about four quid a bag, and some sweaty-looking black olives.

Lucy walked over and gave me another hug. 'Aren't you happy for us?'

Happy, no. Nauseated, yes. I avoided eye contact as she withdrew.

'Cnava drink?'

'Oh, Frank, you're such a charmer.' She tried to make it sound jovial, but there was an undercurrent of exasperation. Or hurt.

'Leave him alone, Luce. What do you want, Frank?'

'Champagne. Can I throw my coat somewhere?'

'Yeah, chuck it in our room but come down quickly, we want to ask you something.'

I went upstairs, feeling a little scared. They were obviously going to give me some duty to perform, and to be honest I just don't do duties, as a rule, they're a bit too close to responsibilities.

24

I had always found their house unsettling. It was, effectively, a miniature replica of both their family homes, perhaps an acknowledgement that their parents had been right about most things after all. Every wall that wasn't cream was magnolia and the doorframes and skirting boards were an unrealistic icing-sugar white. In fact the entire house was a cake, a three-hundred-grand cake: from the outside, it was pastel-pink with three big sash windows again painted pure white, all of which suggested Battenburg. Their tiny bedroom where I was now dumping my coat was baby-blue, with a snowdrift of duvet swathing the wrought-iron bed. The curtains were pale blue and white gingham. There was a Renoir print. The whole thing whispered 'fondant fancy'. I understood the frisson that burglars must feel when they crap in the houses they burgle as I draped my disgraceful brackish overcoat on the bed.

Back downstairs Tom and Lucy were standing parentally by their glacier-white christening-cake mantelpiece, swirling their champagne in their glasses. The huge brass-framed mirror behind them held me in its placid stare. Tom looked conspiratorially at his wife, who nodded at him.

'Well, Frank, we got you here early because we'd really like you to be godfather to our baby.'

He was beaming like a maniac. She was grinning at me with her eyebrows raised. I panicked.

'Oh, my God. I don't have to *do* anything, do I?'

They both thought about it for a moment and then looked at each other quizzically.

'I think you have to renounce Satan, but not much else.'

'No, I mean, if anything happens to you two, do I have to do anything?'

'Well, that's a bit of a negative thought, Frank. We hadn't really got that far.'

'No, of course not, I'm sorry, I just don't want to let any-one down.'

Tom's brow creased. 'For Christ's sake, Frank. Come on! We're trying to tell you that we like you and we want you to be our child's godfather. Ey? Ey?'

He was prodding me in the stomach now.

'Yeah, I know, I'm sorry. Yes, yes, OK – "I'd love to be your child's godfather", or whatever you're supposed to say.'

This was as gracious as could be expected in the circumstances, and I dived for a snout to see me straight. Lucy looked at me a little ruefully and then at Tom. 'Er, Frank, sorry to be a pain, but would you mind if you didn't? It's not for us, of course, but you know what they say, "We've got someone else to think about now", and . . .' Lucy couldn't bring herself to look at me. There was a tiny, important pause as I fought myself like a lion, lighter in one hand, fag cocked in the other. To my amazement, and to that of Tom and Lucy, I got all reasonable out of nowhere.

'Sure, no problem, mate. Do you mind if I slip into the garden and have one?' Or are there some particularly sensitive fucking lupins you're worried about? I saw myself out thank you and sat in their stony high-walled courtyard really getting stuck in to my Lucky. I had undoubtedly scored valuable points with this charmingly executed act of selflessness, but wondered whether they would compensate me adequately for the damage I was doing myself by holding it all in. Already that comma of protein in Lucy's guts was exerting so much power, and not even sensate yet.

As I blasted away, I fixated on it marinading away with its proxy ASH membership, and plotted future godfatherly daytrips to Longleat, the two of us locked inside my car, me chaining my way to emphysema: 'No, I'm sorry, Jemima/Hugo/Candia/Alexia/ Moon Unit, you can't open the doors in a safari park, or you'll get your face ripped off by a mandrill. We'll stretch our legs in an hour or two. Would you like one while we wait?'

This thought gave me sufficient succour to re-enter the house without a scowl on my face, but I knew that I wasn't going to be particularly perky that evening.

By seven-thirty there were about sixteen to twenty people gathered there, almost all of whom I'd met before. Six or seven were in fact veterans of the university parties. I no longer saw any of them apart from at Tom's. They certainly didn't stop by at O'Hare's that often. The remainder were Tom and Lucy's workmates, but indistinguishable in outer appearance from the old guard; tall, with a money sheen rising quietly from their hair and skin and clothes, like vapour from an oil puddle.

I wandered over to Lucy and asked her which girl was the one they'd set aside for me. 'Sadie, over there by the stereo.'

There was a glamorous girl in black with Italianate hair and make-up. I was fearful but excited.

'What, with the black dress?'

'Nononono. The girl next but one to her – in the jeans. Sadie, she's my cousin, down from Gloucestershire to do teacher training. My uncle's a farmer and she was bored with the rural grind. She's fun, I think you'll really like her.'

She was wrong on three counts. Firstly as she was ginger, there was *absolutely no way* I could fancy her. *Not a chance.* I can't stress to you strongly enough how far off my radar gingers are. Secondly, she was a public sector worker. This is a big problem for me. I don't gel with the vocational mentality. Mainly it's because they're all left-wing and skint, which just won't do at all. Thirdly, I didn't deserve her. One look was enough to establish that.

I turned to Lucy. 'I'm not sure she's quite right.'

'Don't be so negative, Frank. Also, she wants a Christmas job, and I said you might be able to get her in at the restaurant. What do you think?'

'Fuck. I probably could actually.'

'Brilliant! Let's go and let her know.'

'OK then.'

My heart wasn't really in it, but we went over. Sadie was in a group of five or so by the stereo. She looked bored and restless.

27

She was about eighty per cent scruffier than everyone else, which made her about twenty per cent sprucer than me.

'Sadie, this is Frank I was telling you about.'

'Hi.'

Uninterested, now she'd actually seen me.

'Yes, he thinks he can get you a couple of weeks at his restaurant.'

'Oh really! Great!'

I shuffled around uneasily and stared at the carpet. It was the colour of marzipan.

'Yerr, we get pretty busy over the holidays. Have you got any experience?'

'A bit.'

'More than enough.'

'When shall I turn up?'

'Dunno. Can you do tomorrow?'

'Yes!'

'You won't get paid much.'

'As long as I get *something*, I'm not that arsed.'

'You'll get something.'

'Sorted, then.'

We were on the fringes of the stereo group. I was too sober as yet to join the conversation. Whitney Houston was doing her airbrushed Brünnhilde act from the speakers. I scanned the CD rack. Opera highlights, U2, Motown's Greatest Hits, the odd jazz sampler. Music for people who don't like music. I felt a soft jab in the ribs. God, ginger, a public employee and sexually voracious, what a nightmare.

'Hello, Frank.' Friendly and open, but maybe with a whiff of patronising irony.

It wasn't Sadie.

'Oh, hi, Sophie.'

A power Sloane from Oxford days. She moved to *mwah* me, but I evaded. A tanned man I didn't know in a sharp cornflower blue shirt was holding court. Sadie and the other two were maintaining shit-eating smiles. If he was boring this lot, he obviously had some special talent for awfulness.

Sophie put a bony arm gently round my back.

'I don't think you know anyone.'

Don't remind me.

'This is Nick and Flora ...' The shit-eaters mouthed silent hellos.

'This is Sadie ...' I couldn't bring myself to look at her, but kept my head high to prevent my double chin pouching too badly.

'And this is my husband Colin,' indicating the cornflower ponce.

'Oh, Colin. Like Colin Bell, the footballer,' I said mock-brightly as we shook on it.

He scowled a little. 'Yes, I suppose so. It's a family name, actually – Scottish.'

'You don't have much of an accent. What part of Scotland are you from? Govan?'

Nick and Flora snickered. I still hadn't looked at Sadie, so couldn't judge her reaction.

'No, not Govan, but quite near Glasgow.'

'Celtic or Rangers?'

'Chelsea, actually. I went to school near London.'

'Near Slough, no doubt.'

'Hmm. Quite near.'

Sophie tried to move us on.

'How's your job going, Frank? Are you still in stockbroking?'

I wish she hadn't said that. Three years ago, in the interregnum between the *Post* and O'Hare's, I had spent six months working as a postboy on the trading floor of a big stockbrokers. If my memory served me, I had somewhat overstated my role to her. To what extent, I couldn't recall. German equities analyst? Chairman?

'No, I'm in the, er, restaurant trade now.'

In the same way that an usherette's in the film business.

29

'Oh, interesting. You were a media industry analyst, weren't you?'

Was I? I had no idea how my mind had come up with this lie, but I cursed it filthily.

'Well, yes, sort of.'

The ponce moved in, sensing my discomfort. 'Sort of? What do you mean?'

'I was training to be a media analyst, but I left before I did any actual, you know, *analysing.*'

'So, what kind of work were you doing?'

'Oh, *précis*-ing reports, general dogsbodying.'

'Which firm?'

'Gellner DeWitt.'

The ponce was warming up.

'Interesting. I know people there. Did you know Tim Locke?'

Why, certainly. Fat loudmouth, third seat up on the Japanese warrants desk, the 'character' of the trading floor. Always had a pint of Guinness on his desk in the afternoons. Never said a word to me in six months, though I doled mail out to him four times a day, hoping to get noticed.

'No, I don't remember a Tim Locke.'

A mistake. You would have to be the veteran of the nursing home not to remember Tim Locke.

'How strange. Most people remember Tim. How long were you there for?'

'Only a few months.' Give it a rest, Colin.

Lucy joined the group. The ponce continued.

'Lucy, you know Tim Locke, don't you? He was the year above Tom at school.'

'Oh, yes. Big noisy chap. Stockbroker.'

'Well, Frank here worked with him for six months, but doesn't remember him.'

Lucy looked puzzled. 'Where did *you* work with him, Frank?'

'Gellner DeWitt, apparently.' Come on, leave off, Lucy.

'Oh, was he in the postroom, too?'

'I don't know. As I say, I don't remember him.'

The ponce was down on me like the Assyrians.

'The *post*room. So you were a *post*boy, I see. No, you probably wouldn't remember Tim, then. Not a very memorable name. I don't suppose our *post*man would remember our name, would he, Sophie?'

Sophie nodded judiciously, but looked embarrassed. To the credit of their sex, all three girls looked embarrassed. I hazarded a look at Sadie. She looked mortified, the blessed little creature. The ponce left me pinned and wriggling, and turned the conversation back to himself. Floored, I took a bottle of champagne back out into the courtyard for another ferocious assault on a Lucky. I perched on a twee little garden bench and sparked up.

Lucy put her head round the door from the kitchen.

'Have I said something wrong?'

'No, Luce. Don't worry, I'm fine.'

'You can't stay out here. It's freezing.'

'No, I'll be fine. Really. I need to smoke.'

She looked at me with eyebrows raised for a moment with what could have been either indulgence or displeasure.

'Have you met Tom's dad yet?'

Tom had arranged for me to be interviewed for a menial job on a men's mag his father was setting up.

'Not a squeak.'

'I'm sure he'll get in touch. He's probably pretty busy.'

'Yeah.'

'Come on, Frank, get inside, we're leaving for the restaurant in a minute.'

'Look, Mum, I'm only halfway through this cigarette. You know I always like to see things through.'

I'd called Lucy Mum sometimes, even before she was pregnant.

She moved to sit down next to me on the bench. I could sense her looking at me.

'You know, we're really pleased you're going to be godfather, Frank. And we think it's great about this interview. Tom's positive it'll come off.'

'Yeah, and I'm really pleased myself, honestly. I'm just not very good at . . . being polite.'

Lucy giggled. I turned to look at her. She had the kind of face that women call beautiful and men call 'all right, I suppose'. She was pale and faintly freckled with a kind mouth that always seemed to be slightly moving; pursing, grinning, pulling itself awry.

'Come on in. You've nearly finished your fag. And you haven't really got going with Sadie yet.'

'I think that relationship's over. It just never quite worked out. I tried my hardest, but it was never meant to be. Anyway I need another ciggie. If I don't average two an hour, I go into a coma.'

She laughed and as she stood up kissed me on the top of the head.

'OK, if you insist. The taxis will be here in about quarter of an hour.'

'Thanks, Mum.'

I then spent an enjoyable ten minutes cannonballing half a bottle of champagne, then lashing Colin to a tree before shooting him in both knees with an eight-bore.

## Seventy-three thou

Tom and Lucy had decided that we were all going out for dinner to celebrate their immaculate conception, but crucially hadn't yet revealed whether they were paying or not. They were already well past the stage when they were earning so much money they didn't know quite what to do with it. They now knew exactly what to do with it. There is a myth abroad that the heinously overpaid yuppie died with the eighties. Not so. It's just that now they've learned to keep a little quieter and spend their money in places where you or I can't see it. This lot of bankers and barristers, if they were doing averagely well for their age and experience, would all be clearing six figures. Sums of money that would turn ordinary hard-working decent folk into a purple fever were to them no more than they deserved.

An example: a year previously, almost to the day, at the end of a drunken evening at his place, Tom had told me that they had just paid off their mortgage with Lucy's Christmas bonus. This was very Tom. Any truth you got from him about the important stuff – how much, how many, how often – only emerged when he was pissed.

'Oh really, that must have been a good one.'

Thirty? Forty? Fifty? Please, Sweet Jesus, no more than fifty.

'Yes, a little over seventy thousand. Seventy-three thou, actually.'

I felt my body trying to cut off the oxygen to my brain. That was five years at O'Hare's in one little Christmassy bundle. And paying off the mortgage rather than slapping it down on an Aston I held to be unforgivable. This is what I mean about the nineties yuppie: so discreet, so understated, so fucking loaded.

Now I was in a lather about whether or not I could stretch to payment. The cortège of taxis were taking us to a new restaurant on Westbourne Grove that was certain to be laughably expensive. I had already developed an unseemly habit of being overprecise when the bill came. I did it partly out of a desire to live up to my Man on the Clapham Omnibus self-parody, but mainly because I am skint. Tom would sit there with the bill and a deck of gilded plastic in his hand, talking the waiter through the details:

'So that's fifty-five each on the gold card, the Amex and the Switch, and what about you, Frank?'

'Fifteen thirty-two, I make it. I only had the main course and a drop of wine. You do take cheques, don't you?' Tom hadn't used cheques for years, the instant hit of cash, plastic and the occasional banker's draft or Eurodollar sufficing for his needs. The cheque to me, though, is the only way to pay. Put the number on the back and it won't, *can't* bounce, and the clearing lag accommodates nasty month-end shortfalls and overshoots. Also if you scrunch it up sufficiently you can buy yourself an extra few days of grace, as the banks are no longer geared up for the front jeans pocket approach to chequebook storage. The fuckers will get to me and my sort eventually, but in the meantime I praise the cheque and its inky, dog-eared, slow-moving ways. I quickly recced my pockets as I got into the taxi and was dismayed to discover that I had left my chequebook at home. I had about eighteen sheets in cash, enough for a minicab back to Clapham and a pack of Luckies tomorrow morning. Even if I had my chequebook it would have been a short-term solution, though. Never mind what I'm going to do about the fact that I haven't got enough money, what am I going to do about the fact that I haven't got enough *money*? I was jemmied into the taxi with four hyenas from Lucy's office, or desk or floor or whatever she called it, and kept schtum. I knew how I was glossed to her glossy mates:

'Really amusing bloke. Great laugh. Total pisshead,' etc. Thanks, Lucy. I should have brought a plastic ball to balance on my nose. To counter the impression they had of me as court jester, I had a Hard Bitten Surly Real Guy persona in play, so that they wouldn't talk to me. It was working a treat. I was being so scary they didn't ask me for any cab money as we pulled up outside the restaurant. Relieved, I determined to lighten up, for old acquaintance's sake, and put my snout firmly and deeply into the booze trough.

That it should have come to this. Tom and I met at university. He was in my history set and had the room next to mine on our corridor. For most of my first term all I remember is thinking that he was from a different planet, like most other people in the university. Planet Popular. Planet Confidence. Planet Born-to-it. As I mouldered in my room with macadamised lungs and cold feet, he held a constant, roaring party next door. Occasionally on my way down the corridor to the college bar to play pool with assorted geographers and college catering staff, I would have to ease my way past the gorgeous attendees at the rolling Mardi Gras. The boys were all six-footers, some Aberdeen Angus, some whippoorwill, in £150 loafers and cashmere cardigans. They emanated health and wealth, their eyes with that good-diet glitter. They were always irresistibly polite to me, and Tom made frequent attempts to get me to join the carnival. I always refused out of the side of my mouth and, without looking him in the eye, would scratch my nose, before scuttling off for another gallon of Belgian lager and a session on the trivia machine with Marje the buttery girl.

It wasn't the boys that put me off, but the girls. Limby, slender, always shaking their glossy hair about and walking with high knees and straight backs. They were quite simply fucking fabulous. In the mornings I would occasionally catch a glimpse of Tom and his current Oaks winner slipping into the shower and would yelp with envy. There was one in particular I remember, whom he told me he was trying to avoid. This was before we became friendly, but he asked me to feign total ignorance of his whereabouts if this girl were to ask me where he was. He gave me a physical description and thanked me heartily. I went off one morning to a tutorial, underprepared and overtired, the pillow creases still red on my cheek, and saw her writing a message on his door, tongue resting in the corner of her mouth. Seeing me flop out of my bunker she asked me the eternal question:

'Have you seen Tom?'

What a fucking specimen she was. No, I mean really fantastic. I mumbled shiftily, trying not to gaze too intently at her high, amazing breasts.

'No, sorry,' and hurried off, terrified by loveliness.

The girls I knew, at home and now here, were at best sweetly pretty. How did the bastard get that kind of action? And this was one he was avoiding! What did he have that I didn't?

Silly question really. I enumerated what he had and I didn't, on the way to my tutor's room: money, charm, the handsome gene, money, a gold-plated accent, money, confidence, money, money, money.

The other thing about Tom was that he seemed to *do* stuff all the time. Drinking six pints would put me to bed for a day with a crepuscular hangover. If I partied with Tom's verve and consistency I would be dead. But he was up at dawn rowing, running, meeting friends for breakfast, driving down to his parents' house and mostly, and most often, fornicating. His bed was approximately two inches from mine, with only a film of papery wall to divide us. I was subjected to a constant chorus of bedspring, flesh-slap, banshee-wail and monkey-grunt. It was like Stockhausen at full volume, all the hours God sent. What kind of drugs did he use? Didn't he ever get chafed? I would lie there smoking hard as he conducted his boisterous sexual trampolining acts, trying not to listen. Sometimes, unavoidably, I would become aroused by all the noise, and nick a dingy onanistic biscuit from his erotic banqueting table. More often I would just lie there in jealous amazement.

We eventually became friendly in our second term, on account of his failure to pass his first set of exams. When the results were posted in our first week back, I looked down the list and expected his name to be picked out in gold leaf. Maybe the examiners would have augmented the initial T into an illuminated depiction of the Ascension into Heaven. In fact, he fucked them up with a vengeance. A straight fail. Oh yes! During term two his social and sexual bonanza abated considerably and he was around the corridor a lot more. He started knocking on my door in the afternoons and coming in for a chat and a biscuit (McVitie's, not masturbatory), to take a break from revision. This ritual was entirely at his instigation, but I came to long for it to come round. New friendships have the effect upon me that new love affairs have on others. I would quite happily have spent whole days talking with him. Rather like Henry does now, he would come and sit on my bed and make me tea, and retrieve my fags from the far side of the room and fix me a bowl of Shreddies. He made out, rather unconvincingly, that he had always been as in awe of me as I had been of him. He also had a tendency to understate how privileged he was. But that was OK, because I would do the same thing, talking up the generic Northern accent, talking down the fee-paying education and the 'ontreprenerr' dad.

For the first time in my life, I even started to develop a crush on another man. As he worked his latest contestant through some rococo moves on the other side of the wall, my eavesdropping self-abuse began to be charged with ambivalence. Whose rapturing face and body was in my mind's eye more? This was a powerful new feeling, and disturbed me greatly. I was from the North, for goodness' sake. The phase took a long time to pass fully, even as long as two years, perhaps. I later decided that it was merely symptomatic of a delayed adolescence. Most boys go through a homosexual period at some time, normally when they're about thirteen. Like many things in my life, mine came later and lasted longer. I still believe now that I'm a late developer. I don't know what gives me that idea.

I became fiercely protective of Tom when my lager and triv mates cast him as just another yah-yah bubblehead. I liked to think that they were only so savage because they were jealous, because they wanted what he had too. Now I realise that this wasn't the case at all. Not everyone is as seduced by Tom's kind of glamour as me (but many more than admit it). In fact, I never did really become part of his social circle, and certainly never got near to entering into his culture. Even when we moved into a house share together in the second year, and I had more direct exposure to his social MO, I was tentative. Take the parties. I just couldn't do his sort of party. My sort of party had grave gender imbalances and not enough booze and tended to sift down to four pasty lads arguing bitterly about D.H. Lawrence. His were straightforward sensual bacchanals where everybody took a little toot, smoked a little draw and had a great time. When they were at our house I would spend the next morning tidying up, wondering why I was the only person who hadn't enjoyed myself. I put it down to the fact that I was a drinker rather than a drugger, and a prole not a party member. My version of a great time was

38

measured by how closely it resembled senility: memory loss, gibbering and impotence. Here were people who liked to laugh and dance around and have sex with one another. What did they know?

Of course, this was just before the great late-eighties drug liberalisation. In the suburbs of Northern towns in the mid-eighties, there was a defence mechanism employed, born of fear of change, that drugs were like tears: strictly for Southern nonces. It was, of course, narcotic Luddism, and the world was moving on regardless. Nowadays, none of the young folk, North or South, drink much any more; they do E and go out and have a lot of straight-up-and-down fatuous fun. An entire generation who no longer associate a good time with vomiting, collapsing and blacking out. Poor lost souls.

My friendship with Tom stayed weekday and one-on-one, but it was none the weaker for that. All my friendships have been based on idolisation, and with Tom this was compounded by my faint, remaining desire to give him one. However, I didn't just adore him because of his confidence, looks and charm. A more crucial element in it was his family. Firstly he had siblings: two rangy blonde sisters. To an only child like me, they inevitably seemed to be great things to have. The real source of my admiration, however, was his relationship with his mother and father. He described to me one January when we arrived back at college what Christmas morning in the Mannion household was like. The children would assemble on his parents' huge bed and the family would spend the morning exchanging gifts and talking. Now, to you this may seem commonplace. If so, then I apologise for being banal. But for years whenever I wanted to fuel a really good dark mood, I would permit myself to recreate a picture of the Mannions on Christmas Day.

The biggest favour I ever did him was to bring him together with Lucy. She was my study partner on a Seventeenth Century European History option in my second year, and would come to our house before tutorials to pick me up. When I first met her I thought she was a real dim bulb. She had this twee way of talking that to me seemed affected. Did anyone ever say 'fab!' and 'lush!' without irony? In tutorial she turned out to be extremely clever. It was the kind of intelligence that I could never have; common-sensical and measured, rather than flashy and over-heated like my own. I also didn't realise for some time that she was probably beautiful, in a womanly, unattainable way, but even then I had no real desire for her. Maybe pit ponies only really fancy other pit ponies. Tom was on to it like a shot. Around the signing of the Treaty of Westphalia he was ardently negotiating terms on dinner dates. By the beginning of the War of the Spanish Succession he was garrisoned in her undergarments on a permanent basis.

One freezing, foggy February morning, trudging to another tutorial I remember breaking a silence by asking Lucy a facetious question, about the character of Mazarin or what Wallenstein did of a weekend or something. She stopped on the pavement and looked at me as if I'd been talking Old Norse.

'Hm? Oh yes.' Very impatient, very far away.

And we continued in silence. I speculated that maybe I was seeing love at close quarters for the first time, and felt all of a sudden bewildered and out of my depth, and truly, horribly envious.

Tom even managed to stay faithful. In his position, this was an heroic feat. He had a kind of perfect magnetism for women; they wanted to fuck him, mother him and be his best friend all at the same time. I mean, even *I* wanted to do him, for Christ's sake, imagine how just-turned-on-to-sex nineteen-year-old women felt. I hung around on the edge of the penalty area, hoping to pick up some of the stray crosses he'd manfully headed out, but didn't even get in a strike on goal. Whilst he spent the better part of two terms lounging in his bower with Lucy, I regressed to my real best mates, Stella, Marje and Triv.

At this point, I moved into my Early-Period Marie O'Sullivan affair. She was in the year below me and had not yet realised that there were better places to start the Big University Relationship than the college bar on a Thursday night. But much more of Marie later. She merits several digressions all of her own.

Tom and I have weathered all the trials of the best-friend relationship. Lucy even underwent a 'Have I ever told you, Frank, that I really want to sleep with you' aberration just after we left university. I believe this is a common occurrence, but it seemed special to me. I remember all the strange and disorienting details. Firstly spending an evening in a dark Tandoori in Shepherd's Bush with her stockinged foot pressed against my groin. While Tom was grinding on at noisome length about pupil masters, tenancy and cheeky-chappy Cockney clerks to my then girlfriend (post-Early-Period, pre-Middle-Period Marie), his fiancée was agitating my balls with her big toe and eyeing me disgracefully. My groin had acquired the density of wet sand. It was fortunate that Tom was still in that phase of his career when he found it intolerable not to be talking about it with a kind of breathless hysteria, because I was incapable of speech. The following morning Lucy rang me in a state of anxious desire from work and said that she had to see me. We met at her flat in Hammersmith and I confected some passion before realising as we writhed noisily on her sofa that I didn't want to do this. I didn't even fancy her. My motives for having come this far were confused, but certainly not good. In an act of superhuman honourableness (and OK I admit it, to some extent to conceal imminent flaccidity), I withdrew, made a fine, stumbling speech about loyalty as I was re-buttoning and left in a double hurry. Had I actually had sex with her? She would have said yes, some form of docking having been achieved, but I don't know. It was sex removed from its primary motivation and incomplete, so I just don't know.

If we had left it at that, the whole episode would have become

41

a forgotten secret. But she persisted, and the next time we were alone together at her place, we went through with it. The fucking was awkward, eyes-closed and joyless, but it cast a shadow of intense excitement. We both felt filthy and low, but also strangely adult, like we had left the hermetic world of Oxford and hit the real world, where real events had real consequences.

Anyway, she saw sense pretty quickly (Did this coincide with Tom's first big cheque? No, no, don't be like that, Frank.) and we had to go through a tedious rite of atonement. We arranged to meet in a pub 'where no-one will know us' and she took me through a slow, grisly tour of her guilt and dismay at ever having *dreamed* of being unfaithful to Tom. She ascribed her motivation to feeling threatened by his commitment to his career, and the absorbing intensity of its atmosphere, which was by necessity tending to exclude her. She said she just wanted to feel some sense of security, and that I provided it. So, in fact the episode had been some kind of cry for help, like a deliberately botched suicide bid. That didn't particularly raise my self-esteem. She cried a lot, and I looked around the pub self-consciously a lot. She put her head on my shoulder a lot. I thought about trying it on, with her so hot, wet and vulnerable all of a sudden, but held back. I mean where could we go? And besides, I didn't fancy her. And besides there was Tom to consider. And besides.

She must have got what she wanted, because a matter of months later they moved in together and she never mentioned her moment of doubt or panic, or whatever it was, to me again. Now here they were, be-mewsed and lathered in confidence and dough, expecting and solid as a rock.

In a way that appals me now, at times when all the full weight of Tom's effortless ability started to get to me, I would summon this bizarre interlude to mind. A grubby strike for the little guy. When he was at his most sparkly and contented, and especially when he was eulogising Lucy in that way he still does, I would look at him steadily and think, Ah, but, Tom . . . and then move on, reluctantly.

# £240 pm

The day after Lucy's gestation knees-up, it was me that needed babying. Thankfully, I had Henry at hand, flatmate, landlord and full-time dispenser of tough, cool love. Henry Stanger has consistently good scores. (There's absolutely no doubt that he is more successful than me.) He breaks down like this:

| 6 | 8 | 8 | 7 | 5 | 4 | 4 | 6 | 8 | 3 |

59. Not bad at all.

He was being good to me that morning, but then again he was good to me every morning.

'Are you going to tell me your version?' He was sitting on the end of my bed with a large mug of tea in one fist and a tuberous reefer in the other. He thumbed his crinkled overlong hair back behind his ears in his very Henry Stanger way.

'Oh, Christ, Henry, I think I've done something very, very bad.'

'That much is evident. Tom just called to see if you got home all right and whether you'd seen a doctor yet.'

'A doctor?'

'There's a large swelling above your right eye, and a trickle of dry blood on your chin. Apparently you punched a banker called Colin in a smart restaurant, vomited in the Philippe Starck sink, headbutted the toilet, and then attempted to curl up with it for the night. He thought the cabbie might have dropped you off at casualty you were in such a state.'

'Oh, Christ. This is very bad. Are you telling me everything?'

'Certainly not. You're not ready for the whole story yet. Here's some tea.'

While flat on my back, I was still occupying that golden place between sleep and waking where it is possible to believe that you're not going to have a bad hangover. When I propped myself up on one elbow to take the mug of tea, how I longed to return.

'Oh, dear. Oh, dear, oh, dear. Oh, Lord.'

'Hangover? How about a bit of this?' He waggled the spliff in his bitten-down fingers. 'Henry's special wake-up recipe – two parts scoopably soft hash to one part fresh grass in a Marlboro Light *nid.*'

I wavered but declined. My mouth tasted like I'd spent the night eating a bonfire.

'No thanks, Henry. Toast would be real.'

'No problem, captain. Real toast on its way.'

He slipped out, and I started trying to piece my evening together. I certainly remembered arriving at the restaurant, and finding myself sitting opposite Sophie and Colin. I also remembered Sophie graciously attempting to rehabilitate me after the postroom revelation. Then I groaned softly as I remembered frotting her during the fish course. Again, undesirable but perhaps not irreparable.

But, oh no, didn't I also make Lucy untuck her blouse so I could get down on my knees and listen to her tummy? Yes, I think I did. And am I right in recalling that I (Oh, please say it isn't true) whispered to her that I'd always loved her? And then . . . I involuntarily cut across this awful train of thought with a loud agonised moan. If I get hit with a flash of embarrassment, invariably the morning after the night before, I tend to launch into a jerky, clenched-teeth rendition of 'I Should Be So Lucky' until the horror passes. This was way beyond Kylie's redemption. Henry re-appeared with a round of toast.

'Yes, Stretch, it's pretty bad, I'm afraid. You'll need to think of a way to make it up to Lucy but I think Tom's forgiven you. Eat, don't think.'

I looked at the alarm clock on my bedside table. 'My God, it's eleven-thirty!' I started to get out of bed in a panic. Gentle Henry bade me stay.

'Don't worry, I phoned O'Hare's. I told them you'd fallen in the shower and were mildly concussed and you'd be there this evening. They were sympathetic.'

'Henry, you're amazing.'

'Toast.'

'To Henry.'

'To Frank. Now, eat up, get up and ablute. We're going for some supermarket therapy.'

I had moved into a ninth of Henry's flat a year previously, by answering an ad in the *Standard*. I had spent two years living in Brixton in a house the personnel of which was in a state of constant flux. Like the philosopher's rowing boat where every plank is replaced over a period of time so that it is and it isn't the same rowing boat, 53 Geffen Road both mutated and stayed

46

the same. Each year one or two new occupants arrived, each week the cycle of food theft and dirty laundry repeated itself. My stay there finally saw me through the start of Late-Period Marie, but apart from that, it was a frozen, footling time. Bits and pieces of work, too much dope, too much TV, too little underwear to cope with the fact that the nearest launderette was six minutes' walk away. A patina of stubborn grime covering everything.

I was never unhappy there. In fact, I told myself that I was having a pretty good time. By the end of my stay, because of the length of my tenure, the place had become my personal fiefdom. I could monopolise the chair that was most precisely squared up to the TV, and keep myself one step ahead on the tea rota. I also had a leading hand in selecting new tenants, a responsibility devolved to me by our benign Spanish landlord. At one stage, I got two French girls to move in, in expectation of a *soupçon* of *l'autre* at *le weekend*. They moved out within a month, appalled at the frowsy sarcastic *Englishness* of it all. I replaced them with a Yorkshire spliff king who sold advertising space and a guy who was trying to make his fortune renovating Fiat 500s, and normal service was resumed. This latter individual was actually the catalyst to my leaving. An invisible sediment of dry filth I could cope with, but an oil-clogged engine block in the bath and a length of rusty exhaust lying in the hallway for two months were too much for me to take. As no-one else seemed to mind, or even notice that their house was being turned into a scrapyard/art gallery, I considered that maybe I was too grown up for all this and started looking for an out.

Enter Henry. The ad read: 'Sngl room for heavy smoker in Clapham flat £240 pm.' Samuel Johnson thought that the art of advertising had peaked by 1745. He'd never seen this little doozy. I breezed the interview, although the high tar content of my Luckies caused him consternation. He served me Marks and Spencer buffet selection followed by pawpaw and mango crush, and rolled me an elegant joint, which had a beautifully fluid, smooth draw. He introduced me to Lottie who had been instructed to eavesdrop from Henry's bedroom, and who gave me the OK. She showed me the scarf she was knitting (which was luridly vile) and asked me if I liked it. I said yes and she told me I could have it when it was finished, because Henry thought it was effeminate, and I moved into their box room two weeks later.

Thinking about it, Henry would have made someone a beautiful wife. In fact, he made Lottie a beautiful wife already, and both of them made beautiful parents for me. He worked from home, dreaming up code for a computer games company, and she did her wool-oriented charity work at the kitchen table. I thought of their life together with unenvious wonder. Him doing his fabulous intricate brainwork, her making things and both of them just quietly hanging out together all day. I'd get home and they'd be lolling on the sofa reading, maybe smoking one, the fridge filled with high class junk food: tzatziki, chicken tikka thighs, fruit fools, parma ham, halva, blueberries, red pesto.

Today Lottie was elsewhere, so Henry and I went shopping together, and he mercifully insisted on protecting me from more detail on the previous night. I was on trolley duty as he mooned around harvesting good things from the fruit and vegetable section.

'Henry, you're pretty hot on probability, aren't you?'

'Well, I'm not bad. What's the question?'

'How many women do I have to meet before I've got a robust statistical chance that the next one is the right one?'

'Augment and clarify.' He was gazing at the star fruit he was holding in the tips of his fingers.

'Well, my current thinking is to treat the process like a series of coin tosses. By this reckoning, about one in every two women I meet should turn out roughly OK, and our relationship should go somewhere. I don't mean all the way to the altar, but maybe all the way to a trip to the pictures or something.'

'Frank, I think the system you're using is a little flawed. And this is Stanger the Man talking rather than Stanger the Statistician. A coin is a very tightly controlled system, there are only two possible outcomes per toss. People are more ...' he was now reading the label on some purple spinach '... difficult. If I were you, I'd base my paranoia on something different. Like a weather system or the football results or something. You know, introduce more factors. Purple spinach. What a gimmick. Let's try it anyway.'

'OK, let me put it this way. I've thrown the woman coin to one degree or another something like thirty-two times, always wanting, let's say, heads. But each time so far it's come up tails. It must get more likely that, the next time I toss, I get a head.'

Henry stopped and shook his head sagely. 'Not much comfort there, Frank. Each toss is a separate event within the system. It doesn't matter how many times you've come up tails, it's just as likely to come up tails the next time. It's plain unreasonable to be more expectant of a head just because you've just thrown a tail. I think there's a play about this. These two characters keep tossing a coin and keep throwing heads. When they finally throw a tail, they both die.'

'Oh, good.'

I watched Henry as he trawled the deli counter for some new exotica to sample.

'Explain this then. England have played 365 test matches. They've won the toss 183 times and lost it 182 times. As equal as it could be. I'm not sure how, but I'm sure that refutes your argument.'

'Maybe, but it doesn't prove yours. They're on tour at the moment, aren't they?'

'New Zealand.'

'Well, then, if they win the toss at the next test match, I would say that you're certain to enter a satisfying relationship by the time they lose.'

'You're being facetious.'

'Do you like carciofini?'

'His early work was all right. When are you going to tell me what really happened last night?'

'Mmm. I think they put a bit too much vinegar in. Let's lob it in anyway. When are we going to tell you? Lucy and I agreed that we'd wait a while. Tragedy plus time equals comedy. We want you to be able to laugh about it.'

'God. Why, fuck, why, fuck, why? Why do I do it to myself?'

'And indeed to others. Don't get too worked up. It's not as bad as your worst imaginings.'

'Did she tell you about that girl they tried to fix me up with?'

'Oh, yeah, she got off with a waiter or something. After *you* tried to get off with her by the fag machine.'

I leant on the trolley and let the heat and noise of my hangover fill the silence. The lump on my forehead was emitting a strong low hum of pain. Henry was now deep in thought at the bread section.

'I think I'll withdraw from social life, Henry. It's just not worth it any more.'

'I thought you already had.'

'Cheers.'

'Just drink a little less.'

'I drink because I get nervous. I just want these fuckers to take me a bit more seriously.'

Henry turned to me with a stern and lucid look on his stern and lucid face. OK, Dad, lay it on me.

'I'll tell you what you can do if you want to be taken seriously. Why don't you go to Lucy's pregnancy party, get appallingly drunk, molest two married women, start a fight with a merchant banker, burst into tears, claim to the assembled party that you are a great poet of the human soul, vomit in the sink, collapse in a toilet cubicle and tell your best friend that he's a squandered talent as he helps you into a taxi. I'm sure that would give you an air of gravitas.'

'Oh, Henry. Tell me you're joking.'

'Nope.'

'Is that everything?'

'Nearly everything. But as I say, you're not ready for the whole truth yet. Anyway, you're broadly forgiven. Stop dwelling on it. In fact that's good advice for you all round: stop dwelling on it, start doing something about it.'

The 'great poet of the human soul' was the real killer. I wasn't fond of the tears either. Or any of it to be honest. The egg-sized contusion over my eye began to wail its reproach. I believed that there was, in fact, very little comedy to be salvaged from this incident. From my humble state the evening now looked like a symbol of Tom and Lucy's increasing weight and stature as human beings. There they were, married, successful, generous, willingly taking on the responsibility of parenthood, spreading their benign and thoughtful influence back out into their society like proper adult people. Wankers – oh, stop it, Frank. But regardless of that, there I was, raging at being cast as some kind of low comedian, acting to type in the most egregious way possible. Subversive behaviour had at one time seemed funny, necessary even, in the face of my friends' inexorable progress towards sensibleness. Now it just seemed like plain rudeness, and rudeness with its source in envy of people who for some reason valued me. Tom's offer to put in a word for me with his dad about the job at *Emporium* made it all worse. I'll call you a wanker, and I do, but I'll still accept your patronage.

There was real annoyance as well, but it was not directed at my peer group any more, just at myself. I used to believe that Tom and Lucy's approach to their lives was a kind of giving in, and that their pursuit of solidity was doomed to failure and disappointment. It certainly didn't appear like that now. And what was more difficult to see was an alternative. My alternative was a restaurant in Battersea and fifty hours of TV a week. My alternative was nowhere, it was nugatory,

51

it was *nada*, nowt, *niente*, null, nix, nil, nought, nothing. My time was up.

For a long time I had nursed a secret belief that, if I wanted, I could be better than anyone at anything, if I put my mind to it. I reckon most people feel the same, most men at least. So Tom looked as if he was making it as a barrister? If I'd *chosen* to be a barrister I'd be a lot better at it than him. So Lucy's a bond trader? That could have been an option for me. So Henry writes elegant, beautiful computer programmes? Mine would be far more elegant, far more beautiful, if I'd ever chosen to give it a proper shot. Now the issue of choice had left the issue. What was I going to do? Take up an adult education course in law, computers and bonds? Furthermore, the evidence for such ludicrous contentions was weak at the best of times. Some strong performances at the junior school debating club, a bit of verbal facility, a knack with quadratic equations; it was never really enough. Now it would be laughable, if I hadn't lost my sense of humour about the whole thing. The reason I gave for not having followed them all was that what they were doing just wasn't worth bothering with. The question of what *was* worth bothering with just wasn't worth bothering with either.

'One day. You'll see.'

Henry paid up and we ambled back to the flat. I resolved to go and revise my maths downward on all dimensions.

That and do an obituary. When I'm feeling in need of cheering up, I do an obituary. It gives you something to work towards. This is the one I worked on when we got back from the supermarket:

### SIR FRANCIS STRETCH QC
### PATENT LAWYER

Sir Francis Stretch, the eminent barrister, has died at his Nash house in London's Regent's Park, aged 71.

Sir Francis was instrumental in the radical reforms of patent law as it related to the emerging information technology industry in the late years of this century. The achievement was all the more remarkable as he came very late to both fields, not being called to the bar until his fortieth year, having completed a computer science degree at the LSE in his early thirties.

Nicknamed 'Golden Bollocks' because of his combination of tenacity and extreme wealth, he was respected rather than liked by his contemporaries.

A wife, Lucy, survives him. They had two step-children from her first marriage, Fortinbras and Clytemnestra, as well as a natural son, Stan.

# Twelve hundred quid

Two things stopped from me from downgrading myself frantically all afternoon. The first was that, as I worked on my death notice, I got a call from Tom's dad's office, proposing some interview dates.

'Hello, is that Mr Stretch?'

'Yep.'

'Cordelia here from Charles Mannion's office at *Emporium*. I'm sorry about the delay in getting back to you.'

'No problem.' I'm used to it, love.

'Well, the reason I'm calling is that Charles would very much like to see you in the next couple of weeks, and I've got some convenient dates which I'd like to try you with. He'd like to do a breakfast if that suits you.'

'Great, perfect.'

'OK, how about the twenty-ninth?'

'That's good for me.'

'The third?'

'That's good for me.'

'The fifth?'

'Fine.'

'The eighth?'

'No worries.'

'The tenth?'

'Couldn't be better.'

'Err, the twelfth?'

'Listen, Cordelia, I'll tell you what, any day at all is fine by me. I'm sort of a . . . a free agent. Any day will be just perfect.'

'OK, I'll get back to you to confirm in the next day or two.'

'Thanks very much.'

I was pretty ambivalent about this whole deal to tell the truth. I had mentioned to Tom months ago that I was considering getting back into journalism, as if it was just one of a whole range of options I was toying with, and he mentioned *Emporium* and said it would be no problem for him to get me in. It was supposed to be 'a men's magazine with a difference' (which men's magazine wasn't? *Manhood – the Men's Magazine that's Exactly the Same as the Rest?*), but Tom reckoned I'd get something out of them, no trouble. They were trying to make it look as overstuffed and glossy as possible, but the backers wanted it done dirt cheap. The only place they could really wield the axe was the writing staff, which left opportunities for has-beens and never-weres like me. But still, the dreadfulness of it all. I'd read these magazines – *Guy Thing*, *Twatted*, *Him* and all those other shinies with their flatter-to-deceive cover shots. In fact, I read them every month. But why do they pretend to be something more interesting and important than the sixth-former wank fodder they really are? In my view, there are only two differences between *Twatted* and *Skinny and Wriggly*. Firstly, the real porn is bound with staples. Secondly, in the *faux*-fuck mags, tanga briefs coyly husband the muffs. In *Skinny and Wriggly* gussets only make an appearance strung between scissoring legs like warm mozzarella. So 'the men's magazine with a difference' presumably meant either *more* crotch shots or *fewer* crotch shots. In either case, I reckoned *Emporium*'s business proposition was terminally disabled before it started.

The only thing that made me say yes to an interview was the thought of Tom's efforts on my behalf, and the sense of duty that these efforts inspired. Well, that and the prospect of the freebies.

Anyway, the second thing that happened that afternoon was that I opened some mail I got in the second post. As I think I've said, I never open mail from the bank. It always ends in tears. I never really open any mail, as everything I get is in some way connected to money that I don't or can't have. But Henry had left a letter for me on the kitchen table *that had a hand-written address on it.* I opened it and was astonished to discover that it was from Bill Turnage. He must have written the note and posted it as soon as I'd left him in Knightsbridge. It was written on some personalised stationery, waxy paper with a quirky little logo of a table in the top right-hand corner. He'd apparently designed it himself. I remembered how brilliant he was in practical lessons. He would be polishing the marquetry on his reproduction Early Georgian *escritoire*, while I was still trying to make a mug tree with branches that slanted upwards.

Bill had been a middle-ranking first-division friend then, sort of an Aston Villa or a Coventry City, and like them he hung around my life without ever really making a huge impression from when I was fourteen until I left school for university. Gaunt and clever-ish, brooding and outdoors-y, he was a lot of people's middle-ranking mate, I guess. He was a lone cyclist and hiker, too independent-seeming, too cagoule-and-walking-boots for anyone really to prize him. I couldn't remember ever having a bad thought about him. Well, maybe he was a bit too bland. Also, he was one of those people who reach puberty when they're about nine, and he turned up at secondary school already able to tuck his cock and balls between his legs and make like a lady. As a consequence, he inspired many sleepless nights of shame and fear amongst his contemporaries, me included. Why was my groin like Action Man's and his like a ferret shop window?

I got over all this soon enough, and we ended up going to the same parties, removing the bras from the same girls, occasionally at the same time, and wondering what we should do *then* for three or four years. He then failed to get into Oxford, and ended up at UEA. I visited him once in my first year and that was that. Five years of easy affection receded into the past as if it had been no more than a handshake. No regrets, though, that's just friendship for you.

His letter went as follows:

*Dear Frank,*
*Don't fall off your chair! Great to see you yesterday. You seemed a bit in a hurry. I hope you enjoyed your party.*
*Any road up, let me fill you in a bit, like I couldn't do yesterday in all the rush. Been married now for nine years (gulp!) to Sue who was at UEA (you met her, but she says she won't be surprised if you've forgotten) and we've got three kids, Debbie (9 – she's the reason!), Ben (6) and Murray (5). Thought about having the snip, but Ben's a pretty good contraceptive anyway!*
*Just to say hello again really and to say you are welcome to come and stay with us in Suffolk any time, we've got an attic (My study – still writing!) you can stay in with a sofa bed. The pubs are good, and have lock-ins, and the sea is wet and refreshing. Drop me a line. Alternatively, just give me a call, but I always hated the phone, didn't I, and still do.*
*Yours 'back from the grave'-ly!*
*Bill Turnage*

The tone of the letter was difficult to judge. There were far too many exclamation marks for one thing. It could, I suppose, have been reproaching me for not getting in touch, but I didn't think so. It cheered me up for some reason, and pathetically I was rather proud of mentioning to Henry that I'd 'just got a letter from a really old friend, inviting me to his house in Suffolk'. He seemed surprised but unimpressed, which was characteristic, as he sat on the sofa watching *Blue Peter* and rolling one up. Lottie was dozing against his thigh. Another tough day in the Stanger household.

'Very good. Are you going to go and see him?'

'Nah. Three kids and a screech-owl of a wife. Sounds hideous.'

'You sentimental old fool.'

'I know, it'll be the death of me. Anyway, I'm off to work.'

'Be the best that you can be.'

I went out to the Cavalier feeling in a relatively good mood considering the previous night's exertions. I had a feeling that I got increasingly less often, which could be summed up as 'things are on the up a bit, things are happening a little'. Admittedly, it usually came to nothing, but was better than its opposite, which consisted of screaming fits and clubbing myself to death with self-hate, so I tried to make the best of it. Anyway, the thought of an evening waiting tables at O'Hare's didn't fill me with a feeling of yowling frustration, as it often did.

O'Hare's is a brilliant idea if, as so many of my friends seem to think, 'brilliant ideas' make large amounts of money for those who have them. It is hard to determine whether the success of the idea was down to luck or judgement. Bart, whose full name was Graham Barton, was the owner and prime mover. He used to work in advertising where, he had told me, he was one of the old guard, up from secondary modern in Poplar and into the postroom rather than skimmed off from the milk round. This background had made him tougher and more devious than his college-boy competitors, and he made it pay. Leonard's, the agency he ran for five years, was old-fashioned, overstaffed and financially imprecise, but had a powerful heritage, still just about marketable, from the early years of commercial television. With this provenance, and a heavily played English Gentleman card, he and the other crooks in charge flogged it to a Japanese agency for a hugely inflated sum in the year of Lawson, 1988. The front page of that week's *Campaign* is framed in the bog at the Battersea O'Hare's: MIEKKO NETS LEONARD'S – AT A PRICE. He once told me that he personally walked out with three times what the place was worth, and he only had fifteen per cent.

With the money he went on holiday for two years, came back and started O'Hare's. The brilliant idea was this: Rip off FUCCERS. What is a FUCCER? Fresh from University, Credit Card, Extremely Rich. Developing this acronym, I believe, had cost Graham at least one sleepless night. 'Fuck' was the unstressed spine of his lexicon. It was as if he couldn't bear to be parted from it, whatever the circumstances. 'Would you like a fucking Jaffa Cake?' was Graham on his elevenses best behaviour. Graham's insight was that to try and open a fashionable restaurant was too fraught with risk – expensive staff and premises, fashionableness giving way to unfashionableness in the blinking of an eye, the need for London-competitive food, which could be anything from Andean peasant to Tex/Belge. So, in classic adman style, he chose his target audience and gave them exactly what they wanted: dark wood, consistency, old film posters, stodgy food, a place to make a noise, a late bar. Bingo. A brilliant idea. After four years he had five restaurants strategically cited in all areas of Part-Qualified Accountant and Articled Clerk Land: Battersea, Wandsworth, Clapham, Fulham and Shepherd's Bush, with another two on the way in Highgate and Hammersmith. He had made himself well versed in the desires of the young and dull in their Gardenia-painted maisonettes, with their Monet prints and complete works of Phil Collins on DAT. After a dusty, we've-just-moved-in-together shag on the Habitat kilim they would crave charred protein and find themselves in one of Bart's joints, revealing their detailed knowledge of the IKEA spring catalogue over buffalo wings and a bottle of Australian Cab Sauv: 'Oh, isn't it lovely to have a friendly little neighbourhood restaurant at the end of the road? No, I think we should definitely have *curtains* in the bathroom.'

Bart had probably made at least another couple of million out of these dreary Fuccers over the years. Eventually they would grow out of his stodgy, expensive baby food and start eating in places that didn't play The Eurythmics' greatest hits on a loop. Bart didn't give a toss, though, because just as one batch moved on, in would come the next, the boys in their M&S crewnecks and chinos, the girls in jeans and blue button downs, positively gagging to be fleeced by their friendly neighbourhood fat bastard. All he did was change the tape: Enya, Mariah Carey, *Riverdance*; gloop music and gloop food for gloop lives.

For a boorish mudhopper from the wetlands of Essex he was doing all right, was Graham. He drove a gunmetal V12 Mercedes S Class with blacked-out windows and the word GRAZER on the numberplate. He sat high up and well back on the creamy hide with his fat baguette forefinger hooked round the base of the steering wheel with no regard whatsoever for speed cameras or pedestrians, constantly growling threats and insults at his managers over the digital carphone. When he wasn't in the Benz, he was in the casino, toying with a couple of grand from the till at O'Hare's.

He carried his twenty stone quite well and wore Ralph Lauren polo shirts, tight old Levi's and whiter-than-white 'Boks in the manner of a Hollywood film director. He liked Rod Stewart. He was so cash, so chrome-and-smoked-glass, so soft-porn, so seventies.

Fat, vulgar, and rich, he felt he could do no wrong, and by his own simplistic standards, he never did. He had a flat in Cadogan Square, a place in Berkshire which he called Hefner

House after his hero, and paraded his ethnically diverse sexual conquests with Sultanic arrogance. He apparently had no friends, apart from his oddjob, Brian the Bat, and spent most of the day staring at a roulette wheel when he wasn't paying unannounced visits to his obscenely profitable restaurants with his latest Sumatran, Geordie or Jap. Having spent his forty-five years on the planet in a constant state of angry pleasure, he was in no mood to stop now. His scores were humblingy good:

| 8 | 9 | 9 | 9 | 9 | 9 | 1 | 1 | 7 | 6 |

68. Good darts, big fella. His score may come as a surprise to some, but not to those who know the extent to which he adores himself. Christ, he thinks he's marvellous. Every little piece of him, from desiccated collar-length hairdo to clean chubby toes, from bloated Merc to tigerskin bedspread, is a constant source of delight to him. With a love like that, you know you should be glad.

After being fired from *The Post*, I had given up on journalism. I temped around for a while, doing nothing in particular, and then pitched up in the Battersea branch of O'Hare's. Bart interviewed me in his car as he lumbered between the Wandsworth branch and the casino. He asked me to start that evening and chucked me out on the Fulham Road, told me to make my own way back over the river, and that was that. I started as a waiter, and had endured many uncomfortable evenings serving people I knew from college.

'Frank, what are *you* doing here?' i.e., where did *your* wheels come off, you sad fucker. Illiterate dullards they may have been, but they knew how to load straight questions with subtext. Especially the men. Thankfully, my contemporaries had largely passed through their O'Hare's phase by the time I got there, and I no longer needed to tell whoppers about how well the screenplay was coming on. I had been promoted to manager about six months previously. Hurroo. All this meant was that I did the count and was in charge of throwing people out when they got too raucous. On a Saturday night, particularly after a rugby international, the choruses of 'Sweet Chariot' and 'Jerusalem' would commence. I'd leave them to it and try to look harassed but amused. But at the point when the boys started slapping their dicks in the dessert, as the manager I had to intervene and chuck the imbeciles out. I'll say two things for Fuccers, though: they never get violent, and they always pay their bill. The English middle-class upbringing can apparently countenance public immersion of undercarriage in the chocolate mousse, but scrapping with the staff and doing a runner? It's just not done.

I stayed because I had no option. Firstly, because to move on it would be necessary to ponder the Great Big Question that bored me so much. 'When are you going to *do* something with your life?' and all that other girlfriend/mother stuff. I didn't feel ready for that type of question. When I did start to tiptoe round such thorny subjects, a voice within me would object like a teenage virgin: not yet, not now, not here, let's wait till later. The Lottery would set me right, or love would come crashing in from stage left in a white Ferrari. Ah, then Frank Stretch would be free and would *do* something with his life.

Secondly, I had accustomed myself to the ritual of working there. It was what I *did*. As I got older, it became increasingly less tenable to make out that I was biding my time until my ambitions had come to fruition. When I had started there it had been simple to say that it was merely a stop-gap. After three years, the thought of being interviewed by Tom's dad for a job on *Emporium* in some ways filled me with dread. I couldn't bear the notion of giving up my routine.

In fact, when I pitched up that night, in spite of the hangover and head trauma, I snapped into action with some crispness.

I was feeling backslappy and chatty, but mostly I was feeling safe. I knew how to do this, for God's sake. Within a minute of me arriving, tables were being reset more to my liking, the blackboard menu was being rechalked for aesthetic effect and clarity and I decided to run a mini-promotion on some noxious Chilean Merlot we'd overstocked. God, I was good, why should I want to leave?

Oh, and anyway, I couldn't leave, because I owed Bart some money.

The whole process had been quite moving in a way, if you're moved by bank manager stories. He had always been a decent, generous man, Mr Frost, and the initial letter he wrote me was suffused with a tone of genuine regret. My account was still held at the Oxford branch, as I'd never been in a position to move it closer to home. He 'suggested' in the letter, in a manner that brooked no refusal, that I go to meet him for A Consultation. When I turned up, I noticed that the place had been transformed into a McDonald's. All the old attempts at gravitas and intimidation had gone. The staff were no longer divided from the punters (sorry, Clients) with bullet-proof glass, but sat in the middle of the floor behind teak-effect desks wearing nylon neckerchiefs and stewardess smiles.

Across the dustless grey chamber strode Frost. He greeted me with a real pumper of a handshake and 'suggested' that we have a chat in the consultation room. I asked him what had happened to his office.

'Everything's open plan now. We're all moving towards flatter structures.'

'What, relocating to a bungalow?' Weak humour is a classic Stretch-is-Nervous stratagem.

'No, no. Flatter management structures. Shorter chains of command.'

So, if a teller wanted to order some new paper clips they no longer had to chew up a valuable two seconds of management time by knocking on his door. I didn't say this. The flatter structures seemed to be getting him down.

The consultation room was the size of a toilet cubicle. We both sat down at the tiny desk, our knees rubbing together awkwardly.

Frost was a mid-30s type of guy. His breakdown looks like this:

| £ | ♥ | ▮ | ♟ | ⊞ | 🚙 | 👤 | ✆ | ! | ♛ |
|---|---|---|---|---|---|---|---|---|---|
| 4 | 5 | 2/9 | 3 | 3 | 3 | 6 | 2 | 3 | 1 |

Summary: £30K and a good pension; 'happily married'; decreasingly satisfied in his job; arid, bookless Beazer home; Mondeo/Vectra/downscale Rover 6; whippy little body (kept in trim by lunchtime squash?); Social life revolving around the bank (work friends score half points); a nice if dullish fish; and a ♛ score in deep decline. Bank managers ceased being GP-ranking 'pillars of the community' decades ago along with teachers and policemen – service-sector slaves who you only notice when they bring you bad news: 'You've been burgled, little Jonny's retarded, you're skint.'

The only real area for debate was the ▮ score. Chances were he was just another lights-off missionary plugger, furrowing away with metronomic dutifulness thirteen times per fiscal year. There was a remote possibility, however, that he was a swinging suburban sex terrorist, swapping, strapping, rolling on the latex and stapling bits of plywood to his scrotum every night. The stifling mix of low-finance, 26-inch HDTV and swagged kitchen curtains can do this to a man. Despite this area of doubt he was undeniably doing better than me, and that's the most important thing to remember.

He wasn't his usual self that day. The familiar tone of ironic indulgence had been replaced by tortuous over-formal politeness. He started to address me as if I was a waxwork.

'Thank you for coming to see us, Mr Stretch. I hope our consultation proves fruitful to both parties and that all outstanding issues can be resolved to our mutual benefit.'

I peered at him in disbelief. 'Is this conversation scripted?'

He looked sheepish.

'Er, well sort of. All Terms of Account Renegotiation Consultations now start with an open and honest statement of objectives. It's part of the bank's Strategic Refocus on Meeting Client Needs.'

I must have looked amazed.

'Oh, Needs and wants. Needs and wants. I always forget that last "wants".'

I masked incredulity with insouciance. You should try it some time. 'OK. I see. Now what was this about "Account Renegotiation"?'

For someone who was in the soup I was acting with some aplomb. He shuffled through a thick wad of papers he had brought in with him. Had he lost his script? Did he want a prompt? 'You haven't read the letters we've been sending?'

'Err, yes, but I can't remember all the details.'

He looked resigned.

'Right then, I note that at close of business on Wednesday, your current account stood at a debit balance of . . .' (dramatic pause) 'one thousand two hundred and twenty-two pounds seventeen pence.'

'That much. Ooh hell.'

'I also note that the account has not passed into credit for seven months. And over your nine-year relationship with us, you have not been in credit for longer than three consecutive weeks.'

That seemed about right, but I was woefully underprepared, and hence had no means of counter-attack. Information is power in these situations. The word 'relationship' threw me a little as well. I fell back on vagueness.

'But I never go over my overdraft limit. Usually.'

He could just about bring himself to look me in the eye. 'Hm, usually. Anyway, there are some new directives that have been introduced by the bank that attempt to harmonise account servicing standards and charging structures across the client base.'

I was nodding with approval, trying to give the appearance of a man who was quite interested in hearing some details about these New Directives.

'The new directives state that clients who do not achieve reasonable credit maintenance objectives may become subject to account review and renegotiation of terms, and in certain circumstances, amicable closure following settlement of outstanding debts. Client incapacity to comply with renegotiated terms in extreme circumstances can result in recourse to legal sanction.'

Whoever wrote this stuff could really pile on the agony.

'I'm afraid you fall into this latter category, Mr Stretch.'

'Last, not latter. There are more than two categories.'

'Oh, are there?' He looked in puzzlement at the piece of A4 that presumably contained this deathless prose. It occurred to me that if this grammatical solecism was corrected because I had pointed it out, I would have cost them thousands in re-printing charges. It was some comfort, but not much.

His gaze met mine again. I noticed that he looked very tired. Beneath the strangulating coils of management speak I could detect a decent bloke trying to communicate. He really didn't want to say what was coming, but he forced it out somehow.

'Simply put, Mr Stretch, unless you repay your overdraft within the month, we're going to foreclose and take you to court. I'm really sorry.' He looked about to break down. 'Thirty days maximum.'

'Oh God. It's that bad, is it? Don't worry, it's not the end of the world. I'll sort it out.'

'There's not much I can do. It's all gone upstairs.'

So there was an upstairs in this Flatter Structure, was there? I thought there might be.

He showed me out, right into the street, and instead of shaking my hand gave me a little pat on the shoulder.

'Good luck. I can't say how sorry I am about this.' He raised his brows and looked at me with sorrowful eyes. I felt like giving him a big hug. How had the bastard managed to do this? Threatened to bankrupt me and then made me feel sorry for him? But I reasoned that it wasn't him who was doing the threatening. Mr Big was elsewhere, in some airconned money mountain in EC2, stroking his jacquard silk tie and flexing his burgundy gut. Frost was just the unwilling kneecapper. He had been emasculated. All his old powers of discretion, the things that had made it possible for him to derive some satisfaction from his work, had been usurped by New Directives until he had become little more than a talking leaflet. On the coach home I imagined him sitting drunk in a hotel bar near Swindon on some infernal Client Service course, hopelessly railing against the new ways, or flopping himself down on his Dralon settee and whingeing at the wife all night about lost self-esteem. 'What I don't bloody understand is . . .' How much time before the laptopped whizzkids at HQ switched from a Strategic Refocus on Customer Needs and Wants to a Strategic Refocus on Firing Half the Staff? Not long, I'll be bound.

None of this indulgence was making me any richer, so I surveyed my options. Theft, prostitution, beggary, abscondment, prison, Bart. By the time I'd alighted at Victoria it was clear to me that Bart was the only way forward. I would rather be in thrall to a fat gangster than become a cat burglar, panhandler or rent boy. I phoned him on his mobile when I got back to O'Hare's for the evening shift and acted in a manner so craven I yelp to remember it. I could hear the dull jabbering of croupiers and Hong Kong Chinese, so guessed he was at the roulette again. After two minutes of my timid greasing I realised that he had already agreed to my request. His only conditions were that it was a personal loan from him to me, and that I had to repay it in full, not in dribs and drabs. He didn't even want any interest. His payment was that he had effectively put me in manacles to O'Hare's for as long as I was unable to save twelve hundred quid. On the money he paid me that was likely to be a very long time.

That night, though, despite the sloughing hangover, the egg of pain on my forehead and a sense of regret, I couldn't make myself care. I bossed everyone about and was dangerously charming to the customers. It was warm in there, nobody knew who I was, and I could do it falling off a log. Work was a kind of deeply provisional happiness. This is the effect a hand-addressed envelope and the prospect of a job interview could have on me. For a brief period of time, obviously.

£2.91

I remembered my job offer to Sadie. The thought brought me down a little. I genuinely couldn't remember trying to get off with her, but I had no doubt that I had done. If she combined that example of my behaviour with my humiliation at the hands of Colin, she probably wasn't currently holding her new boss in particularly high esteem. I think I'd told her to turn up at six-thirty-ish, which turned out to be lucky, because Paolo the chef told me that the witless girl I'd hired a week before had phoned in to say that she was quitting. She had been typical of the general standard. She was Irish, from Kerry, but she was so off the pace she could have been either from the Frozen North or the fourteenth century. She had spent all her time smoking crazily out by the bins and weeping softly into her apron. O'Hare's had had them all in my time there: thieves, mutes, illiterates, screamers and truants. The rates Bart paid attracted people with such ineptitude with the English language and such scrofulous skin that McDonald's would reject them out of hand. There was little chance of Sadie not being up to the job.

She turned up about ten minutes late in a dirty mac and tiny once-black mini skirt. I was standing by the bar putting white plastic flowers into vases.

'Shite. Sorry I'm late, got lost in Clapham.'

She seemed breezily unconcerned that nineteen hours previously I had attempted to tongue her face.

'That's OK, get your coat off and I'll tell you the deal.'

Her hair really was very red indeed. It wasn't sandy or hint-of-mouse-y, it was bright orangey red. She had it pinned back to her scalp and gathered into a complicated curled bun, but you couldn't tone down hair that colour so easily.

When she was ready, I took her over to an empty table and told her the deal: 'Lunchtime shift eleven-thirty till five, evening shift five till eleven-thirty, read the specials off the blackboard, £2.91 an hour.'

*Finis.*

'That's outrageous.'

'Plus tips, you could be clearing well over twenty quid a day.'

'What does it say in my contract about my rights when the boss tries sexually assaulting me?'

'Oh, come on, give me a break. I didn't have to give you this job, you know.' I was aware that this had hit the wrong note.

'I don't have to accept.'

'OK, OK, OK. But try not to mention the . . . incident . . . again. I'm really sorry about it.'

'Don't be sorry, I was flattered.'

'Really?'

'Yes, particularly the bit when you said you don't normally go for gingers or people in the vocations, but I was worth making an exception for.'

'I didn't say that, did I?'

'Oh, yes.'

'That's bad.'

'Yeah, but I'll get over it. How's your concussion?'

'Better. It was more of a blackout, I think.'

'And how's the poetry coming along?'

'What do you mean?'

'Well. You were saying last night how you're a great poet of the human soul, I was just wondering if you'd cranked out any stanzas today.'

By this stage my head was collapsed on to my forearm in grief. Sadie laughed. It was a filthy, masculine, merciless kind of laugh. 'Right. There's a customer. I'm off.'

Part of me had thought that Henry had been making it all up. I contemplated sticking my head in the pizza oven, but instead went out to the bins for a bifter. I didn't speak much to Sadie for the next hour or so, but every time she went past me she said: 'Ah, the Great Poet fixes a drink,' or, 'See how the bard polishes the side plate.' I was beginning to warm to her, to be honest.

At eight, Bart dropped in with Brian. This was unusual. He would occasionally drop in early evening to put the wind up everyone but he wouldn't dream of eating in one of his own restaurants. He sat at a table near the window looking agitated and summoned me over.

'Stretch, how are we doing this week?'

'Good. Ten grand easy already.'

'How many shifts you done?'

'Four so far. The normal.'

'Fucking hell, Frank, why can't you do me a few more? We take bigger when you're on, guaranteed.'

'Oh, you old softie. I can't do any more. I'd go fucking mad. And you won't pay me any extra. I'd have to be a nonce.'

'Don't be a wanker, Frank, do me another couple of shifts.'

'Nope.'

'Anyway, what you say we've taken this week?'

'Ten, ten and a half.'

'Right, that's all right. We're gonna stay for a drink, can you get us a few hundred from the till?'

'There's not enough in yet. I could nip down the cashie?'

'Yeah, good lad, go on then, just three hundred, I'm a bit short and Mossassa's taken me wallet.'

I guessed that Mossassa was the pear-shaped mulatto I'd seen him with a couple of times. I put on the frightful coat and just as I left, called to Sadie: 'Drinks here, Sadie.' And gestured at Bart and Brian.

Out in the wind, I jogged along to the bank feeling a little uneasy. Bart's raiding was up to three or four grand a week, and increasing. I also had the feeling that he only wanted me to do extra shifts so there was always someone around to get him access to the cash. He always said he wanted all that kind of stuff left down to the managers. Tony Ling's glib reassurances weren't working. There was always the possibility that Tony was colluding with Bart against my best interests. That makes me sound paranoid, but you haven't met Tony with his tiny furred little teeth.

When I got back to O'Hare's, Bart and Brian were standing in the street looking pissed off.

'Who's the tart with the red hair?'

'Sadie, she started today.'

'Well, she's fired. Give me the dough.'

'What do you mean fired? What's she done?'

'You can ask her that. We're off.'

I handed over the stiff wad of money and went inside. Sadie was nowhere to be seen. I went into the kitchen.

'Paolo, where's Sadie?'

He jerked his thumb in the direction of the bins. I went through and she was standing there surveying the bedraggled courtyard and smoking softly.

'You're back. Who the fuck was *that*?'

'*That* was the bloke who owns the restaurant.'

'What?'

72

'That's Bart – Graham Barton. He owns the place.'

'Shit. I thought you owned it.'

I didn't know whether to be flattered or gravely affronted.

'No, he owns it. What did you do?'

'Oh, fucking hell.'

'Come on.'

She rolled her eyes and nibbled on her fag.

'OK then – I told him that he was a lousy fat wanker.' She looked at me and started to laugh.

'What did you do that for?'

'Oh, I dunno, he was being annoying.'

'How annoying can someone be in two minutes?'

'He said, "Ginge-minge, get us a fucking drink", so I told him to piss off, and then he called me a tart so I called him a lousy fat wanker, and then he left.'

'So, it was pretty sophisticated stuff, then.'

'Oh, God, I'm so sorry.'

She didn't look all that sorry. She looked amused.

'He told me to fire you.'

She put her head back and looked at the sky, exhaling a miniature weather system of smoke and hot breath.

'Oh, bollocks.'

'Well, are you surprised?'

'I could really do with the money.'

I leaned against the doorframe and looked at her profile. Her nose was snubby and round but the rest of it was quite nice. Her mouth was wide and although her lips were thin, they described quite a sensual line. In the semi-darkness, you could still see the hair colour. Even burnished by clean winter moonlight she was unmistakeably ginger. Deep ginger. This thought pulled me back from my admiring reverie.

'I'll tell you what then, I won't do anything, and I'll wait for him to call me to follow up on it. He won't be back in here for weeks, so if you don't mind, I'll let it go.'

'Really?'

'Yeah, it makes no odds to me.'

She stubbed out her fag. 'Brilliant!'

It looked for a moment as if she was going to kiss me, but instead she squeezed me on the leg as she went back in to the kitchen. The effect was roughly the same: I nursed an ambivalent erection for the next twenty minutes and tried to remind myself of my reasonable doubts about public-sector workers. The red hair prejudice was already ceasing to have much force.

Sadie was, in fact, a pretty good waitress. When I say that, I mean despite the fact she got everybody's order wrong, had a highly developed ability to avoid eye contact with people who were ready to order and dropped everything she picked up, nobody seemed to mind because she was charming and funny. She also had a great walk. She was bandy legged, had ten-to-two feet and her bottom stuck out like a negress mountain cyclist's, but she had a great walk: upright, quick-stepping and pleasurably, controlledly juddering.

I was in my nook at the bar watching her yachting about, sucking very hard on a biro when the phone went.

'Have you f— her yet?'

It was Bart on his carphone. He was breaking up all over the place, but the gist of his message was pretty clear.

'No, not yet.'

'Well, do it. She's a f—cking useless piece of sh—, Stret—'

'Look, Bart, she's all right. I told her who you were and she was devastated. She's doing really well.'

'I don't give a f—. No-one calls me a f—lou—wank— Get rid of her.'

'I think it's the wrong thing to do.'

'Don't be a cheeky c—, Stre—, just fire the bi—'

'Let her stay tonight – and tomorrow – and then when I've found someone else I'll get rid of her.'

'I don't know what's the matter with you, Stretch. You hired her – fire her.'

I watched Sadie casing a couple at a table on the far side of the room. The man was grinning like an imbecile, his girlfriend was drumming her wine glass with her fingers. 'Why don't we give her another go?

'Stupid cu—. No chance. And Stretch, as I say, I want you to do the firing.'

'One more chance.'

'—ck off. You hired the f—, you fire her.'

I got noughty.

'Why don't you do it? You said it always makes you feel better.'

'It doesn't always make me feel better. You're the fucking manager. I hope y— not cuntstruck, Stretch. Very silly, very —cking unprofessional.'

'You know me, Bart.'

'Yeah, I do and you're a —eeky—wat. Are you in over the weekend? I'm going to need a pick-up.'

'Yeah, I think I've managed to alienate my remaining friends anyway, so I doubt I'm doing anything.'

'Shut it and fire her, Stretch, I don't want your life fucking story.'

He put the phone down. Bart seemed to feel that he had the right to crawl all over my life. One thing I'd learnt from three years of studying European history was that rebellion flows from injustice. I was going to tough this one out.

At about midnight we were clear and I was sitting around with Paolo discussing the weekend's menu. Sadie was at the bar skimming a magazine.

'Aren't you going home?'

'I'm getting a lift.'

'Anyone nice?'

'If you like Italian waiters . . .'

I felt a twinge of jealousy. I remembered Henry telling me she'd copped off with a waiter last night. It all seemed to be happening a bit too quickly for my liking.

'Yeah, if you like nineteen-year-old Italian waiters, with six-pack stomachs.'

'That didn't take long.'

'And big cocks.' She started her disgusting laugh again. Paolo nodded and smiled with nationalistic pride.

I turned back to the table and tried not to sound too shirty. 'Fucking hell. No wonder all of Europe thinks English women are easy.'

'Oooo. Is that a little Anglo-Saxon insecurity I detect? Paolo, do you think English women are easy?'

Paolo was still grinning a little sheepishly,

'Beh, it's OK by me. It's not "easy", it's OK.'

'Anyway, Paolo, back to the menu, mate.'

Sadie resumed her flick through *Elle* or *Marie Claire* or *Pussy Whip* or whatever it was she was reading. Those magazines have got a lot to answer for. When did they move from valuing feminine hygiene to prosecuting its polar opposite? '*Explore your dirtbox!! With a dildo!!!*', '*Fucking your colleagues!!?? Why not do 'em all at once??!!! On video?!?!!!*', '*Let him come in your mush tonight!! It's cheaper than Clarins!?!?!*' There is a line, and I thought it had been crossed.

By the time Paolo and I had finished Sadie had moved out of the restaurant, but her lift still hadn't arrived.

I locked the door and pulled down the shutter. She had moved to the edge of the pavement and was looking left and right down the street. I crossed the road towards the Cav. I even found it painful that Sadie, someone who I might never have seen again after the following day, knew that I had to drag myself around town in that disgrace.

'See you tomorrow, Sadie, Good luck.'

I don't know why I said 'good luck', it just slipped out.

'So long, Frank.'

I fired up the car and sputtered off towards the Common. I did a quick mental tally of Sadie's score:

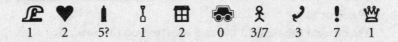

The 🕯 and 🧍 scores were debatable but she was still either a 23 or a 27. I thought initially that she might merit some solid ♛ as well, what with the Lucy link. However, it transpired that her father had downshifted from being a teacher (is it possible to *down*shift from being a teacher?) into smallholding. He had about eleven assorted ill-favoured animals and nine square yards of vegetable garden, and they lived the winter on stewed kale and sheepshank broth. The decrepit score was yet another insurmountable obstacle in my path. It's a rule, a fixed golden rule that I never, *never*, touch anything that has lower scores than me.

I checked my fag box when I stopped at some lights and saw that I only had two left. I did the little smoker's calculation, and decided that I needed another pack if I was to sleep easy, so did a U-ey and headed back past O'Hare's to the petrol station on Lavender Hill. Sadie was no longer standing outside the restaurant. It made me feel reassured that she had found someone who picked her up from work, although for some reason I would have much preferred it to have been a woman.

Then I saw her standing at a bus stop on the opposite side of the road. I pulled in, rolled down my window and hailed her across the road.

'Sadie. Nobody turn up?'

She didn't answer. She still appeared to be scanning the empty road agitatedly.

'Do you want a lift?'

'No thanks, Frank. I'm fine.'

'Well, if you're sure.'

She seemed to think again.

'You're not going to get in too much trouble, are you, with Bart?'

'No. Nothing I can't handle.'

She crossed the road to me and squatted on the road, her arms folded at window level, her chin resting on them.

'I really appreciate it, you know.'

I reached over my left arm nervily and gave her arm a squeeze. You could detect the bones underneath her jacket; it felt like a furled umbrella.

'Come on, get in, I'll run you home.'

She checked her watch. 'Fuck it. OK then.'

I was cheered immeasurably by this development, and treated myself to a fag and turned the tape player up: a hissy best of The Doors collection I'd recorded more than a decade earlier.

'Who's this?'

'The Doors.'

'*Dated*. Like it.'

'It's not dated, it's a timeless classic.'

'Yeah right. That's what my dad says about Jonny Mathis.'

'How old are you?'

'Twenty-three. Why?'

'Just wondered. Where am I going, by the way?'

'Oh, yeah. Battersea Bridge, opposite the council estate.'

I mentally docked a point from her ⊞ score.

I had asked her her age, because I was beginning to develop a theory on why monogamy was impossible, and age was a relevant factor. The Echelon Theory goes like this: when you're sixteen, you don't generally fancy women who are more than a couple of years older than you, apart from a few people off the TV or out of films. This gives you a 'Total Fanciable Universe' of about 5% of the female population. By the time you're thirty, however, you fancy most of the people younger than you, down to the

78

age of about sixteen, as well as being able to see the merits of those older than you, particularly now we all have healthier diets and good cosmetic surgeons. With each year a new echelon of women passes into the lowest range of consideration, *but another echelon doesn't pass out of consideration at the older end.* This was the key point, and the point that gave the theory its incontrovertible force. As you reach thirty, even if you draw the line at women of forty, you still have an effective TFU of around 30%. Of course, as you move into your sixties, everything is totally out of hand. The TFU is up at over 50%. If you take out the under-sixteens and over-seventies (which it is wise to do), it may be that as many as 80% of women you ever come into contact with are in the TFU. No amount of good intentions can withstand the sheer numerical weight of temptation. My rapid if not yet total conversion to Sadie's benefits was bringing home to me the horrible truth of the Echelon Theory. As I heard some tired old American once say, about older men and younger women, 'if you can, you do.' It's a heartbreaking thought, but that doesn't mean it isn't true.

She lived in a road by Battersea Bridge in a row of tall Victorian houses opposite some grey council blocks, which looked like dingy battleships in the sulphurous light. It was nearly one-fifteen by the time I dropped her off, but she invited me in for some tea. Curious to flesh out her life a little, I accepted, and followed her up the stairs to the front door.

The entire house seemed to have been converted into individual rooms. There were two old bicycles leaning against the grubby walls and piles of newspapers and redirected official mail on the stairs. The place stank of damp and bad cooking. Her room was on the second floor. It was smaller than mine at Henry's and irredeemably dingy. There was a narrow bed covered in an orange candlewick bedspread, a cracked sink and a tiny desk. There was little evidence that anyone lived in it apart from two black teacups, a half-filled ashtray and a large, formless nylon holdall, which I guessed served as her wardrobe. A plastic table light gave out a grim yellow glow from the desk. Someone in the house was playing booming jungle at peak volume. As I sat down on the bed it whinged horribly, and Sadie took the two cups, left the room and thumped upstairs to what I guessed was a communal kitchen.

I lit a Lucky and wondered what kind of place she had left that would make living here tolerable. I don't know what student teachers get. Three grand a year? That's fifty odd quid a week. There was no way that this place could cost her more than thirty a week, which would leave her with just under twenty for food and fun, about ten when you took the fag money out. Not great. Substantially less than me, in fact, which was never a good sign. I looked down between my feet and saw a sheaf of paper sticking out from under the bed. I pulled out one of the leaves and on it was a caricature of me as Lord Byron, lolling on a chaise longue. She'd caught my cheeky splendidness quite well. Sadie came back in with the tea. I held up the drawing.

'Weren't you going to show me this?'

'Hah! Was I fuckerslike. Not for a while, anyway.'

'It's pretty good. You've got my pendulous jowls and air of defeat down perfick.'

'I thought it made you look like Stan Laurel.'

'It's more like Oliver Hardy.'

'That's what I meant, the fat one, sorry.'

'Cheers.'

'Don't mention it.'

She sat down. There was a brief silence between us, filled by the BM BM KISHY KISHY KISHY KISHY KISHY BM BM of the music hammering through the floor. I started to feel uncomfortable about sitting on the bed next to her. The atmosphere was becoming strained. I sensed that it may even have become slightly sexually charged. To be totally honest with you, that was the last thing I wanted. I may have been lovelorn but I

80

hadn't become tacky yet, and nothing could be tackier than fucking a workmate after you've given her a lift home, could it? I suddenly had an overpowering desire to leave. She looked at me and smiled, raising her powdery copper eyebrows. I stared down at the teacup. The liquid was colourless and slightly foamy. I looked at her again, and *she* started to study *her* teacup. BM BM KISHY KISHY KISHY KISHY KISHY BM BM. She sang to herself plaintively. 'Lalalalalalala.'

Why had I suddenly pitched up in a Strindberg play? I'd never even *seen* one. I had to escape before she started telling stories of her impoverished upbringing biting the nuts off sheep half way up a Cotswold.

A phone went out in the corridor. She sprang up and flew out of the room, taking care to close the door behind her. Thirty seconds later she was back, tearing her blouse off. 'Wankers, that was Gaetano on his mobile. I gave him the wrong address. He's outside and a bit fucked off.'

'Where are you going?'

'Some club. Chelsea or somewhere.'

'When did you meet this guy?'

'Last night. Just after you started pawing me, actually. Now, would you mind going out of the room. I've gotta change my bags.'

'You don't mess about, do you?'

'God, you really have got some hang-up, haven't you?'

'No. I just . . .'

'Look, sod off, Frank, I don't want to give my boss a look at my thatch on day one. It'll ruin my career prospects.'

'You don't have to talk like that, you know, just because you're in London.'

'Yehyehyehyehyeh. Come on, shoo! Oh, and Great Poet, thanks, c'mere, Ollie.' She put her cool hand on my cheek, gave me a dry but effective kiss and pushed me out of the room.

I went downstairs with a woody gently nosing out across my

abdomen. A twenty-three-year-old. The Echelon Theory had real power and velocity, I needed to flesh it out. Maybe I could get a grant from Princeton to do just that.

On the way home I turned over my dilemma. Bart would be understandably suspicious if I attempted to intervene further on Sadie's behalf, and even if he wasn't, then it was improbable that he could keep her on. However, I couldn't think about her without desperately wanting to be near her again. After the slow descending boredom of Marie and Lucy's cloying mumsiness, here was female company I liked the feel of. She was entertaining and impulsive. To someone as inert as I was, she was almost terrifyingly impulsive. It wasn't sex I was after, it was a sense of *movement*. Honestly. She was still miles away from being a crush, wasn't she? Public-sector, ginger, sub-28 maths, etc.

I was also forming a notion that contrary to appearances she was just a useless little girl, way out of her depth. I had an opportunity to do her a small kindness, to give her a bit of stability as she careered round the city getting insulted, fired and humped by people in the catering business. What was I going to do about it? I wondered what Tom would do, but that was futile, as he was so far removed from her world, he wouldn't know where to start. His approach would probably involve some form of tribunal. Henry would probably try to help her out, but I couldn't guarantee it. With the women on the other hand it was easy. Marie, Lucy, Lottie, all the women would jump to her defence without demur, no doubt about that.

'Doing the right thing' is an area where I trust women's judgement. They don't seem as capable of causing people pain. I don't know how it arises, whether it's biological or inculcated in childhood, but if it's a question of preventing a bit of suffering, I'll back a woman to see the right way through any day of the week. Unless of course it's an issue where I'm involved, in which case they unaccountably lose all their bearings and stick the boot in without mercy. But on the whole, you've got to hand it to women: they're a lot worse than men at doling out the misery. I resolved to get all feminine and approach Bart the next morning with a proposition; I was prepared put more shifts in if he was prepared to give her one more chance.

My magnanimity had something to do with the fact that Tom was convinced I'd get the job on *Emporium*. I could perform my act of goodness, but then not have to deal with the consequences when Charles Mannion spirited me off to the better place. Sadie would be out of there in the week after Christmas anyway. I couldn't really go wrong. I began to enjoy my role in this little ethical parable. Not just because of the rare opportunity I had been offered to act out of altruism, but maybe because I now had, on however small a scale, a sense of power over another person's destiny. The two things must be linked, having the power to help someone out, and deriving pleasure from the exercise of that power. By this reckoning I mused that Mother Teresa must have spent her entire life in a state of constant orgiastic delight. The only reason she went to Calcutta in the first place was so that she could really pig out on power-pleasure. Selfish bitch.

I checked myself out in the rearview mirror.

Oliver cunting Hardy.

## Loose change

When I got home there was a message on the kitchen table from Henry: 'Call Tom re weekend.' Mannion had earmarked me for a weekend at his dad's place out along the M40. I was meant to feel honoured, in fact I felt a sense of dread. I had assumed that my exertions at Lucy's up-the-duff dinner had made it unlikely that I was still invited, and I wasn't too distressed about it. There had been no communication from either of them since. What was Tom going to say? 'We're cutting you dead, you can't come, we've now realised what a wanker you are, get out of our lives, and by the way I've told my dad to cancel the interview. And by the other way just fuck off and die, you pasty Northern twat.'

When I phoned Tom's chambers the next morning I felt sick with nerves. This isn't how you're supposed to feel when you call your best pal. The cocky little Cockney clerk kept me waiting for a minute or two. I imagined Tom putting on his best fatherly reprehension tone and serious brow, ready to give me a real ticking off before dumping me from his golden circle.

'Frank, hi. Sorry to keep you waiting, I was in conference.'

'That's OK, Henry left a message. He said you want to talk to me about the Christmas weekend.'

'Yes, it's a bit of a tricky one, I'm afraid. We want to give you the option not to come.'

'What do you mean the option?' Here we go. *Arrivederci*, Frank.

'Well, Lucy's invited Marie and thought it might be a bit difficult for you, so I thought I'd better give you a get-out.'

How could she do this? She only knew Marie through me. Acquaintance stealing always makes me angry.

'Does Marie know I'm going to be there?'

'Oh yes. She said she isn't bothered about it if you're not.'

Marie would know damn well that it would bother the arse off me.

'And you believed her?'

'I haven't spoken to her, Frank. It's all Lucy's doing.'

All these cowardly hitmen, just acting under orders.

'Is she going to be there all weekend? Maybe I could come on Friday and leave on Saturday, before she arrives or something?'

'No. We're driving down together actually. You know she's just bought a flat down the road in Notting Hill, so we said we'd all leave together.'

I knew that she'd been looking to buy somewhere, but not in Notting Hill. She always thought W11 was a bit too metropolitan and risky. More embourgeoised now though of course, so she'd feel more at home. Everybody's moving up from Fulham, burning the IKEA fixtures as they drive up the Shepherd's Bush Road.

'Well, if she's not bothered, I'm not, I guess. It's probably not a good idea to make us roomies though.'

'That's the tricky bit actually, Frank. She's bringing her boy-friend.'

I tried to speak as brightly as possible through my tight jaw.

'A boyfriend. Who is he?'

Why, where, when, how often, how much.

'He's called David. Nice bloke. He makes commercials. I don't know the details, he produces them or directs them, I can't remember which. Lucy knows him.'

See what I mean about them unaccountably, out of nowhere, spurning the kindly impulses and mercilessly sticking the boot in? And a fucking adtwat, God love us.

'So you've met him before, then.'

'Yeah [sniff sniff], we've had them round to supper a couple of times. They met at ours actually.'

'You set them up?'

'I wouldn't go that far, Frankie. Lucy thought they might get on and they did. He's moving in with her.'

What was he trying to do to me?

'Moving in? How long have they been together, then?'

'A few months, it's three or four months since they met, I think.'

'And they're moving in already. What's going on?'

'Look, Frank, I knew this would be difficult, that's why I called.'

'You're unbe-fucking-lievable, you three, aren't you?'

'Come on, Frankie, don't be like that.'

'Tom, there's something I should tell you. I heard that Lucy's planning to dump you for a forex dealer.'

'WHAT!'

'Don't be like that, Tom.'

'OK, OK, I see what you mean – but *try* not to be like that.'

I *tried* not to be like that. I breathed out heavily through my nose and lit a Lucky.

'Can I call you back, Tom? I need a bit of cooling-off time.'

'Sure thing. I'm sorry, Frank. Call me later, I said I'd call Lucy back about lunchtime to let her know.'

I hung up. I could imagine the thought processes Lucy and Marie had gone through to arrive at this appalling solution. Marie had said that she wanted to stay friends when we finally split. I remember holding my hand like a priest as I stared into the carpet.

'We'll always be mates, Frank. We'll still see each other.'

I had croakily agreed, but only because I thought it was part of the deal. Everybody says it, but nobody really means it. I think she felt the same way. She tried to call me a few times, but I never bothered getting back to her. It was obvious that any meeting would be a torture of teary reminiscence and acrid recrimination, at least from me. Some pub, some car park, some overlong bear hug goodbye, some bleary tube journey home. I was having none of that.

The history of our love was melancholy, but I think if I'd had the maturity, it might have been able to teach me something.

We separate into three phases, Marie and I, as I said – Early Period, Late Period and Blue Period – and the last of these was as limp and unsatisfactory as the first was a full-on robot chubby.

She arrived at my college a year after me, in 1986, and went pretty much unnoticed, at least by me, until the summer term. If I have an impression of her at all, it is of a sense of transformation. When she arrived I was pretty certain that she was middling-horsey; fishermen's sweaters, stretch jeans, suede black boots and her hair tied back in thin black ribbon. By the June in which we first started dating she had evolved into upper-hippy chick, the chief signature of the clothing being diaphany (in the summer, this was a definite boon), the hair now long and ringleted and once, even, an unforgiveable tear drawn on her cheek in kohl. She still would maintain that I overstate the extent of her mutation, but I say, why fight it? What's the point of going to university if you can't dress up and wear masks for a few years? She was brought up in Wimbledon, the daughter of a lawyer and a food writer. They weren't as well off as that makes them sound, but they weren't doing too bad. New Volvos every two years, three kids through private schools, a share in a cottage in the Dordogne. They were good liberal Tories and would be most proud if you described their offspring as 'well balanced', which they all were and are.

They had given her a sense of purpose and a non-specific quite posh accent, and she used to speak to both of them three times a week on the phone, which is how I met her, and I suppose in a way, a contributing element in why we eventually, eventually, *eventually*, split up. I suppose they had also given her that terminally pretty face, not so beautiful as to be scary, but too damned gorgeously, insanely pretty for her own good. I was in college getting morose and fucked on Spar's own-brand vodka at 7PM in some Captain Beefheart fan's room when I decided that I wanted to call a cab home. Some wankers rode bikes in Oxford, but I was having none of that. If the taxpayer wanted me to go to university, the least he could do was lay on a limo. I wandered through the thickening twilight to the phone near the porters' lodge, and there she was, her back to me, Marie O'Sullivan, the receiver in one hand, the other pressed to her free ear, gabbling mirthfully with her folks.

In my experience, nobody is fully fanciable from behind, but here the signs were good. The slightly crazy curly hair was interesting, and she looked thin and flexuous, with the shape of her knickers digging into her soft bottom nicely brought out by the clinginess of her dress. Nothing to start an alarm, though. Indeed, after ten minutes, I was beginning to get irritated with her chuntering, and started coughing and sighing with great obviousness and jingling my loose change. I think she heard me, but her sign off seemed to take another age, 'Say "hi" to Auntie Grace,' and I still remember clearly a reference to 'Shooter', which I took to be a pet, but turned out to be her grandmother. Pet names and posh folks, I don't know.

She put the phone down, picked up her big wicker-y bag and spun round, a big grin opening up her delectable face.

'Sorreee.' And then she slapped my cheek gently as she sauntered off.

Caramba.

That was it.

Infatuated, literally: made stupid, gooned, guyed, fooled, laid open to ridicule, emptied of reason.

I picked up the receiver and inhaled her fabulous scent; sugared almonds and warm bread with a hint of freshly laundered panty. I got through to the minicab place and just shouted 'fuck it, I'll walk' into the receiver. I spent the next five minutes trying to hoover the receiver up through my nose, until disturbed by some Northern chemist who wanted to make his nightly call to The Samaritans.

After this mundane epiphany, I was in lovesick agony for six weeks. I started going in to college to eat, from Tom's house up the Cowley Road, and would hang around aimlessly in front of the dinner hall, looking over people's shoulders waiting for her to emerge. Then I would follow her at a respectful, adoring distance, having invented some urgent business over in her part of college.

As she was in the summer of her first year, she had exams and spent most of the day revising in the college library with a coterie of friends. I had no exams, being a year above her, and could spend hour upon hour hanging out in the library quadrangle, horsing around with people I hated, praying and hoping she would come to join us, or that I could even just get a sustaining glimpse of her.

She didn't appear to have a boyfriend, and spent almost all of her time with other girls. However, that didn't stop me being thrown into nauseated panic every time I saw a bloke so much as talk to her at dinner. I became incapable of holding a conversation with anyone when she was in view, whether she was five feet away in the porters' lodge, picking up her mail (please, please no letters from a distant boyfriend – and I wasn't beyond rifling through the mail in her pigeonhole to check for them), or fifty yards away, walking from the library back to her room with a double-armful of books. Most painfully, late at night I would stand in her quad, watching the illuminated red-orange drawn curtains of her second-floor room until they went suddenly dark, and seethe with ambition to be with her.

I didn't tell a soul about any of this. I was conducting a staccato sex-and-drinking relationship with a burly Geographer at the time, but that wasn't the reason. I held to a strange belief that if I said anything to anyone about her, she would be taken from me instantly.

Strangely, after I had behaved like Young Tristan for nearly two months, the beginning of our relationship was a cakewalk. We kissed the first time I met her properly, if in somewhat anti-climactic conditions. Some power-Sloane in her PPE set was holding a huge summer party in the garden of another college, and Tom got an invite through the Young Boy network. I tagged along, not even expecting her to be there. I was already wasted when I arrived, on Pimm's and dope taken in Tom's tiny back garden with a posse of stripes and ponies.

You become so quickly inured to how beautiful Oxford is that I don't remember the setting at all. As much as I want to deck the memories in gorgeous topography, the images don't come. There's no honey stone, no rhododendrons, no blue-black reflecting pool: just her, face on cupped hands, in an anonymous group of ten or so, prostrate on the lawn. To my amazement and joyous distress, I noticed she was sitting next to someone from my History set, Madeleine George. Madeleine was a tea-and-toast-in-her-room friend of mine, if not an actual one, and had been a two-week crush in my first year. She was no great beauty, but you could tease a wank out of her if you tried hard enough, of which I had empirical evidence.

I went to sit with them on the soft grass, and made an arse of myself, talking the big swaggering talk about getting pissed and stoned, dissing the tutors, swearing like crazy, playing up the Jimmy Porter angle, all the usual gear. It transpired that they were from the same school, and that Madeleine used to go out with one of Marie's older brothers. For some reason they found much humour in this, and didn't reject my sarcastic interjections. We were getting along fine. There were two types of drink available; more disgusting Pimm's and a lurid vodka-based cocktail called Green Mindfuck. Marie and Madeleine were ladling down the Pimm's, whereas I stuck strictly to the Mindfuck. There was some gawky proto-FUCCER who kept on trying to muscle in on our little booze-up, but I kept him out with astonishing feats of rudeness, turning my back on him *directly* and pretending not to hear what he was saying.

The dancing started in a small marquee way at the foot of the garden. By this time I was flying on adrenalin and Mindfuck and asked them both to dance when I heard something by The Supremes or Martha and the Vandellas come on. This was exceedingly uncharacteristic behaviour, but sheer brazenness got me in there. When I dance, which I don't any more, I close my eyes and make like a slow-motion replay; intensely gawping mouth, cycling arms, moonstepping legs. In Northern nightclubs this style had made me a laughing stock, at Oxford garden parties, surrounded by geeks and stripes and dweebs and jerks, I was fucking Nijinsky.

I managed to corral Marie for brief moments, but Madeleine *would* keep on trying to keep it tri-cornered. I wanted to quit when ABBA came on, but Maddy whooped at the first strains of 'Dancing Queen', so I thought I was going to have to stick around. But Marie hated ABBA more than I did, which was merely a further reason why she deserved to be adored, and shouted to me that she wanted to sit down. We left the marquee, and I was streaming sweat like a boxer. The Luckies had already started to bite deeply, and I could feel that my face was terribly flushed. She turned towards me and said;

'Actually, I don't want to sit down, I want to go home.'

'I'll take you then.'

And she burst out laughing.

The walk back to college was a further torture. When her hips occasionally brushed mine, I wanted to throw up. This was sexual attraction. She hummed something tuneless all the way back, we both studied the pavement like Cistercians patrolling the cloisters. These fucking rigmaroles. There has to be a short cut, some system that could be employed to draw the sting from the process. I remember that as we walked I started devising a series of cards containing every possible romantic permutation that the female has to play at specified points throughout the evening:

One dance.

Walk me home, but nothing else, right?

A kiss, just one, at the door to my room.

Kiss now, then coffee, *probably* nothing else.

Tumble on the bed, clothed, if you're good.

Oh, go on then.

Oral/Anal/Suspension. (Delete as applicable)

But when we got to the college gate it didn't matter because she just reached up and kissed me on the mouth. The almond, bread and panty aroma was now supplemented with gin, sweat and damp grass, and it was all over in, I guess, thirty seconds, but Jesus what a thirty seconds.

When she broke from the embrace she still had her eyes closed and scrunched her lips as if she'd just eaten something nice. 'Mmm.'

'Jesus, I'm amazed.'

'Well, don't be.'

92

'How did you guess?'

'Oh, maybe you standing in the quad all night staring up at my window gave me a clue.'

'Oh, Christ.'

'Don't worry, it's nice. But just remember to come up next time.'

'What next time, the next time, like next time or like now?'

'Nope. Revision. Next time.'

'God.'

'See ya.'

And she slipped inside the gate.

When I got home, I lay wide awake in bed for hours, staring at the ceiling and pretending not to notice the keening muscleman in my boxer shorts.

Tom bounded into my room at three-ish; 'What happened to you?'

'Er, I think I've just fallen in love.'

'Great! Beer?'

'Go on then.'

And that was it. The beginning of Early-Period Marie.

And now here we are, some time after the conclusion of Blue-Period, Late-Period, Period (US) Period Marie, and all that positiveness and simplicity has just ebbed away, leaving in my case just an absence, and in hers an impulse to pretend that nothing bad or painful or worthy of regret ever really happened and that everything can be made good with confrontation, time and conversation.

For some reason, the women I know seem to need reconciliation more than the men. Marie was a perfect example of her sex in this regard. She fought tigerishly to maintain connections, whatever the circumstances. Things breaking down or wearing thin or petering out were intolerable to her. She was an emotional hoarder. Her parties were always free mixes of schoolfriends, university friends, new friends, work friends and family, as if she was attempting to create a perfect little society around her. I called her The Collector, which she thought was unnecessarily cynical, but how many people do you know who have a cross referenced index card system and computer database as an address book? My address book is scored with deletions and dusty with rubbings out, a dog-eared emblem of my predilection for the big clear-out.

My having eluded her more direct attempts at re-integrating me into her life, she was now resorting to more subtle methods, now a decent time had elapsed. I thought using Tom and Lucy (obviously now well and truly Collected) was particularly low and manipulative. However, I was desperate to meet her new boyfriend. Pain was what I was after, if I have to be truthful. Pain and a bit of anger. I knew that Marie would be extremely apprehensive about this meeting. The difference between us was that she would think we could talk it through, and everything would be fine. I thought we could talk it through and get a few wounds smarting again. In fact, a revisitation of the scene of past crimes would be just my sort of weekend.

I rang Tom back and tried to be cool about it, and said I'd be down very late on Friday as I had to work the evening shift at O'Hare's, as it would be just before Christmas and everything. This was a lie. I just wanted to prolong Marie's agony a little. She'd had nearly a year, another ten days and then another five hours would do her good.

# Hundreds of pounds

Before I got to O'Hare's that evening I phoned Bart on his mobile to run him through my proposition re Sadie. He was unsure to begin with, thinking it was just a devious way of me squeezing a pay rise out of him. When I told him that I didn't want a pay rise, just another month's grace for Sadie, he was shocked, and predictably accused me of shagging her. When I again protested innocence, he asked me if I'd gone insane overnight, and said that if I had, he would have to fire me instead. His approach to life couldn't permit him any other line of reasoning: if you don't want money, you must want sex, if you don't want either, you must want locking up. And then the idle threat of firing me, the one he made on a weekly basis. It was like the dark intimations he made about the money I owed him. A different sort of power-pleasure. He reluctantly agreed to go with me, probably precipitated by the ball pinging onto the roulette wheel, and signed off:

'If I get a fucking *sniff* of any more complaints, then she's out straightafuckingway. All right?'

I concurred and put the phone down, suffused with a sense of righteousness. Even the thought of Brian the Bat popping in to threaten me couldn't get me down. Not as much as usual anyway. He was called Brian the Bat because, according to unsubstantiated rumour, he kept a range of baseball bats in his office to do Bart's nasty business. A similar build to Bart, i.e. fat as a fuck, but stone bald rather than Rod Stewart-coiffed, he always dressed in a suit and a collarless shirt. He seemed terribly sad to me with his lonely undefined job, his Sierra Sapphire and a botched spider's web tattoo creeping up from under his collar. He couldn't have wanted to end up like that.

From somewhere, perhaps an adult education course at Dalston Tech, he had picked up a scrawny and inappropriate bit of business-speak. For instance, when he came in that night he said that we had to make an extra special 'marketing effort' that Christmas, as 'cash-flow projections' were looking dodgy, what with 'our proposed expansion' in the New Year. When all the old East End spider skins have got MBA-ese you know that one ideology has triumphed and all the others have been vanquished. At any rate, I took his warnings as plain horseshit. He had said something pretty similar every six months since I had worked there and Rome had never fallen. His inspirational suggestion on the 'marketing effort' was that we extend Happy Hour by twenty minutes and he waddled off to scare the shit out of another branch manager before tea. I scribbled out an obit at the bar:

### FRANCIS DEAN STRETCH
### ENTREPRENEUR, RESTAURATEUR
### AND BON VIVEUR

Sir Frank Stretch, owner of the famous restaurant chains Barton's and TFU, has died aged sixty-five.

He made his name in the late 1990s running a small neighbourhood bistro in Stockwell. What appeared to be an unpromising location summoned the great, the good and the glittering across the river (and even across the Atlantic) for many years.

He opened another fifteen restaurants around Britain over the following decade, and made his first millions selling out to Conran in 2006. He then bought another chain, Barton's, from an old boss who had gone bankrupt, and turned it into the gastronomic success of the 2010s. Focused on serving the ever-burgeoning young, urban professional classes, the Barton's name was as prevalent in the thriving cities of the North and Scotland as it was in London. Its dependence on plentiful portions, a late bar and MOR rock played on a constant loop brought mockery from serious restaurant critics, but the concept was so powerful that a new sociological sub-stratum, 'The Bartie', entered the language, referring to the type of person who habitually graced Stretch's establishments. Stretch was famed for high living, and rubbed stomachs with many of the most egregious gourmands of his time. At one famous lunch Stretch and his three eating companions ate foie gras and smoked a Cohiba between each of the eleven courses, each of which was washed down with two bottles of vintage Cristal. The eventual bill, including cigars, was reputed to have been £41,500 plus tip. Stretch later took supper at The Caprice.

He had homes in Clerkenwell, the Upper East Side of Manhattan and Rutland, the last of which was the scene of his death on Wednesday.

He never married, but rather conducted a series of highly publicised affairs with politicians' and novelists'

wives; 'Vote Labour, Fuck Tory and Annoy Writers' was
the motto framed in his Manhattan lavatory.

He leaves a son, a heart surgeon, and a daughter,
Amy, an eminent psychiatrist who specialises in eating
disorders.

That evening, Sadie was as valiantly terrible at waiting tables,
and as breathtakingly adept at securing tips as she had been
the previous day. I was denied the pleasure of describing the
gallant way I had performed on her behalf. I had already told
her that she wasn't going to get fired, so I couldn't very well
tell her that I'd been lying, but that it was all right because now
she wasn't going to get fired anyway. And aren't charitable acts
supposed to be performed on the quiet? I didn't know where
that left Mother Teresa and her whirlwind publicity tours, but
I was sure I'd heard somewhere that you get more credit if
you don't emblazon your good works all over the global media.
Selfish, power-crazed, self-promoting bitch.

Where the credit accrues is another matter of course. I just
hoped it was somewhere that the sex and money gods look. There
you go, Bart, I wasn't totally lost to the world.

O'Hare's gets nasty as Christmas approaches. It is perfectly set up
for office parties and girls' nights out, and despite Brian the Bat's
protestations, we seemed to be doing better than ever; pretty much
rammed from 8.30 till closing, and brisk at lunchtime too.

One Friday about a week after my salvation of Sadie it was
wall-to-wall dreck. We had a hen night clucking and shrieking
down one side, about fifteen of them (I'd say averaging maths
of about 30 each), and about twenty-five estate agents on a
Christmas piss-up the other (with maths of 40, 50-plus maybe
in some cases). The smaller tables were stuffed with FUCCERS
doing that Friday-after-work thing, railing against their bosses,
insulting the waiting staff and trying to fuck the girl from finance.

I was pretty much used to all this by now, as were Paolo and the other regular chefs, Mike and Tony, but the casual staff were more strung out than the money men and adtwats they were fawning over.

I guessed, looking around, that we'd do comfortably over three grand that night. When I say 'we' I mean Bart, of course, with a little left over for Brian. I also guessed that the hen night/estate agent axis was going to be problematic. The girls were service-slave class: seccies and shop assistants and cosmetic consultants. They were on one hell of a bender, ordering thirty vodka and cranberry juices as soon as they sat down. The hen herself was an insanely tall and rather beautiful girl who was probably about twenty-one, with a glossy sheet of blonde hair. She seemed very sweet, and I liked the fact that she hadn't disgraced herself by wearing comedy tits or a chambermaid outfit or anything. Most of the rest of them had really dolled themselves up; there were two in schoolgirl outfits and one had even done the full nurse, which is one of my very favourites. In a different situation I could have spent the better part of the evening planning serial sexual disgrace, but I was flinging myself around the place like a bastard, so didn't have the time. Maybe later.

The estate agents were my main responsibility and started off pretty quiet and controlled. The boys were meaty second-division public-school types with floppy hair and Marlboro Lights all over the shop. The girls were a mix. On the one hand were the lardy, puce-jacketed middle managers with big hair and smokers' teeth, draping themselves over the boys. On the other were a sprinkling of pretty little things in skinny ribs and soft faded jeans who were playing cold pussy with everyone.

After three years, I can spot a cunt a mile off and I had my eye on one of the boys, who was ginger-haired, red-faced and loud. He seemed to be called Rory and even early on started throwing bits of food at the hens. I was cool but firm with him, and he stopped it, but not without shouting 'Farking Sllll-eppazz' at them, while the drooling lard girls fell about.

Sadie was doing the hens' table and was having a 'mare. She looked like she was permanently on the verge of bursting into tears. This was real sharp-end stuff. There were two other waitresses on, both charged with the smaller tables, and I decided to do a swap, moving Sadie to the middle and charging an Australian called April with the hens. I thought an Australian would be in her element surrounded by fifteen pissed-up cultureless proles, and she didn't object.

There was a faint but perceptible lull when all the starters were ordered, and I ducked out to the bins for a Lucky. I started fantasising about the *Emporium* interview, which had been arranged for the following day.

*'Well, Frank, a very impressive speech. Take this Ferrari to the Highlands for a month and do us a think piece. Will five grand do you? And then, how about a piece on LA D-girls for the April issue? Ten nights at The Marmont should be enough, but if you've got any problems, just bell us and we'll wire you another few thou. De Niro's in Vegas at the same time and we said we'd send someone. Available? Fantastic. Yes, and then Juliette Lewis, apparently she's always wanted to fuck a fat, angry Northerner with chargrilled lungs and a biryani paunch. Can you do the honours?'*

Sure thing, Sir Charles, I wheeze.

I went back in to the restaurant and noticed that everything wasn't quite right. Rory, the red pig, had started his food fight with the hens again, and quite a few of the punters in between were obviously getting pissed off. Sadie was pleading with one of them in that manner of hers that made everybody feel even worse.

I approached the Hog: 'Please, sir. Would you please stop throwing the food. Some people are trying to eat.'

He adopted a look of mock indignation. His eyes were pale-lashed, and his top lip was thickly beaded with pigsweat.

'I didn't facking start it. It was those sleppers over there.'

The girls with the bad teeth and weight problems thought this was just hysterical.

'OK, then, sir, if I get them to stop, will you help me out by stopping too?'

'No guarantees.'

More 'hank-hank' sounds as the teeth and flab dissolved.

'Come on, sir, do me a favour, or I'll have to ask you to leave.'

'I told you, they started it.'

He had calmed down a bit though. I noticed that he had his trotter on the thigh of the girl next to him. He probably thought he was in there and didn't want to jeopardise it by having to move on. I've been in that position myself on many occasions. I refuse even to go for a piss if I think I'm going to lose a bit of ground. We were brothers under the skin.

I then went over to the hens, most of whom by now were pretty severely fucked up and lary. Honestly, this job is like being a prison warder when they cut the porn rations.

'Come on, girls, lay off the bun fight and it's a free bottle of champagne. Is that a deal?'

'Ohhh, yeah, awroight! Laverly babbly!'

More cackling. Jesus, the wit levels were unbelievable. Is this what The Algonquin was like? A semblance of calm returned for twenty minutes at any rate, and even Sadie seemed to come off the boil a little.

I went into the kitchen and asked Tony to do something tasteless but tasteless to the swine's main course, if you see what I mean. He had ordered duck, and it was sitting there on the counter as we surveyed our options.

'I've got some mescalin.'

'That'll get us shut down.'

'Speed?'

'Come on, Tony, you can do better than that.'

'Spit's a bit passé . . .'

'Yeah, they almost *expect* that.'

He considered the duck.

'I have got a pretty heavy cold, though.'

We now both gazed thoughtfully at the glazed and steaming item.

'Ah, fuck it, let's just give it a nice, big mucal smear and have done with it.'

Tony did the deed (ooh, did he have a monster cold – it was almost *cancer*) and the duck breast took on a special other-worldly glister as I laid it before pigman. Not a whimper.

I retired to the bar and watched with satisfaction as he tucked in, using a fork-only technique so he could keep his mitt on the water buffalo he was trying to ensnare. Someone else on his table threw his hand in the air. Sadie saw it and went over. As she was turning away, I saw the bloke go for her arse and give it a real tousle. To her credit she just delivered the wine he had asked for without making a fuss.

At least two of the blokes chucked up during the evening. One of them rather touchingly spewed in the sink and left a napkin on top with, SORRY – KHARZI WAS EGNAGED scored onto it.

These people were just incredible. Sex, violence, excrement; this business really gave you an insight into the finer sides of human nature.

At midnight, everybody had cleared off apart from the estate agents. The hens had gone off to some awful club without leaving too much vomit swilling around the ladies, and just when I thought we'd seen it through, it all went wrong. I was used to taking shit off people, but for some reason, as I delivered the last round of sambuccas and brandy to the estate agent zoo, I felt myself spoiling for a fight.

The Hog was now pretty much home and hosed with the

buffalo. Imagine the offspring – pure *Star Wars*. He'd spent the last twenty minutes or so sucking her face. I only hoped he wasn't one of the pukers, for her wretched sake. But this little sexual triumph hadn't shut him up one bit. As I doled out the drinks, he started talking in an overly loud voice.

'I think it's outrageous, being threatened by the staff. We're paying fucking good money to eat here, and all I get is abuse.'

I said nothing, but felt a flash of anger tighten my jaw.

'I would complain, but what do you expect if you come to a shithole like this anyway?'

He hadn't found his range. Slagging O'Hare's off was my favourite hobby, so he wasn't going to get me that easily.

'Shit food, shit service, shit manners.'

An uneasy silence was falling on the table. I finished laying the drinks out, wiped my hands on my apron and gave him a little smile.

'Shit restaurant.'

I was walking away when he finally got me, right in the gut.

'Boy!'

I slowed my stride momentarily, but kept on walking away. Total silence had now descended on his table.

'Boy! I'm talking to you, boy.'

Just one more, you fuck.

'Get over here, boy! I want another drink. Now, boy!'

I turned round, and he turned to the table, his back to me. I strolled over and tapped him on the shoulder.

As he turned his face I smashed him across the cheek with my fist and forearm. I didn't connect very well, but everybody round the table flew back in their chairs simultaneously.

'Get out, you wanker.'

He got up to retaliate, but was too pissed to co-ordinate himself, and stumbled over the table. All his mates were looking at me, and I thought that I was about to get leathered. But Alleluia, the pussy English middle classes, they didn't do *anything*.

103

The Hog was also bizarrely penitent, as he was nursed by his conquest.

'Did you see that? He fucking punched me. A waiter fucking punched me.'

'Yeah, and I'll punch you again if you don't fuck off.'

I have to admit this last sentence was chiefly for the benefit of Sadie who had come through from the bins when she heard the racket.

One of the women spoke: 'OK, I'm sorry about this, waiter. We've spent hundreds of pounds here. I think you should apologise for hitting him. We are diners here, after all.'

One last gamble.

'Diners? *Diners?*'

They all looked taken aback. On he burned.

'You come here, abuse me, throw food around as if you were eating in the fucking monkey house, practically have sex in the main body of the restaurant, ruin every other customer's evening, assault the waitresses and throw up in the sink and call yourselves diners? You are without doubt the most miserable, noisome animalistic bunch of morally spavined no-marks I have ever had the misfortune to have in my restaurant. Now fucking clear off, the lot of you!'

I'd really belted it out. No reaction whatsoever. One of the boys tore at a napkin, his eyes boring into the table. The woman who'd set me off stared at a disc of wine she was swirling in her glass.

I walked away from the table and out to the bins for a trembly Lucky. As I went through the kitchen Tony, Mike and Paolo gave me a round of applause. Indeed Paolo was ecstatic. 'Farkin' bellissimo, Franco. Bravo!'

Sadie came flitting out.

'I bet you don't get service like that in Gloucestershire.'

'Well, it was a little unusual.'

'Yeah, but Sadie, you can only take so much.'

She hung round while we cleared up, and I did the count and I gave her a lift home, which I was trying to build into a custom.

When we got to the house she invited me in and I accepted with alacrity. Human contact, human contact.

She made me some tea. She had bought a little director's chair, so I didn't have to sit on the bed this time, which now made me feel slightly disappointed. Bart was right, of course. Even my protection of her had obviously been some form of sex strategy. Surely I emerge with a bit of credit by saving her from the sack? I believe the principle I employed is called enlightened self-interest.

At least the music was quieter this time, but that room was no place for a girl. The ceiling was half covered by a great beige flower of damp.

'If you don't mind me asking, Sade, how did you end up in this place?'

'Ripped off. They showed me the room on the top floor, which is twice the size and kind of OK, but when I came to move in, they said they hadn't got rid of the guy who was in there, so gave me this for the meanwhile. It's cheap, thirty quid a week.'

The only flat in London, outside Notting Hill, not worth thirty quid a week.

'How long are you staying for?'

'Here, about another month. I've got a place sorted out in Shepherd's Bush. Gaetano, that Italian waiter.'

I felt a gentle flutter in my gut.

'So, you're moving in with him?'

'Looks like it.'

'Are you sure that's wise?'

She looked at me sideways. 'Are you kidding?'

I wasn't kidding, but she obviously didn't want this to go any further.

'So, only ten days left at O'Hare's.'

'Yes, thank Christ.'

This prickled me.

'Is it so bad?'

She softened suddenly.

'I didn't mean that to sound ungrateful. I'm actually quite enjoying it. Especially the punchy Great Poet.'

'Can we drop the Great Poet bit soon?'

'Ten days and you'll never hear it again.'

'I suppose I won't.'

She seemed unable to detect any of the brooding sexual charge with which this comment was infused. 'What I want to know, Frank, is what the fuck *you're* doing there anyway. Lucy told me you went to Oxford.'

'It's a long story.'

'But you people are supposed to run the country, like Tom and Lucy. Not work in restaurants.'

'Oh, really? I hadn't heard.'

'You gonna stay there forever?'

'Naah. Just another twenty years. Bart runs a fabulous pension scheme, and the share options, *whhoo*. I'll retire to Connecticut and paint watercolours.'

She turned her attention from the tidemark on the ceiling and looked at me steadily. 'You're weird.'

'Well, couldn't it be that everybody else is weird and I'm the normal one?'

She resumed her study of the damp patch. At some point over the last week, she had had her tongue pierced. For two days her tongue had swelled up like a tennis ball. Now there was a always a faint whistle and click when she spoke. She was clicking away now.

'Why did you get that thing put in your mouth?'

'What, this?' She wiggled her tongue at me and laughed. The thing was the size of a small grape.

'Don't you think it's, well, *disgusting* mutilating yourself like that?'

'Hey, steady, it's not mutilation. It's just funky.'

'I think it's fucking horrible.'

'*Che peccato*. Italian for "what a shame". I think might do my belly button next.' She clacked her tongue. 'Then my clit.'

'Oh, for God's sake!'

'What's the problem, vicar? Two days' pain, a lifetime of enhanced sexual pleasure.'

Disgust gave way to curiosity. 'Really?'

'Increases the surface area or something. Don't know all the ins and outs yet.'

'Bloody hell. I was born at the wrong time.'

'Why?'

'Being a teenager between punk and Ecstasy. That's why I'm a lager-drinking wet Tory. Fun for me is what people like you call misery.'

'I dunno. I drink lager. It takes the edge off the coke.'

I shook my head, but she couldn't see. 'Anyway, back to me, if we may. I like O'Hare's. In some ways.'

'Oh fuck *awff*. You moan about it all night long, criticise everything. What's to like?'

'I like the routine. Oh I don't know, it's just what I do.'

'Don't you have any dreams and ambitions?' She tried to say it ironically, her tone intended to indicate inverted commas all over the place.

'This is England in the 1990s, Sadie. We don't have dreams and ambitions. Only a vague hope that we'll make it through the day.'

She swung her legs off the bed. 'That is such *bull*shit!'

'Don't criticise someone else's religion, girl.'

She stubbed her fag out fiercely. 'Can't you take anything seriously?'

'What is this, the fucking Oprah Winfrey Show?'

'I'm sorry. But you seem so, I don't know, *beat* and *angry* all the time. I mean, why assault the customers if you're so happy there? What's your problem?'

I must have looked pretty downcast.

'I hope you're not insulted.'

'No, flattered.'

She shook her copper, almost *bronze*, hair out of its bobble and rubbed her face. She was so pretty really, the snubby nose, the swoopy interesting mouth.

'I better go.'

'Yeah, I gotta change anyway.'

I checked my watch. One-fifteen.

'Change?'

'Yeah, Gaetano's picking me up at one-thirty. Some party in Notting Hill.'

Oh oh oh oh ohh! This was intolerable. I urgently wanted to know if this Gaetano character was her boyfriend, but that question is unaskable, as everybody knows.

'What does the dago think of the tongue?'

'He likes it. In its place.' She laughed in that disgraceful way.

'Is he your boyfriend, this bloke?'

'Well, I guess in a way he is.'

'What way?'

She got irritable. 'Fuck, I dunno. What ways are there?'

That got *me* irritable. 'Well, let's count them, shall we; there's the coy-little-snog-at-home-time way, there's the having-the-occasional-shag way, the full-on-rutting-thrice-nightly way, the snorting-Charlie-off-his-bell-end way; do you want me to go on?'

She was standing now, pointing at the door, and shaking her head patronisingly.

'*Jesus*, Frank. What are you doing, you sick idiot? Is this another joke, because if it is, you're only amusing yourself.'

'Well, someone's got to. Everybody else is making me feel terrible.'

'If you're going to sort your life out, Frank, I suggest you do it in private. I've got to change.'

I left in a hurry.

God, I was making a real mess of this wooing procedure. She was so far beyond me it was a total embarrassment: 23, developing coke habit, ambitions include pierced clitoris – you just wouldn't put the two of us together, would you? How the hell was she related to Lucy? That was another miracle. It never ceases to amaze me the human variety that can coexist in one family. No wonder the world's such a shambles. As I toured the Cav back up to Clapham, I began to get angry about it. Why was I stranded in the middle of this arid, money-bent, po-faced, do-it-by-the-book generation? Where was the energy, where were the drugs, where was the casual sex with people you met in restaurants? Particularly this last, where was it? I turned my mind to the imminent weekend at Tom's father's house, and thought about us all desperately pretending to be our parents. Well, not my parents, but Marie's and Lucy's and Tom's. No energy there, no drugs, no easy sex. A bit of piercing perhaps, but not in any way Sadie would understand.

There was something else, though, as well as frustration at being born too early and too late. A quiet voice of resolution that said I wasn't going to give up that easily.

## Crisp notes

The next morning it was up at lark's vomit for the interview with Tom's father. O'Hare's had habituated me to late rising, but Mannion had insisted that I was to be interviewed over breakfast, so when I got up it was still pitch dark outside. His PA had called the previous day and relayed the somewhat worrying news that we were to be joined by the editor of the magazine, one Taylor Bernard, who had been in the year below me at university and was famed throughout the world as a ponce, a phoney, a hack and a twat. He now wrote unfunny young fogey columns in men's mags and had recently published a novel about a dog turning into a woman called *Bitch* that nobody had been stupid enough to buy. Tom's dad knew that *Emporium* would at least get a bit of press with Bernard as editor because all his mates ran the review sections of the papers. I can't say that from what I knew of his work we were likely to find one another congenial.

Of course, what really worried me was that it wouldn't take him

110

long to spot that he would be pulling me up from the gutter if he were to offer me a job. There was no chance of him remembering me from Oxford, which would have been a real shocker, but still, the yellowing cuttings from the *Post*, about parking schemes, post office armed robberies and Sunday football, and the three years in a dive in Battersea put me at a profound disadvantage from a social status point of view. From any point of view for that matter.

The job I was up for was sub-editing the directory section at the back of the mag; it would consist of lists of car prices and specifications, wine and clothes retailers and contact numbers for companies featured in the magazine, and I was also to be given an occasional short feature to write, if I was good. They had sent me a copy of a press release, which was headed:

EMPORIUM
*The magazine for men who eat, drink, drive, shop.*
*And think.*

I have to admit, despite earlier doubts I thought it sounded pretty good.

I had to put a bit of thought into how to dress for once, and was dismayed at how deeply O'Hare's had penetrated into my wardrobe. I had one suit, which I discounted immediately because no-one could wear such a thing in the mid 1990s apart from a temporary filing clerk or a shop assistant in Comet. Everything remotely smart I owned was for work: six white shirts, three pairs of black, what can only be described as 'slacks', and one pair of over-shiny DMs. Whichever way I combined them I looked like a fucking waiter. All else was jeans, cardies, a pair of nonce Samba trainers (like the ones you got laughed at for wearing when you were at school, but which were undergoing a mystifying revival), British Home Stores jumpers holed in the elbow and polo shirts. I think people can spend too long on clothes, but you've got to have at least one thing you look half decent in, otherwise you feel as if you've given up. This was definitely the wardrobe of a man lacking in attack.

In increasing panic I woke Henry and asked if he had anything that might be suitable. He pointed out, through his departing dreams of guava and pipeline-burst cache, that I weighed four stone more than him, and besides he was even scruffier than I am. I eventually plumped for an ex-dress shirt with no collar, my oldest pair of jeans, my awful shorty overcoat and the DMs, aiming at a puritanical-bohemian flavour, and didn't check myself in the mirror before I set off for the tube. The springy knobs hanging from the roof of the creaky Northern Line carriage reminded me of Sadie's piercing and Gaetano's penis simultaneously. I stared at the floor.

We were meeting at a place called The Grill in St James's, near where *Emporium*'s office was situated. It was a bleached cavern of a place with vast plate-glass windows, which cleverly concealed the whereabouts of the entrance. A blithe little dago watched my mime act as I scanned the cliff of glass for handles. He let me flounder for about ten seconds before sinuously drawing back the invisible door with an irritating bow of the head. He didn't seem too well disposed to letting me in, but as soon as I said the word 'Mannion' he started treating me like Elizabeth Taylor.

The other two hadn't arrived, nor in fact had anybody else, and I was shown to a table in the centre of the hangar-sized room, feeling more than a little self-conscious. I ordered a decaf mochaccino from the dapper little waiter, who seemed pleasantly surprised that I hadn't asked for a mug of Mellow Birds with three shugs, and craved a Lucky. I thought it bad form to be found smoking before an interview, before breakfast, before 8AM, but holding the line was killing me.

Mannion and Bernard came in together, Mannion impressive in dandy-ish three-piece and pink shirt, Bernard less so with heavy-metal-length hair and dressed in black from head to toe.

At university, he had been a fey, wet-lipped little Sloane, with brown suede brogues, sludge-coloured cords, tweed sports jacket, the whole nine yards. I wondered if he had any sense of his own ridiculousness, but I doubted it.

I had met Charles Mannion perhaps six or eight times over the previous decade and he scared the living daylights out of me. He was a tall and straight-backed fifty-five-year-old, very much in the prime of life. He had some of Tom's chin-and-brow good looks, but a sense of languid energy all his own. When he did speak, he gave the impression that he was used to being listened to.

He was by no means famous famous, but was at the top of the Nationwide League of the Great and the Good. He had been a political correspondent on the nationals for ten years, before being a surprise choice as editor of *Axis*, an American politics and finance magazine launched in the early seventies. He ceased being a working journalist about three years later, moving into finance and management, from where he had turned the firm which published *Axis* into a tidy little earner for its Yank owners. Through the eighties, under their aegis, he launched a series of coffee-table mags about travel and business for the burgeoning class of London ABs who no longer read books, but still thought that it was important to be seen with the right badge of text. As was pretty obvious to anyone who'd seen his house in Gloucestershire and his DB6, he'd done OK for himself. There was family money too, although inevitably, Tom tended to disguise the actual amount. It had never occurred to me to do Charles's maths, but I ready-reckoned them as I shook hands with him:

86, staggering, in fact, a new high for someone I had actually met. I had even marked down his ♥ and ▮ scores a little due to lack of information, although I knew that he was on his second wife, who was ten years his junior, so kept him well above 5.

I thought of him again on that baronial bed at Christmas, surrounded by his gorgeous, successful children, all doling out the Krug and Cartier. Then I thought of my own Christmases in rented accommodation with Dad (another business gone west) in Urmston or Wigan or Crewe, me handing over a ten pack of Hamlet, dad reciprocating with a grudging soap on a rope.

His greeting words were unsettlingly brusque: 'I don't know if Tom told you, but we've only got half an hour.'

I was thrown by this as it revealed that he had no knowledge whatsoever of how the meeting had been arranged, which was entirely through his PA. I had assumed that he would have given me at least some thought before now, but obviously not. I was just the least important of a string of meetings he had that day, just an obstacle meeting to negotiate before the real deal began half an hour later.

Bernard did most of the talking. He described the magazine as 'a new paradigm in publishing, acknowledging that intellectualism and consumerism are no longer in opposition in post-Thatcherite Britain', which seemed fair enough, but hardly stimulus for conversation. In fact I was tongue-tied for most of the thirty minutes, nodding and humming muted little monkey noises of agreement whenever either of them said anything. I had ordered Full English Breakfast, which was a little embarrassing as both of them had gone for wholemeal toast. I must have looked as if I was hoovering the freebies somewhat, but they didn't seem to mind.

Bernard's conversation consisted entirely of slagging off every other publication remotely in competition with his own. I had read some of them and had no strong views either way on most, but just kept on agreeing. He seemed to hold in particular disdain everywhere he had ever worked, perhaps neglecting his own contribution to their vapidity, grossness or triviality.

When the thirty minutes was almost up, and I was beginning to get anxious that I was there under false pretences, Mannion checked his watch and addressed me directly: 'Right, what do you bring to the party?'

I had a mouth full of fried bread and black pudding, which I swallowed with theatrical eyebrow movements and an elaborate throat-clearing farce. I had rehearsed a pithy little speech as I lay in bed the previous night, but realised that it didn't particularly connect with the content of the discussion thus far. My performance under pressure was lacklustre and strangely irrelevant to the question posed: 'Yes, well I couldn't agree more with Taylor, really. It sounds like a fantastic idea, and I relish the prospect of being involved.'

Mannion looked a little puzzled.

'Cars is your thing, isn't it?'

'Oh yes. I really love cars. I really do.'

'What are you in at the moment?'

'Oh, an X reg Cavalier. I call it my dapple dawn drawn dauphin.'

Mannion looked blank.

'Oh, my Chevalier!'

Bernard cleared his throat on the back of his hand. I felt I'd better add something. 'Hopkins. The Windhover.'

A look of consternation momentarily darkened Mannion's face, which passed as he summoned the bill. Bernard was slouching back in his chair, and apparently took no notice whatsoever of what I had said.

Mannion paid, in crisp notes I noticed, and said that he was going on holiday for three weeks before Christmas, and that they'd let me know.

As they were leaving, Bernard turned towards me: 'Local press, nice way up – get the basics mastered.'

115

He then winked and clicked his finger and thumb together.

Fight, you wanker? I thought to myself, smiling at Taylor and winking back.

The first issue was due out at the beginning of April, so I estimated that they had to tell me sharpish, but I wasn't holding my breath. Formal interviews aren't really me. I reveal my best qualities during long, liquid evenings, one on one.

When I got home, I prepared for the lunchtime shift at O'Hare's, to wit, I sacked out on Henry's sofa with a fag and the remote contol.

No Sadie till the evening. The thought of getting through the day without seeing her left a hollow in my chest. It always happens so quickly. It probably happened in the first half second, when I was at Lucy's ovary bash and convinced myself Sadie was too good for me. It's the cliché: the defence mechanism. Even then, behind the anti-vocational, ginger-baiting carapace, a warm, faintly repulsive desire was writhing around. Now I was a complete spastic. I couldn't think about her without simultaneously getting a glasscutter hard-on and my mind turning into a benign soup. I tried, as I surfed through the pastel, frictionless murmur of morning TV to put it all out of my mind. With Tom's Reconciliation Weekend looming, I didn't feel ready for any more emotion.

I like daytime TV. It promises that everything can change. I watched a ragged homunculus in blue-grey Mr Byrite become a monochrome lounge lizard, crying when they turned the mirror on him. Simultaneously, I watched a mattress and rubble boneyard become an eighteenth-century water garden. It was all done in half an hour. At the end, they pictured the stringy thirtysomething social worker who owned the place rocking backwards and forwards on a little swing. She was repeating over and over: 'Perfect, just perfect.'

I realised why it all has so much power: it's alchemy. They momentarily turn dross into gold. I could do with some of that. I could do with whatever TV was giving out.

My mind turned to my obituary:

### FRANCIS DEAN STRETCH
### TV DON AND CRITIC

Frank Stretch, Emeritus Professor of Comparative Literature at Cambridge University and ex-Chairman of the Royal Television Society, has died aged 76.

Stretch came late to academia and television, after re-entering serious study when aged thirty in 1996. Shortly after publishing his PhD thesis, *Seven Other Types of Ambiguity*, he became much in demand on late-night minority-channel talk shows, and for twenty years had high paying columns in the *Daily Telegraph* and the *Radio Times*. His radical and severe views on modern politics, art and culture made him the darling of the chattering classes.

He continued to publish serious academic works, *Medusa's Reflection*, his treatise on television's influence on literary form, being perhaps the most famous.

His was a quiet, stable and fulfilled private life, revolving around a university sweetheart called Marie and the 3.30 from Cambridge to King's Cross. His television series on Rupert Murdoch, *A Lavish Enterprise*, made for BSkyB on the event of Murdoch's death in 2008 was seen by many as mere hagiography, but as he said in answer to his critics 'you can buy a lot of claret with hagiographies nowadays.'

He died peacefully in his sleep at his seventeenth-century cottage in St Neot's. He leaves a wife and three children, all of whom work in television.

The darling of the chattering classes kicked back from his landlord's pine dining table and let out a throaty roar of embarrassment: 'I relish the prospect of being involved.' Oh, dear me.

# Five quid

On the Friday of Tom's weekend I wrapped at O'Hare's at four, went home, watched four hours of children's television and packed in nine seconds. I holed up in the dauphin at nine, planning to stop off and eat bad food *en route* to arrive at Mannion Mansions around midnight. Tom's parents' place was on the Oxon/Gloucs border, a journey that was an hour and a half's airconned cruise in Lucy's Disco, two-and-a-half hours' belching kangaroo in the Cav. I impacted with the M40 at Acton around 8.30 and found myself in the middle of the Friday-night jam, ten thousand people shuffling out of town like a morose chain gang; five yards forward, halt, three yards forward, halt. They've even got their own spirituals to intone as they go: 'Jesus Christ, when's this going to end?' as they thump their steering wheels; 'Oh Lord, please let me go!' as they crane out of the window to see what's holding them up. I was invisibly manacled to the back of a cake van which bore the somewhat Proustian legend: 'We haven't forgotten how a good cake should taste.' It dragged me jerkily up to Uxbridge where we were briefly paroled, and I got the motor up to 65.

Alone in the Cav, heater on at level nine, and an old compilation tape specially selected to make me feel full of hurt and nostalgia about my relationship with Marie, this was excellent thinking time. I hadn't seen her since the crack-up, and in fact both of us had endeavoured to evade one another. The two previous times we had broken up, we had re-formed but on both occasions in a different register, which was progressively lower and more sombre than the previous. Neither of us could stand doing it all over again, and maybe the reason that we had studiously avoided meeting was that we didn't trust ourselves enough to believe that we wouldn't give it one last shot.

Now, the tape hissed and wobbled, and was all the more atmospheric for it. The music that we both liked didn't survive our first split, because as we faced the increasingly autumnal colouring of that later part of our relationship, memories of the earlier broad daylight were too poignant. But as I listened to it now – The Smiths, Costello, Sinatra – it all seemed to relate to Middle-Period Marie, and the discords and shards of themes that dominated it.

The Woody Allen line is that when the sex goes, it all goes, but for Marie and I the second time round it was the fun that went while the sex, in a modified, biological way, survived. University sex was new and torrential and taken whenever and wherever, like toast and tea or like laughing. I loved the way she dressed, translucent and cotton-y, the way she was so easily distracted from her books, the way she was as often the initiator as me, the way it all seemed so unimportant and never very far away.

When we started on our Middle Period, this had all changed. She was in London by now, first doing a law conversion in

Lancaster Gate, then at some huge City firm called Smethwick's, but we didn't live together. She was sharing with some old schoolfriend way up in Highgate. Sex became confined to weekend mornings, when she could bear to stay with me in Brixton, or snatched joylessly between the end of the movie and the commencement of the journey home:

'I've got to go back, because I've forgotten my pills/I haven't got a clean blouse with me/I need a book from home.'

'I've got to go back because I've got to interview a councillor/a copper/a dustman first thing.'

It was all too fragile for us to contemplate living together: we had only recently separated after she started a silly fling with someone in her English set the year I went down. As a consequence of our geographical distance, and our extended periods of student poverty, with me at Harlow and her on her course, we were always trying to make love happen again on a schedule and on a budget.

But I don't think this was why the fun went. We both spent all our time tiptoeing round fissures in the ice, and our preoccupations elsewhere in the world made us reluctant to notice this. From my perspective, these cracks were related to her minor infidelity, her frantic and impatient career orientation and my perception that she thought I was pissing my life away. From hers, I never really found out, but I think she felt that I'd lost something as I'd left university. Something, at the risk of sounding too literary critical, to do with my irony. At college it was representative of a spark of youth, questioning, curious and incisive, but it started to become more like cynicism. I was twenty-three and already jaded, and maybe even then, for no fathomable reason, shading into bitterness.

The results weren't unusual, I don't believe: our conversations came to comprise snippets of baby-talk, inexpressive and repetitive, which allowed us to make sounds to one another without having to transmit meaning. And, late at night, in bed, we would have different conversations, this time spread out over long confusing silences. We would take faltering steps towards 'talking things through', but always, so it seemed to me, through hostile, rising ground. And always talks about talks, not the actual deal itself.

*'Frank, do you think we talk enough?'*

*She can sense I don't want to answer. I can sense her sensing me.*

*'Frankie.'*

*Sigh. 'At the moment, I think we talk too much. Come on, babes, I'm reading. Go to sleep.'*

*She can't sleep, I can't read.*

*I put my book on the floor, and settle down to spoon her. I can feel my own coolness against her legs. Somehow, though she is utterly still, I can feel her wakefulness.*

*'I'm worried.'*

*'It's too late now. You always want to talk when it's too late. We can talk tomorrow morning.'*

*Oh, Christ, nobody believes that.*

*Then that feeling, when the wavelet of fear subsides, and is replaced by acceptance. The greater good prevailing? Relief at damaging things left unsaid? And then our favourite little wordgame to take us through to sleep.*

*'What do you love me, Frankie?'*

*'Insurmountably, Marie. And you?'*

*'Oh, mmm . . . interminably, that's it.'*

*We snuggle down, turn off the light and stare into the darkness. And for me at least, a sense that there is someone else in the room, maybe draped in the armchair, someone lethargic, greedy and unwilling to be drawn.*

And, unsurprisingly, the Middle Period didn't last long, about nine months, taking us into another hot summer. As soon as Marie started on her closing comments, in her Nova on the way back to mine from a tedious dinner party with some of her

FUCCER friends from Smethwick's, I got in first, and managed to staunch any emotional incontinence. It was over in, what, ten minutes or so, and when I got out of the car in Brixton I didn't for a minute think of looking back at her.

I was about halfway to Tom's now, and it started to snow, the flakes bobbing and diving like a storm of moths around the motorway lights.

The Chevalier surprised me by thrashing itself up to 75. We had been slung back in the chokey at High Wycombe (two-mile tailback, at *10.15!*). I decided to break across country. Reminiscence often makes me want to drive. After tunnelling under the wire at J5, I did a bunny run down mazy, thicketed, increasingly treacherous B roads. I next put my head above ground at a roundabout at Burford or Bicester or Bisley, only to see Marcel the Cake Maker's Transit swing by unforgettably. You can't beat the system. I needed some time to compose myself, feeling a little tired and weepy, and even went so far as to eject the nostalgia tape, and switch to some comforting local speech station. I thought I'd better eat, being too late for dinner at Tom's, and I took my time over a tepid, glistening five-quid All Day Breakfast at the first Happy Eater I saw. I find these places morale builders because they are always stuffed with real sub-20 material: women with pelican-bill upper arms and red-throated roll-your-own-husbands troughing towards their coronaries with the silent intensity of battery pigs. I felt like a king in there, a nice inoculation against the beautiful people who awaited me at Tom's, and one beautiful person in particular.

I stored up on nicotine, anticipating stringent regulations, and dumbed down with Ooh Ahh the *Daily Star*, which was being given away free to all the tits-and-footie lip-movers. I decided to take it with me, to appal Marie's boyfriend, paid up and backfired off towards Mannion Mansions limed with grease and newspaper ink, temporarily a very happy eater indeed.

Tom's dad's place was an early-nineteenth-century mock-Palladian affair that looked as though it had been designed by someone tracing round a primary school geometry set. My mood of chipperness began to dissolve. In the gravel arc outside the porticoed front door, I nosed in next to Lucy's Disco and a chubby Audi coupé, which I guessed was the adtwat's, lit a Lucky and put my head back. I pictured Marie entwined on a sofa with her new boy, sheathed in the glow of fresh sex, and felt deep-down sick. I even considered turning round and limping home, but the front door opened and Tom wandered down the steps, shirt untucked to conceal the fine dining paunch, hands in pockets, grinning his big, rich, glamorous grin. He tapped on the window as I smoked away.

'All right, Frankie boy.'

I rolled down the window which jammed about three inches down.

'All right, Tom. How's it going?'

'Not too bad. Can I give you a hand with your stuff?'

I held up the little fabric sausage bag in which I carried my gear.

'No, I think I'll manage.'

'Are you coming in yet?'

'Maybe just one more tab.'

'Suit yourself. Marie's making coffee. Do you want one?'

The mention of her name gave me a little wobble of nausea again.

'Tea would be good. She knows how I like it.'

Tom went back into the light of the hallway. I hoped that when he said, 'He said you know how he likes it', she'd get a flash of guilt. Only two people have ever made me tea just the way I like it: Mum, all those years ago, and Marie. That thought gave me a sharp blast of sadness, which I tried to sustain for as long as possible. I remembered when I was a kid I used to try and make myself feel sad by imagining my dad dead in a car

124

crash. Now I could do it by imagining my ex-girlfriend making a cup of tea. Growing up has tenderised you, Stretch, just as you hoped it wouldn't.

# £200,000 a year

Three cars in the snow-frosted drive. Just this grisly fivesome, then, two couples and a spare prick. I went into the house and turned into the door first left off the hall. It was a hot, over-cushioned room containing the house's only TV and bookcases stuffed with Freddie Forsyths and Joanna Trollopes. Tom called it the 'snugger'. Family words, always likely to inspire rage and regret. New Boy was lounging on the sofa watching the TV with a bottle of lager. He stood to attention when he saw me.

'Hi there. You must be Frank. I'm David, pleased to meet you.'

I shook his big, firm hand, cool from the bottle, and eyeballed him equally coolly.

'Hi, Frank Stretch.'

It was worse than I'd dared think. He seemed about a foot taller than me and I guessed about five or six years older. He was wearing a cashmere fawn polo and good new jeans, and was wide shouldered, thin and rangy. There was a deep scar over his left eye, but he was definitely a high 3 or low 4 on beauty points: smiley mouth, quite cheekboney and a bum-chin. Why not a fatso? Why not a baldy? Why not a midget?

As we sat down, I saw a pair of Marie's loafers kicked off by his feet, and felt a little breathless. I sat on an armchair in front of the sofa, my face hopefully out of David's eyeline. There was some gaudy low-rent chat show on the box, but I didn't pay any attention. I was knotted up in anticipation of Marie's entrance. I could hear her coming down the hall giggling with Tom. Some 'isn't Frank funny' gag no doubt. She came in with a big tray of tea and coffee, and arranged herself on the floor milking and sugaring. Her hair was getting longer, and she was dressed in a long black skirt and blue button-down shirt that was too big for her. David's? I guessed so. Neither of us said anything. I stared at the wankers on the screen, trying not to look at her, and thought about what it used to be like watching telly with Marie's head on my lap. I tried to take my mind away by doing David's score, but I was low on information and high on distractions, so I gave up. The early intimations of high-70s-ness were also discouraging. Lucy came in and sat on the arm of my chair and kissed me on the top of the head. She had a scan picture of her baby, which she insisted on showing me. It looked like a smudged thumbprint when I first looked at it, but then in a moment of gentle shock its human outline became clear. The oversized pear of the head, the folded arms, its legs curled up together, it looked like a little high-diver in tuck position. I felt moved and disoriented.

Marie stood up, shook her hair out of her eyes and handed me my tea in the way she always had, hand cupped underneath, two fingers calipering the rim, the handle of the mug proffered towards me. Why couldn't she change these little characteristic details, just for this evening?

I sat up and took the mug from her and involuntarily thought of those fingers tracing over David's face, or interlaced with his as they read together in bed, or (don't do it to yourself, Frank) wrapped around his cock. Pain and anger, pain and anger. I tried like hell to lighten up, conscious that my silence was creating an atmosphere, and made some dismissive comment about the pink, perky nonsense on the screen, and everybody seemed to relax a little. I noticed that Marie hadn't resumed her position next to David on the sofa, but instead was prone on the floor with her ankles crossed (Marie's TV-Watching Position Number 2). At one point, David tried to hold her foot, which she moved out of his reach. She was obviously trying to be gentlé with me, the sweetheart. An air of awkwardness persisted as we all tried manfully not to think about how I must be feeling. Probably unconvincingly, I yawned and asked Tom where I was sleeping. He offered to show me and I grabbed my sausage bag from the hall and went up with him.

They had given me Tom's room, and I was grateful they hadn't put me in the room that Marie and I used to stay in, up in the attic.

'Who's up in the roof?'

'David and Marie.'

Of course.

'You all right, Frankie?'

'Yerr. Bit knackered.'

Tom tried to be as normal as possible.

'Have you had that interview with Dad yet?'

'Yeah, last week. He was cool.'

'I'll call him when he's back from holiday, to put another word in.'

'Cheers, Tom. Think I'll turn in actually, if you don't mind.'

'Sure, go ahead. We're going walking tomorrow, down to Harlingford and then lunch at The White Hart, if that's OK.'

'Yeah, great, give me a knock.'

Nine quid for a shepherd's pie, just what I needed. He gave me a pretend sock on the chin and left me to my brooding. I imagined that they had organised the walk so that Marie and I would be able to talk a few things through in the open air. The entire weekend was designed to let me down easy. I started to feel conspired about, like a dog someone was trying to sneak to the vet without it knowing. I stole a Lucky out of the window and then got under Tom's Playboy duvet. His parents had kept the room exactly as it was when he left home, as if he were dead. I lay there with the light on, my ears straining for the sound of Marie and David stumbling up in to the rafters for some gorgeous, sleepy Friday-night sex. I hadn't heard anything by the time I fell asleep and dreamt about Bart snapping my bones.

I woke to find Lucy sitting on the bed. More tea, but Earl Grey this time. Dreck. And some toast and Marmite. Were they taking turns to pander to me?

'Come on, sleepyhead, it's eleven-thirty. Get your boots on.'

'I haven't brought any boots.'

'You can borrow some of Tom's dad's. He's got some wellies that'll fit. We're leaving in ten mins.'

She left me to dress in my country gear, to wit, my city gear plus a cagoule that screwed up to the size of a pair of women's knickers and stored in its own hood. I fished the blue pod of nylon out of my bag and rolled on the crinkled, cellophane item. Checking myself in the mirror as I did my teeth, the fact that I looked a disgrace was unavoidable. Grungy shapeless silage hairdo, a bagel of extra flesh ringing my chin, the cub scout windcheater. As I took a piss, I noticed a fritillary of white tissue paper unflushed on the downslope of the toilet bowl: Marie all over. Perching Marie, always off somewhere else. Restless, lively Marie, forever in transition, flitting off towards a more promising destination. Silly fat fuck, no wonder she'd left me for somebody else. But, of course, she hadn't left me for someone else, originally she'd left me for nobody else. I'd been deemed worse than nothing; if you subtract a minus number you get a plus. With such calculations I descended the deep-pile staircase, past the unregarded pictures, military, operetta, horse and hound, and resolved to be good.

David and Marie were kicking their heels on the gravel outside the front door. She'd pinned back her hair and had given herself a natural outdoorsy look; a trace of brownish lippy, a Barbour (when did she get *that*?) and pristine Timberlands. I hate natural looks, so I didn't feel too bad. I like it when they cake it on and tart it up. David was swathed in a battered Driza-Bone and Rupert the Bear scarf, really playing up the way the wind was sweeping back his fabulous wavy locks. He had the look of someone who'd just spent the night giving your ex-girlfriend the pasting of her life. I slipped a Lucky out of the velcro-ed marsupial pouch in my cagoule and started to smoke it in my cupped hand, trying to look a little feisty and blue collar.

Tom locked up and off we scrunched. The sky was now bright blue and the world was looking coyly gorgeous with its light dusting of snow. Five is a bad walking number as it's impossible to stay three abreast so someone always gets tailed off. I was determined that I wasn't going to be the straggler, so I glued myself to Lucy, a few paces behind David and Marie. This position had the dubious benefit of allowing me to appraise their love antics with a critical eye. Tom took up the rear, really playing the countryman game, in his dad's flat tweed cap, vast green wellies and walking stick. We started off into the wind, just our breath and the swish and swoosh of our clothes audible. Talk in the fresh air is different; more candid, less encumbered.

'I'm really sorry about that shambles at your do, Luce. I hope I didn't embarrass you too much.'

'Don't be silly. It was nothing, it was fine.'

'How did that mate of yours react, that banker bloke.'

David's hand was grazing over Marie's right buttock.

'Oh, he was pathetic about the whole thing. After you left he had a big slanging match with Sophie. He said that she'd been letting you grope her and he stormed out. They split up a couple of days later. He moved out and went to live on some friend's sofa.'

Oh yes!

'But they were married, weren't they?'

David's hand was really burrowing away now.

'Yeah. They'll get back together, but she thought he deserved a bit of time to work out what an idiot he was.'

'So they separated because of me?'

'Well, not really, Frank. She'd been talking about it for a while. That night was just a bit of a catalyst.'

Still, I felt pretty good about it. Maybe she'd given me such liberal frotting access because she fancied a bit of Stretch love while Colin the Ponce cooled off on his mate's sofa. But my sense of well-being was somewhat diminished by the self-conscious love drama going on ahead; nestle, nuzzle, cuddle, grope, slap, tickle. *This is for your benefit, Frank.*

Lucy and I walked in silence for a few minutes down a wooded path. But it wasn't really silent at all. The path was alive with signifying noises; the reedy swish of my cagoule, the more robust scrape of Lucy's stiff, brand new multi-layered ski jacket ('Whistler. We love it in Canada: no white trash.'), my panting, Marie's coyly terrorised giggles. 'You are poor, your friends are rich, you're out of shape, you've lost your girlfriend', they seemed to whisper. Lucy started humming, very softly and tunelessly, Marie style. She was either embarrassed at David's blatant animal-world attempts at establishing ownership or she was about to tell me something. She coughed.

'Frank. Are you all right?'

'I'm a bit out of breath.'

'No, you know what I mean. I mean generally, are you all right?'

'All right'. Both of them concerned about whether I was 'all right'.

'I don't know what you're getting at.'

Lucy breathed in loudly through her nose. 'Neither do I really. It's just that you seem to be a bit down. And you don't call us any more. As if you were trying to shake us off or something. Tom just says we should leave you to it, but I don't want to. You weren't offended that we tried to set you up with Sadie, were you?'

'No no no.'

Yes. She must have known my moral opposition to ginger teachers at the time. Now I was their biggest supporter everything was worse. Why didn't she just leave me be?

'I just want to understand if we've done anything wrong.'

I put this down to a hormone-inspired desire to gather things in. The sprout in her guts was making her want to be everyone's mother all of a sudden.

'God no, Mum. I'm just going through a quiet patch, keeping my head down a bit.' Like a known criminal.

'How's O'Hare's?'

This is one of my least favourite questions. Very *unmanly* of me to want to avoid talking about my job. If I ever asked Tom about his work, I would receive a four-hour dissertation on the state of the British justice system and his pivotal role within it. It's part of growing old, this ability to animadvert endlessly on one's career. Listening to Tom, you could sense that he was beginning to find himself increasingly worthy of comment. Most of the men I knew seemed to be getting like this.

'Oh, you know, the same as ever. Same old shit. Nothing, really.'

End of story. Lucy didn't press the issue.

'You don't mind David being here, do you?'

'No. I mind Marie being here *with* David.'

That shut her up. We had come to a wooden bridge over a stream. David and Marie were bending way over the rail like two little kids. Tom arrived in his dad's countryman cap, with the seams of his too-tight jeans describing a lazy 's' along his mighty hams: closer to forty than eighteen, ancestor worship now upon him.

'Pooh Sticks, anyone?'

Everybody concurred, except me. They selected and discussed their techniques and chosen sticks in that tone of mock-seriousness always adopted by fooling adults.

'I find a bigger stick, dropped firmly, can often be beneficial.'

'Ah, no, you see, what is needed is a light stick and an easy arm action.'

I sat the game out on a tree stump. Pooh Sticks is just not part of my repertoire. If they wanted to recreate a moment from childhood Saturdays that I could understand, why hadn't they brought a TV so I could watch *Football Focus*? I volunteered an occasional ironic heckle and got Lucky. The boys inevitably took charge of the regulatory fineries:

'You're not allowed to lean over so far, Lucy.'

'And no bombing, just because I'm winning.'

The sun was now streaming through the piebald sky. Marie had inevitably brought her camera. The familiar cadences of our relationship momentarily returned.

'Frank, come and take a picture.'

'What's the point? You've already got about a million that are exactly the same.'

'There's no point, I just want a photo.'

Now she was someone else's I had to capitulate rather than escalate the argument. I took the camera from her and they lined up on the bridge. Again, I guessed to spare my feelings, Marie slipped away from David and put her arm round Tom instead. Through the viewfinder they looked anonymous and oddly permanent as they jostled together. Just another photo of just another group of friends on just another twee wooden bridge. There probably are millions of such photos lying around in boxes and plastered into albums all over the country, all of them with similar stories to tell. This one, when disinterred in years to come, would relate a touching little tale about Frank Stretch and how it had all gone a bit wrong – his love, his friends, his usurper, taken with his unerring ability to make everybody look shifty; 'I wonder what became of *him*?'

At lunch I got my first proper look at David. The first thing I noticed was his wallet, which was emblematically tall, slim and glossy (mine is emblematically short, fat and beaten up). It had a rank of cards in it as long as a squash ladder. His cash position was also quite strong, a futon of sharp twenners stacked in the wallet's shiny pocket, and produced with a happy disregard. He wore a very pricey looking watch, a wafer thin oblong, but I couldn't quite read the manufacturer's name, not for want of trying. The conversation centred on country versus London, where he held his own with a humourless defence of the city. He referred to 'friends in New York' with unnecessary frequency and was commonplace on the downsides of living out of town – the family-oriented multiplexes, the lack of decent restaurants, the loneliness.

At one point he said; 'My brother's lived in New York for eight years now.'

Tom asked him, 'Is he the architect?'

'Well, no, he *was* an architect, but now he's a dancer.'

Tom sounded interested. 'Quite a career change.'

'No, not really. Architecture, dance, they're both so much to do with space.'

'Worrgghh!' I nearly choked on a chip.

David continued, blithely unaware of my incredulity: 'It's interesting, because all the family are talented – spatially. Daddy was a fine sculptor, although he made his living in the law.'

I sniffed and cut in: 'And what about your mum. An astro-naut?'

Marie looked at me murderously. Tom to his credit was trying hard to suppress a giggle.

David looked puzzled. 'No. A photographer. And again, of course, photography is just so much about capturing the *meaning* of a space.'

I wasn't going to let him get away with this.

'The *meaning* of a space?'

'Yes, a good photograph is a type of spatial lyric, I think, where light is organised by the photographer to give structure to apparently formless content.'

'Oh, come on!'

That was me obviously.

Marie tried to drown me out: 'Yes, I think that's interesting. Mapplethorpe is a . . . a . . . spatial poet in that sense.'

'For Christ's sake, Marie! Spatial poet? It's just big black cocks! What's the poem? "Ode to a Big Black Cock"?'

A cloud of silence settled momentarily over the rest of the pub. Lucy managed to move us on to talking about the food, the weather and the time, but when David went to the bog Marie couldn't resist a little go at me.

'Frank, just make an effort, for God's sake.'

'But he's a wanker.'

'Just because he's different from you, that doesn't make him a wanker.'

'I don't think he's a wanker because he's *different* from me. I think he's a wanker because he's a wanker. If I'd ever said anything that pretentious you'd've crucified me.'

'Well maybe I've changed, maybe I only did that because I was under your grinding, negative influence all the time. Have you ever considered the possibility that some people actually mean what they say, and not everyone who expresses an interesting view is pretentious? Anyway I think photographs *are* about space and light.'

'Good one, like it; everything grinding and negative – me, everything spacious and light – this pretentious twat.'

Tom was getting impatient: 'Come on, you two, cool it.'

135

David returned serene and oblivious.

'Hey, Dave, what's the khazi like? Enough space for your formless content?'

He laughed thinly, and I must admit it was a slightly pathetic comment. Yeah, but still, what a wanker.

And spacial poet for fuck's sake.

As lunch continued I could see that Marie was very respectful of him, which I found painful. I was hoping that maybe she was just cock/cash-struck, and would regard him with the stupid longing eyes of a pleasured puppy, but she actually seemed almost in awe of him. It was obviously more than just tummy tickling. They also had a pretty convincing physical contact routine going, which suggested a hinterland to their relationship I didn't feel ready to see.

The most significant impression he created was that of a 'serious person'. Despite the fact he was pretentious, he was together, measured and sincere. In comparison I felt half formed. Even Tom was still only playing at seriousness in comparison, still highly susceptible to flippery and rudery. David had obviously crossed some rubicon (35? £200,000 a year?) where it was important to be a real, decisive, confident grown-up. He didn't laugh much, but he wasn't straight-faced in a sullen, adolescent way. It was more that we were all operating well within his scope and that he'd heard it all before. Instead of making him appear an uppish twat, to my alarm, it started to make me want to be liked by him.

It transpired that he was a commercials director. He operated at the top end of the market; cars, beer, airlines. The one commercial of his I had seen was a ludicrously bombastic epic on the theme of the two centimetres' extra leg room available on Thai Air's Lotus Business Class. I remembered Anthony Hopkins reciting the strap over a shot of a Big Top Jumbo banking away into the sunset: 'Up there in all that space, a little more space.' Total fucking drivel, of course, but lucrative drivel. And how do you actually go about

136

doing that, filming a 747 at thirty thousand feet with just the right amount of twilight glint igniting the wingtips? Where do you start acquiring the knowhow? Not in a restaurant in Battersea, that's for sure.

From what I'd gathered so far, high 70s was beginning to look optimistic. Walking back to the house in silence alongside Tom I tried to make Marie and David's relationship into a credit to me, as if it was a natural progression from me to him. It didn't work. He was so obviously a step-change in quality it was almost embarrassing. There was no field in which I felt able to drive home superiority. I was like old technology; more unwieldy, slower, with a couple of design faults built in, worse in every respect.

Only one area remained untested. Maybe I was a better *drinker* than him. With all that continence and lack of irony, he bore every sign of being a two-pot screamer, a drink blouse. It wouldn't be much, but at least it would be something. I resolved to find out.

# Thirty a bottle

After a mute and languorous afternoon watching the football scores on Ceefax whilst everyone else pretended to read the papers, I went upstairs for a purging bath. The vital scenes from Blue-Period Marie flickered across the back of my eyelids as I rocked myself slowly up and down the tub. There was no particular cause of this final collapse, just that she was going one way, infatuated by some notion of progress, and I was staying put. Rows at her place, rows at my place, bitter silent dinners out together, her always paying, rows in the car. What seemed like scores of those. The last day, in a ring of trees in Green Park, me carrying a bag of her clothes she had left at my flat in error, exhorting, blaming, adopting postures of mock-disbelief. We played those last, archetypal, voided conversational games until with a single shake of the head I turned from her as she attempted the final sealing embrace. My last view of her walking away from me north towards Piccadilly, not once mopping her eyes, and this time it was she who refused to look back, holding the bag of clothes over her shoulder like a schoolkid. Two back views, one in the porter's lodge, one in a London park, the unexpressive bookends of our relationship.

I started drinking in earnest at dinner. Tom and Lucy had cooked a vast fish, which I bolted down with some unbelievably delicious wine from a case supplied by David. How was it possible for something to taste so nice? It had a fantastically exotic name, filled with e acutes, zs and xs, and just begged to be glugged in huge erotic mouthfuls. I was practically sucking it straight from the bottle by the time the Häagen Dazs arrived, so determined was I to get the lion's share.

'Jesus, this stuff is fantastic. Where did you get it from?'

'I order it straight from the *négociant* in France. My father has bought wine from them for nearly forty years.'

I knew a bit about wine. One of the few perks of working at a restaurant is that bibulous reps turn up twice a week and forcefeed me with their latest offering, unaware that I have no power at all to actually order the stuff. The game here, however, was to appear as philistine as possible, to play the working-class card, and to play it hard.

'Forty years, fucking hell. What is it, claret? No, that's red, isn't it, like Aston Villa, claret and blue.'

'It's burgundy.'

'Burgundy? I thought that was red, too – burgundy slacks and all that.'

'No, you can have white. Chardonnay, that's the white burgundy grape.'

'Right. Interesting. Is it expensive?'

'It depends what you mean. It's expensive compared to your average bottle of plonk, but we get it much cheaper than you'd pay in Oddbins or somewhere.'

'What, a tenner a bottle?'

'This one is more like thirty a bottle.'

'Thirty quid! Fucking hell! You can get a quarter for that, or three Es!'

'But you don't get the same pleasure.'

'Speak for yourself, pal.'

'No, I disagree. That's the problem with drugs, isn't it? All the interest focuses on the effect rather than the means of getting to the effect.'

'I'm not with you.'

David picked up an empty bottle of wine and cradled it, examining the label.

'Think of all the generations of expertise in grape growing, in maintaining the *terroir*, in upholding the integrity of the process. When you're drinking good burgundy, you're participating in a cultural and historical event. It's silly to drink it just to get *off your face*.'

His italics.

'You can use vodka for that. Or dope or Ecstasy, as you say.'

'But it's all escapism, isn't it? It's all just sensory indulgence.'

'Yes, perhaps, but of different qualities, I think. The motivation for going to see *Parsifal* is probably much the same as that for going to see Oasis. But one experience is qualitatively superior to the other.'

I was in an awkward situation, as Marie was listening intently, and she knew that I was in agreement with David on this one, although a little unsure as to what *Parsifal* was precisely. Did people go and see mosaics? If so, how was this comparable in any way to Oasis? Broadly speaking, though, I am an enemy of relativism. In fact, as you may have noticed, the impulse to classify according to absolutist judgements is my thing. I was forced to take another tack entirely.

'So where does the advertising fit into all this, then?'

'What do you mean?'

'Well, you make your living from the lowest form of everything. Doesn't that make you feel a bit bogus when it comes to casting judgement on the quality of other people's pleasures?'

'Not in the slightest. I'm only in advertising until I've got the credibility to get a movie to direct. It's a means to an end.'

'Like dope.'

'A bit like dope, but hopefully the end will be more constructive than slumping in front of the TV with a pizza and giggling at stuff that isn't very funny.'

'But they'll be watching your films, won't they?'

David raised his eyebrows and laughed gently.

'Oh, you've got me there. I guess they will, yeah.'

In my increasingly boozed state I felt quite triumphal. In fact I had probably been stupidly aggressive, because Marie looked at me and shook her head tightly, for my eyes only, as she always used to when I was making someone feel uncomfortable. The joy was that her disapprobation had no power. She now bore no responsibility for my behaviour; and as she had no responsibilities, she had no rights, simple as that.

I eschewed the ice cream for more burgundy. We were sitting in Tom's parents' dining room, which Lucy and Marie had lit with candles. Everybody looked more attractive in the gloaming, and the cutlery and glassware were refracting and reflecting with soft yellow light. Lucy put some classical music on the stereo – bland, wintry and slithering. The conversation fell to unrememberable mundanities. Tom produced an ancient bottle of armagnac. It was if we were starring in our own ad for Making It in Western Europe. My thoughts, however, were largely elsewhere; Bart, Henry on his dull, steady holiday, Sadie, Mannion and his tawdry magazine, cigarettes. Mostly cigarettes, to be honest. I was by now sweaty and mute with drunkenness. The room started to pitch and revolve, as if I was on a treacherous sea crossing. I excused myself and went for a wander outside.

I sat on a stone rail by the Cav and sparked an ill-advised Lucky, which negated the beneficial effects of the cold, misty air. I was involuntarily scripting a furious monologue in my head on the subject of complacency and soul death. Precisely whose complacency and soul death I was getting so lathered about I was unsure, but it was making me feel better, so I kept at it.

The scan picture of the foetus in Lucy's belly kept reappearing in my scrambled mind. I began to be overwhelmed by a rage I made no attempt to suppress. Tom called me from the porch.

'More booze, Frankie?'

I didn't respond. He came towards me. 'Are you OK, mate?'

'What is this sudden fucking obsession with my well-being with you two? I'm fine, all right?'

'Goodness, sorry, Frank. I was just trying to ask whether you were coping with the Marie situation.'

'Like a dream.'

'I love you, Frank. I knew it would be all right.'

He was as pissed as me. Tom's drunkenness was slurry, boyish and merry in marked contrast to the stern, lucid intensity of my own. He wrapped his arm around my shoulder and kissed me on the ear, which softened me up considerably.

'Come on, big fella. Let's get legless.'

'I'm already legless, Tom.'

He started to squeeze my shoulders tightly.

'Don't you worry about David. He's not a patch on you, mate.'

'Yeah, too right. What's a millionaire film director next to me?'

'Ahh, bollocks, Frank. That's bollocks. You're the best, mate. Fucking A1.'

His transition from gentleman farmer to vault drunk was almost complete. In a moment he would presumably start a shadow-boxing match with me.

'Come on in. Have a lager to sober yourself up.'

'Yeah.'

We went back into the house. David and the women were in

142

the snugger, not watching TV but just talking. Marie was curled up on the sofa, her head against David's upper arm, her arm extended across his chest. He was gently twining her hair around his fingers. They were binding themselves together before my very eyes. I started to feel very dangerous to myself.

I slumped on the floor, my back to the wall. 'David, when you were doing that Thai Air ad, what was it like?'

'Well, I was quite nervous, it was a big project.'

I produced a Lucky and put it in my mouth.

'Yes, I bet you were a bit nervous. All those big planes. All that space and light.'

Marie interjected with a familiar strain of headmistress in her tone. 'Frank, you know that Lucy doesn't want you to smoke.'

'Mind your own business, Marie. I'm not fucking smoking anyway.'

Tom giggled. 'Just like the old days.'

Lucy was probably the only sober one, I couldn't tell. She was certainly keeping very quiet, hunched watchfully over her belly on the arm of the sofa.

'Anyway, anyway, back to this ad. Do you think it's any *good*, David? Do you think it's adding anything?'

He was trying to stay very cool. 'No, not really. Just to my reputation.' He paused and looked at me steadily. 'And to my bank account, of course.'

Ah, very clever. Very good. He'd latched on to this bone of contention between us with admirable pace.

'Of course, your bank account. Though there are some things that money can't get you, David, aren't there?'

The question was laced with drunken sarcasm and threat.

'Stop it, Frank.' This was Marie again.

'No, no, it's all right, Marie, I can look after myself. I'm interested to know what the things are that money can't buy you.'

I felt the alcohol roaring around my ears. 'Have you ever fucked

Lucy, David?' My stomach whooshed up into my throat as if I was on a big dipper. Tom started to look more serious. Lucy now took her turn to intervene.

'Frank, just drop it. What's the matter with you?'

'Nothing's the matter with me, Lucy. I just asked David a straight question.'

'No, of course I've never ...'

'... fucked Lucy. No, I didn't think you had. Well, you see, there are some things that money can't buy you, David, like Lucy for instance. I didn't have any money at all when I fucked her, did I, Lucy?'

Tom's eyes narrowed. He was about to say something, started, but cut himself short when he saw that Lucy had burst into tears. I ploughed on.

'No, those afternoons in Hammersmith, you weren't paying any attention to how rich I was, were you, Lucy? Money didn't come into it at all.'

My mouth was clogged and the alcohol continued to boom in my ears. 'Rutting away with your fiancé's best mate, totally oblivious.'

Tom stood up stumblingly. 'What the fuck is going on?' he bellowed.

I suddenly felt amazed with remorse.

Marie drew herself upright on the sofa. 'You fucking snake, Frank.'

'What does that make her then, Marie?'

'You sick fucking snake.'

Lucy ran out of the room in a welter of tears, and Tom went after her. 'What is this? What is this?'

I heard Lucy scream as she pounded up the stairs. My hands were shaking uncontrollably. I looked at the carpet, and felt the room pitch again. I could sense Marie in my peripheral vision staring at me.

'What are you after, Frank? What are you trying to do?'

'Fuck off, you whore.'

She stood up and took a swing at me with her stockinged foot, which I fended off with a stiff, outstretched arm. I remember that she made a strangled, hating noise that genuinely alarmed me. She then left the room, leaving David speechless on the sofa. I looked at him. He was shaking his head very softly.

'I feel sorry for you, I really do.'

'Fuck yourself.'

'I really wanted to like you, Frank. Really.'

He got up and left me alone with my disbelief.

After about five minutes of silence, I got to my feet and went out to the car. I took the keys from the pocket of my jeans and probed for the lock. When I had the door open I looked up at the first floor windows. I saw that Tom was looking down at me, but couldn't see any expression. I got into the front seat and started the engine. I was still so pissed I couldn't figure out which way to turn the wheel as I reversed over the gravel. After God knows how long shuttling backwards and forwards, I drove off down the path and on to the narrow road. I waited at the junction for an age, carefully studying the road for signs of traffic. I pulled out and headed off at a snail's pace, the experience of driving made hyper-real by all the alcohol. The engine seemed to be howling like a crazed tiger, the knob of the gearstick felt as big as a basketball in my hand. I jerked on for about a mile and then stopped in the bulge of a passing place and tried to take stock. I got nowhere. I could hear myself breathing in over-melodramatic pants, as if I was in a film, as if I was putting on a performance. The last thing I remember seeing was a huge fox in the road, its eyes illuminated amber by my headlights. I turned the lights off and closed my eyes.

# Sixer in coin

I woke at four-thirty. There was no sign of dawn. If anything I felt worse than when I had fallen asleep. There was a swingeing poisonous savour of brandy at the back of my throat and my head was strafed with bizarre pain. It was as if my skull was full of metal plates and shrapnel, and each piece of ironmongery was taking it in turn to flash, hum or sing. I was furiously thirsty, but I couldn't think of anything that I wanted to drink. Fruit juice? Too acidic. Coke? Too gaseous. Water? Too watery. Deep down my body was craving replenishment, but my mouth and lips didn't feel up to delivering it. As my senses groaned back to life I became aware of an icy cold feeling between my legs. I rubbed the area with the numb mitten that my hand had become and realised that I had pissed myself. To hold at bay a sweep of nausea I clenched my jaw and felt it pulsing involuntarily as it attempted to quell the revolt in my oesophagus. I swallowed down several gulps of bitter sputum and started to breathe desperately through my nose.

No good. I started to unwind the window, but it stuck, and I vomited with huge force through the fingers of my right hand, lifted to my mouth in a final gesture of suppression. I managed to get the door open for the last dribbling retchings, my stomach contracting as if pressed by a huge cold foot. I stayed still for a minute, leaning out of the car door panting at dry air. Gouts of puke were sliding down the inside of the door. As soon as my olfactory sense began to function, my nose and mouth filled with the awful tang of rotten fish and stale booze. I retched again but produced nothing more than a syrupy string which swung heavily for a moment from my wide open mouth before attaching itself to my chin.

I got out of the car and went to sit on the bonnet. The road was black and the wind moved through the high hedges and trees roaring like ocean waves on shingle. I was hoping that all that ionising fresh air would clear me out, but I just got even colder and I started to shiver – a bad actor's parody of a shiver. I went round to the boot to find a blanket or a tarpaulin or anything to clean the car and my clothes with. The only thing remotely suited to the task was a crisp, wrinkled chamois leather, filthy from its usual application as the windscreen cleaner and dipstick wiper. I used it to scrape the worst excesses of vomit from the car door and my poor belaboured jeans. I had left my sausage bag at Tom's, so stripped the jeans off and threw them in the boot. I sat at the wheel in my piss-drenched, holed boxer shorts and, after checking that I wasn't in imminent danger of puking again, started the engine and headed off back towards London.

I was very low on petrol, so I nursed the Cav along at a steady thirty until I got to a Murco on a dual carriageway. The boring yellow streetlights revealed gobs of vomit drying on the top of the dash. It was still only five-thirty and the garage hadn't opened yet. I parked on the forecourt and got into the back of the car to try to sleep for an hour or two until the mong showed up with the keys. By curling myself up very tight, I generated enough warmth to see me into a light, strobelit doze.

I was woken by the sound of a car pulling alongside. It was now six-twenty. An insolent pallid teenager with the sides of his head shaved and a greasy slick of black hair plastered back on his scalp knocked on my window. 'Orr roight. Oim opnin up noi.'

I got out of the car and took a weird moment of solace from the realisation that his car was worse than mine: a ten-year-old Seat Marbella he had sprayed black. He had stuck the word 'Smokin'' in tangerine on to the lower body panel. The first 0 wheels score I'd seen at close quarters for some time. He cased my vomity shitbox with what looked like equal derision, and pimp-rolled off to the antique kiosk. No fresh-baked crusty brown loaves, parma ham and espresso here, just flagons of engine oil, mainstream fags and a desultory porn selection. I waited while he turned the pumps on. He gave me an impudent thumbs-up sign through the kiosk window and started to potter around his sad little castle.

I had a twenty in my wallet, and about a sixer in coin, which had to last me a week. I figured that I could eat off O'Hare's all week, so the only real concern was fag money. I put a tenner in the Cav and walked into the kiosk, conscious that without my jeans on I must have presented an alarmingly dishevelled prospect. The mong had unwrapped a pack of Regal and was idling over a skin mag he'd taken down from the rack. I was craving some human contact, and felt determined to start a conversation with him.

'Any papers?'

'Nah. Not till aboot seven-thirty, mate.'

'Fuck.'

I stood at the magazine rack. The lower shelves were made up of those terrible women's weeklies with their mournful tales of suburban deceit and dysfunction: *My Husband's Sex Swap Tragedy, Stepdads and Stepdaughters: Our Shocking Survey, Sexy Secrets of the Soap Stars*. Sibilant shitwash shitehawks.

'You arfter anythin' in partickoler?'

'Just browsing really.'

Higher up there were strange car and truck magazines, which seemed to specialise in just one model: *Escort Driver*, *Your Golf* and *DAF*, and then up to the inevitable contorted pout and splay of the 'adult interest', although I didn't know many adults who were still interested in this cheating dreck. One of them was called *Escort* too, and another called *Fiesta*, which I'm sure the Ford marketing department wouldn't have found too amusing. There was also a new specificity emerging which was faintly intriguing. Alongside the mainstreamers was one called *40 Plus*, subtitled *Women over 40 with over 40" Breasts*, and *Asian Panties*, which as far as I could tell consisted entirely of Japanese girls revealing their gussets. How long before they had *Plumpish Middle Class English Girls in Floral Summer Dresses with Small Feet, Blonde Bobs and Freckled Shoulders*? I'd subscribe to that one. *Ginger Teacher Monthly*? That one too.

As I stood there, mouth open, head back, surveying them, the mong spoke again:

'Go on, mate, do yourself a favour. No-one's looking.'

'What do you mean?'

'Get yerself a mag down. No 'arm dun.'

Christ, I hadn't bought one of these things in ten or twelve years. I'd seen quite a few, as Tony kept a stash in a cupboard by the cistern in the staff bog at O'Hare's. I thought it all terribly sad for the women. Not the women in the mags, that was up to them, but the wives and the girlfriends of the men who bought them. Sure, some of them must be bought by the adolescent, the lonely and the lost, but not all of them. What do Tania, Ondine and Amelia, with their babyish underwear and fibs of constant availability, give that the wives and girlfriends are so unable to? I suppose there is also a failure of women spoken of also, an inability to connect on some level. But as with most things, it's the men who are in control, indulging their worst instincts, letting it spiral out of all control, and hoping to emerge with a percentage.

With a fast beating heart I decided to buy one. No 'arm dun. I selected *Asian Panties*. At least I could pretend that I had bought the thing out of sociological interest, if challenged. This thought partly helped to assuage my sense of guilt.

The mong seemed a little surprised: 'Ooh, right. Everyone's different I suppose. I like the American ones better. More 'ardcore, more quality.'

Seventeen and an aficionado. It made me feel angry and impotent. A real porno mood.

'Fuck yourself.'

'Keep your hair on, mate.'

Reluctantly, I was also forced to buy twenty B&H, Luckies being on strictly metropolitan distribution. I'm not ashamed to admit that the solidly put together gold box gave me a little glimmer of well-being, and they turned out to be better than I remembered once I'd acclimatised to the extra carbon monoxide.

Back on the M40, I made an attempt to browse *Asian Panties*, listen to the radio, smoke, stave off vomiting and drive simultaneously. I was glutting my senses to prevent the consideration of the previous evening's disaster. I was broadly succeeding, until a capricious flat-sided van careered into my path near Marlow, and I felt it wise to drop the pantie mag from my repertoire, slinging it on to the back seat. In a curious inversion of the matronly warning, I couldn't bear the thought of being found dead with all that clean underwear around.

How bad had it all been? The order of events was difficult to remember through the washes of nausea, but Marie's kick and Tom's silly, hoarse shouting remained most strongly. Would a desperate pleading call from a phone box work? I didn't have the number. Anyway, there was nowhere to start. I imagined how the mundane, low-rent details of my curtailed affair with Lucy had been unravelled through the night. Spats of rage, low quiet disbelief, inarticulate lungings. Tom would be raw with lack of sleep, the last thing he could be expected to do was give me a big, magnanimous pardon over the phone. Marie would be raging, her collecting, organising, taxonomic impulses thwarted utterly.

I swung down the M25 and into town on the M4. I should have chosen the Great West Road – so much more poetic. A nebulous sun was coppering the roads and glassy office buildings. London was still scratching its stubble and shuffling into its Sunday slippers, and the roads were quiet. Left almost to myself tooling down the Embankment, the Thames thirstily lapping in its gully to my right, I began to feel an uprush of tearfulness. I don't know what it is about hangovers, but they make me weepy at the best of times. With Marie I was always at my squishiest the morning after a drunk. I was also at my horniest, all those cells madly performing their reparations, bidding increase.

I drove motivelessly into Battersea Park and parked by the tennis courts. It was nine o'clock and still freezing, but two girls were already playing. They were in their mid-twenties, I guessed, and muffled up in thick cotton sweats, breath steaming into the tangy morning air. I was still dressed only in my boxer shorts and shoes from the waist down, so I inched the Cav up to the fence and watched them from the car. The one nearest to me was all in white with her hair in a thick pony tail. She was chubby, and looked like the Pilsbury dough man from behind. Each time she prepared herself to receive a serve, her round bottom swayed from side to side. She was useless; swatting air, ping-ponging the ball over the net by making it bounce her side first, ballooning simple forehands back over her head off the racket frame. All the while both of them were laughing like parrots. I felt terribly, overpoweringly protective of both of them, especially my dough girl. I was willing her to win a game, and when her partner double faulted three times, and then spooned an accidental dropshot out of court, I peeped my horn appreciatively. They paused and conferred at the net and then Doughlene turned round and walked towards the car through the chicken wire gate. Not wanting to be seen in such a state of squalor I tried to start the engine, but before it caught she knocked at my window. She was about sixteen, not twenty-five as I had originally reckoned.

'What do you want?'

I held my hand up, and continued to turn the ignition key. She surveyed my naked lap and then caught sight of the splayed, bedraggled mag on the back seat. She hammered on the roof with her racket.

'You fucking perv.'

I got the wretched car started and reversed away quickly. As I sped up the path I heard her shout 'Tosser' and couldn't disagree.

I got home at nine-fifteen. The flat was very clean and tidy, which seemed grotesquely inappropriate. Henry and Lottie had gone away for the weekend to see his folks in Preston. I turned the TV on and flitted through the education and kids' programmes for half an hour. There was one black Yorkshire woman I returned to repeatedly, who was gradually assembling a symphony orchestra from household objects; the hoover was a bassoon, a plastic mixing bowl with clingfilm stretched over it a whatever-the-singular-is-of-timpani: Timpanus? Timpanum? Timpanorum? She gamely made a violin out of a shoebox and an elastic band before I got overwhelmed by a sense of dread at what use she might put these awful things to, and turned off.

I had a horrible closing-in feeling. I could either fight it or give in. Fighting would mean bathing, shaving, changing, popping out to buy the papers, looking up what was on at the Tate, tubing up to town, browsing, lingering, returning, flicking through the address book to find a Sunday evening cinema partner and starting my memoirs. Giving in would involve sacking out with *Asian Panties* and sleeping until Monday. No contest. I bedded down with Mitsuko, Hiroko and Chiasa, fogbound in sweat and anxiety, and resolved to sleep it all off.

Henry and Lottie were due back late. I had set the alarm for 3PM and spent the late afternoon dutifully fluffing and plumping the flat for them. I even bought them a ready meal and some drinking yoghurt with the shards of money I had left, in case they hadn't eaten on their way down. I had an itchy feeling of anticipation at the thought of them being back. A cosy spliff, a civilised natter, a nice cuppa, nothing could be better. When I heard the key in the door, I sat up a little straighter. I've really held it all together since you went away, I've been just fine, no need to worry about Frank. Lottie went into the bathroom and Henry hung himself around the doorframe from the hallway.

'Hi, Frank. How's it going?'

'Pretty good, Henry.'

'We're going to turn in. Knackered. Seven hours it's taken us.'

'Fucking hell.'

He made a strange little plocking sound with his lips.

'What was Tom's like?'

'Fucking miserable. Marie was there. Horror show, with me in the lead.'

'Downer. Listen, are you around tomorrow morning?'

'Yeah, should think so.'

'Right. I need to have a word before you go to work.'

'A word?'

'Nothing too heavy. Just a quick word.'

'Fine.'

'Night night.'

'Wake me up tomorrow, if I'm not up.'

'Sure. See you.' He went off to bed. So they're getting married, I thought. He'd got down on one knee halfway up some drenched brackeny hillside and popped the question. There goes another one.

# The nine hundred mark

Henry was shifty the next morning. He brought me a cup of tea and a blueberry muffin with apricot jam, but seemed keen to get me out of the sack.

When I eventually emerged he was sitting on the sofa leafing through some computer mag. Lottie was still hidden away in their bedroom, which was ominous.

'Sit down, Frank.'

I obliged warily. Henry eyed me steadily and made a tense little exhalation through his nose.

'This isn't very easy to say, so I'll just say it. We want you to move out.'

It hit me very hard. Although it was an obvious possibility, I had never really considered it. Henry's flat was one remaining positive constant, and I never thought it could just end like this. Although I suddenly felt very weak, I put on a brave face.

'God, well, sure. It had to happen eventually.'

'I'm sorry it's come out of the blue but we've actually been thinking about it for a while, and we just thought it best to tell you before we go away for Christmas.'

'No, thanks for that. No problem.'

'We don't want you to go straight away, but we thought end Jan would be reasonable. Should give you enough time to find somewhere else.'

End Jan. Five weeks of slogging round Stockwell and Kennington peering into slums. Not a great way of fighting New Year blues. I made a decision.

'No, fuck that, Henry. You give me my deposit back and I'll be out in two weeks.'

'Jesus, mate, don't take it hard. We don't want to force you out.'

'No, it's OK, you don't understand. I just want to get moving.'

He thumbed his hair behind his ear and looked deflated.

'It doesn't mean that we're not still mates.'

'No, Henry. 'Course not.'

Lottie edged out of their bedroom. She drew back her bottom lip sheepishly.

'Morning, Frank. Another cup of tea?'

'Yeah, cheers, Lottie.'

She slunk into the kitchen. Was she the brains behind the operation? I didn't think so. Henry was one of those old-fashioned straight-as-a-die Northern bastards. He wasn't a hired hand. He crashed me a Silky. Noisome, dry, dull fags.

'Was there any particular thing I did that brought it on?'

'Naah, honestly. It's just that me and Lot have never really lived together properly, and I got a load of money for this game I've been working on, so we don't need your rent. Circumstances have changed, you know, and we just thought it was time to move on a bit.'

'How much did you get?'

'Eighteen grand.'

'Jesus.'

We smoked in silence until Lottie brought the tea through. In her leggings and WWF sweatshirt she was a pretty unappetising sight at that time of the morning. I noticed that her podgy ankles were bearing a fortnight's stubble. I wished strangely that I'd gone far enough with Marie for her to feel comfortable letting her leg stubble grow. Even at the end we were keeping up appearances with one another. Especially at the end.

'Yeah, Henners, honestly, I'll be out in two weeks if you give me that dough. How much is it, can you remember?'

'Four hundred and fifty quid. Two months' rent. Minus that sixty you owe me, but let's call it four hundred. I know you're a bit pushed.'

I did a little calculation; four hundred from Henry, and two weeks at Christmas from O'Hare's, about four twenty after tax, plus the forty quid or so bonus we usually got. I was up to about the nine hundred mark. I made up my mind there and then to leave town. I didn't know where I was going to go, but I couldn't tolerate another year bumping along the bottom with no Marie, no Tom, no Henry to keep me from sludging to a halt. Bart would never find me, as I didn't know where I was going myself, and as for Sadie, well I'd put her down to experience and that would be that.

I felt a sense of tearful elation as I set off for O'Hare's later that morning. The dun Cav had become a little symbol of freedom as I got in and started her up.

'Two more weeks, mate, and we're off, you and me. AND the fire that breaks from thee then!'

I shouted along insanely to Sinatra singing 'Too Marvellous' as I razzed down to Battersea, and nearly fucking killed myself sliding across an icy junction at Lavender Hill. I was skating towards a bus stop peopled by twenty old ladies, frantically twisting the wheel this way and that. Frankie was now belting out 'Tender Trap' as I hurtled into the maw of an oncoming bus. The Cav stopped about two feet from from its great flat face and I howled with laughter for about two minutes. I saw one of the old ladies clasping her mate with terror. They obviously thought I was a madman, so to indulge them I tried to roll down the window and started doing Jack Nicholson in *The Shining*: 'Wendeeeeehhhhhy. Wendeeeeehhhhhy. Stop swinging the bat, Wendeeeeehhhhy.' But that *fucking* window stuck again, so I guess I looked even madder with my face crammed into the gap, and even quite like Black Jack. I got it together and drove up to O'Hare's feeling like a sail come loose from its mast, flapping crazily, me and the Cav together rebuffing the big wind.

## Spending limit

As Christmas week staggered by in its Santa hat with its dick hanging out, I calmed down a bit. There was still no word from *Emporium*, and I hadn't followed up the interview with a grateful letter as Tom had advised, but I was beyond that now. An internal voice of quiet certitude replaced the strafed gargoyle rantings that had preceded it: 'You're out of here, Frankie boy. Keep it sweet.'

Brian the Bat came in and did his customary mood-crushing speech about how the place was faring. He told us that while we were doing well, O'Hare's as a whole was still in some sort of trouble to do with the two new branches, and we all had 'to pull our pinkies out'. Of course, everybody ignored him.

On Christmas Eve I was doing the evening with Sadie and April, and we were pretty quiet. April crassly asked me what I was going to do the next day. We were out by the bins, predictably. I tried to think of something I'd never do in a million years.

'I thought this year I'd do the entire Ring cycle in one day.'

I was under the impression it lasted for twenty-four hours, which is probably wrong, but April wasn't equipped to pick me up on the niceties: 'Why are you riding your bike on Christmas Day? You'll freeze your goolies off.'

'Yeah, but the roads are quiet.'

'Yeah, giss so.'

'What about you?'

'Aww, get pissed with me mates 'xpect.'

'It's what the little baby Jesus would have wanted.'

'Yip, I giss.'

Sadie was more problematic. The thought of her on her own on Christmas Day was awful. In that room. BM BM KISSHY KISSHY all day long. Or with this Gaetano character, shagging off the mince pies.

As we were clearing up I asked her if she was leaving London. She adopted a tone of resigned levity.

'No. I'm staying here and feeling lonely.'

'Not going to see Lucy?'

'Naaah. She's nobbing off to Scotland.'

I made a sudden lunge.

'I'll tell you what, why don't we have Christmas together? I've got a free flat, and we can nab all the food from here.'

She looked at me through narrowed eyes. 'You sure about this?'

'Yeah, it'll be great. We'll just watch telly or something, and I'll take you home when we start getting worried about anything happening.'

She was turning a glass around her cloth-wrapped hand and looking into the middle distance. Come on, Sadie, you know it's the right thing to do. That glass was turning like crazy now. She eyed me again.

'No heavy duty?'

'Swear.'

159

'No insults?'

'I'll try my best.'

An agonising extra few twists on the tumbler. That glass was as dry as a nun's nasty by now.

'OK. Let's do it.'

'You could come back now, save you –'

'I'll see you tomorrow at two-thirty, Frank. What time's the Queen do her thing?'

'Fuck, I don't know – four-ish? Nine? Three in the morning? Make it two o'clock, and we'll have a little present opening ceremony beforehand. The only rule is you've got to buy it from the garage on Clapham Common. I did this last year with Henry. It lends a sense of occasion.'

'Deal. Only don't spend too much, and make a girl embarrassed.'

'No danger of that.'

I took home an unused chicken, some tired-looking but serviceable vegetables and five bottles of reasonable wine. I was in by twelve-thirty and started frenziedly to tidy the flat. My bedroom was looking particularly bedraggled, and with wild optimism I gave it a makeover. I put the bedding into the washing machine and channel-surfed ardently until it was ready, turned the thermostat up to 45 so I could dry it all off and went to bed. The heat was intolerable. I was being casseroled alive but the permeating aroma of Alpine freshness made it all seem worthwhile. I took a leisurely saunter through *Asian Panties* but held my peace for the morrow, if you see what I mean. I turned the lights out at four AM and threw out vivid mountain-air-infused dreams of tongues and teeth, abandoned hosiery and languid soapy showers.

I was up before nine, and wandered over the Common to the petrol station. The Asian guy on the counter wished me a Happy Christmas, and I wished him a Happy Diwali, which just made him laugh. They must think we're all so ignorant. The choice of presents wasn't very good. Ginster's Sausage Bites,

Ginster's Sausage Rolls, and several packs of sausages dominated the chiller cabinet: antifreeze, Turtle Wax and Shell Multigrade the open shelves. The confectionery selection was pretty poor and I thought chocolate would be a bit naff anyway. I began to get a bit panicky. The present was supposed to be cheesy, but *sweetly* so. I couldn't get her a Snickers and some screenwash. Batteries? No. An *A to Z?* No. Some sachets of Cup-a-Soup? No. *Razzle?* 'That's just a present for you, Frank, isn't it?'

I ended up getting her a Chocolate Orange and five scratchcards, which was a bit above my intended spending limit, but what the hell. When I got home I replaced my bedding (it made me want to sing *Edelweiss*, so I did), chucked the chicken in and watched the telly. The Ceefax clock seemed to move at a glacial pace: 12:28:41, 12:45:32, 1:02:40, 1:03:12. I was driving myself mad flicking back and forwards between a carol concert and the teletext, inspecting the chicken every three minutes, and trotting into the bedroom to check that *Asian Panties* was unfindable. I moved it from under the mattress to under the rug to under the carpet. I finally settled for under a floorboard, under a pile of towels in the airing cupboard. Attempting to slow my pace, I turned the sound on the TV down and tried to read something. I got the familiar feeling whenever I try to read nowadays, that I'm missing something crucial on the TV, so in the end I settled for MTV and nervously looking out of the window for Sadie to arrive. I then moved *Asian Panties* into the loft. Behind the water tank.

At two-thirty there was still no sign. I gave up on looking out of the window, and settled into MTV. They were playing videos on a loop, all the presenters presumably back with their folks in Stavanger, Lugano and Harpenden for Christmas, crunching ice to stave off the cocaine cravings. At 2:42:18 (yes, I was back on that by then) the buzzer went. I flung myself to the entryphone like Dino Zoff:

'It's Sadie, I'm sorry I'm late. Got caught up.'

As she came up the stairs I tried to compose myself. I'd shined up my Docs and was sporting my newest jeans and a cleanish shirt. I didn't know whether to be seated or to stand as she came in so I sort of perched on the arm of the sofa and smoked.

I was a little disappointed in her appearance. She was wearing leggings and an old sweatshirt under her mac, and hadn't put any make-up on. It didn't look like she had any intention of seducing me, that was certain.

'Nice flat. Posh. Is it yours?'

'Nah, I share it with a friend.'

'Lovely.'

'I think the chicken's nearly ready. I'll just check. Again.'

I went into the kitchen and plotted my next move. Dinner with generous sloshings of wine, followed by curling up on the sofa, taking a centimetre of territory every ten minutes throughout the Bond movie was my current idea. By ten we would be in the Appalachian springtime of my bedroom, shagging, which would mean I could easily be back in front of the telly for *Billy Liar*, which Channel 4 was showing at midnight. This was the ideal scenario, although I was prepared to forgo *Billy Liar* if she'd rather watch *Annie Hall,* which clashed. In fact, watching *Annie Hall* would give me the opportunity to show off my ability to laugh *in the right places* in Woody Allen films – you know, the places where *Woody* would laugh – rather than in the places where *everybody else* laughed. In *Annie Hall* 'it must be a tremendous hem', and, 'I want you to touch my heart – with your foot', are crucial moments. The only problem is that I hadn't worked out which one was 'the right place', and which was an 'everybody else'.

This maundering was getting me nowhere, so I boiled some water for the vegetables and went back into the sitting room with an opened bottle of wine. Sadie was coiled on the floor browsing Henry's CD collection, which was pretty embarrassing.

'Are these records yours?'

'Mmm, no. Hardly any of them. Wine?'

'Not just yet. Who or what is Tangerine Dream?'

'Dunno, it's my flatmate Henry. Pomp rock freak. Old-School New Age type ... thang. Are you sure you don't want any wine?'

'No, I'm fine for now. What can you recommend?'

'I think there's a Sinatra in there somewhere.'

'*Frank* Sinatra?'

I sat on the sofa with a big goblet of wine and filled her glass despite her demurrals.

'Yes. My namesake. My dad called me Francis Dean – Frank Sinatra and Dean Martin. The ratpack. They were dad's role models. Priapic crooners with Mafia links and drink problems.'

'Could have chosen worse.'

'Yeah, Engelbert Cliff Stretch would take some explaining.'

'Was your dad a singer then?'

'Only in his bedroom when he was pissed. So most nights, I suppose.'

She turned towards me. 'Don't tell me. Gritty Northern hardship.'

'No, not really. We were usually pretty well-heeled. Ish. He was a compulsive entrepreneur. A sort of serial dreamer. He put his faith in pet shops.'

'Did he ever make it?'

'He got close once or twice, but he was too much live-for-the-moment. If he was doing well, he'd spend it on a big car or a holiday home. He always had his suits made, that kind of thing. He'd sell two hundred live chinchillas and buy his girlfriend a coat made out of dead ones, for twice as much as he'd made.'

Sadie laughed. This was good. Women don't like good-looking, glamorous, confident men with sports cars. They like men who make them laugh. Yeah, they like to potter round the shops with the men who make them laugh, then they go home and fellate the guy with the MG.

'God, rodent economics.'

'They're the most difficult sort.'

'You speak of him very past tense.'

163

'What, Dad?'

'Yes, your dad.'

I swigged my wine. She was right, he was past tense to me now. I hadn't really noticed.

'Haven't seen him for over five years. I think he was in debtor's prison for a while, that's what someone told me, and then I got a letter about three years ago from him in Chicago. He said he was "back on his own two feet". Then we had a sighting. My aunt said she saw him in Tipton, near Wolverhampton, a couple of years ago, and he basically ran away from her, she said. Silly fucker.'

There was a warm, dusty, afternoon silence. She finally chose a CD: The Cranberries. Ginger showing solidarity with her Celtic origins. She moved to sit cross-legged on the floor fiddling with a ring and looking at me intently. 'What about your mum?'

'Fucking hell. She died when I was fourteen. The big C. But by then I was living with my aunt really, because my parents were divorced and my mum was ill for a long time, and Dad was doing his thing, setting up pet shops, groping barmaids, never around. He made me move back in after she died. Well, I moved back in with him at any rate. God, I must be boring you to death.'

'No. It's really nice hearing you talk, actually. Not just bantering all the time, or getting aggressive or defensive.'

'Shit, I am sorry about that night.'

'Forget it. So back to you. Where are you from? You sound like a Scouser to me.'

'Jesus Christ, nobody's ever said that before. If I was still at school I'd hit you for saying that.'

'Sorry.'

'I'm not really from anywhere, I moved around: Stoke, Wigan, Poulton-le-Fylde, St Helens – the Northern grunge belt. Went to school from fourteen in North Manchester and travelled from wherever, although we were mostly in Lancashire by then.' I poured myself some more wine. This talk was getting me down badly, but for some reason there was much more I wanted to say.

'The chicken smells nice.'

Maybe this was the cue for me to move on to lighter topics, like Bosnia for instance, or structural unemployment. I went into the kitchen. The chicken may have smelt nice, but he looked awful. Shrivelled but still pale, as if he was being eaten away from within. I compared him with the honey-bronzed picture in Lottie's cook book. I'd obviously done something very wrong.

I slammed the tray back in and shouted chirpily to Sadie: 'Another few minutes yet.'

I took another bottle of wine through and wondered where to start next. Sadie helped me out.

'Do you think all that family stuff affected you in any way?'

I rebutted hastily. 'No. Absolutely not.'

She was promisingly on the other end of the sofa now, and this time looked at me with raised eyebrows.

'No, straight up I don't think it did. It's like Liza Minelli, y'know, about being Judy Garland's daughter, I didn't know any different. It was just the way it happened for me. I'm pretty content anyway, not like most of the whingers you get: "I'm from a broken 'ome, m'lud, that's why I raped the old gent." It's bullshit.'

Sadie was rapping her tongue stud against her teeth.

'That just sounds so unconvincing.'

I tutted loudly. 'Well, why just believe the orthodoxy? Why assume that everyone with bad or dead parents is fucked up in some way? Why not take it from the horse's mouth? Some of us are just fine.'

'Oh, yeah, I guess so, sorry. I'm not trying to intrude.'

'More wine?'

'No, thanks.'

I glugged out another half pint for me. Henry's goblets were heinously large, and I reminded myself to be careful.

'Oh, shit, I nearly forgot. Your present.'

I went into the bedroom and retrieved the Chocolate Orange

and the scratchcards. I handed them over to her, masking my embarrassment with mock solemnity.

'There you go. Something a little bit special.'

She laughed and we did the scratchcards. She won a tenner, which was perfect in some small way. She delved in her handbag.

'I got you these.'

A caricature of Bart dressed in S&M gear, tongue blorting, being penetrated up the rear by Beelzebub, and two Ginsters pasties.

'You shouldn't have. Especially the pasties. They're exquisite.'

'The choice was a bit limited.'

'I was actually hoping for some screenwash. They have my favourite kind in that garage – Raspberry and Mint. It's a bit too good for every day, but I like to treat myself every once in a while.' She laughed again. Gaetano probably had a sports car.

She was so lovely, but as she looked at me I saw that she was a trillion miles from me sexually, romantically, in terms of love, whatever. I suddenly felt at odds with myself over planning to get her drunk. Was that much better than the dad-battered oik raping the war vet? God, I thought, why can't I reconcile myself to consent? Why was I always on the cheat?

An hour later we were feasting on our Christmas dinner: microwaved Ginster's pasties and baked beans with bacon burgers. The chicken just didn't make it. By the time we took the joint decision to bin him he was the size of a chaffinch with the complexion of a newborn piglet. Sadie reckoned I'd had the oven on too low. I contended that it was the lack of a basting pipette that did for him. Either way he died in vain.

It was fiveish and I was wrecked. Sadie on the other hand had barely touched a drop. Although now fully reconciled to not getting any action on a basis of a meeting of minds, I'd started to ponder going for the pity fuck. Before dinner and during we'd

166

spent most of our time talking about O'Hare's, and what she was going to do in the summer once her course was over. She was toying with the idea of going to America for a few months, but before that she was going to get pissed more often. That was all simply dealt with, and despite my anxiety at the thought of never seeing her again, I managed to keep on an even keel, only occasionally lurching into wordless grief.

We started on the Chocolate Orange for dessert and she swung the conversation mercilessly back to my family.

'Don't you ever think about your dad?'

'Almost never, actually.'

'Don't you want to see him at some point?'

'Nope.'

'You said that too quickly. What are you thinking now?'

I took a defiant slug. I was thinking that I was developing a drink problem.

'You must think about him *sometimes*.'

I pushed my arms out over the table and bowed my head.

'Maybe. Gaaaarrd, I dunno. You're right. Sometimes I *do* want to see him and really have it out with him, y'know, like where the fuck did you go, what are you doing, why do you never get in touch?'

Sadie nodded at me, seemingly encouraging me to elaborate. I kind of blurted, 'I tell you what I think about. I'll be totally honest. I think what I'd like to do is go on a walking holiday with him up in the Lakes and get him up in the Langdales somewhere and just sit him down and let it all pour out. I don't know why there, but I went a couple of times with school and I just thought it seemed exactly the right sort of place. Simple, spacious – you feel like you can throw everything off there and start again somehow. Basically, I've got pretty clear pictures in my mind. First of all I see him with his head bowed in this big confessional huddle really letting it flow, all the apologies, for not being there, for putting our house on the line every six months, for all the uncertainty, for the absences, for basically abandoning Mum when she was ill, and before, and all the refusal to take responsibility, I mean *any* responsibility *at all*. He gets all this out and then he starts sobbing, then throwing his arms around me and begging for forgiveness. By now I'm pretty racked but I decide to fend him off for a while, you know, cold but rigorously fair, and then when he's a husk, when he's totally spent and broken, I make the grand compassionate gesture – I always see me offering his bent head some strong tea from a flask, and when he's sipped a little, and his shoulders have stopped shaking, I fold myself around him, really wrap myself around him and tell him that it's all OK, and that I always loved him regardless, and that this can be a new beginning, and it starts to rain as we head back towards the B&B, and we walk in silence, but a good, strong silence, and when we get back to the road we hug and say that nothing ever happened, and we both bless Mum together and resolve to speak every week and . . . and . . .'

I lifted my head and saw that Sadie was looking at me with consternation, or disbelief. My eyes were pulsing out tears with hot irregularity. I poured out yet more wine to flood my drying mouth.

'Fuck me, I'm sorry about this, I don't really talk about it very often, you've set me off a bit. I'll just go and have a wash.'

She spoke softly: 'Yeah, you go, fine.'

I stumbled off to the bathroom and stared at myself in the mirror. My lips were crusted purple, my teeth Medievally stained. I swooshed myself vigorously with cold water and had another look. What kind of short-sighted angel could even pity-fuck the piece of human wreckage there displayed? Oh, fucking hell. Oh, fucking hell. Fuckfuckfuckfuckfuckfuck. Cunts. Fuck. Wank.

I scrubbed my lips with the toothbrush till they were numb and went back into the sitting room. Sadie was standing with her mac on.

'Where are you going?'

'I think I'd better go back.'

'Oh, don't go back yet, let's watch a film or something.'

'I'm sorry, Frank, but I think I'd better go back.'

'What've I done?'

She tutted and shook her head slowly. 'Oh Frank, come on, lad. You need some time to yourself. Look at you!'

I'd just looked at myself twice, I couldn't bear to do it again. I reached for a bifter. 'Shit! I think it was those pasties.'

She burst out laughing. She really did have an industrial effluent-strength laugh. 'I'm sorry, I shouldn't laugh.'

'Oh, no, you laugh away!'

And she did. She laughed so hard she doubled over, hands on knees, her burnished hair reaching for the floor. She kept saying over and over again: 'I'm sorry, Frank! I'm so sorry! I'm trying not to.'

Then, unaccountably, I started to laugh too. It started as a weak, nervous nasal snort, but within ten seconds I was squealing and screwing my eyes up and hiccupping like a toddler. This made her worse, and she fell on to her backside and juddered on. With her head nodding up and down and her legs splayed out she looked like a doll being electrocuted.

After three or four minutes we both calmed down, and were left in the embarrassing place where too much laughter leaves you. She looked at me from the floor, 'Ah-herr. Whoo! It was the pasties comment that got me. I wasn't laughing at you.'

'Never mind. It's pathetic. By the way, as you can tell, I never think about my dad.'

She half laughed and then went silent. She stood up and walked over and turned her chin up to me: 'I'd really better go.'

Then she stretched up and kissed me firmly on my pins-and-needles mouth. I tried to drag her back as she pulled away, but half-heartedly.

'Ooh, no. Not yet, Frank.'

She turned and left the flat, stopping only to flutter her gloved hand at me from the door.

Not yet. The most promising, denying, liberating, enslaving phrase on earth.

# £15,525

New Year's Eve has always been an anti-climax for me. That year, for once, the sense of bathos gave me no anxiety. For the previous two years I had been working at O'Hare's, and had to endure the screeches of forced jollity from a position of harassed sobriety. That year, with Henry and Lottie away in Scotland, Marie, Tom and Lucy out of the picture and Sadie an enigma, I decided to take a few days off and was free to have it all my own way.

I got up past noon on the 30th and spent the next three days doing precisely what I wanted. I wore my dressing gown all day, ate what I wanted, drank what I wanted and made a terrible mess all over the place. I didn't shave or bathe, do laundry or the washing up. Inevitably, I ingested television. I tried out two new brands of cigarette, both, it transpired, with highly appropriate names. Royals: cheap, gaudy, and made in Hanover, and Pall Malls: dusty, fusty with a savour of cheap scent, like a high-ranking civil servant's underwear. I ate pizza

171

and sugary chocolate deep into the night. I got myself into a mild lathering delirium over my bowel movements, each one heavier, richer and smoother than the last. Willingly I gave myself over to a state of nature, glutting my senses and shutting down my brain. When men are free, this is what they do.

My only responsibility was to complete my Annual Review, which in a perverse way I was staving off because I was looking forward to it so much. It is uncharacteristic of me to delay any pleasure that might be there for the taking, but I was convinced that this would be my last ever Review, and I didn't want it to go too quickly.

The Review draws on many information sources, and as that year I had six years' records to draw on, represented an encyclopaedic store of knowledge about my life. I had harmonised the data with my success scoring system, and thus had a definitive understanding of how everything had come about.

Let me provide you with a management summary.

FRANK STRETCH
ANNUAL REVIEW 1995

£ An average year. After a disappointing £14,270 in 1994, there was some marginal improvement. Total gross income in calendar year totalled £15,525. On a positive note, this increase was comfortably above RPI, and Henry had decided not to put the rent up, as he himself had a very good year financially. Total debt had decreased, as I had graciously written off the money I owed Bart. Despite the hardening of interest rates in '95, which was bound to have had some deleterious effect on my credit-card position, as I had no idea what that position might be, I wasn't unduly concerned. All things considered, it would be unrealistic to permit the overall score to be affected by any of these fluctuations, particularly in the light of some no doubt spectacular gains made by friends/competitors.

For some reason I was convinced that there remained reasons for cautious optimism, as long as it was kept fucking cautious. Score: 2.

LOVE ♥ A bad year, as you have probably been able to determine. Score: 2.

SEX ▌ Disappointing to relate that in terms of both quantity and quality, 1995 was the worst year since records began, with only one Partner and with Events falling below the dreaded double figures rubicon for the first time:

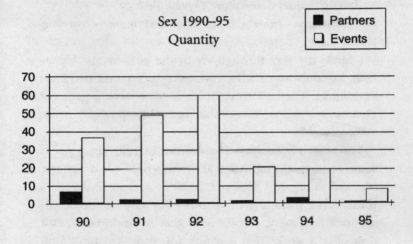

Sex 1990–95
Quantity

■ Partners
❑ Events

In terms of quality in '95, there was, unsurprisingly, little positive news to report. No amount of innovation and intensity could compensate for such a dreadful overall lack of action. For those who are quietly impressed with the Partners score in 1990 and the Events score in 1992, perhaps there is the need for some explanation. 1990 was Middle-Period Marie rebound year, and the numerical success achieved was not matched by any qualitative improvement. Most of the partners were in fact achieved in a one-month period after I left the *Streatham Post* and worked as a filing clerk for BP. About three hundred of us were recruited to

173

help with the relocation of their finance department. I was ascribed to the F-G-H-I-J section, and spent the entire day moving Crystal files from a huge cupboard into orange crates. (£2.37 an hour I remember. There's real dough in the oil business, I can tell you.) The sexual frustration that built throughout these unspeakably tedious hours was immense. Everybody was constantly gagging for it. The smallest, driest phrase would become charged with erotic tension.

'We need some more [Pause] Crystal files.'

'What? [Pause] Some more Crystal files?'

'Yes. [Pause] More Crystal files. And more [extra long pause] more . . . crates.'

I made my way through six of the girls in my Alphabetic Region, two of whom were Australian and two New Zealanders. They all treated sex as if it were a game of *Pictionary*; a bit of forgettable fun. How England needs them now.

The relatively healthy Events score in 1992 again needs some contextualising. After all, it was only 62 'occasions' (defined as orgasms achieved *inside* or *onto* some part of a woman, not including the hand – I'm sorry if the details are a little queasy, but I think they're important). Just over once a week. This is about how well Winston Smith did in *1984* when he was married to a Party automaton who found him physically disgusting. It's not that great a score.

These were the Blue-Period Marie days. Vicious circular day-long arguments, and silent tearful sex to make up afterwards. Quality was generally low, unless you like your sex glistening with tears and snot, gummy-eyed and exhausted at five in the morning.

My single sexual adventure of 1995, isolated on the graph, was strongly contrasting. Henry's younger sister was called Barbara, but had changed her name to Tamara when she left home to go to university. This should have been warning enough. She came to stay on Henry's sofa over the summer holidays, her first time in London, and watched television for a month.

Tamara seemed *old-fashioned* in some ways. When I was in my late teens and early twenties, the prevailing ideology in female dress was Northern industrial agitprop: donkey jackets, furry crew cuts and clompy Docs. The girls looked like navvies. However, they still behaved like girls: friendly, gentle and fun. Only in Tom's milieu was it deemed suitable for girls to look and behave like girls. Now, when I wandered around Notting Hill or Chelsea, it seemed that a total inversion had taken place. The girls didn't just look like girls, they looked like the Ur-girls of eternal male fantasies. Skinny rib sweaters stretched over alert, pointed breasts. Buttocks suspended in soft 501s, the little red tag bobbing like a rabbit in the long grass. Long straight shiny hair (oh how we love long straight shiny hair). But now they didn't behave like girls at all. Now they would go to nightclubs in order to dance all night and go home together. Now that they had men slavering on the carpet like the courtiers of Louis Quatorze, they didn't seem to want them. They got all their fun from homespun chemical factories in the Netherlands. 'Take this man outside, have him hosed down and pass me a Dove.'

But as the world zigged, Tamara zagged. Gloomy, unhygienic and moon-pale, Tamara was the last of the Goths. She was eerily quiet. I spent the first few days of our acquaintance thinking that she was a mute. Her lipstick looked like damson jam applied with a wooden spoon in the dark. Maybe she had glued her mouth up? But no, because she smoked Marlboro and drank sweet cider with appalling rapacity as she hoovered up daytime TV.

She was experiencing Swinging London through the local news programmes while waiting for *Emmerdale* to start.

Like all Goths, it was hard to tell whether she was attractive or not underneath the panstick, kohl and black Einstein frightwig. But along with her dated approach to street fashion went similarly old-fashioned sexual mores. She fucked men. Well, that is to say, she fucked me.

I got back from O'Hare's one night, about three days into her sofa-in and sat down to watch the end of a B-movie with her. Henry, the early girlie, was already abed, dreaming of kumquats and gigabytes. Farrah Fawcett was blubbing on the tube.

'What's this about?'

'Abortion.'

She took a swig straight from the cider bottle. Oh, right. A start, I suppose.

'What, has she just had an abortion?'

Silence. Farrah was now wringing a hanky and staring out of a plate glass window at the ocean.

'She wants an abortion.'

Five seconds later, the screen was obscured by a miasma of black hair. Tamara was kissing me. She was languid but insistent. The smell of hairspray, smoke and crushed apples filled my nostrils. I noticed that she was still holding a lit Marlboro that was supporting a crumbly tower of ash. I was just lying there with my mouth open like a corpse. Maybe that's what got her going. She pulled away.

'Come on then.'

'I'm sorry. I was taken a bit by surprise.'

'Fucking hell.'

Two minutes later she was gently chewing my cock. At least she'd had the decency to put her fag out. I watched her mournful, ruminative sluicing with detachment. Did Goths do sex differently? Was it necessary to draw blood, for instance? Would it all end like a tableau from Russian Orthodox iconography with me bound up in a red velvet shroud and her sprinkling holy water on my feet? Apparently not. Once she judged me to be in a sufficient state of arousal, she removed her knickers (white, which came as a pleasant shock) and sat on me. A high bouncing lover she wasn't. A low grinding lover, that's more like it. Two minutes of weighty toil later, it was all over and we were back to the movie. She crashed me a Marlboro, which I took as a sign of appreciation of my performance, and unscrewed another bottle of Scrumpy Jack.

One week and eight insertions later, I tried it on with her during *Newsnight* and I was rebuffed.

'My boyfriend's coming down tomorrow.'

And that was that. To my surprise, a moment of anger gave way to a kind of grief. Not at this specific situation, but at the goddamned, suddenly revealed *modern-ness* of it all. She was an aesthetic conservative, but a moral radical. Easy come, easy go. In, out, no strings, no hang-ups, no regrets. Go with the flow. I had had her attention for a week or so, but now there was something better, cheaper and more promising to think about.

I am as unsuited to the free market in sex as I am to the free market of capital. They seem to travel in chaotic tandem: all the barriers are down and sex and money rush in and then take flight as the mood takes them. In both areas I tend to come over all redistributive and protectionist, a sexual as well as an economic socialist. Of course, I'm neither. The trouble with socialism is that it might make you feel morally righteous, but righteousness doesn't get you any more sex or any more capital. Socialism is like self-help books: good on diagnosing the problem but weak on what to do about it. What can you do about it? Nothing. Feeling disenfranchised, undersexed, poor, weak and unpopular? That's because you *are* disenfranchised, undersexed, poor, weak and unpopular. Some people are. It's in the genes, it's in the air, it's the figure in the carpet. It's just the way it is.

A long way of putting it, but my SEX score for '95 bore some resemblance to my SEX score in '94. A desultory 1.

WORK ♊ What work? One more week to go and then out. If you remember, the governing question is 'are you happy in your work?'. At that time, I was ecstatic, but only at the thought of having *no* work, which somewhat defeated the system. Looking at it on a strictly short-term basis I was still basically a waiter in a terrible restaurant in South West London. To go any higher than 3 would be a terrible delusion. A 3 it had to be.

HOUSE ⊞ What house? What fucking house? I wished I was a snail with a little shell upon my back. Urgghh. A 0, my first ever straight 0 in six years of Annual Reviews. And I always hoped things would just trend gently upward all my life, not crash, stall, flop and lurch into reverse or a tailspin or whatever it was I was going through.

WHEELS 🚗 The Cavalier, which that day I re-christened the Roundhead for no reason, got me to Battersea and back every morning and would soon get me out of there altogether. Added to which, Tamara liked it, because it conformed to the demands of the kitsch-driven value system of the terminally trendy: what's bad, cheap, gaudy, twee and gross is good, what's good, expensive, understated and tasteful is bad. She would probably give it a 5. It was still a 2 to me.

PHYSICAL ⚸ Fingers still tapering and delicate, grin becoming less winning and more lop-sided. Hair still a formless clod of silage and internally, Luckies really digging in to the soft tissue. It was only fair to reserve judgement on a downgrading until I had some disfiguring accident. I stuck at 3 for the time being.

POPULAR 📞 1995 Account:
   Total incoming social calls – 58.
   Total outgoing social calls – 39.
A balance in my favour, but still nothing special.

| | |
|---|---|
| Visits to the pub with Henry | 31 |
| Visits to the pub with someone other than Henry | 19 |
| Dinner parties attended | 4 |
| Dinner parties held | 0 |
| Parties attended | 3 |
| Parties held | 0 |
| Visits to cinema in company (including Henry) | 9 |
| Dinners in restaurants * | 7 |
| Nights spent sleeping with woman | 5 |

TOTAL NIGHTS OUT                                          78

* Restaurants other than O'Hare's obviously.

78 out of 365: 21%. This performance was achieved with a 'no reasonable offers refused' policy in operation.

New friends made                                          0

A 'new friend' is someone you arrange to meet for a social occasion *more than one time* after the first meeting. This basically stops happening after you leave college. Even my friends who work with the like-minded don't beat this average by much. The problem with friends made at work is that you don't find out until after you've stopped working with them whether they're really friends or not. Almost invariably, they're not. That's why Sadie didn't count. Not yet.

The typical pattern for ex-colleagues who you think are friends is as follows:

*Meet in large group and talk about the 'old days' three times a year.*

179

*Meet in smaller group and talk about the 'old days' twice the next year.*

*The one ex-colleague you find the dullest rings you up twice the next year, but you only meet once. You talk about the 'old days'.*

*You bump into one of the ex-colleagues you thought you liked in Soho and grab a quick pint and talk about the 'old days'. You both swear you'll ring each other the next day to sort out 'a proper session', perhaps including some of the other ex-colleagues.*

*Neither of you bothers.*

*Six months later you catch sight of either the dull or the nice ex-colleague in a record shop in the West End. Both of you pretend you haven't seen each other. Ah, the good old days.*

The overall picture for 1995 was neither disgraceful nor air-punchingly positive. Without Henry, it would all have looked a lot worse, but I reckon everybody has one person who puts a healthier glow on the ♪ score than is really merited. As for Sadie (yes, her again, and again and again), who could tell? Friend or foe? Trick or treat? Shoot or fuck? Who knew, brother.

I gave myself a steady 3.

INTERESTING ❗ I believe that if only people gave me the chance, they would realise what a fascinating individual I am. I only bore myself to death. My score hadn't altered in the six years of Annual Reviews. 1995? Still that life-enhancing 6.

CACHET ♛ In retreat, the older, poorer, more disenfranchised, friendless, homeless, cultureless, dickless, fuckless, cuntless, wankless, twatpissshiteknobarseless I got. 2.

Grand Total: 28. Not good.

I finished the Review at 2.30 in the afternoon of 1 January 1996 and channel-surfed until 3.30 the following morning. Then I tucked myself up with *Asian Panties* and a box of

Belgian chocolates and ravished myself till dawn. Happy Fucking New Year.

# Forty-eight pounds sterling
# and nought new pence

The way the Christmas bonus was handed over by Brian, you would have thought he was a wise man bestowing gifts on the Christ child. The solemn little ceremony took place at one o'clock on a piss-freezing day just after I'd returned from my refreshing New Year break. I was out by the bins, snouting, writing a few enigmatic, angry yet curiously beautiful valedictory letters.

I was turning the phrase 'when a man must answer the call of his conscience' round in my head when Brian tapped me on the shoulder: 'All right, chief.'

'Howza, Bri.'

He snuffled and reached a fat hand into an inside pocket of his nasty double-breasted suit. He left it there, and vainly attempted to look me in the eye.

'We think you've done a great job last year, chief, so Bart slipped an extra few quid into your bonus to get yourself something nice.'

'Fucking hell. Don't embarrass me, Bri. It's not a job for me anyway, it's a labour of love, you know that.'

'Yeah, well anyway. He's put an extra few quid in as I say.'

Another snuffle and he slipped me the little buff envelope before fucking off back to the Orient on his camel. Funnily enough, I think he was actually from Leyton, so it all tied together in a sense.

I didn't know what I had been expecting. My previous year's bonus was thirty-seven pounds fifty pence (if you write it out in longhand it has a weighty, old money feel to it, and feeds a family of four for a month). So, I dunno, a ton? Maybe a ton fifty? Either would put an extra week between me and the *Big Issue*. I fingered the envelope and heard the worrying clink of small change.

Forty-eight quid. Even longhand couldn't rescue forty-eight quid. Even forty-eight pounds sterling and nought new pence couldn't rescue forty-eight quid.

£48.

This was after three solid weeks of FUCCER troughing, with O'Harc's grossing over two grand a day. That means that I, the manager, orchestrator, circus master, grand vizier and all round champion ego-stroker had creamed off approximately one thousandth of the place's Christmas takings for my exertions. Let's just have a look at that as a vulgar fraction, shall we:

1/1000th.

Still doesn't do justice to the pathos. What does it look like as a decimal?

0.001.

Forty-eight quid.

I stuffed the money into my jeans pocket and looked out at the bins. How many hours had I spent just standing at the back door gazing at those bins? I felt a burst of affection for them all of a sudden. The way they were arranged in the little cabbage-and-chicken-bone courtyard, both standing there so nobly as the rain pelted on their rubber lids, it was comforting and sad. I started to talk to them softly:

'I'm off soon, you lads. You won't see me again. Yeah, but don't you worry, I'll think of you. You're good lads, you know, I've got real respect for your sort, just standing there doing your duty, never complaining. This is my private tribute. Don't forget me, lads.' I put the last knockings of my Lucky into the side of my mouth, and stood to attention before saluting the bins with the exaggerated formality of a marine passing out of West Point.

I then started to bark, like that same marine replying to his sergeant major: 'SIR! YES SIR! FORTY-EIGHT POUNDS, PLEASE SIR! SIR! YES SIR! FOUR THOUSAND EIGHT HUNDRED FRESH NEW PENCE PLEASE SIR! SIR! YES SIR!'

I then turned on my heel and marched back into the kitchen, past Paolo who was reading *Gazzetta dello Sport* as usual, and taking no notice whatsoever. When I saw Sadie come in for the lunchtime shift I had stopped soldiering but had arrived at the precise midway point between laughter and tears, that is, simultaneously laughing like a lizard and crying like a snake.

The Sadie issue had been resolved by the Christmas Day fiasco, at least as far as she was concerned. The tingle-inducing promise offered by 'not yet' seemed to have been broken as soon as made. Since Christmas Day our exchanges had been courteous, but conducted through three feet of icy wind. She gave the impression that she was off somewhere soon and pretty quick, and I was no more in her thoughts than the apron she wore at O'Hare's.

I constantly turned over the meaning of the phrase 'not yet'. It means 'not yet', doesn't it? Not 'not ever', or 'don't even think about it', or 'I may never speak to you again apart from to ask about what shifts you want me to do'. It means 'soon', or at least 'some day'. That's what it meant to me, whenever I asked myself when I was going to get out of this hard-faced, business-like, transaction-obsessed city: 'not yet, but some day. And soon.'

It was becoming so easy to leave London behind. Six years, hundreds of weeks, thousands of mornings waking up under the opaque big city sky, all receding to the vanishing point at light speed. The only things I'd leave behind were minus signs: a few ex-friends, a lack of a home, love that never really got started and unhonoured loans. I'd exit the city accompanied by the sound of anti-matter leaving a black hole; astro-silence, the quietest thing you will never hear.

I worked all the overtime possible in that last week, trying to get my fugitive fund up to a grand. On what I'd decided would be my last day, Friday, pay day, I also nicked about forty in tips from petty cash. That was Sadie's tips for the day gone: tough luck, girl. I'll reimburse you some day – but not yet.

I walked out into the street with that straight-ahead stare that's a sure sign of wrongdoing. No thoughts of looking back, for many reasons.

My progress was interrupted by a kerb-crawling Tony Ling hanging out of the window of his Laguna.

'Frank! Where you going?'

'I'm off.'

'I've gotta do the cash.'

'Go ahead.'

'But where are you going?'

'East of Iwo Jima, mate.'

'What do you mean?'

'I'm finished, I've had enough, now if you'll excuse me –'

'Wait! Have you told Bart?'

'What do you think. And if he wants to get hold of me, tell him to try fucking off.'

'What about the safe. I need the keys.'

I took out my key ring and lobbed the keys to the safe into his open window.

'Fleece him, Tony, any way you can.'

He laughed, tiny tallow teeth agleam, and spun the repmobile off into a side street. I felt that it would have been a lot better had I not seen him. He was a henchman if ever I saw one.

Anyway onwards and sideways.

I was home by three, and was relieved to find that Henry and Lottie weren't around. The first thing I did was count my cash. I'd been living on fags and one gallon of four star a week since mid-December. Apart from Sadie's Christmas present I couldn't recall having spent *anything* in the previous month apart from the aforementioned bifters and petrol. My liquidity was pretty good:

£370.00 – left over from Henry returning my deposit
£427.00 – two weeks' Christmas payment from O'Hare's
£293.00 – last week at O'Hare's
£44.00 – nicked tips
Forty eight pounds Christmas bonus (don't forget that)
Six quid of shrap

Total £1,188.00

I tore the corner off the *Daily Mail* where I'd been doing my addition, cut round it with a pair of scissors and mounted it behind the plastic window in my wallet.

As I looked at it an awful thought struck me: given one more week, one more *day* at O'Hare's and I'd be able to pay Bart off forever. Just one more FUCCER-raddled Saturday and I would be, in one sense, free for the first time in ages. (Of course, I had no idea how much I owed the bank or my credit card, as you know. But, as my old man would say, 'What you don't know can't hurt you – today'. Admittedly, minutes later an insolvency practitioner and a rottweiler would come crashing through the front door, but I still think it's the best bit of advice he ever gave me.)

So really I was on the verge of a kind of normality. I was able to summon up a fetching vignette of recovery: Bart paid off, another couple of weeks at O'Hare's while I looked for a better restaurant manager's job, a warm little bedsit somewhere new (Tooting or Streatham perhaps, both *so* on the up nowadays), a lovely little Norwegian waitress with a tobacco farmer father.

I turned on the telly and surfed and smoked while the possibilities circled in my head. I couldn't decide which would be the more cowardly: staying, which even with attempts made towards reparations would be fudging the issue, or going, which with its logical conclusion of eventually having to come back would also be fudging the issue. There, in front of two-frames-a-second kids' TV, the world seemed so forgetful, so separated from ramifications. I watched a pretty Scottish girl on MTV interviewing some washboard stomach from an American boy band:

'*A year ago, you were working as a waiter in Hollywood.*'

'*Well, it was a little over a year ago, but yeah, I waited tables for a coupla years, did singing and dancing lessons in my spare time, met Mike Cooper from Sony, and he put me together with Davie and Lyle, and it's happened pretty quick, yeah.*'

'*It's so amazing.*'

'*Yeah, it's amazing, but we work real hard, and we know exactly where we're at musically and in terms of image, so it's amazing, but we've put the hard sweat in.*'

'*So, is that your advice to all your fans out there, like, work really hard?*'

'*I would just say – just follow your dreams and never give up, and if you keep reaching for the stars you'll never be left with a handfulla mud.*'

'*Aw, that's great, that's fantastic.*'

'*Peace.*'

What a philosophy, and so well suited to the rehab clinic

courses he'd be taking within the year. However, though I'm ashamed to admit it, it hit home in some way. I didn't begrudge him what he'd achieved; he probably did work hard and know exactly where he was at in terms of music and image. And who could criticise the motivation? If you want to be English about it, you could say that we all end up with a handful of mud. If you wanted to be *really* English you could say that we all end up *as* a handful of mud, but I didn't feel like being English at that precise moment.

There was another key moment approaching. If I'd sat there surfing for another five minutes, I would have stayed in London, no doubt. The TV would have soothed me through the evening and into the following morning and beyond. I would have gone to O'Hare's in the morning and looked for a flat share in *Loot* all afternoon. But instead of being piloted back into my life as was, I thought of my boy band guru, pressed the standby button, and made a decisive step towards changing everything.

You've got to fight the TV at some stage. Already you can almost feel the air crackle with signal. Satellites are swathed round the world like chainmail. TV is snaking into homes through the rock and soil, cables are being laid on the ocean floor, way down with the deep sea anglerfish, and they're not going to stop there. What they really want is to turn our skin into a receiver and eyes into screens, your mouth into a supermarket. Watch the in-retina advertising, taste the sweeties on your tongue, lock the jingle into your inner ear, for future listening pleasure. We won't stop them as long as *Friends* and the Premiership are available on demand.

I'm not pessimistic about all this. I won't complain about becoming my own multimedia system, decoding, consuming, browsing for the rest of my life. In fact, I look forward to it. For one thing, it'll be so nice and quiet. In the meantime, while technology was attempting to catch up with my fantasies, I turned off the TV and resumed packing. I wondered if the decision to go had *really* been affected by the philosophy of a twenty-two-year-old LA hardbody superstarlet. I didn't have a Clapham softbody no-mark philosophy to counter him with, so maybe it had.

My bedroom at Henry's was about twelve feet by eight, yet housed all my possessions with ease. The accumulation of material possessions was not a priority for me in my twenties. I had bought two three-foot-high red-white-and-blue stripy plastic laundry bags at Balham market. You see Asian women lugging them around Tooting, bulging with yams.

I packed it all, wavering over a veteran anglepoise lamp before including it to furnish the desk in some future garret, and wrote a note to Henry:

> *Dear Henners,*
> *I'm offski. Thanks for everything. Keep all the crap I haven't taken. 'I have no need for it in the place to which I'm going.' All the bedding's in the washing machine, and I've done the washing up (for once). Sorry, no way of doing that sentence without the two 'washings'. An inelegant ending from an inelegant lodger.*
> *Good luck with everything.*
> *Francis Dean Stretch*
> *Hugs to Lottie*

Bleary with tears, I loaded up the Cav and at about 5.30PM on Friday, 9 January 1996 I blew town with £1,188 and an anglepoise lamp on the passenger seat for company.

## £45

What a time to choose to change one's life. I thought I'd head north, because there was more of it, so I would have longer to go without having to turn back. A simple intention, to point the nose of the Cav away from London and not to think once of turning it around until something happened. But the traffic, the traffic at 5.30PM on Friday, January 9 1996, it didn't want to let me out. It wanted me there in London, throbbing dangerously on the South Circular like an embolism.

By seven I'd reached Mortlake, by nine I was at Wembley. Three and a half hours into the great escape and I was nine miles from home, totally shagged out, with sciatica kicking in. I wanted my bed, I wanted Henry, Lottie, Tom, Lucy, Marie, Sadie. I even wanted Bart. More than that, I wanted to pay Bart a lot of money and give him a big hug.

But on I went. By ten I was south of Luton, by half eleven north of Northampton, by midnight I was closing in on Doncaster and far enough away now to risk stopping. I pulled off the M1 at a service station about twenty miles south of Leeds and wandered around the compound, trying to look purposeful. The Happy Eater and the Boiger King were the only things still open, but I didn't have the stomach for either. I walked over the glass bridge and watched the traffic go by. All the bright white staring eyes streaming away from London, all the sore, red-sockety eyes racing towards it. That didn't seem quite right.

What now? What now? There was a prefab hotel attached to the service station advertising £29 rooms at weekends. I walked into the dustless striplit reception area and browsed the tariff. Inevitably, because I hadn't booked in advance, and wanted breakfast and an *en suite* bathroom, it was going to cost me £45, but that was fine. The bloke on reception, who looked about seventeen, was reading Chekov. I thought he must be some A-Level student working for a bit of E money, but surely they didn't still do Chekov at school? I thought they stopped at Lloyd Webber and Inspector Morse nowadays.

'Hi, I'd like a room for the night, please.'

'Sure thing.'

He shuffled around for some form or other. There was a badge on his polycotton blazer that read MOHAMMED IS HAPPY TO SERVE YOU!, which offered an unconventionally customer-focused vision of Islam.

'Yeah, I'm on my way from London to visit friends up in Aberdeenshire.'

'Right.'

'Came over all tired, so I thought I'd bed down, and head off first thing tomorrow.'

'You're the boss.'

He was farting about on a PC.

'Can I get a wake-up call?'

'Two pounds, sir. What time would you like it for?'

'Oh, seven, please.'

I'd almost convinced myself now that I had a grand house party to attend at the Marchioness of Wester Ross's place.

'Seven, that's fine. Can I have your credit card details, please sir?'

Fuck.

'Oh, I'll pay it all in cash now, if you don't mind.'

'No problem. An address?'

'Err, 82 Exhibition Road, South Kensington, London, SW7, er, 3PQ.'

'Flat number, sir?'

'No. It's a house.'

Fucking hell. A house on Exhibition Road. Who did I think I was? The Brazilian Ambassador?

'OK, sir, that's £51. Smoking or non?'

'Non, please.'

Weird, but true, I asked to be in a non-smoker. This is the equivalent of ordinary people asking for a non-breather. I flopped out my wad of cash and peeled off two twenners and a ten, taking care to shuffle the dough around a bit so he could see how much I was carrying.

'Luggage?'

No way was I going to let him see my polyurethane laundry bags.

'No, no, fine, I'll do it myself.'

So the transaction was complete, and a homeless, unemployed emphysemic ex-waiter from Clapham had successfully passed himself off to an eighteen-year-old Pakistani Russianist as a cash-rich non-smoking aristocrat in the diplomatic service. It may have been pointless, but it kept me amused for a couple of minutes.

I dumped some overnight stuff in my room and then spent forty minutes chain smoking in the reception, storing up the nicotine so I didn't get a case of the abdabs in the middle of the night. Mohammed just kept on reading. At one-ish I decided to turn in.

'Goodnight, Mohammed!'

'Goodnight, sir.'

He didn't even look up, lost in his pursuit of the man within the man. Don't pursue with too much enthusiasm, Mohammed, because you might find out there isn't a man there at all, just a little boy with a furious face throwing his toys around and crying like crazy.

The room was nondescript to the point of genius. In my memory I can just make out grey, cream, beige, buff, manilla, and that was the pictures – a willow athwart a pond, a swan in flight over a pond, a pond scene. This focus on ponds no doubt to make the pond-life that schlepped through this room feel at home: lower-middle managers (extruded snack salesmen? Stapler reps?) not phoning the wife, sleeping in as much as they dared, wanking to the GMTV weather girl before their next stop at a retail park in Rotherham. 32 to 35 range probably, dependent mainly on valve count/luxe rating of company car. Just nudging me out, although my scores had inevitably taken a nosedive even in the eight hours since leaving London.

I lay on the slate-hard rail that passed itself off as a bed and stared into the beigey buffness. Sleep was the last thing on my mind. In my position, what was sleep *for*? I had nothing to get up for and every reason to want to avoid my dreams. I didn't need sleep. I needed a *plan*, and not just a plan to get me through till Monday, but one to get me through to the millennium and beyond. I got a little wavelet of positive thinking all of a sudden. Maybe all those middle management dreams had seeped into the pillow and were rising back up into my head: Establish Stretching Objectives! Strive for Total Quality Delivery! Add Value to the Process! Master the Competitive Endgame! Keep Reaching for the Stars! Fuck your Secretary in your Lunch Hour!

Anyway, whatever it was, I was at the Formica writing desk in a jiffy, gently quivering with desire to write *a plan*. My first step wasn't promising. I scrawled the words 'Oh, Christ!' on to the SupaLodge headed paper in three-inch-high letters, and spent twenty minutes filling them out and colouring them in:

# OH, CHRIST!

became,

# **OH, CHRIST!**

which was more in keeping with the scale of the problem.

I then went down to reception and smoked three bifters on the trot. Mohammed was still there, still buried in his book. I wanted to talk:

'Can't sleep.'

'Mm.'

'Always the way.'

Silence.

'[BIG WHOOSHING TYPE OF SIGH].'

Silence.

'What time do the newspapers arrive?'

Mohammed coughed to himself and looked at me over the counter.

'We don't get newspapers for customers. We just get the *Express* and the *Financial Times* here on reception, but you can't take those away.'

The *Express* and the *Financial Times* just said it all about that place: one pretending its hardest not to be a tabloid so all the Mancunian undermanagers could retain a bit of respect. And the *FT*, I mean come on, in a SupaLodge outside Leeds? The pretension was astounding: 'I'm going to Grimsby to sell nine Twixes to an Indian corner shop owner, so I'll just catch up on the Canadian long bond yields. Oooh look, the Federal Reserve has shaved base rates by twenty-five points. Maybe I should try

194

to flog him a couple of Bounties as well.'

Mohammed wasn't playing, basically, so I had one last stab.

'Any whores around here?'

He looked up at me again, and slid his old-fashioned silver-rimmed specs up his nose.

'We don't get many, being on the motorway. Maybe one of the cleaners would take her teeth out for a fiver.'

'It was more of a theoretical question than a practical one.'

'That's what they all say.'

'I bet it is.'

He looked at me impassively.

'I can easily re-book you into a smoking room, you know.'

'No, it's OK. I'm only smoking as a delaying tactic.'

'What are you trying to delay?'

'The rest of my life.'

'Can't argue with that.'

I checked my watch. Ten past one. Not quite the time 'when it is too early to do anything, too late to do anything'. Had Sartre spent any time in SupaLodges, I wonder?

'What's Chekov like, then?'

'Boring, man. Totally boring.'

'Why bother reading it? Are you studying it?'

'It's part of my drama option. I'm reading it because it's a bit less boring than sitting here doing absolutely nothing.'

'Can't argue with that.'

I stubbed out my last Lucky and went back to my room. Trying to keep my eye off the stationery, I ran a bath and emptied the Roseapple Moisturising Bath Oil into it. The water was scalding hot and chin deep. I lay fragrantly in state for about twenty minutes. After playing Kiki the Dolphin Swims on his Fluke a couple of times (don't bother, girls, it's a boy's game) and watching my fingers go Auden, I towelled down, dressed in my cleanest clothes and went back to work.

The problem I had was formal. How do you write a plan? A

series of bullet points? An essay? A spreadsheet? A sine curve? In the meantime I embellished my earlier work thus:

Just as I was completing the curlicues at the bottom left of the page, I planned ahead in the only way I knew how: obituary.

Thoughts of death to stave off thoughts of living. Something was the wrong way round.

## FRANCIS DEAN STRETCH
### ACTOR/DIRECTOR WHO REVOLUTIONISED
### THE ENGLISH THEATRE

Frank Stretch, the grand old man of the English Theatre, has died aged eighty-four at his manor house in Dorset.

He came late to acting, not entering RADA until 1996, when aged thirty. Noted amongst his contemporaries for being able to combine vigorous conviviality with extreme hard work, he surprised none of them when he secured his first West End lead while still in his second year of study. This performance, as Doctor Faustus in Marlowe's eponymous play, immediately established him as the brightest leading actor of his generation.

He decided not to complete his course at RADA, but instead set up his own theatre company, The Enlightenment Drama Group, which went on to become the most popularly successful and critically admired company of the late years of the last millennium.

It was during this time that he managed to raise £3 million to build his own theatre, which he did, on the site of a restaurant in Battersea. The South London Mummers, criticised by one contemporary as 'a plasterboard Bayreuth set up by a tinpot Wagner with a tissue-paper talent', played to full houses for the next ten years, all under Stretch's direction. As well as bringing his own physical and attacking style to the classical repertory, in 2002 he started staging his own plays. The first of these was *MeMeMe*, a devastating satire on the 1990s, where Stretch played a megalomaniac TV presenter and media owner who dies extremely slowly and painfully at the hands of a gangster with a pathological aversion to redheads. Following *MeMeMe* came *Gauleiters of SW3* and *Sugarshock*, as well as a stream of other hits. Although mainly satirical, many of his plays had a linguistic energy and pungent characterisation that transcended their topicality.

Stretch had affairs with many of the most beautiful actresses of his generation, in addition to two marriages, first to Lolicia Cadiz, a porn star who Stretch

transformed into a fine character actress, and then to
Sadie Dineen, now a dame, and the greatest Rosalind,
Cleopatra and Lady Macbeth of the century.

Despite a fallow period in his forties when Stretch
became somewhat mired in cocaine and supermodels,
he came back strongly in the 2020s with his dramatic
tetralogy *The Work and the Life* and the first volume
of his autobiography *Having it All.*

He was writing and performing well into his seventies.
His King Lear was to all who saw it one of the most
electrifying theatrical experiences of their lives. He never
worked in TV or films, 'because, dear, I don't have to'.

He is survived by his wife Dame Sadie, and seven
children.

It was now two-thirty. I made myself a cup of tea (Earl Grey
again; the nation was suffocating under the stench of bergamot)
and dunked some dusty shortbread. Even the biscuits felt like
decline. I was feeling like a nineties Camus. This gave me
an idea:

## FRANK D. STRETCH
### NOVELIST

The literary world was devastated to discover yesterday
morning that Frank D. Stretch, the young American
novelist, died in Las Vegas at the age of thirty-eight.

Stretch burst on to the scene in 1997 with his self-
published *roman à clef Ozark Love* about a young boy
from Arkansas growing up in the 1970s. The authen-
ticity of his tone and the honesty of his self-analysis
redeemed the novel from charges of sentimentality and
self-indulgence, and it was number one on the *New York
Times* bestseller list for thirty weeks.

There were many who were suspicious about his provenance, mainly because of his strange almost English-sounding accent, and the apparent absence from his life of parents, siblings, schoolfriends and so on.

His second novel, *The Men who Loved America*, a picaresque story about a Mid-West family whose various scions go on to dominate American public life, was another huge commercial success, selling over a million copies in its first year of publication. Many hailed it as The Great American Novel, which indeed it had been subtitled by the author. Money hit him hard, and the last two years of his life were spent in a suite at the Luxor on the Las Vegas strip. He lost the great majority of his fortune on stud poker, and then made a lot of it back at blackjack.

His literary agent, Judy Spitz, said yesterday that his last, unfinished, book would be in the shops by the spring, priced at $18.95. He was unmarried.

Three-thirty, confidence ebbing away. I had a little tootle through *Asian Panties*. All these girls just *couldn't* seem to keep their hems under control – all caught unawares by some knicker-seeking Asiatic scirocco.

One more obituary for the road and then – and then something or other.

## LORD STRETCH OF POULTON-LE-FYLDE
## POLITICIAN, HISTORIAN AND PLUTOCRAT

Lord Frank Stretch, the last man in Britain to be made a hereditary peer, died yesterday at his mansion near Cirencester aged seventy-eight.

His magnanimous liberal intelligence, uncanny political nous and fabulous wealth made him one of the most dominant public figures of the century so far. The Oxford College which he founded and which took his name . . .

The phone rang. I lifted my head from the desk where I'd fallen asleep. All of a sudden I became aware of the chill in the room and the hum of the water pipes. I looked at my watch: 7AM, my alarm call. I went over to the phone and picked it up, whereupon it went dead. Fully-automated, terse, anonymous.

I rubbed my face and blinked to try to assuage the gravelly pain accumulated behind my eyes. Outside it still looked like night, the airport-like complex of lamps around the service station barely illuminating at all. Each one suspended downspread fantails of off-white light which barely reached the ground.

For a few moments, I watched the cars and lorries perform their meaningless stochastic patterns of shunt, crawl, stop and go. What are they all doing at 7AM on a Saturday morning in a service station near Leeds? In the dark? In the rain?

# £875,000

I wandered over to the Happy Eater for an Olympiad breakfast, and read almost every word of the papers. Tories in the soup, soap stars fucking each other blind, cows skating, slithering and raving all over the shop; the usual dreck.

Having reviewed my obituaries I wasn't that cheered up. I wondered whether since I had lived in Poulton-le Fylde for only three months (when Dad opened and then promptly closed a pet shop there in the mid-seventies) they'd let me take it as my Lordship name. I also wondered if I hadn't gone totally insane driving up the M1 the previous day. RADA, I ask you. I hadn't been on stage since I was coerced into playing Laertes in a secondary school *Hamlet*. I was the worst thing you've ever seen. *Everybody* loathed me: the teacher who was directing it, and who couldn't fire me, the other kids, who refused to talk to me because they thought I was cacking it up for them, the teccies because whenever they tried to test a lighting angle I was mysteriously just in its penumbra.

In rehearsals I kept saying, 'Why can't I do it more *naturally*', which wasn't a precocious commitment to Stanislavsky, just that I froze whenever I went on. My mouth opened but would only emit a dying croak of dry air. My arms tended to stiffen and swing *alongside* my legs as I walked up to the dying Hamlet. This understandably detracted from the pathos, or at least added to it but in a somewhat unexpected way. Even after dress rehearsal, I wasn't prepared for the difference between *watching* a play (boring, but restful) and *really being in it* (the most terrifying experience on earth). All that light flooding into your face, and a sense of two hundred invisible people watching you with mockery in their eyes. I thought if I kept it natural, mumbled under my breath, no-one would notice me and I'd be able to survive. Streaming limelight on to someone as self-conscious as I was, magnifying that self-consciousness to an all-encompassing level, was an unmatched cruelty. Eventually, on the last night of the three-night run in the gym, I reached an accommodation and shouted out my lines like a sergeant major, really screaming them out so the time on stage would pass without any other thought entering my consciousness:

'. . . AND FOR HIS PASSAGE THE SOLDIERS' MUSIC AND THE RITE OF WAR SPEAK LOUDLY FOR HIM!'

My performance was so poor yet distinctive that I must have wiped all other memories from the audience's mind. They didn't remember to clap for about twenty seconds after I bellowed: 'GO BID THE SOLDIERS SHOOT!'

They cut my seven lines from IV.IV, the bastards.

Dog tired I went back to the Lodge, and asked the receptionist what time I had to check out.

'Noon, or we charge you for another night.'

'Gimme another night then,' and I peeled off another £51, intending to sleep until Sunday.

\*    \*    \*

I dreamt of runway lights, spotlights and the lights on the Vegas strip, and woke disoriented at about 9PM. It hadn't been a great twenty-four hours. By now, Henry would be deeply into his second sixteenth of the weekend and I would be a smudge in his memory. News might have got to Bart that I'd not turned up for work again, and if it had he'd be suspicious that I'd buggered off with his twelve hundred quid. Sadie would be sashaying chaotically around O'Hare's pouring tepid carbonara sauce down the back of peoples' necks and getting twenty-quid tips in recompense. Ah, no, she wouldn't, because Saturdays were her day off, so she'd probably be at some cheesy disco in Marble Arch being dummy fucked by Gaetano. Tom, Lucy and Marie would almost certainly be at a dinner party, quite possibly the same one, where it is extremely unlikely I'd get a mensh. So the only person with whom I was still an issue was Bart. He wouldn't forget twelve hundred quid in a hurry. How I hoped that I never saw that vicious fat wanker ever again.

I went down to reception for a smoke. Maybe I could make like a character from a Henry James novel and live in a hotel for a season. I could set up a stable little rhythm; sleep from 7AM till 9PM, dine at the Happy Eater, bathe copiously, doodle for six hours, pay out another £51, take breakfast at the Happy Eater, mooch about the car park evaluating sales reps' cars, back to the cot, round and round, Eater, doodle, bath, £51, Mondeo, snooze, for ever and ever amen. I worked out how much it would cost. If only I had £875,000, I felt as if I could be quite happy living like that for ever. However, being by now over £874,000 shy, I had to think of something else.

When I went to take supper at the Eater, I noticed that there was a job going as a trainee waiter. It occurred to me that I could probably get it. It also occurred to me that maybe after that I could progress to being a dinner lady at a local primary school. After that, who knows? Maybe head dinner lady at a further education college. I even went as far as picking up an application form. I *even* went as far as starting to fill it in, but I failed at the first hurdle; namely the 'Address' box. There were also a couple of questions on the top of the form that did for me: 'Enjoy working with people? Thinking of starting a career in catering?'

I chewed my way through a lasagne, which was like eating a tarpaulin interleaved with damp soil, and trudged back over to the Lodge. Mohammed had taken up his seat and his book, and when he saw me come in he looked alarmed.

'Evening, Mohammed.'

'God, I thought you were only staying the one night.'

'The party in the Highlands was cancelled, so I thought I'd catch up on, er, a little business.'

'You're the boss.'

He returned to his book. I felt a horrible urge to talk. My mouth had effectively been closed for over a day, apart from to expel smoke and ingest oiled carbohydrate. I just needed to talk.

'Actually, Mohammed, I never did have a party to go to in the Highlands.'

He looked at me, with an expression that could have been fear. Maybe he thought I was a serial killer. I certainly had the haircut.

'I'm not really going anywhere. What I mean is, I don't know where I'm going.'

He had splayed his book on the counter now, and was nervously nudging the bridge of his glasses with a curled forefinger.

'I'm not sure there's much I can say to that.'

'Yeah, I know. I don't expect you to. I actually feel OK, so don't worry, I'm not going to break down or anything. I wouldn't mind a chat, though.'

'A chat? I'm supposed to be working and the manager,' he checked his watch, 'the manager'll be round in a few minutes.'

'OK, I'll tell you what, I'll sit here –' (I indicated the teak and tangerine reception chair) 'and we can chat a bit, and I'll just tell him that I'm waiting for someone.'

Mohammed looked unconvinced.

'Come on, it says on your badge that you're happy to serve me. I only want a bit of conversation. It's not as if I want a blow job for God's sake.'

He started to move his head from side to side, as if he was weighing it up.

'Go on. Just a few minutes.'

'It makes it more difficult with you putting all this pressure on. I mean, you can't just sit there and say "let's have a conversation". It'll just become stilted.'

'All right then, if I promise to keep it all moving along, and shut up when your manager comes round, what about half an hour?'

'Half an hour? You said a few minutes.'

Jesus! How could it be so difficult just to get to talk to someone?

'OK, a tenner. I'll give you a tenner if you'll talk to me for a bit. That's fair, isn't it?'

'Are you sure you're OK?'

I was fishing in my pocket now.

'Absolutely fine, mate. Look, I'll even pay you up front, there.' I slapped a moth-eaten tenner on to the counter.

He looked at it for a moment, sniffed sharply and picked it up. 'You're on.'

'There you go. Excellent. Now, what shall we talk about?'

'I think you should make the running. I don't know anything about you.'

'Fine. Right. OK, let's start with that book.'

'Do we have to?'

'I've never read any Chekov.'

'Don't bother. It's basically shite.'

'Which one are you reading?'

'*The Seagull.*'

'What's it about?'

'Look, sir, this isn't really a conversation. I feel like I'm back at college.'

'Bloody hell. OK, don't call me sir, call me Frank, and don't tell me what it's about, just tell me why it's so shite.'

He sighed and twisted his lips into a little duck's bill. 'Well, they're just so fucking miserable. They're sitting there in this big mansion watching plays and they just keep on going on about how fucking miserable they are.'

'It sounds pretty good to me.'

'Well it's not. It's shit. Listen to this, this is how it starts: "Why is it you always wear black?", "Because I'm in mourning for my life."'

'That sounds like The Smiths.'

'Who's The Smiths?'

That was a bit of a shock to me, but I didn't want to dwell on it.

'Don't worry about it, they're just some maudlin band from the eighties.'

'Well, that's why I don't like Chekov, basically. Miserable Russian bastard.'

'But I thought all teenagers were miserable.'

'Not the ones I know. They're bored, but they're not miserable.'

There was a moment's hiatus.

'You see, it's not so bad having a conversation, is it?'

'It's all right.'

I'd decided I quite liked the sound of Chekov. 'Can I borrow that book off you?'

'Naah, sorry, pal. I've got to finish it tomorrow.'

'Tut. Give me another couple of quotes that you thought were really miserable, then.'

'What are you on about?'

'I collect miserable quotes in my spare time. I just wonder if there are any good ones in there.'

'You need to sort yourself out, mate.'

'Go on, it'll cheer me up.'

'You know, I thought you were going to try to bum me when I saw you come back in, but you're weirder than that, pal.'

He thumbed around the book a little, puffing out his cheeks. 'What about this one: "There won't be anything in two hundred thousand years, nothing." I mean who gives a fuck about two hundred thousand years' time?'

'Not bad. Not very *relevantly* miscrable though, is it?'

'It's quite *pointless* though, isn't it?'

'Pointless isn't enough.'

'All right, I'll find a better one.'

Mohammed put himself studiously to his task. I don't know about him, but I was having the time of my life.

'This one, then. I don't know whether it is a good one actually: "Women never forgive failure".'

'Ooh, that's a good one all right, that one's spot on the money, Mo. It gets me *right there*.'

I punched my chest hard, and folded up into a coughing fit.

'Yeah, well I've only had one girlfriend and I chucked her because she got off with me mate.'

'You did the honourable thing,' I spluttered through my convulsions. 'How long have we had?'

'About ten minutes.'

'Brilliant.'

There was another silence. Mohammed seemed to be losing interest, so I hit him with one: 'What do you think I should do?'

'About what?'

'About the fact that I have to pay people I've never met before to have conversations with me, about the fact that I'm living in a motel on the M1, about the fact that I haven't got a clue about what to do next.'

'Fuck, I don't know. Go home?'

'I haven't got one.'

'You gave me an address yesterday.'

'Yeah, yeah, but I don't live there really. My *real* home is a 1979 Vauxhall Cavalier. My real home is rusting to death in that car park.'

'Why don't you go and see your mum and dad?'

'Not an available option.'

'Go and see your mates?'

'They're all a bunch of tossers.'

'You must have one who's all right.'

'They're all all right, it's just that they're a bunch of tossers. It's too complicated to explain.'

He began to look a bit puzzled. 'I don't know, sir, really. I'm only seventeen.'

'Yeah, it's all right, I'm sorry for asking.'

'It's a bit sad if you can't go and see your mates.'

That's when it dawned on me. Bill Turnage. The Chippy Chippy. Not only was it possible that I could go and stay with him, he'd specifically *asked* me to go and stay with him. A little pastoral interlude in Suffolk. I could lie through my teeth about why I'd left town, pay him a bit of housekeeping and start planning for my peerage. Well, for my re-entry into civilised society at least. I wouldn't say that I was excited by the notion, but it made the prospect of saying goodnight to Mohammed a little easier.

'I think I've had enough now, if you don't mind, Mo. I think I'll turn in.'

'You're the boss.'

'How long now?'

'Fifteen minutes.'

'Are you going to offer me some of my tenner back?'

'No chance.'

'Fair enough.'

I got up and went towards the corridor where my room was situated.

'See you, Mo.'

'See yer.'

'And thanks.'

'You're the boss.'

It was too late to call Bill there and then, but I took his letter from my address book and double-checked that he had actually asked me to come and stay with him. It was always possible that in skim reading it I'd failed to decode a subtle 'fuck off, I hope I never see you again' message lurking in the textual undergrowth. But no, there it was, in black and white:

*Just to say hi really and to say you are welcome to come and stay at ours any time, we've got an attic (my study – still writing!) you can stay in with a sofa bed.*

Incontrovertible.

To celebrate, I re-retrieved *Asian Panties* from my overnight bag. I had once been told that girls from Japan had horizontal vaginas, that is, running laterally across the pubis like mouths. Although my biology O Level had discounted this possibility, there stayed within me some shady notion that *maybe* there was a grain of truth in it. Some hill tribe, perhaps, retained this unusual anatomical feature from pre-history. Of course, *Asian Panties* was no use to me in these researches, as all gussets were firmly snapped into place. Nevertheless, the striking image stayed with me as I browsed the pages. However after about ten minutes, a sense of vapidity overtook me. I can't explain it, but I started to feel scooped out. My conscience departed my body and looked down from the foot of the bed. Twenty-nine years of age and reading *Asian Panties* in a motel? I must be able to do better than that. Reach for the stars! I got out of bed and stuffed the pathetic little magazine into the bin in the bathroom, taking care to wrap it in a plastic bag, so the cleaners (whom I had never met, and who could never have any idea who I was) wouldn't think ill of me.

I then turned in, turned out the light and tried to think of

209

something constructive. It wasn't long before I was back in my electrically lit dreamworld, but this time at least, the lights seemed to be leading somewhere, in fact, down a broad avenue towards a gentle, restorative idyll in the Suffolk countryside.

# Over eighty pounds

'Jesus, it really does sound as if it's in the middle of nowhere.'

Bill had just finished giving me micro-directions to his house.

'Yeah, it is.'

The sound of hurtling screams and a sporadic boing-ing noise, like somebody hitting a gong, continued. They had provided the soundtrack for our entire conversation

'I said it really does sound as if it's in the middle of nowhere.'

A dog (A wolf?) had begun to bark in the background.

'It's where?'

'What?'

The noise was unspeakable.

'I said . . .'

'WILL EVERYBODY PLEASE SHUT UP JUST FOR ONE MINUTE! Sorry about that, Frank.'

There was a brief lull in the noise, broken only by the occasional whorfing of the dog.

'I just said – it doesn't matter. Are you sure this is all right?'

At least one of the kids started keening, really bawling its little heart out.

'It's great, believe me. Really good. I'm sorry about this bedlam.'

The noise was back towards peak levels as we sorted out the logistics.

'I'll be there sort of early evening.'

'Fine.'

'And you're sure there's no problem.'

'Absolutely positive. It would be – BEN, IF YOU DON'T STOP SMASHING THAT PAN I'LL ... I'LL ... WELL, YOU WON'T LIKE IT ANYWAY. Christ. No, honestly, I'm looking forward to it.'

The boing-ing continued.

'Brilliant.'

'SUE! SUE! Shut them up, will you, stop dithering. Listen, I better get off the phone, we're in meltdown here. I think it's tartrazine or something – WILL YOU –'

'No worries, Bill. I'll see you at six-ish.'

But he was already off the phone.


I set off at ten-thirty, after making my anglepoise friend more comfortable on the front seat. He was a pleasant, unassuming little fella, and he was my pal.

Even when you're effectively off-grid, as I most certainly was, there's nothing good about Sundays. The motorway was sparsely populated, the weather dull steel. Childhood Sundays for me, an indoors type of boy, always seemed this colour. I never really dreaded school, never had to attend church or family gatherings, so it was difficult to figure out what was so enervating and dry about them. I think it was something to do with the bad TV. For some reason, TV on Sundays seemed to have a duty to be bad when I was growing up. It was probably the fault of some patrician liberals who thought putting on bad TV would force all the bored teenagers into taking up bob-a-job or learning a foreign language. All the kids I knew just watched the bad TV. A lot of them even began to prefer the bad TV to good TV, simply on the grounds of its badness. Bad TV was what we talked about on Mondays: 'God, did you see *Aap Kaa Hak* yesterday? Wasn't it shite? It was brilliant', or '*Songs of Praise* was just bobbins yesterday, it was boss, wasn't it?' Thus they were prepared for a lifetime of preferring bad things, on the basis of their badness, which could be ironised and made 'fucking top', to good things, which could only ever be simply good.

The consequences of bad Sunday TV in the eighties and nineties were, therefore, far reaching. *Carry On* films and *Neighbours* were elevated to the canon, for one thing. People bought ABBA records. John Major won a General Election. I'm not knocking it, I'm just pointing out that all those patrician liberals got their calculations wrong. Another thing is that everybody who grew up watching bad TV on Sundays in the seventies ended up *making* bad TV twenty years later: that wasn't the point at all.

That was how it seemed to me, anyway, as I came off the M1 at Leicester, following signs for Peterborough on the A47. Ah, the evocative music of middle England. Bill lived in a village called High Elder, near Yoxford, thirty miles north-east of Ipswich. Once I'd got beyond Norwich, I seemed to be in a country where the places were named by second-rate comedy writers; Beccles, Bungay, Wissett. I even saw signs to Wangford.

The topography was flat, there was no doubt about it, but instead of feeling low down, I felt as if I was rolling along on the brow of the world. There was nothing above fifteen feet high to make me feel small, apart from the vast darkening sky, which seemed unlimited. It was very much like the sky should be at the end of somewhere. By five it was pitch black and raining heavily. Bill had told me to go to a pub called The Two Geese in Yoxford, and ask the rest of the way to High Elder, as it wasn't on my road map. The pub was very un-chocolate box; a flat-faced redbrick building, next to a crescent of ten or so council houses. Inside it was very brightly lit, and there was country and western being played very loudly on the jukebox. I remember the carpet, an amber and purple paisley swirl, because it was like the one we'd had in our hallway when I was a kid. There were five or six people in, all standing round the bar. They didn't look very country. There were some distinctive but unpleasant haircuts: one sported a squaddie crop which started about an eighth of an inch above his eyebrows. Another had classic male-pattern baldness, but had grown the back and sides into a glossy sheet that extended half way down his back. This latter looked at me as I came in, not threateningly but steadily. His beergut was epic. His T-shirt was riding up it like a sleepy eyelid, displaying a deep, fleshy bellybutton and a strip of khaki underpant.

'Hi, I was just wondering if someone could tell me the way to High Elder.'

I addressed the question to the assembly. They sniffed, snorted and pawed their feet like water buffaloes disturbed at feeding time.

The Long Haired Beergut drew on his rollie: 'It's just up the road there.'

I thought this was a prelude to a fuller explanation, but from the way he was looking at me, obviously not.

'Right, OK. And which way up the road?'

'Which way did you come in?'

'Sort of that way.' I gestured in the vague direction of the North.

'That's the wrong way in really. You should of come in 'tother way, down past Peasenhall.'

'Well, I didn't. I mean there's not much I can do about that now.'

'He should of come in down past Peasenhall.'

This was the squaddie.

'OK, I'm aware of my mistake, and I'm sorry. However, despite this error, for which I apologise, could you please tell me which way High Elder is?'

They were all looking at me now. Long Hair spoke, again without threat, but with a little bit of hurt in his tone: 'There's no way you should start gettin' smaaart about it.'

They started sniffing, snorting and pawing again.

'I'm sorry, I've been driving all day, I've come all the way from Leeds and I just want to know where High Elder is.'

'You down from Leeds, you say?'

'Yeah, well just outside.'

'I just don't know why you didn't come down past Peasenhall.'

Then the squaddie: 'It makes it a lot easier if you take the Peasenhall road. 'Ticularly if you coming down from Leeds.'

Another bloke came out of the toilet. He looked about seventy and was dressed in a mauve shell suit and massive Nike trainers. Long Hair addressed him: 'This bloke's down from Leeds, looking for High Elder.'

'Which way did he come in?'

The crowd at the bar gestured northwards.

'He should of come in down past Peasenhall.'

'That's what we told him, but he didn't take no notice.'

I became exasperated. 'How could I take notice? I hadn't even met you before I came in. Obviously.'

There was a horribly long silence. They all looked as if they were wrestling with the categorical imperative. More sniffing, more pawing.

'Don't follow you, I'm afraid.'

'Oh look, is there anywhere else in the village I can ask?'

One of the men who hadn't spoken, youngish, with a Fred West bubble perm, piped up: 'There's a place just back up towards Peasenhall.'

Then Long Hair stepped in: 'Well, sir, you turn right out of the car park, turn left at the phone box, follow the road for about half a mile. You'll go past a big pair of white gates. Turn right and High Elder's just there. It's only three houses, so you'll find it fair enough.'

'Great, thank you. I'm sorry I got a bit tetchy.'

'Right you are.'

I left the pub thankful I hadn't been fed through a threshing machine, and set off for Bill's.

High Elder was in fact a little more than three houses. It was three houses and a caravan. In the darkness it was hard to ascertain whether it was a charming little hamlet or a godforsaken shit-hole. Due to my recent resolutions, New Frank inclined towards the former, at least for the moment.

Bill's house was the last of the three, a long, white low-built cottage facing right on to the road. I parked up on a sodden grass verge and went to the door, feeling unaccountably nervous. I thumped the heavy knocker. Behind the door I could hear children shrieking and the dog still honking away. I even thought I could hear a pan being boinged.

The door opened slowly and the face of a great dane appeared in the aperture, ropes of spit suspended from its blackened jowls.

A woman's voice was remonstrating desperately: 'Flash, it's all right, Flash, gotoyourbox, gotoyourbox.'

Flash started to bark with an eerie softness of tone.

'Is that you, Frank?'

'Yes.'

'I just need to calm the dog down, then I'll let you in.'

She closed the door again, and I stood there in the road, getting soaked. All sorts of things were going on in there, tearing, growling, yelping, thumping. Was there a place to which the adults could retire, and smoke? I hoped so.

Another two minutes of getting pissed on and I was almost

ready to go back to the SupaLodge. Then the door opened and instead of the dog appearing, Sue greeted me with a look of over-exaggerated relief.

'Goodness, I am sorry about that, but Flash is very good, really – a bit of a handful – but he's great for the kids – they all love him really – and of course he makes you feel so secure – not that there's much crime around here – but it gets worse every year, doesn't it? And he doesn't take that much effort, but he costs a bit, vet's bills and what not, over eighty pounds for a toe abcess, I ask you – you must be exhausted BEN, STOP THAT NOW you must want some tea – or I think Bill got some beer in, a few bottles, knowing you were coming – he doesn't drink that much himself DEBBIE! DEBBIE! WHAT HAVE I SAID ABOUT LEAVING YOUR SHOES IN THE KITCHEN but when he gets the chance he'll sink a few – have you got any bags? I'll get Debbie to help you in with them, she's very good around the place actually for a young one *DEBBIE!* . . .' I saw Debbie's tiny, nightie-wearing figure fly through the hallway and heard her scramble up the stairs giggling seditiously.

The place was a shambles. The tiny low-ceilinged hallway looked like an untended store cupboard, piled up with anoraks, boots, plastic mini go-karts and dog toys. As Sue diarrhoea-ed on about nothing I followed her into a long thin kitchen that smelt of dog breath and cheap meat. A child, who I took to be Ben, had rigged up a pan-based drum kit on the bench-width table and was arrhythmically boinging away. The walls were plastered in crap crayon portraits of Mum, Dad and Flash. I noticed that in most Flash towered above the stick adults like a T-Rex.

'Bill's sorry he's not here but he had to go over to the workshop what with all this rain he's worried about a leak he's had in the roof, he listened to the forecast but it said it was going to be dry so he thought he'd leave it till tomorrow BEN PLEASE STOP

217

THAT! UNCLE FRANK'S HERE NOW! but he won't be long I know he was really looking forward to seeing you and the workshop's not far, just up beyond Peasenhall – did you come in that way?'

I nodded, to avoid a re-run of the farrago in the pub. Flash was flinging himself against a glass sliding door that separated the kitchen from another little room. Along with Ben's Evelyn Glennie act it was pretty easy not to concentrate on her gibberish. 'Oh, I always think it's better to come straight down from Bungay, that's what I tell Mum and Dad, and they're living up North now, near Harrogate – you're up there, aren't you – Leeds, Bill said – I believe it's quite lively now, but of course anywhere seems lively if you live in High Elder, apart from Peasenhall!'

She laughed loudly and humourlessly. I made a note to myself to visit Peasenhall. It had obviously made an indelible impression on anyone who had ever visited it. I shoe-horned a word in and said that I'd get my bags myself. I was worried that if I stayed in that kitchen any longer when Bill got home he'd find a child with a wooden spoon up its arse, a wife with a cushion over her face and his house guest's carcass being picked over by his dog. To spare him such an embarrassment I sat in the Cav for a few minutes, and smoked.

It wasn't just that she talked so much, she looked so terribly beaten up. Bill had written in his letter that I wouldn't remember her, but I did. When I met her ten or eleven years ago she was from the mousily pretty gene pool: shortish and nondescript, but not totally out of the question, if you found yourself on your own with her in a tent in the Pyrenees for three weeks, as Bill had. I remembered that she had worn pink ankle warmers, which put her totally out of possible consideration for me, but she wasn't a public disgrace. Now she was sagging and collapsing like an old bridge. OK, I wasn't exactly a himbo myself, but the way she had her hair cut into a crop, the baggy-arsed leggings, the utility

218

sweatshirt, it was all too much. She looked as if she had come to the end of sex.

I gathered myself, and my stripy bags of doom and went back into The Somme.

Almost as soon as she had let me in again Bill arrived. He was carrying a huge tool box. He was dressed in a navy blue smock and grey cords and was wearing three days' stubble. Then I remembered his testosterone supercharger and figured that he probably hadn't shaved that hour. He greeted me with slightly disturbing affection: 'Oh, Frank, how great to see you.'

He gave me a malodorous bear hug, which I half-heartedly returned, and held me by the shoulders at arm's length.

'God, it's great to see you again. Ten years.'

I couldn't really look him in the eye, and shimmied out of his grasp.

'About that. Apart from December in Knightsbridge.' I was trying to introduce a little bathetic reality into the scene. I really can't bear the big fuss.

'Yeah, but ten years.'

'I'll make you both some tea – where did you put those beers, Bill – I've looked everywhere – can't find them anywhere – or would you rather have coffee, Frank – or we've got some Ribena – we're allowed the Ribena, aren't we, Bill, as it's Sunday – but oh didn't we finish it last week – I think we did and I meant to replace it when I went to Kwik Save but they only had the Light stuff and Ben can't drink it, says it's too sweet – not that there's any difference of course, but you try telling that to him when he's in one of his strops . . .'

Bill put his toolbox down and slipped off his smock without so much as attempting to engage with what Sue was saying.

'Let's go to the pub.'

'Are you sure Sue . . .'

'Oh, I don't mind, you blokes go off to the pub and catch up. I've got plenty to do here – we're having mutton tonight I hope that's all right with you, Frank – well, the kids of course, they're having French Bread pizzas, can't get proper food down them – no, you two go off to the pub, I'm fine . . .'

Bill flashed her a shockingly angry look. 'I'll shut up now, of course. Sorry for rattling on – I'm a stupid old rattler, aren't I, Ben?'

The vile little drummer boy stopped for a moment.

'Yeah, you're bloody stupid, Mum.'

She exhaled with a strange half-laugh and disappeared out of the kitchen.

Bill looked at me without reference to what had just happened.

'Come on, let's go down The Geese.'

# Nearly seventy

Bill said he'd drive. He had a monstrous old Transit van that obviously doubled as a shed. The floor was carpeted in old rags and newspapers, there were two watering cans on the passenger seat and the dashboard was inches thick in leaves, work gloves, sawdust and tins of varnish. In the passenger footwell there was a thick length of rubber tubing that tangled my feet. I kicked at it in irritation which caused Bill to stop the van in a hurry.

'What are you doing?'

'There's a hose or something down here.'

He reached under my seat, grabbed the hose, took it round to the back of the van and threw it in. We continued the drive in silence, Bill continually, almost obsessively, reaching over to the windscreen and rubbing it with the back of his hairy hand. In profile he looked grim and thirsty.

We walked into the pub and the water buffaloes were still *in situ*. As we walked to the bar one of them said something out of the side of his mouth and they all started laughing. Bill acknowledged them. Long Hair raised his hand slowly.

'All right, Billy boy. How are you doing tonight?'

'Good, Len. Can I get you a pint?'

'Oh, I don't know about that, Bill. I've got to go down past Peasenhall tonight.'

They were really scoffing now. Bill looked at me and shook his head. 'They didn't pull that one on you?'

'It appears that they did.'

'What way is that to treat a visitor, Len?'

'Well, it's just that he's such a *waaanker*, Bill.'

At this the laughter trailed off and they all turned back into their ragged semi-circle. Bill ordered two pints of bitter. I would have told him that I don't drink bitter on principle, but I was wary of what reaction it might inspire from Len. We sat in a corner. I made sure I kept my back to Len. I have an alarming tendency to stare at people, particularly those who have shown hostility towards me. It's not an aggressive impulse, just a kind of fascination. Actually, I think I do it as a means of trying to connect with them in some way. The last thing I want is to offend people, or make them think ill of me. Well, the last I thing I want is to be glassed by a pissed farm hand, but honestly, conflict of any sort is always intolerable to me.

Bill still wasn't talking. He was hunched forward over the table and twisting his head in a strange way. He would stretch his neck out to the left, with lips tightly pursed, until there was a dull click, and then move it out to the right until the noise was heard again.

'This your local, then?'

'Yep.'

'It's nice. No-one has a local in London, really.'

'It's a big place, I suppose.'

I offered him a fag, which he accepted. He smoked it very inexpertly, with stiff fingers and inhaling very deliberately with his mouth remaining open all the while.

'What made you come to live out here?'

He looked at me as if I'd criticised him.

'Bringing up the kids, better for the kids.'

'Yeah, it's gorgeous round here, isn't it?'

He absolutely and utterly missed the sarcasm.

'Never liked cities, even Norwich was a bit too much, and she –' He jerked his head towards the window, 'she was brought up in the country.'

'Right.'

I watched him closely. He had stopped his stretching ritual and was now doodling with his finger in a pool of spilt beer. His face was wide, but the skin was sucked to his bones. His thinning black curly hair was plastered to the seamed forehead. He looked impressive and real in some way. Some people (me mainly) have a fleshy amorphousness to them which makes them look temporary and half-formed, as if they haven't quite fully emerged into being. Bill, in contrast, looked defined and individuated, as if he had arrived at his personality's destination.

'How's the work?'

He exhaled sharply. 'My work's good, but that doesn't mean anyone's buying it.'

'Right.'

He became more animated, visualising his story with his tiger-strangling hands, but still staring at the table.

'I mean, Sue says, and she's maybe right, that what I really need to do is try to sell it to the big places in London, get in that way, but I've tried. Like when I saw you last year I was at this design fair and it was to be honest a fucking humiliation, watching all these people look at my stuff and look at me, and think, "Oh no, a real no-hoper this one", and move along. I just don't really understand it all, because I really believe in the work, but when I was there I felt like a charity – understand? – like people were only stopping at my display because it looked a bit sad, and they were trying to make me feel better. I remember the smiles as they left, sort of wiping themselves over their faces, you know, looking into the middle distance, patronising. Humiliating, really, as I say.' He was pretty tightly coiled, old Bill.

'Did you sell anything?'

'It's terrible, it's terrible, because I paid them a hundred and fifty-five pounds for two days' rental at the display, and I hired a van for nearly seventy, but I packed up just after lunch on the first day, loaded it all up myself and drove home, just couldn't stand it. Wrong thing to do I know, but just had to. Peace of mind.'

'What kind of things do you do?'

He looked at me now, practically for the first time.

'Of course, you've never really seen anything I've done, have you? I'll show you. In fact, why don't we go now, over to the workshop, it won't take long.'

'Sure.'

We left our half-finished pints and headed back into the sodden car park. The workshop was two or three miles from the pub, down a badly maintained track. It had a corrugated iron roof which was making a noise like a football rattle as the rain battered it. Bill undid the heavy padlock on the wooden door and forced it open with his shoulder.

'This front bit is the sort of showroom.'

He pulled a chain inside the door, and three exposed bulbs glowed dimly overhead. The furniture was all kept under mangy dustsheets. He went round the room enthusiastically pulling the sheets off. I don't know anything at all about furniture beyond its most basic properties; you can sit on a chair, eat off a table and put things you don't want to think about in a drawer somewhere. Despite this ignorance, or because of it, I was extremely impressed, almost awe-struck by his work.

'What I do basically is combine metal with wood, like this – this here is a pretty good example of what I try to do.'

He was squatting on his haunches stroking the curving metal arm of one of a set of six dining chairs. I'll not be able to do them justice here, but they looked pretty cool. It was amazing to me that anyone could make things that looked that good. I couldn't work out why he wasn't fêted by society as some sort of genius. I can understand why footballers get paid forty grand a week, because there are just so few people who are any good at football; perhaps five hundred in the whole country who are brilliant at a sport which every fucker now professes to adore. But there are hundreds of thousands of solicitors, accountants and people who work in marketing, each one of whom is instantly replaceable. Even the lowliest of these clockwatching arselickers would earn, I guessed, at least three times as much as Bill. Even I could be a lawyer or an adman, but not under any circumstances could I ever have made a set of six chairs which were so, well, *beautiful.* I became alarmed at the somewhat William Morris sentiment I was displaying and tried to rationalise Bill's situation. I supposed the poor bastard was born with the wrong gift. Maybe he should have considered retraining as a design consultant and start making executive pen holders.

Bill had now moved to a table, which had a rustic-y style oak-y sort of top and elegant zinc-looking legs (I'm really not doing him justice, am I?).

'You see, Frank, I think it's good work. I go through the catalogues from the London shops and think that this stuff is just as good, and if I do ever sell it round here I might get a few hundred quid, but if I sold it in London I could get a couple of thousand.'

'I don't know much about it, but I think it's brilliant.'

'I could do you a deal on something, if you really liked it.'

The table really was magnificent. It was different from most tables I'd seen, but not so different that you'd feel exposed when you showed it to your friends. It wasn't a *boring* table, but it wasn't a *risky* one either. This is about as close as I get to an aesthetic standard.

'How much for this then?'

'The table? Six hundred?'

'God, Bill, I'm not sure.'

'Five fifty?'

'Well . . .'

'Why not for Christ's sake? If you think it's brilliant?'

'Well, I think you should know a few things.'

He locked up the workshop and we headed off back to the house. On the way I gave him a summary of what had happened, only missing out the bits I couldn't even admit to myself. He listened in silence. It was useful to me for him just to listen. Relating everything to someone who didn't know anyone or anything involved made it all seem manageable somehow. I could also gloss things in my own interest a little. Certainly, the weekend at Tom's parents' house was recast as a tale of righteous anger; Hamlet and Gertrude rather than Faustus farting at the Pope, which was its real theatrical precedent.

Bill wasn't exactly sympathetic, in fact he didn't utter a word, but he didn't attempt to put the case for my prosecution, and as we stood outside his front door he squeezed my shoulder and said: 'Look, if all you need is some time out, you can stay here for as long as you like.' As soon as he said it I felt guilty. I realised that this response had been my intended prize throughout the entire description of my bad Christmas. I'd left him no choice. I resolved to do right by him, if I could.

It occurred to me as we sat down to dinner in the sweaty kitchen that Bill had told me in his letter that he had three children, but that so far I had only met two, Debbie the elf and Ben the percussionist. Sue had locked the children in the TV room by the time we returned, so I still didn't have an opportunity to meet Murray, the youngest. Flash slumbered fitfully by the stove.

'I hope you like mutton, we get it straight from the farmer over there, you don't get it much nowadays I suppose but I was brought up on it and it's Bill's favourite on a Sunday, isn't it? Which reminds me you'll have to go over to the farm shop tomorrow because we're low on basics and I've got to be at school early tomorrow because John's preparing for an inspection, so we'll have to get the kids ready early, I'll just dump them in the library and get Joanna to pick Murray up straight from there – yes, so you'll have to drop me off at eight if that's all right, and I'm sure Frank can entertain himself –'

Bill had returned to his brooding taciturnity. He shovelled his food into his mouth without lifting his eyes from his plate. Sue filled in the gaps in the conversation with aplomb. She told me that she was the secretary at the local primary school and then started on what I found out over the following weeks was her Grand Theme: 'Of course it would be so much easier if we had the second car, because then Bill could come and go as he pleased, and I could take Murray to Aldeburgh after Debbie and Ben were settled. I've cleared it with John and he's said that would be fine, I could just work a bit later if there was anything that needed doing to make up the time I lost and we wouldn't be so reliant on Joanna's good nature. Not that she minds –'

'Sue, I think we've been through this.'

'But it brings it home, doesn't it, when I have to be in early or whatever? Because it's all so inconvenient –'

'It's not that inconvenient.'

'Well, no, but it's not ideal, it just seems that for a few hundred pounds we're –'

'Sue. Enough. C'mon.'

She fell silent, reluctantly. It wasn't easy for me to piece together the story. Why did Murray have to go to a different school? I sensed there was some difficulty attendant on the issue, and that they felt that it could only be broached obliquely, so I didn't follow it up.

Sue regained a bit of courage; 'You see, Frank, we used to have a second car, it was only an old Allegro, which was mine, but we sold it last year because we'd been a bit short, and since then it's been a rigmarole, to be honest, living way out here with only one car, because you have to drive everywhere really, to get anything, there aren't any buses around High Elder, I mean of course there aren't because we'd be the only people who would use them anyway, and it wouldn't solve the problem of getting Murray to Aldeburgh every day, would it? And the weekends when Bill goes off to the market then I'm pretty much stranded here with them all –'

Bill was shaking his head. 'I'm sure Frank doesn't want to hear this.'

I was already pretty embarrassed. Sue seemed to want to use me as some kind of jury on the issue, which was a role I was very unwilling to adopt. I also thought that nobody should have been subjected to the Tale of the Forsaken Allegro, it was just too mournful. How much could they have got for it? Eighty quid? How 'short' must they have been? I meditated with horror on the prospect of not only being poor, but being poor and having three children, and not only having three children but having a fantastic talent that was of no economic value. Why wasn't Bill constantly screaming with grief and rage?

After the mutton, which was gamey and pungent and tasted far too much of dead animal, Sue left us, to put the children to bed.

'I'm sorry I didn't say anything then, Bill.'

'What could you have said?'

He looked at me with his haematite eyes, his hands splayed in forgiveness. 'Chess?'

'Sure.'

He brought a large, solid chess set to the table.

'I made this.'

The pieces themselves were heavy, stylishly simplified versions of normal ones with zinc strips round the bases, and the board was two colours of dull metal.

'It's . . . brilliant.'

228

Bill looked jaded with the limitations of my critical vocabulary.

'I think it's a piece of shit.'

Chess is not a strong suit of mine. I get three moves in to a game and want to sue for peace. I am totally satisfied with a negotiated settlement that means that neither side loses face. My early style, which married Kasparov's sense of tactical daring to 'well I know most of the moves' technique, might let me beat Marie, but it usually left me pretty exposed against anyone who didn't spend the entire game eating figs, doing their nails and phoning their gran.

Bill played slowly but with what to me looked like skill. Despite the horrific noises emanating from upstairs as Sue tried to put the children down, he remained fixated on the board and had the annoying tendency of giving a little definitive-sounding sniff when he had made his move. He beat me four times on the bounce within half an hour. Sue came back to the kitchen when some modicum of order seemed to have been imposed upstairs, and looked in at us. Bill still didn't lift his gaze from the board. We were starting game five.

'Oh, I'm sorry I didn't mean to disturb you.'

I heard her singing tunelessly to herself in some other part of the house for a few minutes. She then started clattering around in a cupboard in the hallway. Bill half turned round and frowned, but didn't say anything.

'OK, boys, I think I'll go up now,' Sue trilled from the hall.

There was a moment's silence. We continued to play, and I heard her trudge upstairs to bed.

# Money

I came to a deal with Bill that I would pay him £40 a week for as long as I stayed. This meant that I had a bolt hole from which there was no chance of being evicted. The money meant too much to him. The more he told me about his finances, the luckier I felt. This is saying something. He told me that not only could he not sell his work, but he was locked in a negative equity trap, having bought the cottage in the late eighties when all the first-wave yups were buying second homes. Since they had all receded to their Wandsworth villas in the early nineties he reckoned it had lost about a third of its value. As he'd managed to wangle a zero deposit mortgage he was well and truly fucked.

He said that if he sold one larger piece of furniture a month, clearing about four hundred for himself, he was doing well. Out of that he had to buy his wood and metal and tools and run the car and pay as much of the mortgage as he could. Sue paid the rest of the mortgage and child benefit bought food for them all.

When they talked to each other, which was not frequently, it was about money. Money was a constant conundrum, an unshakeable weaseling presence, always spinning through their minds. It dramatically foregrounded itself every couple of days: one of the kids' birthdays was approaching, Ben had cracked the bay window in the TV room, Debbie needed a school dress. For Tom and Lucy, money was a cashmere shawl into which they buried their faces, for Bill and Sue it was an oily sheet they used to shore up the holes in their existence. Always temporary, always causing more damage than it repaired, never quite doing the job properly.

Along with money, and the need for a second car, Sue's other daily issue was Murray. When he was two he had been diagnosed as having a behavioural problem. He was very weird-looking, thin with a huge head and fair, wispy baby's hair. Debbie and Ben, on the other hand, were both thin, but wiry and gypsy dark. Murray seemed very placid, and rarely said anything, but Bill told me that he would occasionally fly into unassuageable fits of anger and grief that could last for hours. Because of his unpredictability, he had to be taken to a special school in Aldeburgh every day. They said that one day he might well turn out to be fine, but they also said that he might be like this forever, it was impossible to know.

When Bill first told me about Murray's problems, I was amazed he could be so sanguine about it, particularly when compounded with his financial position. However, after watching him and Sue for a week or so I realised that they didn't seem bothered because they had simply had to accommodate it as part of their lives. There was obviously no alternative. With Murray, Bill was indulgent and watchful to an extent, but with the other two he seemed blasé to the point of neglect. They would all come home together at about five o'clock in Bill's Transit, including Flash who spent the days around the workshop. Every night, when Sue came in she would be babbling about what they'd said at

231

school about Murray, whether he'd had a good day or a bad day, how his reading was coming on, how many times he'd chewed through an electricity cable and so on. Bill didn't even listen. I was usually in the kitchen, and he would come in, pour himself some milk and read the local paper sitting at the table as Sue warbled away. I know a bit about inattentive fathers, but even I thought his behaviour was a bit rough. With the other kids, too, she was constantly updating Bill on how they were doing, what the teachers were saying about their work, who they had made friends with, all the usual stuff, but he just wouldn't respond. She talked herself to a standstill for an hour, and then got on with fixing the dinner.

What was strange was that the kids seemed to hate her for it. Ben in particular would cling to Bill as his mother spoke, and just interject an occasional contradiction or insult: 'No, Mum, don't be thick – God, Mum, you're such a spasmo – leave me alone, Mum, you saddo.'

It was sort of too much for me. I remembered that Marie had once told me, when I was bemoaning my lack of one, that 'families are tough places to grow up in' (which I thought was a quote she'd nicked from some American daytime queen), but seeing the reality of it was almost sickening. I couldn't say anything, of course, it was nothing to do with me.

The attic where I was staying was full of old concertina files. Bill had told me in his letter that it was his study. I remembered from school that he was always writing something, usually surrealistic playlets he'd read out during lunch break. The files were all scrawled with cryptic phrases: *Monitor 2, Bill's Bullshit, Overhang, The Cabinet Maker, What's Left, Teflon Pete,* and scores more. The second week I was there I decided to have a poke around some of them. I felt almost as if Bill wanted me to. He kept saying things like 'I hope they're not in your way, those files,' and 'I'll move them if they're causing you any hassle,' as if deliberately trying

232

to draw my attention to them. A couple of times since I'd been there, he'd taken one of the files downstairs and sat at the kitchen table scribbling on it, as if he was making vital amendments to a final draft. He would leave the file open while he watched TV or read his paper, again as if he wanted me to ask about what was in it. I never did. Tom had showed me an early draft of his art theft novel years ago, and I got pissed and told him I thought it was 'shite'. He told me he'd got a deal for it. I told him that deals probably weren't so hard to come by when your dad owned the fucking company (a statement which was both extremely cheap and wildly inaccurate). Anyway, it caused a bad atmosphere for a few months, so the last thing I wanted to do was volunteer an opinion on my host's most treasured thoughts.

But I couldn't help wanting to have a look. The primary motivation was, of course, a desire to see what he'd written about me in his diary, or whether I'd featured, thinly disguised, in one of his plays.

One morning, about a fortnight into my stay, I made myself a vat of tea and decided to have a good rootle. There were scores of files, but you could easily tell which were the more recent ones. What I found was for the most part pretty unremarkable. The first file I looked at was *The Cabinet Maker* which was basically a *roman à clef* filled with vengeful spite, directed particularly, it seemed, at IKEA and metropolitanism. Nothing unusual there. A couple of the other files contained plays, which seemed to have been worked on over and over again. They were totally unreadable. I tried to commit some of the lines to memory, but as soon as I thought I'd got a speech down pat, it would slide out of my mind like a marble running off a table. I'll try and give a flavour:

BILL
*Oh, if only I had never met her.*
JOHN

*But you cannot think thus. You have met her, and she is*
*your life.*

BILL

*Ah, but I can think thus, because I do not want this life any*
*more. I want the one of which I dreamt when young, glittering*
*and pure and full of promise!*

JOHN

*But promise is ne'er attained, and in that truth lies the truth*
*of all of us! You MUST learn to love your failure.*

BILL

*But if we love failure, what becomes of our dream of love?*

JOHN

*This, too, must perish!!*

And so on.

The one marked *Bill's Bullshit* contained a series of hardback exercise books. They were his diaries. The first one I opened was dated 1990 and was the standard stuff: paragraphs of rank self-indulgence and sexual fantasy unreadably combined. I browsed through a couple more of the books, but they were too repetitive to be interesting. I noticed that the more recent ones had started to become infected with odd little calculations; you couldn't go three pages without coming across one. It was easy to work out that these sums related to his finances. After a bit of cross-referencing they even allowed me to determine what Sue's exact salary was (£7,500 a year if you're interested), and how big their mortgage was (about £130,000). The numbers would break into the text unbidden, or scrawl themselves into the tight margins, unrelated to what was written beside them. It was tiring and depressing reading, and I closed the volume I was looking at and replaced it in the file.

Then I found his current diary. It was a fat black hardback notebook with no dates. By now, practically every page was

234

stuffed with calculations, some extremely elaborate, some simple additions and subtractions repeated over and over again. There were graphs with projections into the future, most with 'optimistic' and 'pessimistic' scenarios. The most commonly occurring type was a four- or five-row addition, which I worked out was his weekly account, because the last one had my £40 included, next to my initials. In between the arithmetic were short, dense paragraphs of his neurotic handwriting. There was an entry every two or three days, which tended to run for three or four pages, numbers included. It was effortful to read, not because the handwriting was so dense, but because the only subject was money. Not thoughts about the meaning of money, or speculations on the future of money, just money. This month's money, this week's money, that day's money. The writing was cryptic and larded with acronyms, clearly it was all intended purely for Bill himself. The tone was chiefly a contingent, short-term kind of hope. The pattern of a typical entry would be: *'If X happens, and I can do Y, then, as long as Z can be delayed, then everything will be fine, for a week or two.'* Occasionally, however, there were sharp swerves into despair, where the logical formulations gave way to Tourette's syndrome, the words dug into the page, ignoring the feint lines:

*'FuckcuntfuckyouCUNTthisisfuckingshit – thisisfuckingshit – youCUNTyouCUNT – this is fuckkkkkingshit.'*

When I had kept a diary at college and in my early twenties the intended audience was: Marie, my dad, Tom, my boss, i.e. all the people I wanted to have something out with but didn't have the nerve. If I were ever to die in a bus accident, the diaries would let everybody know what I really thought of them. Oh, such tears at the crem. In other words, for me, keeping a diary was a disgusting and egotistical act of self-consciousness. Bill's diary wasn't in any way a pose. It was the real deal.

At the end of some of the entries, every two weeks or so it seemed, there were short lists in two columns, that always

contained the same items, sometimes in different orders. I copied
one down:

| | |
|---|---|
| *Sue* | *Work* |
| *Murray* | *Debt* |
| *Ben & Debbie* | *No friends* |
| *My talent* | *This book* |
| *Belief* | *Lonely* |

The list was pretty obviously a kind of balance sheet. I thought
it strange that he always separated out Murray from the other
two kids, and that he put Sue on the plus side. In fact, I thought
for a moment that the left side could be the minus side, if you
felt like being cynical. Not that the list could be reversed, with
the minuses becoming pluses, but that *both* sides had a pretty
minus-y look to them to me. I thought it strange that he repeated
this list so often, and checked back to see if I could work out why.
The only correlation I could determine was that the list appeared
after most of the gloomier entries, and almost always after the
outbursts of Tourette's.

I took a swig of cold tea and set about returning all the
books and papers I'd looked at to their original positions. I'd
been burrowing in Bill's psyche for over three hours and the
experience hadn't been uplifting. I went downstairs and surfed
daytime TV for a while feeling scooped out like an old orange.
For the first time, I noticed that Bill's furniture was scattered
throughout the shabbiness and squalor of the room. The TV
itself was on an elegant dull metal stand, the coffee table, although
bruised with mug marks and sharp ends of childrens' toys, was
recognisably his work. Even the bookcases built into the wall
were detailed with metal strips and studs. For some reason I
found the single-mindedness of his approach, his unswerving
commitment to his own style, very moving. Those words *belief*
and *talent* obsessively repeated in his journal were the only two

things he had left over which he had any control. Then I snapped out of feeling sorry for him; at least he had *belief* and *talent*, the jousy bastard.

That evening, the raggle-taggle crew got home at the usual time, in the usual manner, and the usual evening ensued. The kids had begun to accept me as a welcome distraction. Even Flash had got over his initial slavering animosity and now spent some minutes every day snuffling and drooling over my groin. Sue told me that this was him showing trust (though not in so many words). To me the proximity of his moist, slapping jaw to my nuts made it feel more like a threat.

Of the kids, I'm ashamed to admit, it was Debbie who got most of my attention. Part of my deal with Bill was that, when asked, I'd do some driving duties for the family. During the days I rose late, watched TV, drove and smoked in the mornings. After a pork pie lunch, I'd go to the post office for them, maybe get some groceries (tinned, bland or waning past eat-by date) or pick up Debbie and Ben, if either parent was unable to. It's amazing how you can kill days, particularly in winter. If I got up at eleven, I only had about five hours to dispose of before the Turnages got home. If I drove to the coast, bought a paper, threw pebbles into the sea and drank tea in a café then I'd done a good day's work. By the time I got back to High Elder it was nearly time for dinner, and after a game of chess, and perhaps a pint down at The Geese, it was time for bed again, occasionally broken up with commutes to the primary school or the Co-op and back.

The car journeys with Debbie and Ben were split exactly 50/50 in terms of pleasure/pain. Debbie was energy, wriggliness, verbal invention, good questions and as cute as a button. Ben was hoarse, grinding, unrelenting, violent, ill tempered and smelly. I always sat him in the back, but within eight seconds of starting the engine he was swarming between the front seats like a pillaging infidel, all pivoting knees and deadly aggression, some part of the car wedged between his teeth rather than a scimitar. Debbie on the other hand, would sit and burble as if I were her special-ist friend in the world. Her special-ist friend in the world was some lucky, lucky bastard called Keith Mottershead. When she first mentioned Keith, looking at me out of the corner of her eye, grinning manically and twisting her lips around, Ben commented, surging over my shoulder:

'Yeah, yeah and everyone at school says Keith looked at Debbie's bum at dinnertime.'

Debbie's response was to roll her eyes and sigh exasperatedly. I elbowed Ben firmly in the chest. He laughed like a drain.

Debbie kept asking me what I did, and was I retired like Grandad? I just said yes.

'I like Grandad, because he keeps a supply of Creme Eggs all year, so I can take them to school when no-one else has got 'em, like in winter.'

I longed to be as inventive and considerate as Grandad.

I hated it when she danced to pop videos, and imitated the pouting singers, lifting her skirt, putting her finger against her cheek and crossing her arms over her bony chest. I imagined her five years down the track, sitting on a wall by the bus stop near the pub, hair badly bleached, an Embassy on, a bottle of Hooch and Gary the pot man's tongue down her throat.

I *was* her fucking grandad.

Maybe I could look after her, somehow. With what? Good intentions and an anglepoise lamp. Grrrrr.

She was the most elusive, flirtatious, gorgeous beast I'd ever met. Her sexiness was a disgrace. It's almost too much to recall her appearance; it makes my heart hurt with fondness and guilt. She was nine years old, a bag of bones and downed with straight fine hair from forehead to ankle, like some forest child. Her eyes were like Bill's, a metallic dark grey-brown, and she used them like a weapon, stunning anyone out of a tone of reproach with one volley. Sue cut her hair, and because you couldn't get Debbie to hold still for more than

238

a moment if she didn't want to, the fringe was graded in strata, and the rest of it looked as if it was cut with some imprecise blunt instrument. A letter opener perhaps, or Flash's teeth.

I had no idea how I was supposed to deal with a nine-year-old girl. What's allowed, what isn't? Too many idle lunchtimes reading the newspapers at O'Hare's had rendered me incapable of feeling relaxed in her company. All those abuse stories piling up day after day, with their obsession with the tiny behavioural details; what came into contact with what, when, under whose supervision, how often, under what pretence. I felt so sad about it. I wouldn't let her near me, brushing her off me like a spider if she got too close. That, of course, would just inspire Sue to harass the poor girl:

'What are you doing – leave poor Frank alone, you're always mithering him, come over here, stop showing off –'

What I really wanted to do was scoop her up and give her a breathtaking bear hug and a big humming kiss on the nose. Ah, but the doorstepper, the care worker and the cops. The fucking *Daily Mail*, the lousy fucking *Sun*. It's not just that kids have been robbed of childhood, it's that poor bastards like me have been robbed of children.

I usually helped her with her homework. She was bright, but butterfly-minded. Her favourite thing was 'projects', which seemed to be mostly about TV programmes, and I would help her cut pictures out of magazines and stick them into her books. I'm so cack-handed most of the time she would have been better off without me, but she obviously thought it was important in some way to have me on hand. Also, doing homework meant sitting at a safe distance at the kitchen table or on the telly room floor. There was no risk of bad thoughts or misinterpreted actions at such distances.

One night we were cutting and pasting pictures of birds from old magazines the school had given her. She spent most of the

239

time trying to smear Pritt over Ben's face, which far from resisting he seemed to encourage. In retaliation, he made several loud references to Keith Mottershead's widgy.

I hadn't got anywhere near Ben, and I got the impression that his parents hadn't either. He was infatuated with discordant sound, and quite happy being left alone to generate it. His banging, shrieking, droning, nee-naw-ing was the constant soundtrack to life in the house. If we went out for a walk, with percussive aids limited, he would just shout. He was exhausting at first, because you entertained some notion that he could be controlled, but after a while I got used to him, and he seemed no more than a minor irritant, like a drunk uncle at a wedding.

Murray was scarily quiet and almost completely static, as he was that night. Sue monitored him constantly out of the corner of her eye. I was there for a little over a month in total, and he didn't fit once, but the longer the period of quiet lasted, the more you were certain that it was just about to end. For all that the other two sapped energy, it was Murray and his threatening, pressure-cooker silence that tired Bill and Sue out the most.

I realised why Bill separated out Murray from the others in his gnomic lists. He remained largely detached from Debbie and Ben, but spent large portions of time with Murray. He would sit on the floor with him murmuring encouragingly, or simply looking at him like an artist emerging from a trance, mystified by his own creation. Murray was different, and Bill gave that difference the respect and admiration it deserved.

I also started to see what connected Bill and Sue as the days passed. In a way it was disheartening, because the connection was so much based on Sue's admiration for him and her refusal to admit that he could do anything wrong, but he was in such a bad way I supposed he deserved some coddling. Sue particularly lionised his work, always telling me how it was just a matter of time before he broke through in London and got the recognition he was due. He would just grunt and deny in response. Her honesty and kindness made me feel terribly guilty about my original reaction; she might well look as if she had got to the end of sex, but she certainly hadn't got to the end of love, and that's the most important thing, I guess.

Debbie and I stuck a few more nightjars in her book, Ben wailed and squawked himself to apathy, Murray lay curled up in front of the regional news, Sue broiled some brisket, dirging to herself, in the dripping kitchen, where her husband read the *East Suffolk Gazette*, doodling mathematically on the Games and Puzzles page. With Flash in a guttering snooze in the hall, what a picture of domestic contentment we must have looked.

# Seven hundred left

After three weeks I was beginning to feel that it was time to move on. I still had about seven hundred left of my thievings from O'Hare's, which I thought was getting dangerously close to destitution. If I were to get a flat, then I'd need a few hundred quid deposit. Allowing a week to find work, and at least a week waiting for my first paypacket, seven hundred quid effectively equalled zero. I had finally come to an uneasy peace with myself about where I should go next: it had to be back to London. I felt that I needed to start making my reparations and discharging my debts. I was also still able to fantasise that the Sadie situation was recoverable, and that thought more than anything was turning me back south. How much longer could 'not yet' be?

One night after dinner Bill suggested we go down to The Geese. He seemed very agitated. His normal mood was lugubrious and grimly unexpressive, but that night something was definitely rattling him. As we drove he sniffed constantly and thrummed the steering wheel with his powerful thumbs.

As soon as we sat down with our drinks he started on what had been on his mind: 'Frank, I've been speaking to Sue, and I just want to apologise.'

This had a familiar feel to it.

'What for?'

'Well, we, I mean I invited you here under false pretences.'

'What do you mean?' Three in a bed? The Moonies? Virgin sacrifice?

He spoke very deliberately, neck bent, staring into his cello-brown beer.

'The only reason I asked you to stay, it was a last resort. I – it's pretty embarrassing – but we were getting desperate and I thought what with you living in London, and I remember when I saw you at university you seemed pretty well connected, I thought you might be able to help me sell some work.'

Christ, how disappointed he must have been that first night when he heard about all those severances.

'Aren't I the one who should be sorry?'

'God, no. And then I told Sue about the rent deal, and she was livid, inviting you to stay and then charging you for the pleasure.'

'I wouldn't have offered if I didn't think it was the right thing.'

'Well, here.'

Bill reached into his back pocket and pulled out eighty quid in brand new twenties and laid them on the table.

'Here, we insist you have it back.'

'Bill, don't even think of it.'

'No, really, I can't imagine what I was doing. It must be such a miserable experience for you anyway, Sue clattering on, the kids so wild, and me moaning in the corner.'

I kept thinking of the diary. Eighty quid could blow a huge

243

hole in his entire year's financial strategy. I also thought about those weird little Tourette's outbursts.

'Look, Bill, you don't know how much I appreciate you letting me stay with you. I don't really now where the fuck I'd be if I wasn't here. I can't take it back.'

He started shaking his head rapidly.

'Oh, God, this is a mess.'

'It's not that bad. And besides, I like kids. They make you less selfish.'

Expert parent, after three weeks.

'No, I don't mean that, not just this, the money, it's the whole fucking thing.'

'I'm not with you.'

He now put his hands up to his mouth in the praying position. His fingernails were long and filthy.

'It's OK, Frank, it's too much, it's so fucking *infantile*.'

He was rocking his head, now, his mouth concealed by his hands.

'I'm sorry, Bill, I still don't really –'

He suddenly stood up. He quickly stuffed the money into his trouser pocket, as if by speeding up the action it might not really have happened.

'No! *Fuck!* I'll be back in a minute. Excuse me.'

He strode out of the pub, smoothing both his hands over his head.

I looked around the pub, a little insecure about being alone. It was a Wednesday night, and the pub was pretty quiet. The Geese only ever seemed to be busy at Sunday lunchtime. The rest of the time it was the water buffaloes and their ticks who provided most of the trade. I don't think I'd been there once when Len the Belly hadn't been standing at the bar. Tonight was no exception. There were a couple of other blokes in whose company I'd seen him before, but tonight he obviously wanted to be alone. He was extremely pissed, leaning his bulging frame steeply against the bar rail and breathing heavily through his open mouth. He seemed reduced without his court around him. The long sheet of hair that had flowed so imperiously down his back three weeks ago now straggled over his face and shoulders like a stringy stole. All these lonely men, why did they have to go round being so *openly* lonely? I guess they're seeking sympathy, seeking the love they never got from those who were supposed to give it. But where are all the lonely women? Women must suffer their privations. I can only assume that they do the decent thing, and keep their loneliness to themselves, their window seats and their cigarettes.

Bill had been away for five minutes now, and I was beginning to get anxious. I left my pint and went out into the car park. The Transit van was still there, and nobody seemed to be in it. I banged on the rear doors a few times, but nobody answered.

It was a deep February evening, cold to the heart and swatted with wind. I walked out into the street and looked around inefficiently. No sign of Bill.

I felt at a loss. His exit had been surprising, but not surprising enough for me to alert the police, or to worry Sue. I went back over what we had talked about. Nothing really. I figured that Sue had made him take some money out of the machine, aghast at the thought of my paying him to stay with them. As it tends to be with other people's embarrassment, I couldn't work out why either of them should be embarrassed at all. He had then appeared to be on the verge of telling me something. I speculated that he had been fucking the local dairy maid or farmer's wife, and was dying to get it off his chest. I would have thought it a shame, but I could have forgiven him.

Just as I was turning to go back into the pub, the engine of the Transit van started. A volt of shock raced down my chest. I looked at the van. The headlights had come on, so I couldn't see who was in the driver's seat. The lights flashed manically as the van started moving towards me. I shouted out, in a reedy unconvincing voice:

'What's going on?'

The van drew up to me and the driver opened the passenger door.

'Get in.'

The voice was thick and hushed, but recognisably Bill's.

'Bill, what the fuck's going on?'

'Getingetin.'

I got into the cab and closed the door.

'Bill, what are you doing?'

Not looking at me, he moved the van into gear and we moved off.

'Frank, I'm going to do something very bad.'

Oh, Christ. I had a flash forward to being strapped to his workbench, being chafed to bubbling pulp with a power lathe.

'What the fuck are you talking about, Bill?'

He was driving extremely deliberately. I couldn't tell where we were, but we certainly weren't heading home. I could see his lips pursing and repursing in profile.

'Bill, come on, man, this is bad shit. Talk to me.'

When he spoke, his voice still had an eerie thickness to it: 'I'm sorry it has to be you, Frank, who's with me, but that's just it. I've thought it through, and there's no way you can be blamed.'

'Bill, what the fuck are you saying?'

'This puts you in a bad position, I know, but I thought of you as a kind of last hope. It was ridiculous, I know that now, I knew it then, but when I realised that you couldn't help me, not that I should ever have thought you could, I sort of – freaked.'

'You're not fucking saying this. You're not saying this.'

'I am, Frank. I've thought it through.'

I felt something in the passenger footwell. Jesus Christ, it was the rubber hose. 'Bill, this is *insane*. This is just insane.'

'Look, the plan is, in a minute I'm going to pull into a side road, you're going to get out of the van. You don't know where you are, but I've hidden a map telling you how to get back to the pub just near where I'm going to pull up. It'll take you about twenty minutes to find it. The directions in the map actually take you a long way round –'

'Bill, look, this is madness, I'm not going to walk off while you fucking kill yourself. Who do you think I am?'

He paid no attention to me, just closed his eyes momentarily in impatient disdain. We started to pull in to a pitch-black side road.

'By the time you get back to the pub, you must call the police and tell them you found my body –'

'Bill, what the fuck are you saying?'

He sniffed aggressively and turned towards me. His breath stank of alcohol. 'Frank, I have a contingency if you prove difficult. Either way, I do the deed. If you do it my way, you don't get hurt.'

'You're not – you can't do this, it's –'

'WHEN you've spoken to the police, it'll only take five minutes for them to find me. I don't want to be found by someone from the village. I don't want to be found by Sue. If I went missing, she'd know to look here.'

I moved one hand on to his forearm and put my other round his shoulder.

'This isn't right, Bill, can't you see that this is just stupid, it's fucking ridiculous.' He made a sudden move with his right fist towards my head. I caught a glimpse of a bottle in his hand, but he was so pissed or his position was so awkward that the blow landed heavily but painlessly on my chest. I struggled to stop him attacking me again, pushing my forearms over his neck. If he'd been sober I would have had no chance, all that manual labour had really brawned him out. As it was, I could just hold him at bay.

'Bill, you must stop this, think of Sue, for God's sake, think of *Murray*, you selfish bastard.'

He didn't respond, just tried to lever himself on top of me

247

by pushing his legs into the floor of the van. I heard something splinter and crack. He had pushed his foot through the floor of the cab. I so badly wanted to be out of that van, but I thought if I did bail out, the crazy wanker would just hurtle off and gas himself on some other fucking dirt track. I was now not frightened, just exhausted at holding him at bay. If you've never had a fight in a Transit van with a suicidal carpenter, don't; it has zero entertainment value. I looked at the crowded dashboard for a blunt instrument with which to fight back. I saw a couple of tins which didn't look quite heavy or sharp enough. Then, as he made another lunge for me, the bottle he was holding spun out of his hand and into my footwell. I reached down to pick it up and in a superhuman feat of timing, crashed it into his face. The blow wasn't hard enough to sedate him, but forced his hands up to his eyes. I now pushed him with all my might, and as he screeched in pain made him tumble out of the cab onto the track's gravelly verge. I tumbled out after him, still holding the bottle, and just as he was regaining his feet hammered him over the crown. The bottle blew apart like a nail bomb. He made a weird cackling noise and crumpled at my feet.

Then I burst into tears. I dropped the bottle and shook like a rag in the biting wind. I staggered around for a moment like a rubber man. My entire body seemed to have turned into soup. I had to sit down. I tried to smoke a cigarette, but the combination of the wind and my juddering hands wouldn't allow it. I flung my cigarette away, regained my feet and started trying to drag Bill's slumped form back into the van. I laboured for ten minutes to get him into the cab, but didn't have the strength, so I opened up the rear doors and after a freezing, sweating struggle got him hauled up. In the pale sheen cast by the van's interior light he looked dead. I felt for a pulse at his wrist, but couldn't remember how you were supposed to do it; is it thumb or finger? I tried both; with my thumb it seemed to be racing, with my fingers, wrenched and numb from heaving him about, there appeared to be nothing.

I pushed my face to his mouth to try to detect some breathing, and felt a faint brush of whisky-infused air. I waited for a few seconds and felt another. I suddenly started panicking even more. That horrible cackle, was that a death rattle? What is a death rattle?

I slammed the rear doors, and got into the driver's seat of the van. My co-ordination was wrecked, but I got the thing going and headed off God knows where.

It was only about nine o'clock, but I didn't see another car for fifteen minutes. I came to junctions which had signposts listing places I'd never heard of; Sibton, I remember, reappeared over and over, always one and a half miles away in the other direction, and a laughably sardonic Rotten End. I was flying down these tiny roads now, terrified either that Bill would die, which would be bad, or wake up, which would be worse. I found a road that looked more major and followed it until I reached a small town. As I lurched around its empty, low built side streets I heard Bill stirring in the back and felt my scalp bristle like a porcupine. He started to retch and I could hear him trying to get himself on to all fours. To prevent him I sashayed the van around making it lunge wildly on to its spongy wheels. I heard him being bundled over, and as I turned back on to the high street I also heard the sweetest sound in the universe, the siren of a police car.

I stopped dead, which threw Bill into the back of my seat, and me into the steering wheel, and leapt out of the cab with my hands on my head like a Bronx drug dealer. I can't remember exactly what I said, but I think it was something like: 'I surrender. Don't shoot.'

The two coppers frisked me up against the side of the van, handcuffed me and one of them hauled me to their pathetic Mini Metro panda car as the other went back for Bill.

The place where we'd been arrested was, it turned out, called Leiston, but they didn't have two cells there, so we had to be taken

249

to Saxmundham. A gentle, cheerful policewoman took a garbled statement from me, and told me that they would have to keep me in at least overnight because Bill had been sent to the local hospital. She took my wallet, which had a rather suspicious three hundred quid in it, and my belt ('We don't want to come down tomorrow and find you 'angin' from the light fitting.'), which I thought was quite touching.

They asked me if I wanted to call anybody. I said no, as long as they would call Sue, but that was apparently already done. Someone had already been sent to take her to see Bill in the hospital.

They took me to my cell, where they let me have a cigarette. I lay down and slept dreamlessly for what felt like a hundred years.

# Four twenty-pound notes

They let me out late the following morning. Bill had told the copper at the hospital what had happened. He wasn't seriously hurt, just concussed, in need of a few stitches and he had severe alcohol poisoning. He had drunk two-thirds of a bottle of whisky between leaving me in The Geese and picking me up in the car park. That meant he'd necked about a pint of Scotch in ten minutes.

Sue had left a message at the station for me to bring the van home. She said in the note that she had been to the hospital, but had no intention of staying with him for longer than was absolutely necessary. The note also contained an embarrassing flow of thanks and apologies. I thought it would be worth pointing out to her that I had not undertaken any pre-meditated acts of kindness. I had merely flipped under pressure and bottled her husband unconscious.

When I got back to the cottage, there was a car I recognised outside. It was Sue's friend Joanna's, and I guessed she had taken the children overnight and packed them off to school that morning. Joanna terrified me. She was only in her mid-thirties, but had the massive practical sensibleness of a sixty-year-old farmer's wife. She was, in fact, divorced and owned a couple of children's clothes shops in the area. She had met Sue and Bill because her daughter was at the same special school as Murray.

She opened the door to me. 'Well, you have been in the wars, haven't you.'

'I certainly have.'

She took me inside, sat me at the kitchen table, made me a mug of tea and some thick toast.

'Sue's asleep. She was with that bloody idiot practically all night.'

'Did she know that he was liable to do something like that?'

She snorted as she cleaned the work surfaces. 'Oh, God, yes. She said that she even knew the side road where you'd beaten him up. He's done the same thing three times now; the Scotch, the van, the side road, the hose. You're the only new element in the enterprise. Added a bit of vim to the storyline.' Her derisive matter-of-fact-ness shocked me.

'Has he ever got close?'

Joanna was now polishing the taps.

'Has he blazes. It's all a lot of bull, and so unfair on Sue and the kids.'

'He seemed to be pretty serious last night. He had it all thought through; a pre-placed note telling me how to get back to the pub, he'd worked out how long it would take me to get help, all that sort of thing.'

'It's a lot of bull, I'm telling you. The furthest he got was the second time he supposedly tried, deciding to drive home after drinking half a bottle of whisky, and colliding with a fence post at low speed. Bloody rubbish.'

I watched her on her knees now, scrubbing away at the cooker door. I hoped she was right and that Bill was merely pathetic. I just had a feeling that last night it was a bit different. I told Joanna I was going to have a bath and change, and went back up into the attic. I looked for his current diary in the *Bill's Bullshit* concertina file, but it wasn't there. I bathed, got dressed and told Joanna I was going for a drive. I wanted to find two things: the diary, and the note with directions he had left for me down the side road.

It took me an hour to find the road. I didn't recognise it at first, but when I got out of the Cav, I saw the shattered whisky bottle and a riot of tyre tracks. There was also a shoe which I thought was a little clichéd. One of Bill's brown cornish pastie jobs.

The place looked so bland and harmless in the daylight. Last night it had felt like the last exit to hell. Struggle, pain, coldness, the promise of loss. In fact, it was no more than a rutted farm track which curved round to a five-bar gate. Beyond the gate was a dull, cambered field of mud.

I remembered that Bill had said it would take me about twenty minutes to find his note. In the daylight I found it a lot quicker, wedged into his diary, under a football-sized stone by the gatepost.

The note itself was simply giving tortuous directions back to the pub. It was placed between the last two written pages. On the right hand page, the handwriting was uncharacteristically clear:

*Dear Frank*

*I am so sorry. You can't imagine. You will find out that I've tried to do this before. I know it won't come as anything less of a shock, but this time, it's too desperate.*

*Reading back this note, it seems so weak. I have left a note for Sue under the steering wheel. Tell the police.*

*Bill*

Reading it back, it really did seem weak. I thought of Debbie and Ben. Then for longer I thought of Murray, the gentle little stranger. How confusing, how baffling to them it would have been if he'd succeeded. Confusion, disbelief. In time, Joanna was right, it would probably be the sense of unfairness that replaced the lack of comprehension. Unfair; such a childish word, and maybe that's why in this case it seemed so right, on so many counts.

I remounted the Cavalier, put the diary into the glove box and headed back to the cottage. On the way, I stopped at a phone box and called the police in Leiston. I told them about the note to Sue, and they told me that they'd found it already, and destroyed it.

The Transit was outside the cottage when I got back. Sue was sitting in the kitchen, small hands wrapped round a tumbler of wine. She looked very freshly scrubbed and well-rested, which came as a surprise.

'Oh, Frank, you're back.'

She twitched a strand of fringe out of her eyes.

'Yeah, I went for a drive.'

I sat down opposite her. 'Can I get you anything?'

'A new husband?'

I smiled, in a very phony way, but she didn't seem to mind.

'I'm so sorry, Sue.'

She sighed with her mouth wide open. 'What am I going to do with him?'

I became very self-conscious suddenly. I could tell she was greatly pained and embarrassed, but I had no idea how to make her feel better. I made an indistinct sympathetic noise, 'Khaer.'

Sue tapped her wedding ring on the tumbler.

'Oh, I've just remembered.' She got up and rummaged in her handbag, which was on the side.

'Bill forgot to give you this.'

She held out the four twenty-pound notes. I thought quickly.

'Oh, didn't he tell you? I told him to keep it as a deposit on a table he's selling me.' She looked suspicious.

'Yeah, it's six hundred or something, so I said he could keep that as my first payment. In fact, if you wait a mo –'

I got up and went out to the car. I counted out two hundred and twenty, added it to the three hundred in my pocket and went back inside.

'I may as well give you the full amount now, as I've got it to hand.'

I splayed the money out on the table. After accompanying me around for a month or so, it looked a bit beaten up. Something happened to money in the eighties. I remember when Dad was doing well, he'd keep his cash on a pin and when he took it out (which was frequently) it fluttered and lolled as if it was made of some fine cloth. Now new money slices your thumb. It seems constructed of some millennial material, some way between a metal and a gas. It's boned with titanium, downsized, all round sharpened up. It feels as if it's worth less. My cash, lying there browned and crinkled, looked like a throwback. It seemed to be worth a lot. Which it was, to Sue and me at least.

Sue looked astonished.

'He didn't say anything about this.'

'Well, it probably wasn't the first thing on his mind.'

'I suppose not.'

She looked at the money as if it were about to spring into life. 'But he also said that you were a bit, a bit down on your luck.'

I liked the old-fashioned ring of that. It made me sound like a washed-up cabaret singer, or a hereditary peer who's moved out of the manor into the gamekeeper's croft. Lord Stretch of Poulton-le-Fylde hoved briefly into view again, in his cavalry twills and leather-patched jersey.

'I over-exaggerated. In fact I'm going back to London tomorrow to start a new job. Going back to journalism.' I started to feel a sense of moral elation, the Mother Teresa Effect again. 'Yeah, it's pretty good, writing features for a new men's magazine – *Emporium.* Which reminds me, did Bill mention the car?'

'The car?'

'Because he gave me such a great discount on the table, I thought I'd give you the car.'

'Frank, that's ridiculous, you can't give us a *car.*'

'No, honestly, it's fine, I pick up a company car in a couple of weeks. That thing's only worth a couple of hundred quid, I checked in the local paper. But it runs fine, it's more use to you than it is to me. I can't be bothered with the hassle of selling it to be honest.'

'When did you sort all this out?'

'Oh, a couple of days ago. He probably wanted it to be a surprise.'

Christ in a basket, that was undoubtedly the corniest thing I'd ever said in my life.

'Flip. I don't know what to say.'

'Really, it's nothing. Have you seen the table? It's so nice, I feel like I'm practically stealing it for six hundred quid. Honestly it's fine.'

I started to feel the elation recede and a cold, unyielding sense of worry enter my guts.

'It'll be a bit of a help, as you probably know.'

'Oh, sure, but I'm trying to fix him up with a few of my London contacts. I'm sure it'll only be a matter of time, once he gets – better.'

'My London contacts': the man who doles out the gruel, the girl from Centrepoint who cuts your beard at Christmas, the trench foot doctor. I went upstairs for a bath and considered my recklessness with intensity. That was it: the billet, cash, the car, gone in one five-minute conversation. I briefly attempted to do my score, for the first time in over a month. The effort made me laugh hysterically. The steady 28–30 of the previous six years had nosedived to under 10 in six weeks. I was playing out the last

256

futile moves in a zero sum game. 29 was always a very bad score. 9 was the preserve of those in a persistent vegetative state.

I dried myself frantically with the sandpaper towel Sue had issued me with, and went for a much needed lie down.

Later at dinner, Sue told me that Bill would be out of hospital the following day. I would have to get to him in the morning, and brief him on my stupendous lies. It occurred to me that I could spin the same trash about the job and the car to him, he wouldn't know or care.

As it was my last night, I tried to be extra-avuncular with the children. I helped Debbie with her maths. She was learning how to draw a bar chart. She was thrilled at my expertise. Once they'd bathed and changed into nightclothes, I went to say goodbye to each of them; Ben and Debbie shared a bedroom, Murray had his own.

Murray was his peaceful, ignorant self. He was lying on his side in the battered cot, his eyes open staring at some strange inward enactment. I laid my hand on his head and felt his secret warmth. I wished him all the luck in the universe.

Ben batted me off when I went to kiss him, and continued with his harrowing yells.

Debbie sat on the edge of her bed fingering a plastic necklace.

'See you, Debs.'

'Bye, Uncle Frank.'

I took my chances and gave her what I'd promised myself; a breathtaking bear hug and a big humming kiss on the nose. She kissed me back on the neck with an over-emphatic smacking noise and as I lowered her back on to the bed, she kicked and wriggled for fun.

I walked out on to the landing and treated myself to a little weep. I felt like I had come to the end of something. I *prayed* that I had come to the end of something. But a small rational voice was telling me that I wasn't quite at the end, not yet.

# Forty-four pounds eighteen pence

The final routine had a reassuring sense of closure to it. I got up at nine, drove over to the hospital in Saxmundham and dropped off a long explanatory note for Bill. When I got back I was forced to do an inventory of my possessions: now I was car-less, at least one of the refugee Louis Vuittons had to go.

The inventory was hugely unimpressive, so much so that I made a note of it, which I reproduce below, with commentary where necessary:

<u>Eighteen LPs:</u>
- 3 x Frank Sinatra (Capitol era)
- 1 x *Tchaikovsky's Greatest Hits* (which doesn't have on it the bit I actually wanted, which I think now probably isn't by Tchaikovsky anyway)
- 1 x *Hits From the Shows* Box Set

1 x *Randy Racquel Talks You Off* (a 21st Birthday present
from Tom)

1 x *Glory, Glory* (a compilation of the team songs of First
Division football clubs, circa 1978)

1 x *Your Hundred Best Hymns* (again, without the one I
wanted, which goes at one point 'There is another country
I dreamt of long ago' or something)

1 x *Out of the Blue* by ELO, gradually swinging back into
fashion, I fancy

2 x Smiths albums

2 x Elvis Costello albums

1 x *Eye in the Sky* by the Alan Parsons Project (a gift from
Early-Period Marie)

1 x Rick Astley album

1 x *The Doors* by The Doors

1 x *Wombling Free* (the rare *second* Wombles album)

1 x *Erwartung* by Schoenberg (bought in a later-regretted
fit of cultural purism. Surely some of the most horrible
noises ever produced by humankind)

0 x anything to fucking play them on

Filing Case

Contents included: every bit of paper I'd received over the
previous three years that I was too frightened to throw
away, to wit: unopened bank and credit card statements,
fragments of film scripts embarked upon, a couple of job
rejections (that promised to keep me 'on file'), tissues, bus
tickets, yellow stickies with provincial phone numbers on
them, some cuttings from the *Streatham Post*, love letters
(unsent, mainly). The filing case also housed all my scoring
paraphernalia: charts, reviews, progress reports, archive,
workings out. I even toyed briefly with binning it all,
feeling as I leafed through some of the more abstruse

sections (*The Importance of the Number Four in My Sex Life with Middle-Period Marie,* and *Bar Chart: Percentage of Friends Earning Over Twice Average Household Earnings – Updated Quarterly*) that it was in some way of decreasing relevance. In the end I elected to keep it, at least partly because I saw one section I hadn't turned my attention to for a while: *Problems Encountered/Solutions Found: Ratios 1988–1993,* which had a promising timbre to it.

## Clothing
- 2 x crew neck M&S sweaters, one swamp green, one marsh brown
- 1 x pair of black jeans, now mid-grey
- 4 x white shirts, 2 Van Heusen
- 3 x black waiting slacks, shiny knees and arse
- 6 x pairs of black socks, gauzy thin and baggy round the tops
- 4 x pairs of tanga briefs I held on to despite Late-Period Marie's protestations
- 2 x boxer shorts she bought me as a counterweight to the above, but which always annoy me because they give me severe wedgies if worn in bed

My agitprop shortie overcoat and Docs

My Adidas Sambas

A sample of crap, sloganising T-shirts: 'War on Want', 'They're Happy because they eat Lard!', 'Sisters are Doin' it For Themselves', 'Public Enemy'

## Books
Thirty or so books bought recently, mainly True Crime, American cop books and drillerkillerthrillers and a number of screenwriting 'How Tos'. All my university books had

been pawned when the temp work had dried up for a while years ago. I still occasionally pine for 'The Faerie Queene', de Tocqueville and *The Decline of the West.*

Yeah right.

There were also a couple of books Marie had given me. I'd never read more than the blurbs, the author biogs and the dedications and acknowledgements, which always provide good scoffing opportunities. She was the only person I ever knew who read modern literary novels. On the train, in bed, on the bog, at the bus stop, while the telly was on, during breakfast, during dinner, during sex (at least two times I noticed), during rows. She was pretty undiscriminating, and seemed to think of reading as a form of entertainment, a truly singular notion in the nineties, dear. I often tried to read them, but always gave up on page three shaking with boredom. *The Peregrinations of Senor Borrego's Parrakeet, Wankered!, Danton's Dingus, The Famished Magic of Meaninglessness. The Extremely Portentous Title;* what were they trying to say to whom and why?

The two she had given me were of such marginal relevance to existence that you could think they were deliberate jokes on the purchaser. The first was *Magnetic Islands,* 'a heartbreaking tale of illicit, impossible love amongst the urbanised immigrant underclass of Auckland'. I mean come on, New fucking *Zealand.* Maybe I'd enjoy the bit where the heist goes wrong and the cop's chick gets skewered in the crossfire. Sorry, wrong blurb. Maybe I'd be enthralled by the first tender, inarticulate sexual fumblings of the railwayman's son and his tubby Samoan bumchum. Maybe not.

The other one was a footie novel. Too despicable an idea even to be contemplated.

## Two Caricatures by Sadie

One of me as bloated poet/fat, bowler-hatted comedian, one of Bart as the devil's sexual plaything. Not mementoes usually associated with a great romance.

<u>My passport</u>
  The old-fashioned hardback sort, with a photograph of me
  as a wiry revolutionary and no stamps. I haven't been
  anywhere. Maybe that's one of the problems.

This mangy list represented a lifetime's work: doubleplusungood,
Frank. I took the stuff to a charity shop near the hospital. They
took most of my clothes, my books, the anglepoise lamp, my
LPs and posters and the filing case. I was left with the contents
of my filing case, my passport, Bill's diary, two days' worth of
clean clothes, my terrible shortie overcoat with two caricatures
in the inside pocket and nothing else. Most of it fitted into my
one remaining bag. My files were too bulky to take with me.
It was obvious that they had to go. I drove around for a
while, looking for a skip. When I found one, I couldn't bear
to leave my life's work on top, vulnerable to public gaze, so I
spent twenty minutes tearing the pages up and screwing them
into balls. I distributed the remnants like scruffy flowers among
the rubble and chipboard. Untraceable. I held on to my most
recent Annual Review, the caricatures and Bill's diary, but I didn't
understand why.
  I felt neither relief nor regret as I drove back to High Elder,
just that small nub of satisfaction that surfaces when some minor
administrative task has been completed. I let myself into the
cottage and stood for a few minutes in the TV room feeling the
stillness. I put the Cav keys on the kitchen table, wrote a last note
of thanks. I called a taxi and let myself out, posting the house
keys back through the letter box.
  The cab took me back to Saxmundham. I ate a cheese roll,
which had the consistency of Kevlar, in a café near the bus station.
I bought the *Telegraph*, because it had a picture of a beautiful
woman on the front and the promise of an article about Brits
making it big in New York. I boarded the growling coach at
two-thirty. I noticed as the driver opened the hold in the bus's

flank that even my luggage wasn't out-classed in this company; seventies vinyl sports holdalls, great high-sided leather-look suitcases in retirement tan or bungalow grey, orange nylon rucksacks, cagoule-blue nylon rucksacks, a couple of stuffed and Sellotaped KwikSave bags. I speculated that with all that plastic about if the engine overheated the whole lot would merge into one semi-liquid morass. When we got to Victoria we'd have to stretch our hands into the toxic fondue to recover our smalls.

There were only about twelve or thirteen other passengers; a few young and studenty types, the statutory scary middle-aged manual labourer and a group of three elderly couples. The old folks sat at the front. The men were in zippered knitwear that co-ordinated with their suitcases and the women were all buttoned up to the throat, eyeing the other passengers birdily from beneath vaporous silver hairdos. Sunday best for London. They looked so clean, I thought, and so vain.

I sat near the back and counted my money. Forty-four pounds eighteen pence, perhaps two days' worth of existence. I tried to sleep, but was kept awake by a persistent draught and a building sense of panic. By the time we reached the London suburbs I was writhing on my seat. My memory had gone completely. I couldn't afford to contemplate what had happened. The city night was climbing into the sky in front of me, blacking out any possibility of reflection. Just the persistent boring question: 'what on earth are you going to do tonight, Frank?'

As we came through the West End I stared at my face in the coach window. The downlight chopped it with shadows and made me look skeletal and ghoulish. I had to be very, very careful. I was trying to spook myself. I could feel that this was dangerous, even as I did it. I tried to re-impose a bit of calm, a bit of clear-headedness, some purpose.

I got off the bus at Victoria at about five and lugged my sack to a pub and read the *Standard*, nursing half a lager. The pub was definitely major terminus: the carpet was beaten to dusty thinness, the chairs were made out of that wood that's as shiny as a conker, the bench seats were dark pink velour-effect, pitted with black remnants of chewing gum and neat fag burns. All the frightened tourists in there were waiting for the next bus out, gathered transitorily round the edges of the tables, keeping a watchful eye on their bags. I sat on a rocky, high stool at a ledge near the door, smoking my first Lucky since January. Rothmans had been my tipple in Suffolk. The woman in the post office where I bought them had thought I was some kind of toff because I didn't buy Dorchester's or Lambert & Butler. It was good to be back on the Luckies; so autumnal in flavour, so bitter on the lips.

At seven-thirty I decided to move, a decision without a motive. On the pavement outside the pub I twitched my nose at the air; a mild night, thank God. I started off dragging my bag up Buckingham Palace Road towards Green Park. The rough, scraping noise emanating as I jerked it along behind could have been made by a lame third limb. By the time I reached the train station my shoulder muscles were already whining their disapproval, so I checked the bag into an overnight locker, taking the time to retrieve an extra sweater and my passport.

I considered my next step. West into the depeopled wedding-cakery of Belgravia and on to Knightsbridge, then High Street Ken, up to Holland Park and sheepishly into the arms of Tom and Lucy? Or Chelsea Bridge, Queenstown Road, across the mud and dogshit knocking shop of Clapham Common, to Henry's stoned, surprised face? Or along the Embankment, Battersea Bridge, a short hop through the council block ghetto of beached dredgers, to Sadie?

I headed off northwards, eastwards. I didn't know anybody northwards and eastwards. Wandering up Buckingham Gate, trying to keep my head up and my back straight, I looked pretty much like everybody else. I stopped a young black girl and asked her for a light. I had my lighter and two boxes of matches in my pocket, but I wanted some contact. She rummaged impatiently in her handbag, held the lighter towards my face, screening it from the wind with her free hand. There was an embarrassed little scuffle as the flame went out three or four times and I tried to flick the wheel with my own thumb, she tried to resist, and poked me in the eye. We got there eventually, and I thanked her. She said 'No trouble' and walked away swiftly, as if she thought I was going to follow her. Having initially felt in some way validated by the interaction, I felt a little depressed at her walking off like that. Perhaps I already gave off the whiff of desperation. This was strange, because inside I had begun to feel quite free and peaceful.

I walked into Green Park. There was still a thin stream of office workers walking down to The Mall. I looked into a few faces, imagining what occupied them, what dramas pressed behind the middle distance gazes: imminent assignations, professional advancement denied, mortgage arrears, uncompliant children, the fear and excitement attendant on a new sexual relationship. Whatever it was it didn't show. I reached the circle of trees where Marie and I had terminated our Late Period. I tried my hardest to feel something, but couldn't. One year on, only, and already so unaffecting. So done with.

Instead of walking up to Piccadilly I struck out into the middle of the park. The ground was mulched, skiddy and black. I felt like I was backstage at some great outdoor theatre; the lights and rumbling noise of the city continued yards away but in this ill-lit place you could be totally unconsidered and prepare yourself quietly for a later entrance. I walked towards a pair of benches. One was unoccupied but a dark figure was curled up on the other. In the misty outer reaches of the streetlights the figure could have been a statue. I thought of the image replicated throughout London, in doorways, in other parks and under bridges, a new public statuary, commemorating not those who commanded the city from its bridge, Nelson, Gladstone, Churchill, but those who clung to its hull like barnacles.

266

I sat on the empty bench and, inevitably, lit a cigarette. The figure next to me stirred and lifted his head. He peered at me steadily for a moment, shifted to a sitting position stroking his thick dark beard and asked me for a fag.

'Sure.'

'Bless you, sir. I'm Gordon.'

He had an RP accent. The hand he extended for me to shake was pale and feminine, each fingernail long and rimmed with black filth like an inverted pint of Guinness.

'Just been made redundant?'

'No.'

I think I sounded a little over-defensive.

'That's a common cause of mid-evening bench sitting around here.'

'Well, it's not my cause.'

'Mm. Lost love?'

'No. Not really.'

'So, lost love then. It's always one or the other.'

'I just said "no, not really".'

'"Not really" means yes. You learn this much if you hang around Green Park for long enough.'

I looked at his boots as he stretched out his legs, trying to rid them of sleep. He was wearing two pairs of trousers, some thick woollen ones over a pair of jeans.

'It's not lost love for me. I'm just waiting for someone.'

'Knob jockey then.'

'What?'

'Knob jockey. That's the only *other* reason you might be here – redundancy, lost love, homosexuality.'

'I'm not – gay.'

'Don't worry about it, you get to be pretty open minded living around here.'

'I'm not remotely worried about it. I'm just not gay.'

This really did sound huffy.

'Hit a nerve, have I?'

'No you haven't hit a fucking nerve. I'm just not gay, all right?'

'Have you got a girlfriend?'

'Well, no, but that doesn't mean I'm gay.'

'True.'

He continued to stretch his legs out.

'Lost love then.'

'Fucking hell, you crash someone a fag and all they do is try and annoy you.'

'Sorry.'

He was pretty cheery for a dosser.

'Got any booze?'

'Not on me, no, sorry.'

'I really fancy a drink.'

'I don't know how you drink that stuff, you lot.'

'What?'

'I don't know how you drink that stuff – Tennent's Super, HSL, all that crap, first thing in the morning.'

'I don't drink that stuff, you cheeky bastard.'

I was momentarily taken aback by his vehemence.

'You people are all the same, just because I sleep outdoors you think I'm some sort of cunt.'

'No, sorry, it was a thoughtless comment.'

'Fucking right it was.'

He ground his fag end into the path and stood up, stretching his arms out in front of him and bending his back. I felt plucky.

'Well, what about you then – redundancy, lost love or queer?'

He raised an eyebrow at me in a sort of fatherly way.

'To be totally truthful, my friend, the lot, the whole lot.'

He started to laugh. 'The whole fucking shooting match and more besides, in fact.'

I started laughing with him. I suddenly felt enormously grateful

268

and warm towards him. Without really meaning to I said, 'Shall I go and get us a drink?'

He put his head back and whistled softly. He looked at me. 'That would be *good*.'

'What do you fancy?'

'Red wine?'

'Suits me. I'll be back in a tick.'

'I'm not going anywhere.'

I went off to Shepherd Market. I could sense that I was probably doing the wrong thing. How long before he offered me a hand job for a fiver? How long before I accepted? However, there was this counterbalancing sense of freedom. It's difficult to explain, but I felt as if I was light, uninvolved, running downhill with the wind. Bill and his pretend madness, the encumbrances of Debbie, Ben and Murray, the mortgage, the weekly calculations, Bart's imprisoning contract, the terrible mistake of the weekend at Tom's, the Sadie farrago and old fashioned, disappointing Marie; I felt as if I had thrown it all off like a bout of bad flu.

I found a Nisa-type store. I bought two bottles of Bulgarian Suhindol, a sleeve of plastic tumblers, a corkscrew and forty Luckies. When I got back, Gordon wasn't at the bench. Maybe he'd split because he'd decided he didn't fancy me.

'Gordon!'

A voice emerged from a black clot of bushes behind me. 'I'm just taking a shit.'

For some reason, this revolted me. I knew there were public bogs at Green Park tube station, two minutes' walk away, but his laziness wasn't the reason I was disgusted. There was suddenly something else going on inside me that I couldn't fully under-stand. The downhill feeling had evaporated to be replaced by something else. A sliding feeling. I opened the first bottle and filled two tumblers. Gordon joined me and examined the label: 'Hmf. Balkan shite.'

'Cheers.'

This word performed the dual role of ironic gratitude and toast. We both tasted the wine. The wine was too cold, the air was too cold, so the only sensation was one of wet astringency. Gordon twirled the tumbler in front of his eyes.

He narrowed his eyes; 'An hysterical little vintage.'

'And I think you'll be defenestrated by its intransigence.'

Gordon laughed half-heartedly and turned to me. 'So go on then.'

'What?' Get your knob out? It's felch time?

'What *are* you doing here? This friend of yours hasn't shown.'

'To be honest, Gordon, I'm doing pretty much the same as you.'

'And what's that then?'

'Trying to get my act together.'

He nicked a fag from one of the unopened boxes I'd placed on the bench.

'That's not what I'm trying to do.'

Christ, he was trying to come over all mysterious.

'Come on, spit it out.'

He lifted the opened bottle of wine to eye level.

'We're going to need more booze.'

'We've got an hour's worth.'

He looked at me neutrally. His eyes glittered.

'You don't get me, do you?'

'What do you mean?'

'How much money have you got?'

I was reluctant to tell him the real amount, in case he thought it was worth mugging me for.

'Tenner, fifteen.'

In fact, this wasn't too far away from the truth. About twenty quid far, in fact.

He muttered to himself, 'Tenner, fifteen. I can get you a free breakfast, you know?'

'Right.'

'I mean I *will* get you a free breakfast, if you'll get some more of this.'

He shook the opened bottle at me, drained half a tumbler of wine in one and poured himself the remainder of the bottle.

'Does that get me your life story as well?'

'Thrown in, free of charge.'

'OK, I'll get some more.'

I was thinking that this time I'd get up and not come back. He was beginning to frighten me, and I'd noticed that he was pretty big. Big enough to turn me over at any rate. As I got up I stretched trying to appear nonchalant. I thought if I left too quickly he'd figure me out.

'Off I go, then.'

He looked up at me, his face twitching under his beard. I felt as if he was reading my mind. 'I'm coming with you this time.'

# Forty p

I was woken by my own shivering. The usual second or two of disorientation lasted for what seemed like minutes. What didn't take long to establish was that I was in a sleeping bag in a kind of hexagonal shelter. In front of me was a fenced broad lawn with a few ancient trees unevenly spaced around it. They spread a vast wiry mesh of branches between me and the sky. Men and women in dark suits and white shirts were strolling by with an air of self-possession and a sense of their own seriousness. I had a sudden dreamy panic that I was back in Oxford. It was the first day of finals. I was under-revised and under-dressed. A part of my mind started to reach frantically for essay themes; The Petition of Right, Tariff Reform, the Poor Laws.

Then reality began to broaden out and clarify. I was in Lincoln's Inn Fields. Gordon had brought me here and we'd talked late into the night. This is where he came for his free breakfast, dispensed by some conscientious female barristers. When I had started to get cold, he'd given me his sleeping bag and a musty pile of blankets. I looked around for him. Nowhere. Struggling out of the sleeping bag, still in my overcoat, I waited for the hangover to hit. To my amazement, it didn't. I remembered that I hadn't been drunk at all, just talkative and tired. I stood up and stretched. It was still mild. The day was overcast and had a dull metallic feel. I remembered that my dad called this kind of day 'soft weather', and that felt right. The absorbed, gentle-seeming people walked soundlessly on the soft tarmac paths. They talked softly as they walked, and the range of heavy buildings that surrounded the square was softened into monochrome by the grey light. I stood forward on the steps of the shelter and started to look around for Gordon.

Then I saw Tom. He was walking towards the shelter down the broad path, no more than fifty yards away. He was with a small, older man and they were laughing heartily. Tom was bouncing a heavy briefcase against his legs like a schoolboy and spraying out his free arm as if scattering seeds. There was no way that he wouldn't pass within a few yards of me As they approached the shelter I put my hand up over my face and stroked the bridge of my nose. They passed, and as they did so, Tom, without stopping walking or talking, looked at me for a brief moment before returning his attention to the older man. He then looked towards me again, turning his head quickly as if taken up in surprise. I froze for an instant, then shielded my face by making my hand into a visor. The two men walked on. He must have recognised me. I recognised him instantly from more than fifty yards away. Why didn't he stop? Astonishment? Shame? Kindness? I looked at my immediate environment. It was impossible not to conclude that I had slept rough that night: the sleeping bag and the blankets were piled around my feet and my shoes were laid on the top step, evidence of my one concession to civilisation. I pondered running after him to explain myself, but feared that I would be unable to be coherent. Instead I decided to find some breakfast and consider what to do next. I felt in my jeans pocket for money; a fiver and some change, about eight quid in total. I then checked my coat; nothing. I waggled my head to clear it. The thirty quid, my passport and the key to my locker at Victoria I expected to find had gone. I punched round in the sleeping bag trying to find them, and then realised why Gordon had gone AWOL.

'What a fucker.'

I kicked the pile of blankets in frustration. It felt good so I did it again about twenty times shouting incoherently all the while. Panting sharply after a minute or so, I took a breather but then started again, this time kicking the blankets down from the shelter across the path and on to the lawn. They were strewing out around me, and I was booting out in all directions, growling and grunting my head off. I got attention from the passers-by this time, but not much: just a few head-turns, some longer-ranged pointings, nothing else.

I started to act up, still kicking away at the blankets:

'Look at me now, ma! Look at me now!'

Pretty exhausted, I fell on my arse and looked for a fag. He'd nicked them as well. I started to throw the blankets around:

'There just . . . they're just such beautiful shirts.'

Ahh, fuck it, nobody was watching anyway. After a little lie-down, I tidied all the blankets into a pile in the shelter and headed off to the Underground. I was disoriented. Ten years in London and I'd never had any reason to come here before. I meandered aimlessly past a wig shop and a pub that had PRIVATE BAR etched on to one of its glass doors. I was in Carey Street. I had heard the name before, and knew it was famous for something, but I couldn't remember what.

I found my way to Chancery Lane. There was a tailor's which had a sign, STATE LEGAL MUNICIPAL ACADEMIC, above one of the windows, which seemed to me an accurate summation of the mood of this place. The gates and entrances were hung with plaques resisting entry: THIS IS A PRIVATE ROAD. THIS

IS A PRIVATE THOROUGHFARE. I got to Holborn and the banal flat-faced commerciality felt bracing. Two minutes later I was fully merged into the mid-paced, dully coloured crowds of the Underground. The locker at Victoria was empty, except for Bill Turnage's diary and the few files containing the highlights from six years of The Maths. I got myself some Luckies and sat in a café on Eccleston Street and eked out a weak, sugary tea. With nothing else to do I started flicking through Bill's diary. A thought struck me. I unpacked the Maths file. My thought was confirmed. An outward observer could have concluded that they were written by the same person: obscure, malevolent calculations, bizarre attacks of bad language, an unhealthy focus on the sickening, self-pitying soul. It was as close as I'd ever got to a moment of self-realisation. I got the feeling that I'd had at Tom's weekend. A sense that some heavy object was speeding towards me, intent on causing damage, and that heavy object was Bart. Instead of feeling scared and sick, however, I started to will it towards me. I wanted some kind of closure, a big black full stop, a moment of inertia that could somehow bring something to an end.

I walked out of the café, dumped my files and Bill's diary in a bin on Pimlico Road, and continued south towards Chelsea Bridge.

I spent ten minutes watching the bungee jumpers at the south side. They had started doing two people at once, trussed up together like hostages. I watched a couple plunge and snap back. It seemed to happen at two speeds; the terrifying pelt downwards stretching into slo-mo as they reached the bottom. Their screaming turned to laughter as they bobbed to a halt. As they were being winched back the girl spotted me and called out:

'You've got to do it! You've got to do it!'

The boy was waving at me. I waved back and bellowed: 'I'm just about to!'

Twenty minutes later, I was outside O'Hare's. It must have

been about ten o'clock, an hour and a half before opening, but there were people moving around inside. I went in. It was being gutted by a group of dusty workmen. One was attacking the bar with an axe, a couple of his mates were crashing around in the kitchen.

'Dyouwant?'

'I work here, I was just wondering what's going on.'

'You what?'

'I work here.'

'No you don't, mate. It closed down two weeks ago, we just come in to strip it.'

'What do you mean it closed down?'

'It fucking closed down, I dunno, bankruptcy or something they said. Somebody's bought it and we're doin' the refit.'

'Fuck me.'

'Looks like you'll be needing another job, mate.'

He started chuckling and carried on belabouring the bar. Then he stopped abruptly.

'Oi. What's your name then?'

'Frank Stretch, I used to be the mananger.'

The axe man paused for a moment, sniffed and went off to the kitchen, stepping over the orange flexes and piles of plasterboard. I went back out to the street. I couldn't make it compute. They'd had the best Christmas ever, and were planning to open two more branches. How had it happened? The only thing I could think was that it was some elaborate tax scam.

There was an estate agent's over the road. I walked in and asked one of the proto-Sloanes if he knew what had happened. He tiredly looked up from his *Daily Mail*. 'We don't know exactly, but somebody here spoke to one of the chefs a couple of weeks ago. Said the accountant had disappeared with a bundle and that the owner was stealing from the tills to pay off some gambling debts. They had five or six branches, apparently, and they've all gone straight down the toilet.'

276

'Jesus.'

'The police got involved last week. Apparently someone came over in the middle of the night and tried to start a fire. I mean there are flats over the top of it, they could have killed someone.'

That was Brian the Bat, almost certainly. I walked over to the plate glass window of the estate agent's and looked back at O'Hare's.

'Are you looking for a place round here?'

'Me? No, mate. Definitely not. The place is crawling with yuppie Sloane wankers.'

'Yar. 'Tis a bit, but nice though, I think.'

I went into a café next door and tried to work out what to do. I spent sixty p on a can of Diet Coke. I was now under the quid level, with my clothes worth maybe eight p on the black market.

I was stumped. The idea had been to go crawling back to Bart and beg for a job. I couldn't believe the silly cunt had blown *everything*. Fifteen minutes later I left the café with no idea what to do next. I stood on the pavement looking around aimlessly and constructing the obituary of the street sleeper who married a duchess. Just as I was scrunching the Royce into the stableyard, I heard a white van screech round the corner from Clapham Common. It lurched to a halt up on the wide pavement outside O'Hare's, and the driver's door flew open. It was Brian. He leapt out and shouted across the road.

'Oh yes, Stretch, oh yes.'

'Brian. What's happening?'

I checked the traffic and trotted halfway over the road. I saw that Bart was in the passenger seat. Brian was breathing heavily. He was in a lime green shirt and grey tracksuit bottoms.

'Nuffing, nuffing. Tell you what, you wanna come with me and Graham?'

'Come where?'

I saw Bart lean over and say something to him.

'Come wiv us, we got some money for you, severance pay like.'

Brian continued breathing heavily. I saw Bart stretch something out of the cab to him, which Brian tried to conceal behind his forearm. That's when it all became clear. I tried to cross back to the estate agent's, but there was too much traffic. Brian wasn't so timid, and I turned to see him smash the bonnet of a car as he stepped out in front of it. I darted out in front of a bus, which blared its horn at me futilely, and started running back up towards Clapham Common. I ran without looking back for about twenty seconds, but then came to another road flushed with fast-moving traffic. I turned into the gravel drive of some big block of flats and tried to carry on running. I couldn't: the side return of the block was barred by a gate. You couldn't film this, it would be the shortest and least dramatic chase scene ever captured on celluloid. I tried to look calm and unfazed, and walked back out of the gravel drive to meet Brian, who, with his ludicrous wide-armed, head-back style, was doing his best ever fat wanker's run. He juddered to a halt in front of me.

'All right, Brian, I understand, I understand.'

'Oh, no, you don't, mate, no you fucking well don't.'

I noticed that he let a short, black truncheon fall from behind his forearm.

'Now I wouldn't try running away again, Frank, I really wouldn't.'

He escorted me back to the van, and chucked me in the back. Bart didn't say anything. Sitting there amongst the rags and sticky-rimmed tins of paint, stomach crunched with nerves, I understood those momentary flashes of impending violence, but made peace with them fully. I just wanted it to come quickly, now. They had some easy listening station on, The Eagles were the first thing I recognised, then John Denver, which Bart sung along to atonally.

'Come thrill me again' in tender diminuendo.

I could only catch an impression of the route through the front window: I mostly saw the heavy sky, with corners of tower blocks occasionally sliding through the grey. The van rattled and swayed along what seemed to be a faster road before Brian wrenched it hard left. We slowed to a crawl, before swinging slowly right and jerking to a halt. They both got out, and I heard them murmur and stamp around for a moment outside, as if they were finalising some meeting arrangements. Brian opened the back doors: 'Cammon, darlin'.'

We were in the middle of a new, well-maintained housing estate. It was low built and solid red brick, a cramped facsimile of suburbia. The windows were clotted with fancy net curtains, and porcelain dachshunds and crystal ballerinas perched on the window sills. I knew we must still be in South London as we hadn't driven for more than ten minutes, but I might as well have been in Minsk. Us middle-class lads, even if we're down to our last forty three pence in all the world (which I was), don't hang around on the estates. Not even the net curtain and Franklin Mint variety. I don't think I'd ever *met* anyone who lived on a housing estate. Well, for ten years I don't think I'd ever *met* anyone, apart from Bart and Brian. As they were about to beat the living daylights out of me they weren't much of an advertisement for getting out more often. They led me, Brian quietly gripping my elbow, down the side return of one of the little houses. Bart fiddled with a vast bundle of keys, heavy and spiky like the head of a mace, and let us in.

The kitchen was gleaming; beige and pink lino, dark mock-mahogany units, some with mock-leaded glass fronts, mock-marble work surfaces upon which rested some mock-reproduction crockery. I had time to take all this in because the boys had left me there for a few minutes. There seemed to be some conversation going on upstairs. A few moments later, Bart's girlfriend Mossassa, she of the barrel arse and the Polynesian/Cuban complexion, came into the kitchen in a flappy leather coat. She grabbed some keys off the side and looked at me. Her brow was creased and her mouth twisted into an expression of sympathetic regret.

'I'm so sorry, luv.'

Before I could respond, she was out the door and Bart was calling me from the sitting room.

'Stretch, come on in here.'

I went in, calm but dry-mouthed. Bart was at the stereo: he put a Celine Dion CD on, quite loud, and gestured for me to sit on a dining chair that had been placed in front of the fireplace.

'Oh, dear, Frank, you really shouldn't have got yourself here, you know.'

I didn't know what to say.

'I mean, you're a good lad. But you wouldn't be able to guess it, from what you done.' His tone was unnervingly solicitous.

'Which thing in particular?'

'Fucking hell, don't be silly, Frank. Forty thousand quid, mate. You can't fuck off when you owe someone forty thousand pounds. You can't just fuck off.'

'Forty grand?'

'Ow, come on, don't do that, for fuck's sake. You're better than that. We'll get Tony too eventually.'

I looked down at my hands which were clasped in contrition on my lap. Tony: what a silly boy.

'Now, if you hand it over, that'll be it. All over.'

Celine Dion's wailing was reaching some interim climax. I was drifting into it, in spite of myself, unable to focus on the matter in hand.

'Frank, talk to me, for Christ's sake. The money.'

'I can't.'

'Steady now, Frank.'

'No, I mean I really can't.'

'What have you done with it?'

280

'This sounds so feeble, but I ... I just didn't do it. I don't know anything about it.'

'Oh yeah, oh yeah, so the day after you disappear, Tony Ling disappears and forty grand disappears, and you don't know anything about it.'

'Honestly, Bart. I really don't know.'

Brian purred unnervingly: 'Tell us where it is, Frank. It'll all be over.'

I shook my head. Bart dropped his voice too: 'The alternative's not very nice, Frank.'

I lifted my head and spread my hands at him in supplication. 'Look, Bart, I don't have it, I haven't got any money, not forty quid, not forty p, really. I didn't do it. I honestly don't know what you're talking about. C'mon, I wouldn't have the nuts for one thing.'

Bart shook his head. 'I don't fucking get it with you. You were doing all right, Frank, before this, I thought you were all right. A good straight-up kind of boy. What are you doing? Just trying to fuck it up for yourself? Is that what you want? You're better than that, mate – running off with a Chinese accountant and forty thousand quid – you *knew* you wouldn't get away with that, Frank. This is London. This is real. Here, right here where you are now, it's all real.'

He was standing tapping the window sill for emphasis with his fleshy claw. 'Some people, I could understand it, but you're not that stupid.'

'Looks as if I am.'

He stood up and walked over to the window.

'Are you saying then, that you're not going to give me this money?'

'I'm saying I want to give you this money, but I can't.'

'And Tony Ling? Don't tell me: you got no idea where he is.'

'Look, can we just get this over with?'

'We will, don't you worry.'

He walked over to me and hovered the great bovine head above mine.

'And if we don't get Ling soon, we'll be back for you.'

His breath was sweet and minty. He was always a personal hygiene freak. Personal hygiene: random violence's ugly sister. He walked away.

'One last thing, Frank. Don't go to the coppers on us. We got people all over dying to set you up.'

'But how's that? I really . . .'

He started ticking off a list on his fingers: 'Three months of taking money from the bank, sometimes up to five grand a week, all in cash, no record of it anywhere. They got vids at the cash machines, vids in the branches, we got mates all over the place. You're fucked.'

'Ahh! What a sucker.'

'You said it.'

He stood up and rubbed his face with both of his steak-like paws.

'Bart, can I ask you a couple of things?'

'Be quick.'

'How did you find me this morning?'

'The lads in the old O'Hare's. Briefed to look out for you. We knew you'd come back eventually.'

'What a sucker.'

'Is that it?'

'Last thing. How did you manage to go bankrupt?'

'I didn't. It's tactical.'

'So you don't need this forty grand then?'

'Don't be silly, Frank.'

I had a thought, and reached into my coat pocket.

'Oh, Bart – I've got a present for you.'

I extended Sadie's caricature of him being humped by the devil. He looked at it, made no comment and shook his head slowly.

'I did it.'

'Oh dear, Frank.'

He drew the curtains, tugging at them carefully until all the daylight was shut out, and went out of the room. Brian stood up, stretched back his shoulders and picked up the truncheon from the mock-mock-reproduction sofa.

I remember thinking three things: firstly that I could take anything but my teeth splintering out, secondly thank God for the sweet relief, thirdly that I really truly genuinely hate Celine Dion more than anything on this earth.

# Zero

Brian had done a thorough and comprehensive job. It was the work of an expert: nothing was irretrievably damaged, but everything was in a pretty bad state. When I woke up in the hospital my right arm was in a sling, my face was swabbed and bandaged, my chest whinged with pain every time I breathed in or out and my legs felt numb and swollen. I checked my teeth in a sudden panic with my sore right hand: all in place. I noticed that they'd put me in pyjamas. They smelt of babies and launderettes. The beds either side of me were unoccupied, which must be some kind of miracle, but the rest of the ward was pulsing with activity. It was like a Delhi bus station: bustlers, loiterers, snoozers, shriekers and weepers. God bless the NHS, it's a fucking national treasure.

I tried to crane my neck to check the time. Brian had got there too, his loving attention to detail ensuring that no movement was possible without excruciating pain, apart from a gentle eye swivel.

I lay there, staring at the mustardy brown ceiling and started to laugh softly. This caused a riot of agony in my chest, which just made me laugh more. The face of a black nurse floated into view above me. The name-tag pinned to her deep-cushioned bust told me she was called Cressida.

'Goodness me, sir, you don't have nothing to laugh about.'

'What time is it?'

'It's three o'clock, near enough.'

'What are all these people doing here? It's like a refugee camp.'

'They're visiting their friends and relations, nothing wrong with that. I expect you'll have some visitors before too long.'

'That's not certain.'

She started tucking in my bedclothes and put her cool hand on my forehead.

'What happened to you?'

'I got into a fight and lost.'

'Oh, deary me.'

'I never laid a glove on him, in actual fact.'

She tutted and smoothed her front. 'Well, it's not too serious. You're just battered and bruised. Hungry?'

'Nah. Tell me, how did I get here?'

'They found you on the ground outside A&E. Some kind soul had dropped you off.'

'Tuck me.'

'Now, sir, we'll have a little less swearing, please.'

'Sorry, nurse.'

'Now, any more questions? I gotta get on, you know.'

'How long will I be in for?'

'Two or three days. You need a little operation on your arm. Now what's your name? We don't get many in with no ID at all. You're a bit of a mystery, fella.'

'Francis Dean Stretch.'

She scribbled in a little notebook.

'Address?'

285

'Poh. I haven't got one.'

'Oh dear.'

I was loving this conversation. It felt so natural and domestic. I wanted her to invite me back to her place. I don't think she was similarly minded. I wondered if she'd seen my cock. I gave it a quick tweak with my operative hand to check that Brian hadn't been there before me and given it a little sprain. It seemed bewildered but OK.

'Nurse, before you go, can I have a couple of sheets of paper and some stamps and envelopes?'

'Don't you want to use the phone? You can still walk, y'know.'

'No, I want to write a couple of letters. Three actually.'

'Well, sure. Have you got any money?'

I couldn't believe it.

'There was a bit in my trousers, I think.'

'I'll check it out and get the things brought over.'

I had decided it was outright, craven apology time. I was feeling Last Plays Shakespearian: bursting with a desire for peace and reconciliation. I wondered if I, as the injuring party, was allowed to dispense healing. I decided that I was, as long as I grovelled sincerely enough.

There wasn't long: if I didn't get the letters out as soon as possible, they wouldn't be received until after I'd been discharged. The letter was the only form I could feel happy with: unlike the phone and the face-to-face it offered the possibility of going unanswered, and minimised possible conflict.

One of the other nurses, a porridgey gap-toothed Australian, brought over the writing paper, and told me she'd lent me a quid to cover it all. They'd only managed to find forty-nine p in my gear, which was in fact six p more than I thought they'd find.

Tom and Lucy, Henry and, of course, Marie were to be the recipients.

With my right arm snapped and futile, I had to write the letters with my left hand, which lent the calligraphy an unmistakeable air of pathos. Other than that, I don't want to say much more about them. It wouldn't make me look any better. Let it merely be said that they were the most cringing, fawning, abject letters you would ever wish upon anyone, and that every word of them was scorched with honesty. Say what you like about me, but I always try to be honest.

Tom came barrelling on to the ward about three o'clock the following day, trailing a big black coat and impatiently shaking his head. His expression was serious, almost severe. He didn't say hello.

'Bloody hell.'

'What?'

'Look at you. What happened?' The tone was impatient rather than indugent.

'I owed somebody some money.'

'I bet you did. Are you pressing charges?' Like brief to crim.

'No, I deserved it.'

'Well, Frank, that's up to you but I'm not going to be gentle on you just because you're in pain.'

'What do you mean?'

'Lucy told me not to come, you know.'

I tried to relax my body into the bed. I was about to get another walloping.

'It's that weekend, isn't it?'

He'd started shaking his head again.

'That's part of it. I don't really know where to start.'

He had his hands clasped in front of him, and was banging his thumbs together. He obviously had a lot to get off his chest.

'Firstly, whether it was right or wrong of us to invite you, you agreed to come that weekend. Now if that means the whole display was pre-meditated, it's even worse than it looked. Secondly, on to the specifics, that little *farce* about you sleeping with Lucy – what did you think, what did you hope the effect would be? Now, did you really think that I didn't know about it, that she wouldn't have told me? We got it out of our systems years ago. I understand what happened, it was all rather silly, and we've dealt with it.' He then got another burst of energy. He bounced his palm against his forehead theatrically.

'And the most *amazing* thing to me is that you've been sitting there for ten years nursing it. Can't you see how bad that makes you look? Have you spent every moment with me over the last decade waiting for the right moment to tell me that you once slept with my wife? Did you ever consider that there might be consequences? Did you have to save it up until the most important time in our marriage?'

'How is Lucy?'

'Oh fuck you, how is Lucy? She's a lot better now she hasn't seen you for two months.'

'Come on, Tom, I –'

'No really, that's true, it's absolutely true.'

'Was it that bad?'

He made a disbelieving 'huh' noise in the back of his throat. His head had started that fatherly disbelieving shaking again.

'Apart from Lucy, why the hell didn't you call my father about that job?'

'What?'

'I put myself on the line getting you that job. Apparently you made an idiot of yourself at the interview, totally unprepared, waffling, whatever – Dad said he wouldn't let you loose on the tea trolley, but I persuaded him to give you a go, said that you were like that, a bit diffident, but that you'd do really well, and the editor called you about three times and left messages, but all he got was Henry calling back and saying you'd gone.'

'Oh, God.'

'Where did you go, anyway?'

'Doncaster, Suffolk.'

He was revving up for another assault. 'If you think I'm angry, by the way, you haven't seen Marie. Bloody hell, Frank, what are you trying to do to yourself?'

'Well, Tom, you know what I think? I think Marie can stick it up her arse. I absolutely do not give a flying fuck what she thinks. Why did she want me there at that weekend anyway, other than to show off that unspeakable twat of a boyfriend – to really grind my nose in it.'

This set him off again. '"Fuck twat arse", yes, good, Frank, very convincing. She's *fond* of you, for God's sake, or she *was* at any rate. She wanted to stay in touch with you, she wanted to make it easy for Lucy and me still to see both of you, and part of her wanted to say to you, "Look, we may have split up, you may have hurt me, but I'm still coping."'

'*I* may have hurt *her*? *She* was still *coping*.'

My, how indignation hurts your chest.

'It's amazing to me, Frank. You seem determined to make a complete mess of the whole thing. I'm going to level with you, Frank; Lucy and I have put a lot of thought into this. You may have come to think that it's OK to be a waiter for the rest of your life, but we don't.'

*We? We?* What had possessed him to start speaking like Margaret Thatcher all of a sudden?

'What are you saying?'

'I'm saying that you can do better than that, and we think part of your problem, most of your problem, is that, well, you've not lived up to – your . . .'

He sniffed. He was about to arrive at the dramatic dénouement of the whole conversation.

'Well, Frank, as I say, Lucy and I have thought about this a lot.'

'What exactly?'

He sniffed again. 'Well, you've failed us, Frank. You think you're a failure and you spend most of your time going around persuading other people that you're a failure. We've had enough of it.'

'Thanks, Tom.'

'It may be difficult for you to face up to, but we think that maybe now is the time.'

I was silent for a few seconds. Tom had his arms folded on his soft, round gut. He was looking at me without a trace of self-doubt.

'I don't know what to say.'

'Well, you don't have to say anything, just think about it. And perhaps think what you're going to do about it.'

I was thinking about it already. I was also thinking that my best friend had turned into a complacent, self-important wanker.

'Does this mean that you don't want me to be godfather to your baby?'

He shifted a little on his chair. 'It's not top of our agenda at the moment. We'll have to see. That is, Lucy's considering what to do.'

'What? So you're considering dropping me as a friend because I'm not successful enough?'

'No, I don't think that's a fair way of putting it. But, certainly if you carry on behaving in the way that you have been, then obviously there's little point in us continuing to see you.'

He stood up and checked his watch.

'I've always known you were a Tory, Tom, but when did you become a Nazi?'

'I've got to go back. Call me again when you're out. Where are you staying?'

'At your place?'

He furrowed his brow. 'As I say, call me when you're out, and we'll talk again.'

He left. I lay there letting it all sink in. Certain elements of what he'd said weighed heavily with me. It was true that I hadn't considered properly the effects of my meltdown that weekend at his father's house, and I felt full of remorse. I was totally unprepared for the news that his father had been prepared to offer me a job. I didn't, however, feel any particular guilt that I hadn't answered the calls. I would only have turned it down anyway.

As for the accusation that I was a failure, well this was hardly news to me. However I couldn't help questioning his motives. There were two questions, and both could only summon unfortunate answers: a) What sort of person calls his best friend a failure? b) How much of a failure do you have to be for your oldest friend to tell you that you're a failure? I concluded that not only both questions, but both answers were equally valid: a) only a best friend who isn't a best friend would ever say such a thing and b) a lot of a failure.

To validate answer b) I did a quick mental maths. A pretty strong argument could be made for the following outcome:

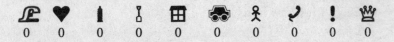

| 0 | 0 | 0 | 0 | 0 | 0 | 0 | 0 | 0 | 0 |

In fact, any argument that contested such an outcome would be full of holes.


About half an hour after Tom had left, I tried to get up for the first time in two days. It was actually not too bad. They were giving me painkillers which made my head floaty, but once I'd gained my balance I could walk without too much pain. Cressida saw me from a distance and I heard her have a good laugh at my progress. I waved to her in a deliberately sickly fashion, which made her hoot, and shuffled down the ward in search of diversion. There was a table at the end of the ward which had a few magazines on it, mainly old women's stuff and ancient car mags. I found a couple of *Country Lifes*, so I took them back to bed to look at the property ads. This was real top-shelf stuff: nine-bed mansion in forty acres Surrey/Berks border; stabling, two tennis courts, indoor pool, all photographed lovingly, teasingly at an explicit three-quarter angle through a greased lens. I checked out Girl of the Week, the eugenicists' nightmare, and read an article about point-to-point racing in Dorset. This is what people refer to as 'displacement activity'.

Just as I was starting on a feature about the new auditorium at Glyndebourne, Marie appeared at my bedside, dressed in her black lawyer's power suit. She looked somewhat less well-disposed towards me than Tom had.

'What happened?'

'Fight. Over money.'

'I got your letter.'

'So Tom passed it on.'

'Mm.'

'How do you think he is?'

'Pissed off – with you.'

'Yeah, I just saw him.'

'I know.'

'Thanks for coming to see me.'

'I don't think you'll thank me when I'm through with you.'

'Oh, no, not another bollocking.'

'What do you expect?'

She paused, but as I looked up into the ceiling I could hear her breathing hard through her nose. 'Totally humiliated.'

'What, me?'

She laughed mirthlessly. 'Very good. No, not you, *me*, of course. In front of David. Both of us in front of Tom and Lucy. That weekend was important to me, Frank, and at every stage you went out of your way to make me feel awkward.'

I looked over to her. She was sitting back on the visitor's chair with her fists bunched on her hips, her head cocked angrily. It struck me as inconceivable that she'd spent six years of her life as my girlfriend. I recognised her demeanour. You couldn't argue

292

with Marie when she looked like that. She would come back incessantly, and always harder. There was so much stamina in her anger.

'What do you want me to do?'

'Apologise.'

'I apologised in my letter.'

She waved her hand dismissively. 'That wasn't an apology, it was a string of crap excuses and pathetic grovelling.'

'Define apology.'

This received no response other than an exasperated exhalation. She stood up and went to the foot of the bed to look at my charts. She softened slightly. 'You're in a right mess.'

'Cheers.'

I watched her study the chart and flick over a couple of the pages. Her once unruly hair was clipped into a super-conditioned bob. She was still pretty and her slender shape was still just discernible beneath the boxy black exoskeleton, but to me she was utterly desexualised. Over-moisturised and cleansed, over-coiffed and glossed, slightly dusty round the corners of the mouth, she was a stiffened and desiccated version of the real Marie. David was welcome to her body. I didn't think he'd ever get anywhere near her soul. I never did.

'Marie, why did we go out with each other for so long?'

She looked up the bed and without pausing said: 'Habit, inertia, boredom, cowardice, fear.'

'What about mutual loathing, you missed that one out.'

She started to button her hard black coat. 'I never disliked you, Frank. I just think I got to the end of you.'

I could never say anything like that to anyone. I thought that maybe my only real disadvantage in life was that I was nicer than everyone else. I tested this theory immediately.

'I apologise, Marie.'

'That's not quite enough, you know.'

'No, I don't think you quite understand me. I apologise for not being more honest with you.'

She bent her head encouragingly, but suspiciously.

'Go on.'

'That bloke you're shagging, that pompous, pretentious, self-loving, tedious, humourless self-righteous charlatan – he's way too good for you.'

I saw her screw her face up into a child-like pucker of rage and closed my eyes as I saw her hand go back. The slap was half-hearted, but my already bruised, pulpy face wasn't equipped to cope. I heard her click off on her Gucci heels. My rational mind started an internal commentary on the events occurring in my nervous system: Oh wow, this is what pain feels like, God, interesting the way it *hurts*, it's uncanny, it's almost brilliant the way it works.

I kept my eyes closed for the next hour, amazed by my own body's capacity for intensity. When I opened them the ward was quiet. Everybody there looked much worse off than me. Cressida had told me I was in a surgical ward. I didn't want to speculate on what some of these poor bastards were going to have done to them. Most of them looked old and poor. There was one woman who was so fat they had her in a specially wide and low bed. When she walked you could see the flesh gathering round her ankles like yards of heavy drapery. How do people get themselves into such a state? Two hours later, when the ringing pain in my cheek and jaw had just begun to subside, Henry came rolling in to see me, swaddled in expensive blue climbing anorak. That's one good thing about Henry: when he came into a bit of money he'd spend it on top of the range anoraks. Such behaviour was proof of his essential goodness, which at that moment fell on me like a balm. He scraped the chair from the wall and sat on it the wrong way round, legs splayed and his crunchy-sounding Gore-Tex forearms folded calmly on the back. I hoped everybody had

294

noticed how many visitors I was getting, and how nice they were being to me.

Henry brought me a bag of lychees, a bottle of Aqua Libra and a six pack of my favourite fromage frais. He also brought me my mail.

'You're in the shitola, Frank.'

'What do you mean?'

'Bailiffs, summonses, threatening phone calls.'

'Threatening phone calls?'

'Yeah, from someone called Brian at O'Hare's.'

'He got me. That's why I'm here.'

'And from Marie.'

'She got me as well. While I was in here.'

'Yikes.'

He looked around the ward moonily.

'Let's have a look at the mail.'

He scuffled in the inside of his coat and slapped a thick pile of state legal municipal academic envelopes on to my lap. Academic, of course, because they were academic: there was nothing I could do to meet their demands.

'I opened them all. Basically, it's the bank and the credit card people, foreclosing and so on.'

'Henry, do you want to beat the shit out of me so I can stay in here another few days?' Henry had cut his hair. His natural crinkles had been subdued, but by no means weeded out completely. He still couldn't resist thumbing it behind his ears.

'Come back to the flat. We'll keep you safe and sound for a couple of weeks.'

'Do you mean that?'

'I mean both bits. Of course you can come back to the flat, but only for a couple of weeks. It's time you got going, y'know.'

'Let's go for a fag.'

Cressida said there was a little fire escape down the corridor where we could smoke. I had to put my old Docs on and my

295

shortie overcoat, because they'd run out of dressing gowns. Once we got outside Henry crashed me a Marlboro Light and skinned up.

'Here, Frank, have a bit of this. Reduce the pain a bit.'

'Ta.'

The cigarette, combined with the painkillers, had already made me flighty. The spliff zoomed me off into the troposphere. After a few moments' giddy swaying Henry dragged me back to bed and urged me to eat a lychee.

It took me a few minutes to recover the power of speech, during which time Henry idled over *Country Life*.

'Henners.'

'Yeah.'

'Do you think I'm a failure?'

'Oh, fuck, that's a tough one.'

'Does that mean yes?'

He continued scanning the mag and turned his mouth down in consideration.

'I would say that while you're definitely not a failure, you've definitely gone through a dip in form.'

'I think that's the nicest thing anyone's ever said to me.'

'Thanks. When are you getting out?'

'Day after tomorrow.'

'Just turn up. Lottie'll be in even if I'm not.'

'Thanks, mate.'

He tossed the magazine on to the bed.

'I better get off. I'm bored shitless in here.'

'Fine.'

He poured me a glass of Aqua Libra, nicked a lychee and turned to leave. 'Oh, I nearly forgot. Some girl's been calling up. Sally, I think.'

'Sadie.'

'Could be. I've got her number somewhere.' He rummaged in most of his anorak's seventy pockets and produced a yellow

296

sticky inscribed in his miniature super-neat scientist's hand-writing.

'Yeah, Sadie, you're right. Give her a call.'

He hunched himself into his anorak and ambled off.

## 0171 299 4563

''ello?'

A man's voice. A nineteen-year-old Italian man's voice. My heart swooped.

'Hi, is Sadie there, please?'

'I think it.' I heard him retreat and shout into the background.

'Sadie! Phone!'

Then there was the sound of a boulder bounding down a cliff face.

''Lo?'

'Sadie, it's Frank here, Frank Stretch.'

She made a noise like a ghost.

'Oooooo – aren't you in trouble?'

'What do you mean?'

'Bart, Lucy, Tom – everyone's after you.'

'Most of them have already got me.'

'That can't be right, you're still alive. Where are you?'
'St Thomas's Hospital. Losers' Ward.'
'I'd better come and see you then, hadn't I?'

# LEVELLING

## Averagely off

I'd insisted that we take my car. A '76 Triumph Herald spotted in the local paper and picked up for seven hundred quid. Convertible – the cat's pyjamas.

We were crossing Waterloo Bridge. It was about a hundred degrees and inevitably we were stuck in a jam. I had that clammy, soapy, nervous feeling you get when you have to put on your best suit in the middle of the afternoon. I gazed absently towards the City. It looked like a cemetery where bereaved families had contended desperately to build the highest, greyest, ugliest, most vulgar tombstone. I reached into the central well to retrieve a Consulate. As I lit it, Sinatra's 'Nice and Easy' came on the radio. I turned it up so everybody could hear.

'I could learn to love this place,' I said.

Sadie was looking wild. She was wearing a black-and-white halved minidress which rode up so you could see the darker band of nylon at the top of her tights. Her hair was piled up in a ludicrously sexy muddle, and her nails were painted midnight blue.

'What time are we due there?'

'Three. I don't want to get there much earlier. I'd rather avoid all the glad-handing.' We were slipping into the Kingsway tunnel now.

Sadie flipped down the passenger vanity mirror and started pouting and crimping her lips.

'I think christenings are *marginally* better than weddings.'

'I don't agree. At least at a wedding you can case the unknown females. Christenings are so incestuous. And all those grandparents looking like they've got a right to be proud – as if they've actually *done* anything worthy of congratulation.'

'You don't get speeches at christenings.'

'Fair point. But you don't get unlimited free ale either.'

We parked the car in an NCP near Holborn and studied the map.

'Right. Across to the south of Lincoln's Inn Fields and turn sort of left.'

Sadie took my hand as we set off.

'What's all this about?'

'Well, you're my date.'

It felt good. You could tell that everyone would think, 'What's *she* doing with *him*?' He must be loaded, hung like a mule, or have a nice personality or something. I was conscious of the cold rind of grease between our hands.

'Sorry I'm so sweaty-palmed. I don't think I'll ever get rid of it.'

'Don't worry. It's quite endearing. It says intense young man. Perhaps even budding Great Poet.'

'One day you'll let me forget about that.'

'Unlikely.'

As we strolled over the Fields I saw a familiar figure snoozing along one of the benches. Gordon. One of my refugee bags was under the bench. I noticed he was wearing one of my jumpers. Cheeky bastard.

'Sadie, hold up.' I dropped her hand and shook Gordon's shoulder. He peered up at me, shielding his eyes.

'Who the fuck are you?'

'I'm your benefactor, Gordon. What are you doing here? Lost love, redundancy or are you just a knob jockey?'

He looked ill and doped. I felt ashamed of waking him. He tried to mouth something but couldn't.

'Here mate, sorry.' I got my wallet out and folded a tenner into the pocket of his jeans. His head dropped back to the bench like a stone. Sadie was looking puzzled.

'Who's that?'

'A friend. I get all over, you know.'

We entered New Square: ancient, sequestered and insulated, it repelled me, despite the prettifying sun. I realised that with its lush but trim lawn and its orderly cleanliness it looked like an eighteenth-century Barratt estate. I told myself to store this one up for Tom.

Sadie stopped me with a jerk of my hand. 'Mmm. Nice. Very Oxbridge.'

'That makes it nice?'

'Very *pretty* and very *quaint*.' She said this pursing her lips in the camp tone of some backwoods dowager.

'I'd like to burn it down.'

'Great Poet and Class Enemy, Frank Stretch – still angry after all these years.'

'Come on, let's go before I throw up.'

The christening was being held in the chapel at Lincoln's Inn, with drinks beforehand in some undercroft-vestibule-cloister. We showed our invite to some deferential old gull on the door, and took a deep breath. The hall was in itself like a chapel, religiously windowed, but pictures of senile lawyers hung high up all around it indistinct up in the shadow and sun-dust. Either scrawny to the gills, or red-faced and bloated like Christmas geese, they gave you the feeling that the painter was intent on having the last word on them.

The place was seething with quality. Thin rich young women, fat rich young men. The noise seemed to hover over the crowd like weather. Sadie and I shuffled uncomfortably towards a corner, me with my back to the throng, her rubbernecking like crazy.

'Can you see Marie?'

'Err, let's have a look, no, not at the moment.'

'What about David?'

'No sign. I can see Tom and Lucy though. God, he's got so *bulky*, hasn't he? He's *spilling* over the top of his shirt.'

'I'm doing that as well, steady.'

'But it's quite sweet with you, because of the shaving rash, and all the blood on your collar.'

My hand involuntarily flew to my neck.

'Fuck, why didn't you tell me?'

'Didn't notice till now.'

'Hadn't you better go and say hello?'

She wiggled her mouth in consideration. 'Not sure yet. Sir Charles is with them. He gives me the willies.'

Just then, I heard Tom's voice booming over the crowd, and his rugby hands thudding together.

'OK, everybody, a bit of quiet please, a bit of quiet!'

He was up on a dais at the end of the hall, now shushing everybody by flapping his hands over his head like a conductor. 'Now, before the ceremony itself, David here, who as most of you know is to be Patience's godfather, wants to say a few words. Not all of you know him very well, but you will soon if we have anything to do with it. David!'

David leapt up on to the dais and spread his arms like a vicar.

'I'd like to thank you all for listening to me for a moment, but mostly I'd like to thank Thomas and Lucy for letting me say these few words on this great occasion in their lives.'

306

There was an uncertain ripple of applause.

'Not only do I feel hugely privileged to be asked to be godfather to the ravishing Patience Phoenicia Mannion, but I would like to say that today I am *truly* the happiest man on earth.'

He paused and beamed around the place. 'Because this morning [Pause] Marie O' Sullivan agreed to be my wife.'

The applause was more determined this time. Some stamped on the wooden floors. The real twats whooped and cheered. David extended his hand down and I saw Marie climb up on to the dais and hug him, like a politician's wife after a conference speech. Sadie turned to me.

'Did you know about this?'

'Naah.'

'How do you feel?'

I stayed silent for a moment, trying to work out how I felt.

'I feel absolutely terrible.'

Tom hopped back on to the dais. 'OK, everyone – through to the chapel now please.'

We milled along with the perfumed crowd. I saw a few faces I recognised and mouthed a couple of insincere 'Hi's. We stepped in to the back row of seats, out of everybody's way. Sir Charles smiled and bowed sardonically at Sadie as he went by, but took no notice of me. Marie and David went by, him grinning into her upturned, supplicant face like a faith healer. He wasn't so absorbed in her that he didn't keep flicking his hair around.

'Sadie, what do you think of Marie?'

'I've only met her a couple of times.'

'That doesn't usually stop you.'

'To be honest, I think she's dull. And I think she's got no idea what she wants. And I think that secretly she's totally embarrassed by the way David behaves in public.'

'Like it.'

'Lucy told me that they never have sex.'

'That was always our favourite too.'

307

Sadie swung her head round. 'Really?'

'At the end. But even before that for a couple of years I used to have to think of other girls to get sufficiently *à point*.'

'God, that's terrible.'

'Yeah, it's funny – went through all the stages. When I started seeing her I used to have to think about Harold Wilson's gusset or the dates of the Saxon kings to avoid popping too early.'

'Didn't you ever get it right?'

'For about ten days in the early nineties I was in perfect equilibrium. After that I was forced to move on to Nicole Kidman and the woman in the bra ads to save face.'

Sadie giggled. And then looked outraged. 'Nicole Kidman's a redhead!'

'She was a brunette when I was shagging her.'

'At least you don't have to worry about that now.'

'Don't remind me.'

The ceremony was only made tolerable because David's reading was so unintentionally funny. Particularly the bit where he choked up. I craned my neck to see if I could detect any embarrassment in Marie's body language. She had her hand splayed over her cheek and was gently tapping the index finger against her jaw. Marie Cringing At The Behaviour Of Her Boyfriend – Hand Position Number One.

Oh yes.

When it was all over Sadie and I walked back out into Lincoln's Inn Fields together.

She nicked a Consulate off me. She yawned and stretched. 'That wasn't too bad.'

'Could have been worse. What are you doing now?'

'I'm meeting this bloke at six. Couple of hours to kill.'

'Which bloke is it at the moment?'

'He's a new one actually. I met him at a club on Thursday. He's called Roger, which is a bit of a problem for me, but he seems all right. He said he was a DJ, but everyone you meet says that at the moment.'

'You do get around a bit, don't you?'

She looked at me mock-indignantly: 'Three blokes in six months this year.'

'I hope you're taking precautions, young lady.'

'I am. No rimming till the second date.'

'Oh, Jeesus, Sadie. It's too much, it really is. We've just been in church, for God's sake.'

The filthy laugh. 'What are you going to do?'

'They've invited me to the evening do, but I think I'll give it a miss. I've got to finish my column today.'

'What's your theme?'

'I'm tossing up between "Is the Media Really Dumbing Down?" and "Deputy Dawg or Hong Kong Phooey: the Debate on Canine Cartoon Sleuths". The editor wants more 25–34s, and I'm his bridgehead.'

'It's going places, the *Clapham Argus*. By the way, what's Deputy Dawg?'

'God, the kids today. One despairs.'

We were back up at Holborn. We stood looking at each other, neither really wanting to separate.

'Where are you meeting Roger?'

'North. Highgate.'

'OK. I'll see you tomorrow then, back at the flat.'

'Sure thing.'

She gave me a hug and I grabbed on for that extra second or two. It wasn't anything sexual, you understand. I just wanted to say thank you.

'Oh, by the way, it's my birthday tomorrow, Sade.'

'God, why didn't you tell me before?'

'I'm trying to keep it quiet.'

'It's not your thirtieth is it?'

'Ish.'

She gave me another hug.

'We'll have to do something.'

'No, me and Henry are going to get stoned and watch the telly. It's all been organised. I just can't disrupt such carefully laid plans so late in the day.'

'Well, we'll do something later in the week.'

'Whatever.'

As she turned to go I called her back.

'Sadie, can I ask you one thing?'

She spun round.

'What did "not yet" mean?'

She held my gaze for a moment. I find it alarming when women look me dead in the eye. It's always a prelude to honesty.

'It meant "not ever" in the way you were thinking, but "some day soon" in the way *I* was thinking.'

'Meaning –'

'Meaning that I thought it would be a good idea for you to cool it, because I knew we'd work so much better as friends than as anything else.'

'OK.'

'I'm right, aren't I?'

'I think so.'

'I am, believe me.'

She was so right. Sadie and I were never meant to be: it was generational, philosophical, psycho-sexual, temperamental, practically genetic. My first instincts were right – she was way too good for me. Now she felt something similar: not that I was too good, but that she could never have made me happy as a girlfriend. For a start she never fancied me. One bit. This way, though, we were in it for the long term – train tracks headed off into the distance, sashaying through the years, never quite meeting, never quite parting. Friends.

She breezed off towards Covent Garden looking overdressed and underprepared. She'd be all right though.

I got back to the flat at five and changed out of my suit. I fired up my laptop, poured myself a glass of wine and started on my column. Writing about TV, it was so obvious really. I had all the right equipment: a lifelong love of the subject, an ability to form instant and pungent judgements, extreme facetiousness: what a natural. The pay was miserable, worse than O'Hare's, but now I was syndicated (Tooting, Wimbledon, the far shores of Croydon) I was beginning to feel like I was on to something. Slowly, month by month, I was paying my way back to solvency. By the time I reached forty, I'd be all square and ready to start afresh. Sitting in my new linen trousers and polo shirt I tried to imagine that I looked like someone out of American aspirational TV. It always puts me in the right frame of mind; I'm kooky and wry on the surface, but underneath there is a steady, penetrative intellect and a firm set of principles. You can like me, but you can also respect me. I'm also fab in the bunk, honey.

I looked at one of Sadie's caricatures I'd stuck to my screen: me, just me, standing with arms outspread and a big grin on my face, captioned 'FRANK STRETCH: 29 AND RISING'. I clattered away at the keyboard for a few seconds and stopped. Brian's lavish attentions gave me occasional shooting pains in my right hand. They'd never got back to me, so I guessed that they'd found Tony Ling. What a state he must be in. At least he'd finally be free of those grubby teeth. I flexed my hand and pushed myself back from the table. We had somehow crammed the Bill Turnage piece into the flat. You could really spread out around it. The population of Sao Paulo could have really spread out around it. I had contacted Bill in the spring and he'd driven it down from Suffolk in the suicide truck. In broad daylight, in London, when I was sober and relatively lucid of mind, it wasn't quite the towering enterprise I'd originally taken it for. In fact, it looked like a piece of cheap garden furniture. I didn't have the balls to tell him. He still looked capable of jigsawing your liver out. I took him for a beer and told him straight that I'd read all his diaries. He responded placidly. In fact, he responded placidly to everything because he was on elephant dosages of anti-depressants every day. He said that they worked but that they made him an orgasmic.

'An orgasmic what?'

'No. One word: anorgasmic. Can't have orgasms, or never want to at least. Doesn't make much difference.'

'They're overrated anyway. I don't bother with them very much either any more. Certainly not with other people present.'

He told me before he limped off that Debbie was really missing me.

'Oh, I must come and visit.' Yeah, some time between now and the contraction of the universe to a teardrop of sub-atomic soup.

I started pecking away again at my TV piece, but couldn't concentrate. I wanted to be outside, but I knew that as soon as I stepped out I'd want to be back indoors again. I was waiting for a woman, you see. For a phone call from a woman, to be precise. Impatiently, I came out of my Journalism folder and opened Personal. For the fifteenth time that week I double clicked the file called 'lovead.doc':

BORED OF EXCITEMENT? Averagely-off man, 30, re-shaping gently after minor deformation, celibate, nice flat, own car, pudgy, outgoing (within limited circle), lively if downbeat mind, SEEKS sensible, fair-minded girl with a view, in the medium-to-long term, to making a settlement with life. Late 20s - Early 30s. Smokers more than welcome.

Sadie thought it was an undersell. She persuaded me to take out the references to my hair being the colour of silage. I myself took out the line which said 'recent tendency to cry and get into fights'. Maybe it didn't seem endearing, just possibly it wouldn't bring out the powerful mothering instincts it was intended to provoke. Maybe I was too old to need that kind of attention in any case.

As I considered the ad, the phone went.

'Frank, it's Tom.'

On a mobile, in a Sports Utility Vehicle, his wife beside him mugging at her new baby, somewhere in West London, presumably knocking chunks out of some blinking loser on the pavement.

'Hi there.'

'Listen, are you going to come along tonight?'

'I don't think I will, mate.'

'It's a real shame.'

'I know. Busy, though.'

'Not good for you to work all night.'

'I know, I know I shouldn't.'

'OK, I'll leave you be.'

'Thanks.'

There was a slight pause before the phone went dead. Something left unsaid. He was obviously regretful about something. We'd sort it out sooner or later. I was forgiven and forgiving, which I suppose was inevitable. Time doesn't heal, but it makes you forgetful.

I went back to my column. Nine words in five minutes:

*Time spent watching television isn't deducted from your life.*

Particularly when you're getting paid for it.

I closed the computer down, bagged out on the sofa and watched television, late, late into the night.